WORTH EVERY
Game

HAWKSTON BILLIONAIRES
RAE RYDER

Worth Every Game

Book Two of the Hawkston Billionaires

Copyright © 2024 by Rae Ryder

The right of RAE RYDER to be identified as the author of this work has been asserted by her in accordance with the Copyright, Designs and Patents Act 1988.

All rights reserved. No part of this publication may be reproduced, transmitted, or stored in a retrieval system in any form or by any means without permission in writing from the copyright owner, nor otherwise circulated in any form of binding or cover other than that in which it is published and without a similar condition being imposed on the subsequent purchaser.

This is a work of fiction. All characters in this publication are fictitious, and any resemblance to real people, alive or dead, is purely coincidental.

PB ISBN: 978-1-915286-05-5
www.raeryder.com

Cover by GetCovers

Editor: Sarah Baker

For anyone who ever wanted to get down and dirty with their best friend's brother, or who just fancies imagining they might. Please, indulge.

Author's Note

Please note this book is written in British English and will include British variations on spelling and vocab where applicable.

You'll find pavements, lifts, tubes (as in metro/subway), boots (of the car), a lot of S instead of Z, and an extra U in places you might not expect. Sometimes an E for an A, too.

Finally, Mr and Mrs appear without the .

Trigger warnings can be found on my website at www.raeryder.com/content-warnings.

This book contains mature content and is intended for those over 18.

1
JACK

"Daddy bought me my first pony when I was six."

I stifle a yawn. I'm unsure if it's because Lydia has been running through her childhood family pets for the last ten minutes, or because this is the third date I've been on this week, with three different women, and I spent the other nights working until after midnight.

I focus on the woman in front of me. She's hot. *Very*. Long dark hair, dark eyes. Figure like a swimwear model. I'd be keen to fuck her if I didn't think I might fall asleep on top of her. The pet chat is even worse than when she was listing her celebrity clients. I couldn't give a fuck what actor or actress she does the PR for, and I've been feigning interest in her conversation for what feels like too long already.

It's possible the whole work hard, play hard thing isn't working for me anymore. Either that, or she's incredibly boring.

I drain my glass of scotch, letting my mind drift back to work, my eyes glazing over as the sounds of the busy bar, and Lydia's voice, fade into the background. It's been six months since I sold my boutique hotel company to the corporate behemoth, Hawkston Hotels, and it's been a crazy ride. With a seat on the board, and a huge share contribution, I'm working myself to the bone to prove my worth. It's exhausting.

My phone buzzes in my pocket. I slide it out to see my sister's name flash up.

Why is Kate ringing me now? She never calls, especially not on a Friday night. Anxiety twists my gut. Ever since our father died eight years ago, I'm the one she calls when she needs something, which to be fair to her, is rare.

Maybe it's a butt dial. If it's serious, she'll call back.

My gaze ping-pongs between the phone screen I'm hiding beneath the table and Lydia. Her eyes are sparkling, and she's talking faster and louder, as if she knows she doesn't have my full attention and is keen to reclaim it ASAP. Maybe I do want to get laid tonight. I could get a coffee somewhere first...

I reject the call and slip the phone back into my pocket.

It rings again. *Kate.*

Twice in twenty seconds? That's not good.

I hold up a finger and Lydia aborts her diatribe about the rosettes she won as a teenage show jumper. I flash my phone at her. "It's my sister. I have to take this."

I get up from the table, accepting the call as I stride away. "What's wrong? What do you need?" I ask before Kate has time to say a word.

"Oh, thank God," she breathes, and my heart rate quickens. "I just got home, and the kitchen is full of bubbles. The dishwasher's exploding. Can you get here and help me? It's making this terrible gurgling noise."

She's calling me for bubbles? "Have you called a plumber?"

"Of course. I tried several, and none of them can come, and the guy who can, can't be here for two hours. There's foam everywhere. It's like one of those terrible gameshows where the contestants flop around in slime in here."

That sounds awful. My instinct is to rush to her aid, but I'm not entirely free to act on it. I glance over at the table to find Lydia staring at me, a coy little smile on her lips. *Tempting.*

I force my attention back to Kate. "Where's Nico?" Now that my sister and my best friend are dating, maybe he can be the one to come to the rescue.

"He's in Paris this weekend." *Damn*. "Please, Jack. It's your flat. Elly's coming home soon and I don't want her to know what a state the place is in."

I perk up at the mention of Kate's quirky flatmate. But I'm not sure how helpful Elly would be in this scenario. "Why wouldn't you want her to know?"

"Because," Kate begins, hesitation threaded through her voice, "I think she did it. We're out of dishwasher tablets, so she must have filled it with washing up liquid before she went out."

"Why the fuck would she do that?"

"I don't know, do I? Because washing up liquid also cleans dishes? It's not completely stupid—"

"Just a bit stupid."

Kate tuts. "She'll be humiliated if she's broken the dishwasher, and she won't be able to afford to get it fixed. Please, Jack. I can't do it all by myself, and you should probably check there isn't an actual plumbing fault."

Damn Kate and her big heart, wanting to save her best friend the embarrassment of knowing she's destroyed the kitchen. If Elly's fucked the dishwasher, she should face the consequences. How else is she going to know not to do it again? But there's no point trying to talk Kate down from this one. I know my sister too well.

I glance back at Lydia, who's running her finger around the rim of her champagne glass. She really is gorgeous, but I'm exhausted and I'd hate to pass out on her after one orgasm. Better I pass out fixing a dishwasher than inside my date.

"Okay. I'm coming. Give me fifteen minutes."

"Thank you, thank you, thank—"

I hang up and make my way back to the table. Lydia flashes me a sexy smile that all but screams '*let's fuck*'. Guilt spears me alongside a little regret. I would have appreciated a blow job tonight. I could have stayed awake for that.

"I'm so sorry, but something's come up. I've got to head to my sister's flat. There's been an emergency."

Lydia's smile evaporates, replaced by a disgruntled pout. "Can't she call the landlord?"

"I'm the landlord."

"Oh." Disappointment rings through her voice and she looks completely dejected. I don't want to totally crush her; I might want sex later this week, and in all likelihood fucking this woman is going to be more interesting than talking to her.

I offer an apologetic smile. "I'll make it up to you."

"Tomorrow night," she blurts, so keen that it's *almost* off-putting. "My friend is throwing a party—"

"Sure. Love to. Send me the details," I respond on autopilot, bending to kiss her on the cheek. "I really want to continue this date." *Sort of.*

On the way out, I pay the bill. Lydia might not be my dream woman, but I won't let her buy my drinks.

Forty-five minutes later, I'm standing in Kate's kitchen, sleeves rolled up, sweat dripping from my forehead.

"We did it," Kate muses, looking delightedly around the clean kitchen. Not a bubble in sight and the dishwasher is purring away happily. "Good as new."

"New? This place needs a total overhaul." I glance around at the flaking paintwork on the walls and the damp patch on the ceiling in the corner of the room. If Kate hadn't adamantly protested that she and Elly love living here, I would have moved them both out six months ago. As it is, I'm letting them run out their leases before I tear the place apart. "I've got those building survey reports coming back soon. I bet a faulty dishwasher isn't the only thing you need to worry about."

Kate *hmms*. "Well, it's never been so clean. You should move in here."

I huff out a laugh. "No. You and Elly are a pair of pigs."

She gasps in mock outrage before her expression turns sincere. "Thank you. I know it's Friday night, and you probably had something better planned."

"Nah. No plans this weekend." I don't want her worrying that she ruined my evening. "Besides, I like being here with you." I pull her into a hug, and she squeezes her arms around my waist.

She releases me and steps back, turning towards the kettle to make us both some tea. We're silent for a few minutes, and the only sound is the incessant drip-drip of water from the leaky tap into the sink. *Is everything in this flat falling apart?*

I try to ignore the noise and take a seat at the cheap Formica-topped table. Kate has her back to me when she says, "There's this other thing I wanted to talk to you about."

A zap of suspicion bolts down my spine. "Oh, yeah?"

She puts our mugs of tea on the table and flops into a chair opposite me. "I want to ask Elly to sing at Nico's surprise birthday party. What do you think?"

My eyebrows rise before I have a chance to stop them. There's so much wrong with the idea I don't know where to start. *What the hell do I say?*

Kate has an expectant look on her face, and guilt expands like gas behind my sternum. The regular rhythm of the water dripping into the steel sink booms in the quiet kitchen.

"You need a new washer on that tap," I say, and my attempt to avoid the question is so transparent that Kate lets out an exasperated breath.

"Forget about the tap. You've done enough plumbing for one evening. I'm asking you about Nico's party. He's your best friend. I want your opinion. I've never thrown a party this big. I want to get it right."

I pick up my tea and slurp it, but the liquid's so hot it burns my mouth. "Fuck." I clench my jaw, squeezing my eyes shut. I wipe my mouth on the back of my hand, but my mind is still stuck on Kate's original question, and clearly she's not going to let it go. "You want to ask Elly to sing for Nico? Elly as in Elly Carter? Elly who flooded the kitchen? *That* Elly?" I sound like my brain is powering down.

"Yeah. What other Elly is there?"

Shit. "Just wanted to be sure." I'll have to tread carefully because Kate loves Elly. Adores her. They've been friends since they were pre-teens and have lived together most of their adult lives. I rest my arm over the back of the chair next to me and lean back just enough to look casual. "I don't think it's a good idea."

Kate quirks a brow. "Why not?"

"You can't have an amateur play at your boyfriend's party just because she's your best friend. He's Nico fucking Hawkston." I gesticulate emphatically with one hand, but Kate doesn't look convinced, despite the fact that Nico is one of the youngest billionaires in the UK, if not the whole world. "If you were dating a regular guy, I'd say yes.

Of course, I would. But not for Nico. The stakes are too high, and it would be your reputation on the line."

"Jack..." Kate says in a tone that's meant to warn me off, but I'm not about to let her make a fool of herself in front of London society.

"I'm not trying to be an arse here. There's a lot to consider; it's not just about Nico. It's his reputation too. The business. The brand. The PR of the damn thing." I tap my hand on the table to make sure she's listening, and her eyes widen slightly. "Everything he does, and everything connected with him, reflects on Hawkston Global Hotels, and therefore, on us." Nico bought out our family business last year, and now we both work for him, but not even this point reduces the resistance emanating off Kate as she crosses her arms and glares at me. I refuse to back down. "You can't invite London's finest to a party and have a late-night basement singer be their entertainment. Be serious. You have to hire a professional."

So much for treading carefully.

Kate sucks in a gasp. "But Elly's great."

Her defense sounds flimsy as fuck, and I reckon she knows it, but she doesn't look ready to concede that I'm right, so I keep going. "Maybe she is, but where else has she performed? Are you confident she could handle that sort of pressure? As far as I'm aware, she's never even sung in the lobby of a Hawkston Hotel, let alone at a party for the CEO."

This seems to penetrate, and when Kate says, "I suppose that's true," I relax a little. But then she adds, "I have total confidence she could pull it off," and I'm back to square one.

Time to offer a viable alternative. "Why take the risk? You could have Amy Moritz if you wanted. She'd probably jump at the chance to play for Nico."

Amy is the music scene's biggest new name, and she's had a string of top ten hits in the past couple of years. She's huge, and she's also one of Nico's best friends, which, to my mind, makes this a no-brainer.

Kate considers this for all of half a second. "I don't have the money to pay Amy Moritz to perform."

I shrug. "Get Nico to pay."

Kate's expression hardens. "This is a *surprise* party. And I don't have access to Nico's funds. I can't splurge the way he could."

"So tell him about the party. Have him book Amy."

She splutters into the tea she's about to drink from. "You really don't have an ounce of romance in your entire body, do you?"

I screw my face up. *What kind of comment is that?* I'm not hanging around if she's going to dismiss all my suggestions. It's late, and I'm tired. I get to my feet and shrug into my coat. "This isn't about romance. This is about throwing the best party you can—"

"For the man I love," Kate interjects.

"Sure. Whatever. But you cannot get Elly to perform at a billionaire's birthday party. It's ridiculous. Not to mention the fact that she's ditzy as hell. She can't even remember to pay her rent, for fuck's sake. It's late every single month. Did you know that?" Kate bites her lip and, to her credit, looks a little ashamed about this. "If she wasn't your friend, I'd have terminated her lease years ago. If you do ask her, she'll probably forget to turn up or arrive half an hour after her set was due to start. Don't fucking do it. If you're strapped for cash I'll lend you money to pay for someone else."

Kate looks perturbed by my outburst, but the expression dissolves as she leans back in her chair, judgment wafting off her. "You haven't even heard her sing, have you?"

My lip curls. "I don't need to. If she were any good, she'd have made something of herself by now."

A loud creak sounds from right outside the front door. *Someone's out there.* Kate's worried gaze locks onto mine. Before I can think, I pace to the door and yank it open.

Elly, half-bent over as if she'd been peering through the keyhole, topples into me, limbs flailing, her curly blonde hair all wild.

I have a split second to realise she's been out here eavesdropping before her fingers are clamping into my quads in an attempt to prevent the crown of her head crashing against my dick.

"Fuck," she swears, digging her fingernails into my trousers. My hands fly into the air, raised in surrender. I'm not touching her. I can't be dealing with any accusations that I'm taking advantage of this situation. *But if she will fly head first at my crotch...*

She's still clinging on when I let out a croak of laughter. "Found your happy place down there, El?"

She scowls up at me and quickly rights herself, dusting down the arms of her sheepskin coat. "Jack." She says my name in the exact tone you might say '*fuck you*'. "I knew you were here. Your cologne is hanging out there"—she indicates the stairway—"like a cloud of mustard gas. I nearly choked on it."

I give her my best smile. "Good to know you've memorised my scent."

She crosses her arms over her chest, and her small but perfect breasts balance on her forearms, the V-neck of her pale blue jumper revealing a hint of cleavage.

Damn. She might not be the best choice to sing at Nico's party, but I can't deny she's gorgeous. Always has been, but I've never pursued her because she's Kate's best friend, and I have plenty of other options that won't get me in trouble.

But today, I allow myself the luxury of taking her in. She's wearing tan leather cowboy boots paired with a sheepskin coat, like a seventies wannabe music star. Beneath it, a short white skirt hits mid thigh. The length of the skirt is baffling, given how cold it is outside, but the glimpse of bare skin is so unexpected that I find myself drawn to it, allowing my gaze to linger on the toned curve of her thighs.

She clears her throat, calling me out, and I drag my eyes to hers, determined not to show a hint of guilt as I flash her the grin that works on all women.

Except, apparently, Elly Carter, who directs a look of pure animosity my way.

"Elly, hi." Kate's voice is a shock to my system. I've been so absorbed by Elly that I forgot she was there. Her greeting rings guilty, and even if Elly hadn't heard us talking about her, Kate's tone is a dead giveaway.

"Hey," Elly replies, her voice hollow. It's so different from how I've heard her with Kate in the past, all bubbly and vivacious. *Is that my fault?*

She shifts and I get a whiff of her scent. My gut tightens as I realise it's as familiar to me as mine appears to be to her, and yet I hadn't known it until this moment. All these years, and *now* I notice? *Bizarre.* It's fruity... like lemons and something else. *What is that?* Without thinking, I lean a tiny bit closer and inhale.

Elly's eyes widen, and she draws back, staring at me like she wants to slit my throat. *Shit*. I must have really annoyed her because ordinarily she'd make some flirtatious comment or tease me. I'm not sure I like this version of her very much.

"Get what you wanted there?" Elly hisses at me.

I dare a grin and run my tongue over my top teeth, hoping she'll stop that nasty scowl. "You smell like lemons." When her expression doesn't shift, I add, "Sour."

Annoyance flashes in her bright blue eyes, then she looks past me to Kate. "What's this about a party? Did you want to book me to perform?"

Wow. I'm stunned and mildly impressed that Elly's addressing this head on.

Kate straightens in her seat. "Yeah, actually. Nico's surprise party. What do you think?"

The pause that follows is a beat too long, and Elly appears to shrink as something like panic mars her face. It contorts her features for a microsecond, but it's long enough to tell me what I need to know, validating every word I said earlier: Elly Carter doesn't have the confidence to perform at an event like this.

She wipes her expression clean and straightens her shoulders. "I'd love to."

Fuck me.

She holds herself upright, and I sense a further hardening of her muscles before she turns to me. "It didn't sound like you thought it was a good idea."

Is that a question? I consider holding my tongue, but the aggressive way she's staring at me feels like an intimidation tactic. As if she's asking if I have the balls to say it to her face.

Does she think I'm going to back down? Retract my statement? Pretend she's better than she is? Out of what... politeness? Decency? I have to swallow the harsh laugh that claws at my throat. Elly might have the brightest blue eyes I've ever seen, but I wouldn't cushion my opinion for anyone else, so why should I do it now? "I don't think it's a good idea. You're not qualified. Nico needs the best, and you aren't it."

She flinches. I expect her to lash out, but my comment appears to have landed somewhere deeper, and I feel the sting of regret.

Her eyes close slowly, like she's holding back a surge of emotion, her breasts rising on a lengthy inhalation.

Why does she have to look so beautiful in her hopelessness? I feel like I swiped a kitten that was pretending to be a tiger, and the urge to apologise swells like a wave. I lock it down. She asked. I answered. If she can't take it, that's not my problem.

"Fuck, Jack," Kate hisses at me, then shifts in her chair to focus on Elly. "He has no idea what he's talking about. He's never heard you sing, or seen you perform. When's your next gig?"

Shit.

Elly's eyes narrow as if she's wondering if we're playing a trick on her. "Tomorrow night. At the Marchmont Arms..." Her eyes flit to mine, and I sense she's uncomfortable with whatever else she's about to say. "In the basement." Ah. My *late-night basement singer* comment comes back to me. "It's after my bar shift. Not until eleven."

"Great. We'll be there. Won't we, Jack?" Kate's tone is clipped, as though this is all decided. "You just told me you have no plans this weekend."

Damn it. The last thing I want to do is spend my night in a shitty dive bar. And then there's Lydia too. "Actually..." I begin as Elly examines me. Her unrelenting stare is making my body heat like tarmac in summer. I grip my tie and tug on the knot. "There is—"

"He doesn't want to come." Elly cuts me off and her gaze slices past me to Kate. "I'm all for a bigger audience, but not when you have to drag them there kicking and screaming like a toddler having a tantrum. It kills the vibe."

Tantrum? "I don't kick and scream," I counter.

"Oh, no, of course not. My mistake. You'd never do that because you're *all man*," Elly teases, drawing out the last two words and rolling her eyes. "You'd just sit there and growl."

Growl? What the actual fuck? "I bet you'd love that," I say, smirking at her suggestively, which is definitely not the response she expected because a soft blush colours her cheeks and her eyes dart away from mine.

"Jack," Kate reprimands, but I ignore her.

"And yeah," I continue, staring at Elly, my tone much sharper now, "if I have to sit through a bunch of amateurs, I'd probably growl about it."

Her furious glare meets mine. "Do you even know what the word 'amateur' means?" she bites out, going all tigress on me again. "It means you don't get paid. And I do get paid. Just because we can't all be Mr Moneybags like you, doesn't mean it isn't still worthwhile cash."

Mr Moneybags? I can't even work out if that's an insult or not. It sounds like a compliment, but it definitely wasn't meant as one. Elly's always taken issue with the fact I have a lot of money, as if me working hard and making millions is something I've done deliberately to annoy her. Or at least that's how it feels when she niggles me like this. *Two can play at this game.*

"Good to know." I make a show of glancing at my watch. "Your rent's due at the end of the week. Keep saving those pennies, and maybe you'll be able to pay on time this month. And if you can't, I'll sit outside the front door and growl until you can."

Elly's mouth opens wide, and her gaze moves to Kate. "How are you related to this arsehole? How is that possible?"

I chuckle, and Elly glares at me.

"Oh, El." Kate's tone is placating and apologetic all at once. "Ignore him. I'll strap him into a taxi and gag him. That way, it won't matter if he kicks and screams."

Kate gives me a closed-lipped smile, seemingly pleased with her joke, and it's right on the tip of my tongue to retort that Elly would probably enjoy having me bound and gagged. She's probably into that kinky shit.

I open my mouth to crack the joke, then stop myself. *What am I thinking, laying on the sexual innuendo in front of Kate?* That's my cue to leave. I'm fucking knackered. If I stay here any longer, I'll say something unforgivably inappropriate. I give them a bow and announce, "Goodbye, ladies."

"Night, Jack. Thanks for everything tonight. You're the best." Kate blows me a kiss, and Elly steps to one side to let me past.

For the briefest second, my entire body is alongside hers on the threshold. The hostility radiating off her is palpable, so sharp it could tear my coat and destroy the cashmere. *Fuck it,* I definitely don't like this state of affairs. Bring back the slightly antagonistic flirtation; that's always worked perfectly for me and Elly.

"Hey, Jack," she whispers, so low I'm sure Kate can't hear it. "If you come and hear me sing, I promise I'll listen to you growl."

My heart gives an awkward thud. *What the fuck is that about?* I pull back to see her eyes twinkling, and a smile creeping in at the edges of her pink lips. *That's more like it.* Seeing my slightly stunned reaction, she looks delighted with herself, like she thinks she's won the match point.

I'm still staring at her when she says, "See you Saturday. Or not." She gives a little shrug like she doesn't care either way.

"I'll be there."

It's her turn to look surprised, but she recovers quickly, giving me a little nod. "Okay."

It's a simple response, but her voice is a husky whisper that echoes in my mind long after the bitter wind outside ought to have blown it away.

2
ELLY

"Elly, table fourteen." Marcia clicks her fingers and points where she wants me to go. She's my boss, and she's always stern—a fact that used to upset me until I realised it wasn't personal. It's how she copes with running a rowdy bar, and when she's not in 'boss mode', she's lovely. I'd never be able to handle a place like the Marchmont Arms, but Marcia can control the punters with the merest raise of one of her artificially thickened brows. She's so competent I spend my shifts half in awe of her.

I watch her drift through the bar, smiling at patrons and giving orders to other members of staff, but I don't move. There's a strange nervous sensation that's sitting in my lower abdomen, and it's knocking me off my work. It's been there all evening. I'm pretty sure it's not about my upcoming set either, because I've played here hundreds of times.

Maybe it's Jack.

I'm trying to ignore the fact that he's supposedly coming to see me play. *Jack Lansen. What a fucking arsehole.* I knew he never took me seriously. He always had half a sneer on his lips whenever he asked me what I was doing, if my music had taken off yet, or if I was going to be releasing a single anytime soon. Oh sure, that sneer was concealed beneath an ice-thin façade of good manners and false chivalry, but I knew it was there, hiding behind that annoyingly handsome face of his. Dark hair, blue eyes, the crook in his nose from when he broke it playing rugby that somehow makes him even *more* handsome, and his jaw so square it doesn't even look real.

The way he talked about me being late to pay my rent... as if it's something I do on purpose, shows he's completely out of touch. How I live, monitoring every penny I spend and having to skimp on essentials so I can justify the occasional night out with my friends, is probably so alien that he can't even comprehend it. I don't have pots of savings to dip into whenever I want to treat myself. I struggle to pull the rent together every single month, and my job here is the only stable income I have.

But overhearing him telling Kate not to hire me... that *really* annoyed me. He was cock-blocking my career. *Arsehole*. But even though I want to get mad about it, I can't quite manage it because... he could be right.

Nico needs the best, and you aren't it.

It felt like a hit to the face when he said that, and I couldn't even disagree with him. If Nico could have Amy Moritz performing at his birthday, why on earth would he want me? He wouldn't. And I *haven't* sung in the lobby of a Hawkston Hotel, let alone at a billionaire's birthday party.

If I had been alone with Kate, I might have made an excuse. Sing for Nico Hawkston? Nope. I can't do that. But with Jack staring at me like he knew exactly what I was thinking, could read every doubt and hesitation as if it were a manifesto that backed up every point he'd made, I couldn't say no.

But—*fuck me*—what have I gotten myself into?

Once upon a time, I imagined I'd make it to the top. Platinum albums and sold out arenas. But after years of graft and constant rejections, I had to be realistic. Maybe this is where I belong. Maybe the basement of the Marchmont Arms is the pinnacle of my career. *Maybe this is where dreams come to die.*

I shrug the thought away. I like it here. It's familiar. Comfortable. I can handle this.

A sharp pinch on my shoulder wakes me from my reverie.

"Table fourteen," Marcia hisses at me. *Oops.* I completely ignored her earlier command. I'm away with the fairies tonight.

I rush through the darkened bar. There's a comedy act going on. Apparently, he's popular on social media and he draws a pretty big crowd; the place is packed. With any luck, a few people will stay on for my set.

I make my way towards table fourteen, but my pace slows when I see who's sitting there.

Jack Lansen.

He's early. It's only half nine. My heart gives a giddy little thrum, which I can't explain.

He's wearing a white shirt without a tie, and the collar is undone at the neck. It's a perfect mix of casual and smart; he rests his elbows on the table and his biceps fill his sleeves. Dark scruff shadows his strong jaw, and I'm pretty sure I can make out the blue of his eyes, even in the dim light and from this distance. Or maybe I'm imagining it…

He's with a woman, who at first I assume is Kate, because they were supposed to come together, but on closer inspection, it's definitely not her. This woman's hair is a fraction lighter, like gold has been spun through it, and her features are less angular than Kate's. Her eye makeup is heavy; thick black liner decorates her top lids, and her lashes are full and dark, but in an overwhelming way. They can't be real. Her lips are so shiny they look sticky, but in spite of all that, I can't deny she's beautiful. Together, she and Jack look like a couple from a magazine shoot—they're so good looking that it's hard not to stare, and down here in the Marchmont Arms, they stick out.

The woman smiles at Jack, her hands on the table, leaning towards him. And Jack—the *arsehole*—is laughing. His entire handsome face is glowing. He's radiating happiness, and it makes my stomach churn.

It's only when he stops laughing, his attention drawn by me staring, that I realise I've stopped walking. I'm standing between two tables, my iPad dangling from one hand.

And Jack Lansen is staring right at me.

The woman with him turns to look too, probably pissed off that she's lost his attention for a second. She gives me the once over and then looks away; I might as well be another table or chair for all the acknowledgment I see in her eyes.

She strokes the back of Jack's hand with her fingertips, and he drags his gaze off me and back to her.

I will my body to move. *Get a grip. You knew he was coming.*

But now that he's here, and with someone I wasn't expecting, I feel a whole commotion of weird emotional crap bubbling up.

I walk over to the table, but right about when I should be asking for their order, I can't seem to open my mouth. Jack's gaze slides over me, but my inability to speak must be catching because he doesn't say anything either.

With a monumental effort, I roll my shoulders and plaster my great big server smile on my face. It's my job, after all, and I need to keep it if I want to pay my rent to my prick of a landlord.

The woman wafts the back of her hand towards me, keeping her eyes locked on Jack when she says, "Can I get a white wine spritzer?" and then continues to chew Jack's ear off about someone they know in common. It sounds deathly dull.

Jack's blue eyes pop up towards me, then back to the woman. "Lydia," he says, and his tone sounds like a gentle reprimand.

"Huh?" She raises an eyebrow, clearly a little peeved that he's interrupted her tirade.

He cocks his head at me. "This is Elly. My sister's flatmate."

"Oh." She shifts sideways in her chair to get a look at me. "Oh. I thought you were the waitress."

"I *am* the waitress," I deadpan, holding my iPad poised to fill in their order. Lydia's glossy lips pucker and her brows shoot up, but I don't acknowledge the caricature of shock she's currently portraying.

"One white wine spritzer and...?" I look to Jack.

"A lager." He holds my gaze way longer than is necessary to order a beer, and my cheeks heat.

"Is that all?" I ask, breaking the staring match.

Jack blinks, confusion skirting his features, like he'd momentarily forgotten where he was, or what he was doing. "That's all."

"So, you live with Kate, do you?" Lydia says. "That's weird, isn't it? Your flatmate's dating a billionaire, and you're working tables?"

So rude. The thump of my blood in my veins suddenly seems too forceful.

"You made it." Kate's delighted voice drifts towards us, saving me from having to respond. She's bustling through the tables, wrapped up in a cashmere coat and scarf. She grabs me in a big hug, then hugs Jack. She's about to slide into the seat next to him when she notices Lydia eagerly staring up at her. She gives her brother a quizzical look.

"You brought a date?" She holds out her hand without waiting for Jack to confirm, and she and Lydia start going through introductions.

Jack strokes his jaw from his ear to his chin, his elbow propped on the table as the two women talk.

A lock of hair so dark it's almost black falls across his forehead, looking artful and casually perfect. He really is unfairly good looking. I want to ruffle my fingers through his hair and mess it all up, just to annoy him. He pushes the wayward lock back, and the motion distracts me from my thoughts. He side-eyes me like he's checking to see if I'm still there. Perhaps suspicious that I've been watching him, ogling his bone structure. *Damn him and his gorgeous face.*

"Can I have a coke, El?" Kate says.

Jack's still watching me as I add it to the order. *Is it hot in here?* It's normally not this warm in the basement, and I am sweating tonight.

"Elly's got the most beautiful voice," Kate says to Lydia. "Jack doesn't believe me." She nudges Jack. "You'll find out tonight, eh?"

Surprise lights Lydia's eyes, and she turns to me. "You're performing?"

"I'm on at eleven."

Her forehead wrinkles. "We can't stay that long." She stretches across the table, laying her hand over Jack's again. *How many times has she touched him?* "I thought we were only here to see the comedy. It's my client's opening night at the Shaftesbury Theatre. We're meeting her after the show." She turns to me, her hand still covering Jack's. "I'm in PR. I deal with a lot of famous faces, and I have to be there."

A slow curl of anger wraps itself around the disappointment in my stomach. *Why the hell did Jack show up at all, if he wasn't going to stay?*

Kate leans back in her chair and crosses her arms, death staring her brother. "You're leaving? But that was the whole point. To hear Elly perform—"

"Jack doesn't need to be here. I don't need to prove anything," I interrupt.

Lydia claps her hands together. "Fabulous." Her glee stokes my rage. "Because there's a party after the show. Some big names in British film are popping in."

Oh, shut up, Lydia. It's unlike me to be this irritated by a woman I don't know, but tonight I can't help it. I tuck the iPad under my arm and then, just because I'm pissed off, I lean into Jack on my way past the table and whisper, "You don't know what you're missing."

I sense him stiffen at my proximity. I don't turn around to catch his reaction as I head back to the bar, but I'm pretty sure I can feel him staring.

I spend the rest of the evening waiting tables, trying to ignore Jack Lansen and his date. I don't know why he bothers me so much. He's a typical money man... only interested in business and cash and all that shit I don't care about. I don't think he has a creative bone in his body. I'd never be interested in someone like him. Too corporate. I doubt he has a soul beneath his suit.

At ten thirty, he and Lydia get up to leave. Kate stays alone, and it ignites a spark of anger that Jack's ditching his sister. When they've left, I head back to her table.

"It's late," I say. "You don't have to stay. You've heard me play loads. Don't sit here alone just for me."

Kate's mouth distorts with a barely concealed yawn, which she covers with the back of her hand. "Oh, Elly... are you sure? I've had a tough week at work. I could really use an early night. I'm sorry about Jack. He didn't tell me he had a date tonight."

"Doesn't he always have a date?"

Kate yawns again, but it's interrupted by a laugh. "True. He has a short attention span."

I put my hand on Kate's shoulder. "Go home. I'll see you later."

"Actually, I'll be at Nico's tonight. You'll be okay getting back? It's supposed to rain. Take a cab."

She's already lifting her coat, shrugging into it as she stands. She gives me a quick hug. "Break a leg."

When she's gone, I clear the table, and there, beneath Jack's beer bottle, is a pile of fifty-pound notes. My fingers tremble as I count them. *Ten*. Five hundred quid. It's the biggest tip I've ever received.

But what does it mean? Is it an apology for leaving early, or is he just in the habit of leaving this much cash everywhere he goes, like a bird shitting when it takes off?

It's probably the latter.

I take the money to Marcia to add it to tonight's tip pot, tormented by the idea that, despite the enormity of the tip and how pleased everyone will be by it, I would have preferred him to stay and hear me sing.

My set goes well, or as well as I could hope. Turns out not many people stayed after the comedy had finished, but that's not new. Most of the time, I'm playing to an almost empty room, or a couple of drunks in the corner. Tonight, I played some covers and some of my own stuff. All acoustic guitar, but my buzz had kinda been killed by Jack Lansen showing up only to bail before I'd sung a note.

I stay until closing, helping to clear everything away, and there's a lock-in afterwards for a few of the regulars, so I join them for a couple of drinks. No need to rush home to an empty house. A tinge of sadness hits me at the thought, but I shove it away.

"Elly," Marcia says, leaning over me as I sip my drink. "Someone left this for you." She slaps a little white business card down on the table and watches as I pick it up to read it.

Granville Entertainment Agency
Robert Lloyd
Music Agent

My heart starts pounding, and my hands feel shaky. *Robert Lloyd*. He's a big name in the industry. There must be some mistake. This can't be for me, can it?

The confusion must be clear on my face because Marcia gives my shoulder a little squeeze. "Thought you'd like that."

She's misinterpreted my silence for the stunned speechlessness that comes from finally winning something you expected to win, rather than the utter shock of winning something you never dared to hope for.

"He said he liked your sound and you should call the office and schedule a meeting."

Wow. "Oh, gosh...I..." *Can't speak.*

Marcia hugs me. "Come back and see us when you're rich and famous, okay?"

I laugh, but I'm still completely dazed. My pulse increases its beat as I grip the business card in one hand. *It's real.* This is what I've been waiting for... this is the dream I thought had died, risen to life like Frankenstein's monster, lurching awkwardly inside me.

The Granville Agency is huge, and Robert Lloyd is the top dog. If I can get representation with him, my career might finally take off.

Suck on that, Jack Lansen.

Excitement buzzes in my veins, and I stay for a couple more drinks, unable to keep the grin off my face. *Robert Lloyd wants to meet me.*

When I'm finally ready to leave, the rain is pouring down. I hoist my guitar, safely packed away in its bag, over my shoulder, and walk out.

There isn't a cab in sight. I know I told Kate I'd take one, but I'm strapped for cash. As though the skies hear me, the rain gets heavier, and water batters my cheeks as a gust of wind pulls my hood back. In seconds, my hair is soaked and rain is dripping into my cowboy boots.

Damn it. Not even I need to save money this much. I pull my phone from my coat pocket, intending to order an Uber.

Shit. It's dead. I forgot to plug it in before my shift.

Nothing for it but the night bus.

The street is quiet because of the pounding rain. I make my way down towards Piccadilly. The deluge is so heavy I can hardly see. I pull my hood back up, but the rain is coming every which way.

Lightning spears the sky overhead, and a bone-rumbling clap of thunder follows soon after. The streets are running with rivers of water. *Crap. This wasn't my best idea.* I hurry towards the bus stop when a car honks. I keep walking, not even looking up at the noise. I don't know when the next bus is, but as long as I'm moving, I'm attempting to sort out this shitty situation.

The horn honks again, twice. Short. Sharp. I still don't stop.

"Elly!"

Weird. Why is someone shouting my name during a storm in central London in the middle of the night? I look around, but I don't see anyone.

I glance over to the car that's parked on a double yellow line, flashing its hazard lights. The vehicle is dark, sleek, and no doubt crazy expensive. Whatever arsehole is driving it doesn't care about the price of a ticket, because he shouldn't be idling there.

A hand sticks out the passenger window. A man's hand, with an expensive watch on the wrist. Two curled fingers beckon me towards the car. I can tell it's the driver, rather than a passenger, because I can see the shape of him leaning across the inside.

"Get in the car."

What the hell?

Cars are blaring their horns, driving past the stationary vehicle, arches of rainwater from their wheels spraying towards me as they pass.

I peer in at the car just as the man leans out the window. "Elly. Get in the fucking car right now."

Jack Lansen.

My heart does a little pitter-patter, then annoyance sets in. Who does he think he is, bailing on my set this evening and then ordering me into his car?

"I don't get into cars with arseholes," I yell.

He moves away from the window and for a second I think he's going to drive off, but his car door swings open and he spills out into the middle of the road, all six foot four of him, and paces towards me through the rain.

"What's wrong with you?" He grabs my elbow. "Your guitar is going to turn to mulch out here. Get in the car. I'll drive you home."

Just as I'm trying to make sense of the fact that Jack Lansen has appeared out of nowhere in the middle of a storm and is screaming at me to get in his car, and has his huge hand wrapped around my elbow, a horn blares, long and loud. It's an orange Lamborghini, offensively bright even in this rain, and it's careening at high speed down the road. It's going to hit that huge puddle so fast, we'll be drenched.

Jack grabs both my arms, pulling me close to shield me as the car roars past, covering both of us in a tidal wave of rainwater. A second car, travelling equally fast, passes right behind, dousing us a second time.

I gasp as the freezing water drenches me from head to foot, but when the water clears, all I see is Jack.

He's scowling, and his hair is plastered to his forehead, rain dripping off the congealed strands, cascading down his face. His suit jacket is a soaked rag against his torso, but he's still holding onto me with both hands. There's a split second where our eyes meet, and something like alarm flashes through his gaze, as though he's not quite sure how he got here, pressed up against me, trying and failing to protect me.

"Fuck's sake," he snarls as he lets go of me and stares down at his soaked clothes. "I should've left you out here to drown."

This whole scenario is nightmarish, but for some reason, I find it incredibly funny.

He's sopping wet, I'm sopping wet, his car door is open, the lights are flashing. Cars are roaring past and honking.

I start to laugh.

His handsome face twists into a mask of disbelief. "What the fuck are you laughing at?" He blinks at me through the droplets that are hanging off his ridiculously long eyelashes.

I bite my lip to stem the unreasonable cascade of laughter that's seeking its way up my throat, but it does nothing to hide how amused I am.

"If you don't come with me right now, I'm leaving you here."

"All right, all right," I say, letting him drag me to the car.

He grabs my guitar from me, yanks open the back door, and tosses it onto the backseat. He slams the door way too hard, as if it's the instrument that's angered him rather than me.

Do I want to get in the car with him when he's like this? Normally, Jack's all cheeky smiles and amusement. I've rarely seen him take anything this seriously. He's not himself.

But he's also right. If I don't *actually* want to drown out here, his car is my best option. I get in the passenger side and Jack gets in the driver's seat.

The windscreen immediately fogs up with the two of us in here, steaming and damp. Jack puts on the air con full blast to clear it, and the buzz of it fills the car. He hauls off his jacket and throws it into the back on top of my guitar case. His shirt underneath is soaking too. It's so wet that the cotton sticks to the outline of his pecs in an alarming way, and a strange coil of arousal that I don't want to examine too closely slithers somewhere deep inside me. Somewhere *intimate*...

Damn it.

He brushes his hair off his forehead and then grabs the steering wheel, glancing in the wing mirror as he clicks on the indicator. The window-wipers clear the screen in a hypnotic double-speed.

I press my spine against the back of the leather seat, crossing my arms over my chest, trying to ignore the straining of Jack's biceps against his wet shirt as he drives.

I've never been alone with Kate's brother before, and definitely not in a small space like this. His presence fills the car, mingling with the rich, masculine cologne he wears and the smell of autumn rain.

"Fucking Lambo drivers," Jack curses. "Who the fuck buys an orange car? The same arsehole who doesn't care about soaking pedestrians. That's who."

I think about commenting that he'd parked on a double yellow line, so maybe he's just as bad.

"I like those cars," I say.

Jack scoffs. "You would."

What does that mean? I don't want to give him an opening to insult me more than he already has, and for a few moments, neither of us speaks. There's a strange tingling sensation spreading through my whole body, and I'm hyper-aware of the rise and fall of my breasts as I breathe. My nipples graze against the wet cotton of my bra. *Has my shirt turned see-through?* I need to say something to distract from the silence that's wrapping around us, tying us together in its stealthy grip.

Jack must be feeling the same way because he blurts out, "Did you get your tip?"

"Yes. Thanks. Everyone was very grateful."

"Everyone?"

He looks genuinely confused, and it's curiously endearing. I rush to explain, driven by an unexpected need to ease his discomfort. "We pool the tips and share them at the end of the night."

"Oh." He taps his index finger on the wheel. "If I'd known that, I'd have left more." He doesn't look my way, but I can sense his awareness of me like a spectral presence. Somehow, it feels like he's scrutinizing me without so much as a glance in my direction.

My chest constricts, and breathing feels suddenly hard. Tension seeps into the air, and this time it's me who cracks it. "Is this a Bentley?"

"Yup."

I snort, and Jack presses his lips together but says nothing. I shift my wet hair off the back of my neck and let it hang down my shoulder. "I didn't realise it was you when the car pulled up. I thought you'd have gone home with Lydia."

"How do you know I didn't?" His eyes flick up to the rear-view mirror as he shifts lanes.

I check the time on the dashboard: 2.22 am. He's had more than enough time to take someone home, fuck them, and come back again. *Ugh.* I rub my hands over one another in my lap. "I don't."

Jack nods, but I sense that he's merely acknowledging my admission of ignorance, rather than confirming or denying anything. Silence engulfs us for a few moments before he speaks again. "What were you going to do? Walk home in the rain?"

"Night bus."

A laugh rumbles in his throat. "You should have called me."

Called him? When have I ever called him? He's called me once or twice when he couldn't get hold of Kate, but it would never have occurred to me to call him, especially not when I knew he was on a date with another woman, and the fact that he's suggesting it feels... weird. My heart flutters. *What the hell?*

"My phone died," I add, although why I'm explaining myself, I don't know. "What were you doing? Curb-crawling?" I imbue my voice with as much disdain as I can muster, despite the fact I'm still flustered at the idea that he wanted me to call him.

"Yeah. I've been scouring the streets for a suitably bedraggled woman to drag into my car and destroy the leather seats with."

I turn sharply to look at him, but his strong profile looks straight ahead. There's not a trace of humour on his face.

"Seriously?"

He shoots me a glance before his eyes roll up to the roof. "No, not seriously. I came back to the Marchmont, but it was closed."

My heart gives an almighty thud, so hard I immediately panic that Jack can hear it, or maybe feel the vibration of it through the car seat. *What the fuck is going on?* I don't like this man. But a little balloon of hope is swelling in my chest. *Maybe he came back to hear me sing.* "Why?"

Jack frowns, and the moment stretches a fraction too long before he finally admits, "I forgot my coat."

Pop goes the balloon. Thank God Jack has his eyes on the road because I'm pretty sure he'd see the disappointment on my face, and I would rather die than let him know he can incite that kind of feeling in me.

3
JACK

I park up outside the Clapham house. There isn't a soul on the street, given the weather and the time of night. It's not raining anymore, but the streets are slick and water runs in streams at the sides of the roads, trickling down into the drains.

I get out of the car at the same time as Elly does. I grab her guitar from the backseat and in a moment, the two of us are standing at the front door of the three-storey townhouse. Elly and Kate share the top floor flat. Normally, I rent the other floors, but they're already empty given my intention to renovate. No lights shine from any windows. The house looks deserted.

Standing side-by-side, I'm struck by how tiny Elly is compared to me—she barely reaches my shoulder. Her enormous curls are slicked down in winding strands at the side of her head, and her coat is soaked through.

Guilt hits hard. I was supposed to watch this woman perform tonight and I didn't stay. I'd kinda hoped I could swing back to the Marchmont and Elly would still be playing, but I'd totally lost track of time, although God knows why because my date with Lydia was a disaster. I had to follow through on our agreement to attend the party with her, but I dragged her to the Marchmont first because I told Elly I'd be there.

Fucking pointless, the whole thing, given I never got to hear Elly sing. I would have been better off not going to the Marchmont at all, or cancelling the date with Lydia, but I didn't want to show up solo to hear my sister's friend perform because that seemed way too intimate. Too much pressure. Lydia was a buffer, of sorts.

When I extricated myself from her clutches, I drove back to the Marchmont. I figured that, maybe, Elly might still be there, and I could apologise, but the place was locked. I didn't lose my coat. I never even took one out tonight. I don't know why I lied, but I'm not about to tell Elly that I came back for her.

Seeing those cowboy boots splash through the puddles, and that tight little body all wrapped up in a giant raincoat, wild blonde curls poking out from beneath the hood, I knew it was her immediately. It was like my guilt had willed her into existence, right when she needed me.

She holds out her hand for the guitar. "Thanks for the lift."

I'm about to hand it over when a thought occurs to me. I pull the guitar back out of reach. Elly's shock is clearly etched on her face.

"Not so fast," I say. "This guitar could be ruined. That was some pretty severe rain. I think you should check. In fact, I think you ought to take it out and play."

"Don't be ridiculous." She stretches for it again. "It's late."

I keep it out of reach. "I know. But apparently, I don't know what I'm missing."

Elly gives a cute little smile, obviously recognising her words from earlier. "And now you won't ever find out."

"But I *really* want to know." I hold the guitar up in the air, vaguely aware that whatever the fuck is happening here is a lot like flirting... but not the regular, banter-filled flirting I engage in with Elly, where we wind each other up, knowing it will never go anywhere. There's a subtle difference, and right now this feels like *actual* flirting. Feels a lot fucking like it, especially given the way she's standing on tiptoes in those little boots trying to reclaim the guitar. She hasn't a hope of reaching it unless she wants to climb me.

Why does that not sound as bad as it should?
Fuck. I am flirting.

Better draw it to a close, pronto. I take a set of keys out of my pocket, intending to unlock the front door, but I can't resist the urge to add, "And I always get what I want, El."

She's right behind me as I stick the key in the lock. "Hey, it's not legal for the landlord to enter the premises without permission."

I glance over my shoulder at her. "Bad storm. Roof could be leaking. It could be an emergency. I'll need to check."

I don't know what the fuck I'm doing here, but before I can think too hard, I've shouldered the front door open and traipsed up the stairs to the first floor.

It's only when my key is in the door to the flat that I realise I could be about to open the door to find my sister. Or even Nico.

"No one's here," Elly says like she's read my mind. "But I didn't invite you in. And for the record, I'm *not* inviting you in. And as for us having sex tonight, just because you picked me up in the rain, that's definitely not happening."

My jaw almost drops to the floor. She's totally called me out on every possible outcome that I may or may not have conceived, subconsciously or otherwise, when I refused to hand her back the guitar. "Woah—"

"I'd rather eat raw fish than sleep with you," she quips.

What the hell? "Sushi's a delicacy. You know that, right?"

She wrinkles her adorable nose, and the piercing on her left nostril catches the light. "Just because your date with Lydia didn't go well doesn't mean you can force your way into the flat and seduce me. I know your game, Jack Lansen."

I ignore the fact she's accusing me of trying to fuck her, because talking about sex with Elly feels... *strange*. A bit dangerous. Kinda like skating on thin ice. If we walk out on it, we're going to plunge right through the surface. Not that she'd come with me, but *fuck it*. Elly Carter is hot, and I wouldn't say no if she asked.

I pull my thoughts back in line. "How do you know my date didn't go well?"

She puts her hand on her hip. "Seriously, Jack." She pauses as though I should immediately understand where she's going with this, and when it's apparent I don't, she blows out a sigh. "You don't want to date anyone who treats servers like shit. That's the biggest red flag there is."

I mentally replay the interactions between Elly and Lydia. "You think she treated you like shit?"

Elly averts her gaze as if this line of questioning makes her uncomfortable. "She wasn't nice."

I shrug because I don't really care what Lydia's like as a person. I figured I'd get laid and go home and that would be it. Never see her again. But the thing is, Elly has a point. Only a few hours in Lydia's company and I could already tell she was more self-obsessed than I'd have liked.

But really, it didn't matter. I would've fucked her anyway—and she was keen. She made that pretty clear when she slipped onto my lap and started grinding her arse against my cock at the after show—but for some reason, I didn't feel like it tonight.

Elly pushes past me with the most irritating smile on her face, like she's won whatever game we're playing, but she stops abruptly, spinning back to look me up and down. "But seeing as you're my best friend's brother, you're soaked through and you brought me home out of the kindness of your heart, I'll make you a cup of tea."

Without waiting for me to reply, she steps across to the open plan kitchen, fills the kettle, turns it on, and gets out two mugs from an overhead cupboard. The handle falls off the cupboard door as she closes it, landing with a metallic thud on the linoleum floor. She picks it up and fixes it back without a word of complaint, making me feel like the worst landlord in history. *Christ, this place is a dump.* The sooner her lease ends, and she's out of here, the better.

I follow her into the flat and let the door close behind me. She grabs a tea towel that's hanging off the oven and chucks it at me. "Dry yourself."

"I'd rather take my shirt off." I undo the top button. "It's very expensive. I'd like to lay it flat to dry."

Elly points a finger at me. "Don't you fucking dare. I'll throw your arse out onto the street if you even think about undoing another one of those buttons."

I lean against the kitchen counter, but I can't help smiling at her as I dab myself dry with the towel. "You seem very convinced that I have an agenda in being here tonight."

She sucks the spoon she used to stir our tea, then puts it on the side of the sink. "That's what you do, isn't it? Jack Lansen. Top class womanizer."

Shit. She's not holding back. "First, you don't know I didn't already get laid tonight. I could be totally sexually sated right now. Second, I came up here to hear you sing, because I felt bad about what I said yesterday, and then about leaving before your set tonight."

She hands me a mug, and I let the towel rest on my shoulder so I can take it.

"Is that an apology?"

"No. I stand by everything I said. You can't sing at Nico's party." I tap two fingers against my lips, then point them at her. "At least not before I've heard you."

"Hmm. Okay. Let's say, hypothetically, you're telling the truth, and you have no ulterior motive in forcing your way in here other than to hear me sing. I'll play for you. But I should warn you, you *will* want to fuck me afterwards. Can you handle that?"

Woah. That was not what I expected her to say, but there's a challenge in her eyes I can't resist, and the smirk of amusement that tugs at one side of her mouth seals the deal.

Her lips are so pink... naturally full and *pink*. *How have I never noticed that before?*

"Yeah," I say. *Casual*. "Course. But you should know that I always get what I want."

"You said that."

I nod slowly. "Right. So, if you're about to do something that's going to make me want to fuck you—"

She inhales, the sound so close to a gasp that it cuts me off. "For that to ever happen, I'd have to want it too."

This brings me up short. I definitely didn't mean to imply I'd ever take something that wasn't being willingly given. "Well, yeah. Of course." I flash her a smile, the one that ordinarily has women simpering, but Elly's expression doesn't shift. *Awkward*. "I'd just wait for you to realise it was mutual," I tease in a bid to lift the tension.

She rolls her eyes, but thankfully looks more amused than annoyed. *Phew*. "You really are the most arrogant arsehole out there. But it's after 3 am on a Saturday, so I'll forgive you." She rubs her eyes, stretches the lids wide and blinks a few times, as though she's waking from a dream. "This is surreal." She blinks again. "Is this weird for you? I mean, what happened tonight? How are we both here, soaked to the bone, in the middle of the night?" She squeezes strands of her wet hair in fisted fingers, letting a few droplets of water fall to the floor. "Let me get changed, and then I'll play."

She potters off towards her room, and I sit on the sofa.

She's right. This *is* surreal. I shouldn't be here. Just as I'm wondering if I should leave again, Elly reappears wearing blue pyjamas with stars on them, and a pair of pink slippers that look like two electrocuted rabbits dipped in neon dye.

I refrain from commenting on them, but Elly must see me looking because she pauses and shakes a foot in my direction. "Sexy, huh?"

I swallow. "Yup. Hot stuff."

"They're my backup. For when you do want to fuck me." She smirks and it's hard not to smile back. "I figure a man like you isn't coming anywhere near these things. They're the fabric equivalent of pepper spray."

I laugh, because... damn it, she's funny. I feel way too comfortable right now, joking around with her. "Yeah, those are pretty hideous." *But it would only take me half a second to rip them off.*

She picks up her guitar and unzips the case, pulls the instrument out, fixes the strap around her neck, and sits in a chair opposite me.

She strums a few chords and makes some adjustments to the strings.

Anticipation fires through me. Part of me hopes she's bad, so I can stand by the things I said last time I was here. The other part is just plain intrigued.

She tilts forwards on her chair a little, and her pyjama top gapes at the neck. *She's not wearing a bra.* The shadowed curve of her breasts is clearly visible. Even the outline of her nipples is clear from where I'm sitting. I'm instantly assailed by images of me sucking her little pink nipple between my teeth, and a shot of heat goes right to my groin.

Shit.

I shift in my seat, mentally warning my dick not to go getting ideas. I'm not about to give Elly the satisfaction of being right. Worse than that—I might actually want to fuck her *before* she starts singing, pink slippers and all.

She sits up, and my gaze slides off her breasts and up to her face. She arches a brow at me. "Ready?"

I nod, and she begins. Her delicate fingers move across the strings, plucking and strumming in a miraculous pattern that weaves a sweet tune throughout the room. I don't know the song, but the combination of chords has chills running up my spine, and when Elly opens her mouth and starts to sing, goosebumps scatter over every inch of my body.

The sound is so sultry, so low and sweet and intense that I swear her voice filters straight through my ears and directly into my bloodstream.

By the time she crests to the peak of the song I'm convinced that I'm sitting before the sexiest woman I've ever met.

How the fuck did I not know she could do this?

I'm barely breathing, held completely captive by Elly and her singing and the notes and her voice, which is like a scrawl of molasses over the carpet between us. I want to sink in it, bathe in it... *drown in it.*

She strums the last few notes, letting the sound echo in the air before she places her hand on the strings to still them. Neither of us moves.

"This really is surreal," she mutters.

A gulping affirmative pops in my throat.

Get a grip.

I propel myself off the sofa. I need to get out of here before my dick gets hard. "It's official." I fist a hand and press the knuckles to my lips, then release it. "You definitely can't sing at Nico's party."

A scandalised look crosses Elly's face. "Why not?"

"Because everyone in the room is going to want to fuck you. Including Nico." If the tension wasn't thick enough before, it increases tenfold. I'm going to fucking choke on it. The colour drains out of Elly's cheeks. "And that really wouldn't be fair on Kate."

She's staring at me like a startled deer, her blue eyes all wide and... *scared*?

"I should get going," I say, edging towards the door.

Her brows draw together, and she continues to stare at me as I move away. I'm convinced she's not going to say a word, not even goodbye, when she speaks. "Hey, Jack?"

"Yeah?"

"It's not real. What you're feeling right now... it's not real. It's just the music." *She knows.* "It wears off a few minutes after the song is over."

I want to tell her that I've listened to a lot of music, and I've never felt like this before. But instead, I say, "So I can go ahead and growl, then?"

If she looked scared before, she looks worse now. Blotches of colour appear on her throat, rising up her neck, and she presses a hand to her cheek. "Gosh. No. Don't do that."

She's flustered. Seeing her that way, and knowing I caused it, thrills me so much that I have to smother the grin that tugs at my mouth. "Okay. But you should probably keep those slippers on until you hear me drive away, just in case."

I don't hang around to hear her response because, honestly, I might be a little fucking flustered too.

4
ELLY

The minute the door closes, I'm acutely aware of the pounding of my heart. I'd been joking when I'd told Jack he'd want to fuck me after he heard me sing. Winding him up. Teasing him. Maybe even flirting... but the look on his face when I finished was... frightening. Like if I'd given him the go-ahead, he would have torn me apart with his bare hands.

I've never been looked at like that before. It was so carnal. So *animalistic*. So different to the way Jack normally looks at me, and I *liked* it.

And to tease me about the growling. *Dear Lord.* I wish I'd never mentioned it. If any kind of deep, manly, rumbling sound had come out of his mouth at that moment, I would probably have jumped up to lock the door and not let him leave until...

Until what? What the hell am I thinking?

I've never spent any time alone with Jack until tonight. I barely even know him, really. He's Kate's older brother who appears at parties every so often, flirts with everyone in the room, and then leaves with some beautiful woman dangling off his arm.

I set down my guitar and tune into the pounding of my heart, and the steady beat of my pulse that I can feel right in my core.

I know I shouldn't, but I slide my hand into the waistband of my pyjamas. I close my eyes, praying a futile prayer that maybe Jack Lansen hasn't turned me on.

I edge lower, my fingers passing over my clit, ignoring the jolt of energy that sparks through me. I shift my legs wider and slide my fingers down to my entrance, only to find it completely and utterly slick.

Not that I needed the confirmation, but the feel of wetness against my fingers is like a blast of inevitability I was hoping to escape.

I drag my fingers over my clit, which is throbbing like it wants me to notice. Wants me to do something about it. I'm breathing slowly, paying attention to all the tiny currents of need and desire flowing through me.

How much do I want to give in to this? To forever hold the knowledge that I brought myself to orgasm thinking of Kate's brother?

It's not a good idea, but I can't stop images of Jack sliding through my mind. His wet shirt over his pecs, the bulge of bicep through damp fabric, the hard expression on his face as he drove. Those eyes, so intensely blue and framed by eyelashes so long and thick it's unfair they belong to a man. And the dark scruff on his square jaw that my fingers practically begged to brush against.

My hand is absentmindedly gliding over my wet slit as the images slideshow in my mind. What if this is more than the song and the intimacy of performing for an audience of one?

What if I actually *like* Jack Lansen?

The memory of his words filters into my mind. *I'd just wait for you to realise it was mutual.*

I abruptly still my hand. *Nope. Not happening.* I am not letting my best friend's brother become my latest fantasy, even if it is only for one night.

I get up and traipse down the hall to my bedroom, my slippers scuffing along the floor. I stare down at them. Massive pink fluffy puffballs.

"You bitches," I mutter.

5
ELLY

I've thought about Jack a lot since our interaction last week. Not deliberately, but I've caught myself zoning out, only to realise a few minutes later that my thoughts have wandered to him *again*. So when Kate asked me if I wanted to accompany her to watch rich men drive ridiculously expensive race cars around a track with the caveat, 'you might find it boring, but I'm going to support Jack and I'd love you to come', I had to rein in the urge that nearly blindsided me to yell, 'Yes please, I'd love that. I've been secretly hoping to see your brother again'. Because watching men battle for dominance in luxury cars in the bitter cold is something I'd never have normally agreed to, and Kate would have known it.

I played it cool, allowing her to badger me into it, feigning reluctance at every step. But here I am, exactly where I wanted to be, on the side of a racetrack outside London. Kate grabs my arm and tugs me against her. "I'm so glad you came."

I give her a tepid smile, still intent on concealing my enthusiasm for the event. I can't have her getting ideas that anything—*however insignificant*—might have occurred between me and Jack, and the fact that I sang for him, and it left me aroused and confused, is a guilty secret that burns in the pit of my gut. I am telling *no one*.

I ease out of Kate's hold and cup my hands to blow into them, warming my fingers. It's bloody freezing, but Nico keeps plying us with beers to stave off the chill, seeing as it was him who dragged us out of the Director's box so he could 'hear the roar of the engines'. I don't like beer, and it's so much liquid that I keep having to pee, but I'm not one to say no to free booze.

"Look, there's Jack," Kate says, pointing.

My heart leaps into my throat at the mention of his name.

Damn it. Why am I having these irrational reactions to the mere mention of him? After knowing him, or *of* him, for nearly half my life, we spend one evening together and now I'm all messed up over it. *Ridiculous.* Absolutely ridiculous, because I don't even like him.

I. Don't. Like. Him.

I watch as Jack steps out, ridiculously handsome even in his driving kit. He waves, and an answering roar fills the stands. I'm pretty sure I can hear screaming. He's peacocking, and the crowd loves him for it. I want to be disgusted by how confident he is, but I can't quite manage it. I'm a mess of nerves at the thought that he's about to race a bullet-like car around the track.

"He's crazy about these cars, and this is the only place he can actually put his foot down. Can't be driving around central London at 200 miles an hour." Kate presses her hands into prayer, brings them to her mouth, and stares down at Jack. She's always worshipped him. "Do you see him? There." Kate points again.

"Yeah." I squint down at the track, as though I haven't been tracing his every movement. Dark hair flops over his forehead, and he's flashing that handsome smile at everyone nearby. He's in his element, and it's hard to look away from him. "I see him."

The truth is, I've spent the entire afternoon trying to be subtle about ogling him. He's been wandering around down there with his racing team, wearing one of those all in one suits that stretches over his broad shoulders and displays his arse perfectly. It's a very different look from his tailored suits and cashmere overcoats, and it's one I can definitely appreciate. When someone in his team wins, he roars like an animal. It's hot, in a weird, primal kind of way, as though he's the kind of guy who could put me over his shoulder and carry me back to his cave, whilst warding off wild animals (or other men) with a giant club. The idea amuses me, and I can't help grinning as I watch, while simultaneously trying to ignore the fact that the idea might turn me on.

I'd never actually hook up with Jack, but admiring him from afar... that can't do any harm, can it?

We sit in silence, watching as he fits his helmet and gets into his car, the engines revving as the racers wait on the starting positions.

I wring my hands, my heart thumping. I'm way more emotionally involved in this race than I ought to be.

The gun fires and the cars burst from the start line, roaring off at top speed. I watch Jack's car weave through the others. I didn't know he was into this stuff. It doesn't take long before he's near the front, his car edging up behind two ahead of him. I had no idea he was this good. Watching him race feels like I've unearthed some crazy, unexpected fact that only makes him more attractive. I have a sudden impulse to start telling everyone nearby that I know the man driving that car, as though I want to claim his ability as mine. To claim *him* as mine.

"Are you feeling prepared for your interview?" Kate asks, her question a shock that draws my attention from Jack and has my heart jackknifing, as if I've just been caught doing something really, *really* bad. *What if she knows? What if she can tell I'm thinking about her brother?*

"Yeah, I guess," I say casually. After Robert Lloyd left his card for me at the Marchmont, I called to book my interview and scheduled it for a couple of week's time. "Robert Lloyd's a big deal. He represents Amy Moritz."

"Amy Moritz. Wow." Kate leans forwards, seeming genuinely excited by this news. "She's huge. I'm thrilled for you. A real step forward. We'll get you out of that dive bar in no time."

I force a smile. There's an edge of condescension to Kate's enthusiasm, and although I know she would never deliberately mean it like that, her final comment about the bar reminds me of Jack, calling me a *late-night basement singer*. I can't let them dismiss my place of work like that. "I like the Marchmont."

Kate peers at me, frowning as though she suspects I can't really mean it. "You don't want to be there forever though, do you?"

I look at her blankly. Of course, I don't want to be there forever, but it's safe and small and contained. It's familiar. *What's wrong with that?*

Nico offers us more drinks, distracting Kate, and saving me from having to respond, and we watch the cars on the track. The race takes longer than I ever imagined it would. If I'd known how long Jack was going to spend out there, I might have thought twice about coming.

Actually, I'd still have come, but I might have worn something more weather-appropriate. Jeans, maybe. As it is, I'm tugging my tiny skirt down over my thighs in a pathetic attempt to stay warm.

As we watch, Kate and I share all our news, have more drinks, and eat a multitude of snacks, but after a while, she turns away, focusing her attention on Nico and his friends who surround us in the stands, leaving me with only her mother to talk to. Mrs Lansen is awful... I'm pretty sure she's never liked me.

"How's the waitressing going, Eleanor?" she asks, not taking her eyes off Jack's car.

Of all our group, she's the only one whose appreciation of Jack can rival mine. Kate's always banging on about how their mum only has eyes for Jack, and she never got a look in. I can see that now, in the way Mrs Lansen nearly explodes whenever Jack's car comes into view.

"I'm a musician," I say.

She flaps a hand as though my statement is an inconsequential irritation, like a buzzing mosquito. "Oh, sure. But that doesn't pay your bills, does it? I thought you'd have given up on that dream by now. How long has it been?"

Inside my chest, something starts shrinking. *She's so judgmental.* I've no idea how Kate turned out to be such a lovely person with this woman for a mother. Then again, my own parents aren't much better. They hated me choosing to focus on music, constantly urging me to train to be a lawyer or something more stable. Where Mrs Lansen bothers to ask, they ignore it entirely, as though my choices are unspeakable. I'm on my own out here.

"I'm never giving up," I state, and Mrs Lansen's eyebrows shoot up in disapproval before she takes a tight sip of her drink. Her lips are squeezed together so hard I'm not sure how she can get any liquid through them. Awkward silence passes between us, swallowed up by the roar of the cars and the people roundabout.

Down on the track, Jack overtakes on the inside in a nifty manoeuvre that has my heart galloping. Those cars are moving so fast, how could anyone survive if something went wrong? I can't imagine how brave you must be to get behind the wheel and race like that. It's insane. This is the craziest hobby ever.

Kate and Nico are both leaning forward in their seats, staring down at the track. I know Nico's brothers are racing too, but I wasn't paying attention to them or their cars. I have no idea how they're getting on. I've been absorbed with Jack.

Mrs Lansen sets her drink down on the ground to clap her hands. "What a man my son is," she says, eyes pinned to his car as he slips into first place. "A champion in every way."

I feel oddly nauseous that watching Jack has me experiencing a similar sensation to the one it clearly ignites in Mrs Lansen, except her claim on him is a real blood tie. Whereas mine is... *nothing*. A surreal evening of flirtation.

I absolutely won't indulge these bizarre feelings I'm having. I'm already here on account of them, but I certainly won't give Mrs Lansen the satisfaction of knowing I agree with her.

"Excuse me, but I really have to pee." I deliberately emphasize the word 'pee' for shock value. I get up abruptly, intending to push my way along the row of seats to the aisle. Mrs Lansen widens her eyes as if to say '*how rude*' and I wonder who the gesture is for. Me? Or anyone who might be watching her? All her actions seem like that... as though she thinks people are paying attention to her every movement.

Her gaze shifts from me to the racetrack. "Oh," she squeaks, jumping from her seat. "Go on, Jack." She screams, and everyone starts yelling as Jack moves into the the final lap.

My heart begins to race as Jack's car zooms across the line so fast it's nearly a blur. Everyone goes wild. Nico is on his feet, punching the air and Kate's jumping up and down, hugging him.

Jack's won the whole bloody race, and I have no one to celebrate with. I'm damned if I'm going to start hugging Mrs Lansen, even if her darling son did seal the win.

We watch as the rest of the cars cross the line, and I keep my eyes on Jack until the moment it's all over and he starts spraying champagne like it's as inconsequential as water from a tap. He's elated, and the energy coming off him is so strong I find myself grinning down at him, wishing I was standing right next to him to celebrate the win.

But I really do need to pee, and now that the race is over, I'll have to run to miss the queues for the bathrooms. As much as I'd like to stay and watch Jack, I have to go. I push my way through and dash to the bathrooms.

By the time I come out, the audience is filtering from the seats, and the corridors back here are filling up with rowdy spectators.

I hear another roar of applause and male voices yelling. More people. How will I find my way back to Kate and Nico? I should have told them where I was going. I start to jog, easing my way through the crowds, back to the doorway I left from. I swing round a corner and there, coming towards me at speed, is Jack Lansen, all wrapped up in that padded suit, sweat-slicked dark hair plastered to his head.

He's not looking where he's going, staring over his shoulder at something behind him. At the last second, he turns to face me, an agitated expression carving up his handsome features. But he doesn't stop before—

Slam.

Pain thumps through me as his hot, hard body crashes into me.

"Shit," he grunts, grabbing my upper arms and pushing me off. His expression is still distracted, and he appears harassed; not at all like the cocksure Jack I know. He looks down at me, recognition flaring in his gaze. "El. Shit. Are you okay? Fuck. Sorry."

I step back out of his hold and rub at my arms. "Ow. Watch where you're going."

"Sorry, I didn't see you. I was..." His words fade, and time seems to slow as we stare at one another. A fizzing sensation bursts to life in my chest, and heat rolls out slowly across my body. Jack's face is red, and he's breathing hard, but he's just finished racing, so it must be that, right?

Whatever it is, it's intense enough to set a fire blazing beneath my skin.

Jack is the first to collect himself. "I didn't know you were coming."

"Last minute decision," I mutter. "I came for the beer."

He must see the lie on my face because his blue eyes go all twinkly, like there's a fireworks display happening inside his skull. "Oh yeah?" He breaks into a sly smile, his gaze intense with innuendo. "It's a long way to come for a pint of beer."

He's staring at me like the cat that got the cream, and it riles me. "You can wipe that delighted look off your face. I didn't come to watch you."

"Whatever you say, El." The deep, seductive timbre of his voice slides under my skin, boiling me from the inside. A gasp sticks in my throat, and Jack's gaze settles on my lips for a second before he winks, which nearly finishes me off. He's doing this deliberately, I'm sure of it. And as annoying as it is to see him so satisfied with himself, I'm basking in his attention. I take him in, piece by delicious piece. The handsome face, the eyes bright with exertion, the muscles on his thighs I can make out through the suit... *I bet this man has stamina...*

He smirks, as though he knows exactly what I'm thinking. The expression is an easy resting place for his features, making me wonder if he gets looked at this way all the time and knows it. But of *course*, he knows it... there's no way Jack Lansen isn't aware of exactly how attractive he is.

A raucous chanting from further down the corridor interrupts us, and I tune into the repeated sound until I can make out the words.

Jack Lansen,
Hottest man on the track.
I'd eat him for a snack.

It's a dreadful rhyme. *Who came up with that?* A burgeoning giggle expands in my chest, but I bite my lip to hold it in because Jack's cocky expression dissolves, and he squeezes his eyes tight shut as though the sound causes some catastrophic internal agony.

Was this what he was running from when he crashed into me?

He throws an uneasy glance over his shoulder before turning back to me, one hand threading its way into his thick, dark hair. "Fuck," he mutters.

I lean past his bulk to see who's responsible for the disruption, only to catch sight of Lydia from the bar last week marching through the crowd, leading a team of women all wearing masks with Jack's face printed on them. They're waving a banner with *'JACK LANSEN WE LOVE YOU'* painted on it. It's absolutely, certifiably bonkers, and I cannot hold back the burst of horrified laughter that pops out of my mouth.

"You have superfans." I nod at the oncoming army, and in response, Jack gives a tiny shudder.

"Jack," comes Lydia's high-pitched squeal.

He braces as though he expects her to launch herself at him like a cannonball, propelled all the way from the other end of the corridor. "She won't stop calling. And now all this..." He waves his hand in her direction, looking so perturbed that I almost feel sorry for him. But not sorry enough to prevent the smile breaking over my face.

"She does look... hungry."

Jack raises a brow. "Don't fucking laugh, El," he threatens, but there's a teasing light in his eyes that tells me he appreciates how ridiculous this scenario is. As he holds my gaze, the two of us on the verge of laughter, I feel a happy glow ignite inside. *Am I bonding with Jack Lansen?*

"Jack," Lydia calls again, an unhinged screech to her voice this time. She's approaching fast, and I don't want her anywhere near us. Not only is she clearly a little insane, but, as much as I hate to admit it, I'm enjoying having Jack all to myself.

He cusses, a desperate grimace warping his features before it brightens like he's been struck by a moment of genius. He grabs my hand and pulls me so close to him that my next inhalation is full of the scent of him, which is somehow fresh like rainwater and the outdoors, despite the sweat. My heart starts leaping around like a kid on a sugar high.

"Kiss me," he rasps in my ear.

Goosebumps spread up my arms like a minor scale played at high speed, and my mind spirals as I process his words, but the moment I make sense of them, a jolting realisation hits me. *I want to do exactly what he just ordered.* I want to slam my lips against his, sweat and all, and kiss him.

But not like this. Not because of *her*.

I have to summon every ounce of self respect just so I can push my hands against his chest—*fuck, those pecs are hard under there*—and shove him away. He steps back, which is just as well, because there is no way I could actually move him. "Yuck. No."

"Yuck?" Jack begins to laugh as though there is *no possible way* I can really mean it.

Lydia is still pushing towards us, waving like a madwoman and yelling Jack's name.

"Yes, yuck. You're all hot and sweaty and—"

"Those your only objections?" All concern for Lydia appears to have vanished as he stares at me. He's still grinning, and that smile is doing wacky things to my insides, melting them into a soupy glue.

"Because I can go take a shower." He jerks his thumb over his shoulder as if the showers are *right there*.

I cock a hip. "I'm not kissing you at all, *ever*, but especially not here and now, so you can avoid dealing with that woman." I nod at the frenzied Lydia who's going to be on us in moments. "How old are you?"

Jack rolls his eyes but still manages to look amused rather than exasperated. "Fine." He bows his head a little and says, "Excuse me while I go and deal with this situation like a grown up." He turns to leave but looks back at me, pointing his finger like he can pin me in place with it. Which he obviously can because I don't move a muscle. "Drinks. I want to see you at the drinks later."

Before I can respond, he turns away and greets the crowd of women. Lydia steps to the front, the mask with Jack's face printed on it dangling from one hand. She's gorgeous, and she doesn't hesitate for a second before she's draped all over him, kissing his cheek, not seeming to care at all that he's all damp and sweaty. He doesn't appear to be pushing her away either. Envy rises in me like morning mist.

For a brief second, it felt like he was interested in me. *Stupid*.

As I stand there in a jealous stupor, her kiss on the cheek somehow becomes a kiss on the lips.

Did she do that, or did he?

The contents of my stomach curdle. *That really is yuck*. I tell myself I don't care. I just rejected him. He's free to do whatever he wants.

I wrench myself away from the sight of them together. It's probably just as well I can't stay for drinks, because I'd only have to watch Jack Lansen fend off all his female admirers. And I don't want him to think I'm staying just for him. I can't give the man's ego any more fodder. His skull will explode.

But even so my fingers are itching to pull my phone from my coat pocket and call Marcia at the Marchmont to tell her I won't be able to work this evening because I've been struck down by a sudden illness.

And maybe I have.

6
JACK

Freshly showered and dressed in a casual shirt and jeans, I walk into the director's lounge. It's the best entertaining space on the track, and I've hired the whole thing. I'm still on a post-win high. Feeling fucking brilliant. Not even Lydia attacking my face, suckering onto my lips like a barnacle, is enough to dampen my mood. I had to physically peel her off. Bizarrely, or perhaps not so bizarrely, any desire to fuck her has completely evaporated.

I put Lydia out of my mind and focus on my surroundings. The director's lounge is enormous, with high ceilings and huge glass windows that look down on the track below. The light is fading fast outside, but the atmosphere in here is a winner. Everyone's happy and the place is heaving with people, their excited chatter peppered with the pop of champagne corks. Most people are well on their way to being completely inebriated.

Near the main bar, someone is singing karaoke, badly. Not sure I approved that, but what the hell. People are enjoying themselves, and that's the most important thing. I spot Nico and Kate over by the window. Seb and Matt are with them, and all four of them are joking around. The giddy sound of Kate's laughter reaches my ears, and both Seb and Matt are smiling widely, clearly on the same post race high as me. It's a normal expression for Seb, but racing fast cars is one of the few things that can get Matt Hawkston to crack a grin.

My heart gives a ceremonial thud, as though something important is going to happen tonight.

Elly. That's what it is. If Nico and Kate are over there, Elly must be nearby too.

The whole time I was in the shower, lathering shampoo in my hair, I was thinking about her. Those cowboy boots and her killer thighs. The little skirts she wears, even when it's freezing outside. The anticipation of seeing her makes me feel like a teenager. Who would have thought hearing her sing would get under my skin so much?

I'm only half-aware of all the people in the room offering to buy me a drink and slamming their hands on my back and shoulders. I'm smiling and thanking them, but if any of them really cared to notice I'm sure they'd see I'm not fully focused.

Where is she?

When I reach our group, Kate throws her arms around my neck and Nico grabs my hand in his, congratulating me with a handshake even as Kate is still in my arms. If anyone can pull me out of my Elly-induced daze, it's these two. They're all smiles and admiration and it feels pretty damn satisfying to be on the receiving end of it all.

Seb and Matt come over to greet me too.

"Just as good as you were in your twenties, mate," Matt says, offering up his fist for a bump. While I return the bump, Seb turns away abruptly, fiddles with something, and spins back. His face has been supplanted by an image of mine. "Hottest man on the track," Seb jeers from behind the mask.

Fuck's sake. "Prick," I mutter, pulling the mask so the elastic snaps and Seb's face is revealed again, looking irritatingly amused. I toss the mask aside, where it lands in a puddle of what looks like beer on a nearby table.

"I was gonna keep that," Seb moans.

"What the fuck for?" I query.

"Target practice."

I roll my eyes, and Matt hands me a glass of champagne. The first gulp tastes so unbelievably good because I've earned it. My mother appears and kisses me on the cheek, making me slop my drink over the floor. I bite back the urge to reprimand her as she says, "What a fabulous performance. That team would be nothing without you. You carried the rest of them, absolutely carried them, darling."

Seb and Matt, who both put in a stellar performance too, are standing mere inches away, and they share an amused look. Mum has a tendency not to consider her audience when she makes proclamations like that.

"He was very good," Seb agrees heartily. "One man team, really. Not sure why the rest of us bothered racing at all."

Nico snorts, then lifts his champagne glass to his mouth to hide it, and Matt busies himself drinking half his glass in one go, avoiding meeting my eye. I'm pretty sure he wants to laugh, but he's too polite to do it in front of Mum.

As everyone is chatting amongst themselves, I take the opportunity to ask Kate the question that's been bothering me since I walked into the room. "Where's Elly?"

She quirks a brow. "How did you know she was here?"

"Saw her out in the corridor after the race."

Kate accepts this explanation for my sudden fixation on Elly's whereabouts. "She had to work. Shift at the Marchmont."

Something inside me drops into an abyss. *She's not here? She's gone back to the bloody Marchmont Arms?* I resolve not to say another word about her, in case I accidentally reveal that I'm absolutely, unreasonably crushed by the fact she's not here when her presence should make no difference to my enjoyment.

Tonight should be about the race, my team, my friends. Not about some girl with curly hair and cowboy boots, who has always kind of irritated me.

But it is about her.

I haven't been this gutted by a no-show in a long time.

Mum tugs on my arm. I turn to find her standing with Lydia, whose big brown eyes are fixed on me. I try to mask my surprise. I just rejected this woman; peeled her off my face like a wet plaster. *Was I too subtle? Too polite?* Fuck it. She doesn't seem remotely deterred, and Mum looks completely smitten with her. Thankfully, Lydia seems to have ditched the banner and pictures of my face. The Hawkstons would never let me live that down.

"Darling," Mum croons. "Lydia says you're dating. She's delightful."

Lydia gives a bashful smile that looks completely wrong on her face. "Jack took me to a terrible little pub in the West End," she says, glancing at Mum. "Dreadful service. And it stank of beer and sweat. What was it called, Jack?"

"The Marchmont Arms," I say, and an odd quirk of pain makes itself known in my chest. I'd have described the Marchmont the same way not long ago, but hearing it come from Lydia in that dismissive tone rubs me up the wrong way.

"Poor form, darling," Mum says to me, her lips curled with distaste.

Lydia lays a hand on Mum's arm. "We didn't stay long. I lured him to a much more glamorous affair afterwards."

"Oh, thank goodness," Mum replies, then leans into me, whispering, "Jack, she's wonderful. You finally picked a good one. I'm thrilled. Well done, darling."

I don't correct Mum, because her knowing anything about my love life is too fucking much. She has a tendency to interfere, and I've made it a rule to give her as little information as possible. But she and Lydia are getting on like a house on fire, smiling and laughing. It's alarming.

I turn back to Kate, but as I do, her face breaks out into a huge grin at something behind me, and she starts arcing her arm over her head. "El," she calls, and a flicker of hope bursts to life inside me.

I spin to find the source of Kate's elation, only to see Elly in the doorway, pushing her way towards us. Her expression is serious, but it melts into a brilliant smile when she catches sight of Kate's erratic waving. Their elation must be contagious, because it shoots through me like an electric shock, and I take a steadying gulp of champagne to stave off the grin that wants to split my face apart.

"Don't you have to work?" Kate says when Elly reaches us. "Please say you don't have to leave."

Elly's gaze shifts to me very briefly, and there's a guilty look in her eye, as though she's about to lie. "They don't need me tonight."

Did she cancel her shift for me?

Kate hands Elly a glass of champagne and drags her off for a chat, leaving me wishing I had a more legitimate reason to talk to her. I can't chat her up all night in front of Kate, Nico, and Mum. She might be here, only a few feet away, but she's almost as inaccessible to me as she would be if she hadn't turned up at all. And now there's the added frustration of knowing she's here and not being able to spend every second with her.

The evening wears on, and Mum continues chatting with Lydia. I try to focus on Seb and Matt and Nico, on *anyone* else, but it's useless because my attention is hooked on Elly.

After an hour or so of chugging champagne, Seb decides to hit the karaoke, performing a dreadful rendition of Annie Lennox's *Walking on Broken Glass*. He finishes to great applause before he stumbles back towards us.

"Who's up next?" Seb says, grinning as he slaps Matt and Nico on the back. They refuse, and it's then that Kate reappears with Elly at her side.

"Kate, you look like a singer," Seb says. "Get up there."

Kate doesn't even bother replying before her whole face lights up, and I know she's had one of her ideas. "Elly can sing," she announces.

Elly's eyes widen and latch onto mine for a fraction of a second. "No, really, I don't think I should. I've had a lot to drink."

"It's only karaoke. And Jack never heard you sing the other night," Kate continues, vibrating with excitement. "This is the perfect opportunity."

Elly stares right at me, her body utterly still, and I know she's remembering that moment in her flat when she sang for me, and the secret of it binds us together. The sensation is so intense that we might as well be back there, because everything else has ceased to exist. Kate's still tugging on her arm, but Elly's looking at me, and I can't look away from her. *Shit*. Someone's going to notice in a moment.

"She's got a killer voice," Kate says, oblivious to whatever is passing between me and Elly. "Come on, show them. Jack wants to hear, don't you Jack?"

I clear my throat, finally breaking eye contact. "Yes. Yes, I do."

Elly gives me a lingering look I can't read before Kate whisks her away. I feel shaky, as though I've bench-pressed twice my weight for longer than I should have.

"Karaoke," Lydia says, appearing as if from nowhere. "It's so undignified. After this, we should take the car to the West End and go somewhere else."

What the hell? She thinks she can join us? And what car is she talking about? My fucking car?

Mum latches onto this idea fiercely, already linking arms with Lydia. "Oh, yes," she says, turning to me. "This place is very glamorous, darling, but I'd love to find a quiet, exclusive venue. We could have some champers and celebrate your win properly, without all these other people."

"I'm fine here," I state. I want to tell Mum that Lydia is one of those *other people* I don't want to hang out with, but I can't be that rude, and Mum has clearly adopted her as a new favourite.

Mum and Lydia continue gossiping as Kate ushers Elly up to the bar to choose her song. The place is so full now, and everyone so drunk, that I can't get a decent view, even though I'm taller than most people in the room. I don't know why Kate is bothering making Elly sing, because no one is going to be able to hear her properly anyway.

A few minutes later, Kate is back at my side. "Just you wait," she hisses in my ear. "You are going to be amazed at how good she is."

Elly must have joined a queue to sing, because the next guy up isn't her, and he's crap. He drones on for what feels like forever, and I've almost forgotten Elly's about to sing when a clear and sensual note pierces the room. The volume of rowdy chatter cuts in half as people stop talking to turn to the sound.

She's singing Alicia Keys' *Fallin'*, and the power of her voice hits me smack in the chest. I haven't heard this song for years, but the way Elly sings it, it might as well be brand new. Kate lets out a squeal, and everyone in our group turns to the bar where the karaoke is set up.

"Fuck me, is that Kate's friend? She's got a pair of lungs on her." Seb's lips part, and his eyes sparkle with delight. "Wow." He blows out a forceful breath. "She just got about a million degrees hotter."

Seb's dimple deepens, and I get a flash of insight into how women must perceive him. Handsome, yet boyish. Unguarded, but still charming. And it irritates the fuck out of me. The urge to grab him by the scruff of the neck and tell him to shut the fuck up hits me so hard, I have to fist my hands and clench my teeth to keep from doing it.

The crowd begins to cheer, realising Elly is the real deal. This isn't another karaoke performance.

"That is fucking sex appeal. Holy shit." Seb brings his glass to his mouth and downs the rest of his champagne, then licks his lips, still mesmerised by Elly. "Is she seeing anyone?"

"Cool it, Hawkston," I warn, and he raises a brow at me, a knowing smile tugging at his mouth.

He doesn't push it any further, but a sensation akin to panic has already taken hold in my gut. I don't know if Elly's seeing anyone, and before now I'd never thought to ask, but the need to claim her as mine consumes me. I want to tell everyone that this incredible woman belongs to me, but it's not true. Up there with the microphone in her hand, she belongs to everyone. And it fucking kills me.

My body heats as I watch her perform. She's a total natural. The entire room is eating out of her hand, and the look on her face... *shit*, Seb is right. Sex appeal is coming out of her pores. The way she moves, the bright glint in her eyes... she's absolutely loving the attention.

A shrieking electronic noise interrupts the song. *What the fuck?* My heart lurches and adrenaline spikes in my system. *Fire alarm.* Screams erupt and rumours of a fire on the ground floor rush across the room.

People begin to panic, but we're near the exit, and Nico is quick to lead the others towards it.

Kate grabs my arm as we're swept up in the crowd. Everyone is yelling and clambering over the furniture to get out. It's a fucking stampede.

In the distance, I can hear the far-off wail of fire engines. *Is it a real fire?*

"Elly," Kate cries, gripping my arm, her eyes wide and desperate.

I glance back towards the bar. I can't see Elly, but she must be over there. "I'll get her."

I force my way against the crowd, and it's a good thing I'm big, because otherwise, I'd never make it. Champagne and beer glasses are falling to the floor, smashing and splintering underfoot, alcohol slopping everywhere.

Elly's half the size of the men in this room, and when I reach her, she's made no progress to the exit whatsoever, and is surrounded by panicking, inebriated people.

I take her hand in mine. "Come on."

She looks up at me, amazed, as though I'm the last person she expected to see, but the shock in her gaze vanishes and the relief that sweeps in to take its place wrings out every organ in my body. *She needs me.* She doesn't resist when I tuck her under my arm and escort her to another doorway. She's so small. *So vulnerable in this heaving crowd.* I squeeze her tighter, and together we make our way down a side staircase. She lets out a cough as the stench of smoke filters over our heads. Not a drill, then. *Fuck, if anything happens to her...*

Others must smell it too, because the screaming increases and the movement down the staircase gathers urgency. People are shoving and tripping. Hands flail and grip my jacket, using me to pull them forward, or trying to push me back.

Finally, we spill outside. There's a bitter chill in the night air, but it's a welcome sign of safety. *We made it.* Around us, people disperse, searching for friends, gathering in clustered groups, and within moments Elly and I are alone in the darkness, standing by the side of the building. My heart is racing, the adrenaline flooding my system making my limbs tingle.

Heaving breaths, Elly stands opposite me, trembling. "You think everyone got out?"

I glance back at the building, where smoke is choking out of a ground floor window. "I hope so."

"Fuck. That was crazy." She tangles the fingers of one hand in her hair. She shifts around, thumping her feet on the ground for a few seconds as though she too is flooded with adrenaline and needs to shake it out, then her gaze snags on mine and she stops moving. "You came back for me," she says, breathless.

I want to tell her that, *of course,* I came back for her. There was no way in hell I would have left her struggling in that mess. I give a careless shrug and say, "Figured a little thing like you would get crushed."

Elly wraps her arms around her. She must be freezing without a coat. If I had mine, I'd give it to her. "Thanks," she says, her breath pearling out in a cloud of fog.

She's shaking visibly now, and I don't know if it's the cold or shock, but before I've thought it through I'm saying, "Come here," and stepping up to her. I slide my arms around her, pulling her against me. She doesn't resist.

"Shit," she mutters, but she lets me hold her until the trembling lessens. It's a risk, having her so close to me because she can probably feel the rapid beating of my heart. With any luck, she'll attribute it to what just happened, rather than her proximity.

Her sweet, citrusy scent surrounds me until all I'm aware of is the woman in my arms. "You okay?" I whisper.

She looks up, and when our eyes meet, electricity surges through me, connecting us in a charged moment. Elly must feel it too, because a momentary look of confusion flits over her face. "The others. We should find the others," she murmurs, but there's no urgency in her tone.

Without thinking, my hand rises to the back of her neck, slipping beneath all that wild hair. Her skin is warm and soft, and the tips of my fingers twist into the curls at her nape. I've never touched Elly like this, and my skin is prickling at the contact. Maybe it's because she's off-limits—Kate's best friend—or maybe it's because I like her. But either way, there is absolutely no passing this off as me trying to comfort her. It's way too intimate. "We should," I admit. "But I'm not in a rush right now."

A stillness descends, and we're trapped, motionless, in the energy field of whatever is happening between us.

Elly wets her lips with her tongue, and when her gaze falls to my mouth, I know I'm not imagining it. She wants to kiss me as much as I want to kiss her. But as I lean towards her, she blinks, breaking the connection, and jerks away from me, eyes flashing with annoyance. "You think everyone's ready to fall at your feet, don't you?"

My laugh takes me by surprise. "What? No." The words are a knee-jerk reaction, which I immediately reassess. "Actually, yes. A lot of the time."

"Unbelievable." She paces away with purpose, but I catch up to her in two strides.

"Have I offended you? Because you should've known when you got up there to sing, the effect it was going to have. This is predictable."

She tosses her hair over her shoulder and glances sideways at me. "What is?"

"Me, wanting you."

She stops and stares right at me, outrage flickering in her gaze. Her pretty pink mouth opens to say something I'm sure isn't going to be complimentary, when—

"Elly! Jack!" Kate's voice cuts through the night air, and only now am I aware of how close we are to the main gathering of people near the track. The buzz of chatter roars in my ears, and I wonder how I hadn't noticed it before. "Thank God you're okay," Kate exclaims, rushing up to us. "It was a fire in the kitchen. Hot oil or something like that. No one's hurt. Barely any damage, apparently."

"That's good," Elly says, and I'm wondering how she's managing to appear normal and maintain a regular conversation when I am spinning from our moments alone and our almost-kiss.

"You have to come," Kate continues. "Mum's determined to go into the centre of town and drink champagne. For her nerves. She's all shaken up."

"Bollocks, it's her nerves. She's been gagging to get back to the West End all evening." I sound disproportionately irritated, and it's more to do with Elly than Mum wanting to leave. Kate, clueless as to the origin of my unexpected vehemence, shoots me a reprimanding glance.

"You know what," Elly says, "I'm going to head home. I've had enough excitement for one night."

Kate tries to dissuade her, telling her its too cold to be out without a coat, and that she should stay with us and take the car, but Elly's having none of it. She gives Kate a hug, promises to take a cab rather than the night bus, and barely glances at me before she walks towards the main road. I will her to turn back, to give me some indication that it's not *that fucking easy* to walk away from me, but she doesn't.

And she takes every scrap of enthusiasm I have for this evening with her.

7
JACK

Everyone is high off adrenaline after the fire and Mum isn't the only one who's keen to get to another venue to have a drink. I'd rather head to bed and rest, especially given Elly's gone home, but I don't want to let everyone down.

Our drivers are waiting to take us to the West End. Me, Mum and Kate get into our car, and the Hawkstons take theirs. Lydia, who's still floating around like a bad fucking smell, gets in the Hawkston car, because I quickly close the door on ours when she heads towards me. She was quick to turn to Seb and cling to him like a lifeline. He can deal with her. She's not my problem.

In the back of the car, Mum pulls an envelope from her handbag and hands it to me.

"What's this?" I ask, bemused, as I open it. A bunch of photographs fall out, and every image is a headshot of a different woman.

As I gather them up, Kate watches, her gaze flicking between me, Mum, and the photographs. She looks as confused as I feel.

"I've put together a list of the most eligible young women in London." Mum reaches out and taps the photos on my lap. "All of these have my approval."

What the fuck?

Next to me, a smothered, spluttering sound escapes Kate's mouth, which she tries to catch in her cupped hand. She must be drunk to be openly ridiculing Mum.

Mum sits back in her seat, a self-satisfied expression on her face. *She's serious.* "I've written their details on the back, so you can decide for yourself. It's about time you settled down. I've picked the best of the best there."

I don't move for at least five seconds, holding a load of images of women I don't know. How Mum moves on so fast from a burning building to this is bewildering. I always knew she was unusual as far as mothers go, but this is next-level craziness. She must have been holding this back all night.

I flick through the photos because what the fuck else am I supposed to do? Some of them are printed, others are obviously cut from magazines and stuck on bits of card. Pretty young society women, smiling up at me, their names and ages and educational details on the back in Mum's neat handwriting. There must be at least fifteen here.

I have no interest in any of these women, especially given my body is still recalling the feeling of Elly in my arms. There's no space in my head for anyone else.

I can't help wondering what Mum would say if she knew I'd nearly kissed Elly tonight. She'd fucking hate it.

"Oh, look. Isn't that Princess Astrid?" Kate says, leaning across to flick one of the pictures.

"Royalty?" I arch a brow at Mum.

"Only the best for my boy." Mum purses her lips, still looking delighted. "You're the heir to Lansen Luxury Hotels, after all."

I lean back in my seat. "Lansen doesn't exist anymore. We sold out to Nico. No one cares."

Mum draws her chin in. "Our hotels were always a cut above any of the Hawkstons', and don't you forget it. The Lansen name means something in this city. We've got to hang onto that."

Kate shoots me a look that says '*our mother is a nutcase*', but I don't return it because Mum's attention is so harshly pinned on me that she'd notice. I shuffle through a few more of the pictures until I hit another face I recognise, flipping it so Mum can see it. "She's married to a guy I went to school with. Do you know that?" But even as I hold the image up, I can see on the back that Mum has noted that she's married, but next to it she's written '*on the rocks?*'

"Yes, but I don't think it'll last," Mum announces as if it's perfectly normal to be anticipating the end of a marriage so you can nab one half of the partnership. "She'll be divorced within twelve months. She'll get a huge divorce settlement too. I heard her husband has been—"

"Thanks," I say, cutting Mum off. "But I'm okay." I stuff the photos back in the envelope and hand them back.

Mum doesn't take them, and her features harden. "You're not okay. You keep flitting from woman to woman as though they're dishes at a buffet. Enough is enough. You're thirty-five. It's time to get serious about your future. And these women"—she nods at the envelope I'm still holding—"are it. One of them is the mother of my grandchildren. I know it."

For fuck's sake. I have not had enough to drink for this conversation.

"What about Lydia?" Kate asks. "I thought you were dating?"

"No, I'm not—"

"I liked Lydia very much," Mum interjects. "She's in there too." She waves at the envelope. "Did you know she's the great-granddaughter of Sir Marcus Compton? A fine family. One of the best." I roll my eyes at this, and Kate smirks, but Mum ignores us both, continuing to pontificate. "A wonderful coincidence that you'd already met her. I think it's a sign, darling, so if you don't want any of the others, I'd be very content if you chose Lydia. In fact, she and I have arranged to go for tea next week. I'd love to have a daughter I could relate to."

Beside me, Kate sucks in a breath. Our mother is the queen of back-handed blows. I'd pull her up on it, but there's no fucking point. She's like a brick wall; nothing you say gets through.

"Lydia? Really? She was wearing a mask with my face on it," I say.

"I saw those," Mum says. "I thought they were adorable. You have a very handsome face, darling. In fact, I might ask her if she has a spare one so I can pin it on your bedroom door and imagine you never left home."

Jesus.

Kate's fists clench in her lap. "Do you want one of me too, Mum?"

"Gosh, no, darling. What on earth would I do with it?" Kate huffs quietly and stares out the window, and Mum continues talking to me. "I meant it when I said you'd picked a good one. Impeccable breeding and wonderful manners." *Wonderful manners?* Elly's comments spring to mind about Lydia treating servers like shit. "We can run with her if you want."

"This is not a team sport," I snap.

Mum looks only marginally affronted before she continues, "Just choose one of them, please. It doesn't have to be Lydia, but she's my first choice. It's the charity event in memory of your father in a few weeks, and I'll invite whoever you choose to that. It can be a casual date. Not too much pressure."

Rage simmers in my gut. This is exactly why I never tell Mum anything about the women I'm seeing. She's always been controlling. Admittedly, never as overtly as this, but in the past, when she's heard a rumour that I've been seen with someone, she never holds back an opinion, and the judgment can be vicious.

"Just take the photos and say thank you," Kate hisses in my ear.

Mum pricks up, sitting erect in her seat as though she heard what Kate said, but she makes no comment. Rather than risk my mother's wrath, I do as Kate suggests and tuck the photos into my pocket. "Thank you. I'll look at them tomorrow."

Mum offers me a tight-lipped smile. "Wonderful. Let me know your preferences and I'll see about arranging that date."

Fuck that. "Great." I knock with one knuckle on the partition that separates us from the driver.

"Yes, sir?" the driver says.

"Can you let me out? I'm going to walk from here."

"Oh, Jack. Don't leave," Mum pleads. "We're just about to pop some decent champers."

"Jack, no," Kate pleads in a whisper-hiss. She's making eyes at me that say, '*Don't leave me with Mum*', but I'm not up for tag-teaming tonight. I was hanging onto the celebrations by a thread, and this bundle of photos severed it.

"Sorry. I'm done. Need the sleep. I'll pass out at the table if I come with you." I feel a buzz of guilt that I haven't said goodbye to the others, but I don't feel like discussing my future wife with my mother over expensive champagne. *Nightmare.*

The car draws up to the curb, and I let myself out.

"Call me. I'll be waiting," Mum sing-songs right before I slam the door.

The car drives off, and I stand on the dark street corner, relieved to be alone.

It's not far to my house from here, but as I start heading in that direction, Elly pops into my head. She must be home by now, alone in that shithole of a flat. I could go there…

Don't be ridiculous.

I shove my hands deep in my pockets and walk home.

8
ELLY

It's time for me and the slippers to part ways. Maybe it was the fast cars or the sweat or the desperate '*kiss me*', or the way he admitted he wanted me, like it was an undeniable fact, but I cannot be dealing with constant reminders of my interactions with Jack Lansen. Enough is enough. It has to end. He's not a viable option for me, and I won't entertain the thought of him any longer.

I slam my foot on the pedal to open the kitchen bin and drop the slippers in. *Goodbye, bitches.*

I dust my hands off like I've just achieved some pivotal 'moving on' moment. *Symbolic.* No more thoughts of Jack Lansen, thank you very much. I have to focus on the important stuff in my life, like my music, and my upcoming interview with Robert Lloyd.

The buzzer goes, and I jump at the interruption. *Who the hell is here now?*

The buzzer goes again. *Okay, chill out.*

I pace to the intercom and press the button. "Hello?"

"It's Jack."

Jack? What's he doing here? Nerves tingle through me, making my knees weak. *So much for my symbolic moving on moment.*

"Kate's at Nico's," I blurt.

He pauses. "I'm here to see you. Let me up." *Oh.* Butterflies burst to life in my stomach. His disembodied voice sounds way hotter than I've ever noticed before, probably because his face is so distracting. And damn it, my heart is pounding at the demanding tone of it.

"Good morning to you too," I reprimand, trying my best to sound like him turning up here is no big deal, and that it might even be a tad inconvenient rather than the most exciting thing that could have happened.

I press the button to let him in, and his footsteps pound up the stairs. A wave of panic seizes me. I'm not ready to see him, not after the intensity of that moment in the dark after the race last night. *Shit.* My insides roil at the thought of it, almost as though I might throw up. I cannot be in the same room as him. Maybe I can fold myself into a kitchen cupboard or lock myself in the bathroom.

But I'm not quick enough. The door flies open, and Jack stands there in his cashmere overcoat, irritation scrawled over his handsome face, my sheepskin coat draped over his forearm.

His gaze snags on me, dipping right to the toes of my cowboy boots, and my breath stutters. After a beat, he lurches into motion again, unhooking my coat—*my favourite coat*—from his arm and handing it to me.

"Oh. Thanks." My voice sounds weak as I take it. I clear my throat and add, "I was about to start mourning for it."

Mourning for it? I cringe. *Shut up, Elly.*

A muscle flickering in Jack's jaw is the only acknowledgment of my joke. "I picked everyone's coats up from the track this morning. It doesn't smell like smoke." He nods at my coat. "It still smells..." His words trail off, and his focus shifts from me to the middle distance. *Oh, crap. He thinks my coat stinks.* He must notice my grimace because he collects himself and adds, "Like you. It smells like you."

Like me? Is that good or bad? He's been here thirty seconds and he has me second-guessing myself already. "Okay, well—"

Before I can finish, he pulls a thick wad of papers out of an interior pocket of his coat and throws them onto the kitchen table.

"There's asbestos in the roof and it's suspected in the external pipework. Maybe in the flue of that blocked-up fireplace." He drags a hand through his hair. "You're going to have to move out."

Asbestos? Is that dangerous? "You're kicking me out?"

"No," Jack insists. "I'm making sure you don't die from asbestos poisoning when we tear the roof down. It's going to be a pain to rectify, but I've got to do it if I want to renovate this place. Look, I'm sorry, but you can't stay."

My body is buzzing, and I can't tell if it's Jack being near, or the panicked thoughts racing through my mind. *Where the hell am I meant to go?* What if I need to pay more rent somewhere else? I'm already stretched to the limit to pay the rent here.

"How long do I have?"

"We need to make it happen yesterday," Jack states, and somehow, through the fog of panic, it occurs to me that this might be what he's like in the office. All bossy and demanding. *Is it hot? Am I finding this attractive?*

Yes.

But then the panic takes hold for real, and my heart is thumping, anxiety threading through my veins as Jack rants about Kate moving in with Nico, building schedules, a buyer in the spring, and the deal falling through if he can't finish the work on time, and I can't follow everything he's saying.

"Where am I supposed to go?" I whimper. "Aren't you supposed to give me notice about this? You can't throw me out."

He stalks from one side of the kitchen to the other, impatience steaming off him. "I'm not *throwing* you out. I was walking home last night, and I thought of you in this shitty flat, and…" He breaks off and stands still, breathing a little heavily, one hand resting on his hip. "I wouldn't want to live here, and the idea of you being here alone most of the time now that Kate's with Nico... it just didn't sit right. And this morning I opened the report, and thought, 'fuck it, let's expedite this'. Let's get you out of here." He aborts his monologue, frowning as if catching himself doing something he doesn't want to.

"That still sounds like you're throwing me out," I mutter.

His eyes shut for a beat. "Do you have friends you can live with? Family?"

Family? There's no way I'm going back to my parents' place with my tail between my legs. They already think I'm a lost cause. Nearly thirty and only just scraping by.

But wait, he *can't* throw me out. "As the landlord, it's your legal responsibility to house me elsewhere for the duration of my lease."

He braces, casting an assessing look over me as I stand in the middle of the kitchen, obviously freaking out, and his own harassed demeanour cools, like he knows he has to calm this situation down before I disintegrate. "I'm not going to leave you high and dry. We can work this out. Sit down." At his command, I sink into the nearest chair. "I'll make you tea."

Oh, phew. He's not going to abandon me. "Thank you."

He starts banging around, getting out mugs, filling the kettle and turning it on. He comes to sit opposite me as it boils, and his concerned gaze meets my own. Is there a hint of last night's heat there? Even if there isn't, I can feel it. *I'm suddenly as hot as the water in that damn kettle.*

"I could live with Kate and Nico," I say, more to distract him from the sheen of sweat that's pearling on my forehead than anything else. Their relationship is new, and I don't want to intrude on their first weeks as a couple sharing a home. They'll probably want to be alone so they can have amazing sex in every room. *Ugh. I might be the teensiest bit jealous.*

He scoffs as though a similar thought has occurred to him. "Sure, ask her."

Okay, fine. "What about one of your other rental properties? I know you have loads. Don't you own half of London?"

"They're full," he replies. "Let me think for a moment."

The kettle reaches boiling point and clicks off. Jack stands and pours the water into the mugs, allowing it to brew before he pours in the milk. He's not talking, but he's soaking up my attention like a giant, hulking sea sponge. A hot one. Even when making tea, he moves with an authoritative purpose that's incredibly appealing. And the way his navy coat fits his broad frame, sliding over his shoulders and hanging down his back is really... *something else.*

I need to stop perving over Kate's brother. *Ugh. He's off-limits. Off-limits.*

He uses the teaspoon to squeeze the tea bag against the side of one of the mugs, and then, to my horror, he presses his loafer to the pedal for the bin, and the lid swings up. He takes one look inside and freezes, teaspoon hovering over the abyss.

My heart leaps up my throat, blocking the air to my lungs, because I know what he's looking at. *My slippers.*

He lets the bin lid close slowly, resting the teaspoon with the tea bag still squashed into it on the counter. My stomach churns. There's no way Jack Lansen isn't going to have something to say about the fact I've thrown away my slippers.

Tension fills the air, and with each inhalation it seems to solidify my lungs. The silence sparks, exploding abruptly when Jack spins to face me. "Three months," he announces.

I lean back from his outburst, both surprised and relieved that he's ignoring the slippers. "Huh?"

"That's what's left on your lease. And you have nowhere else to go." I wait as he seemingly mulls over his own statement, unsure what he expects me to say. Suddenly, his expression brightens with the lightning strike of an idea. "Move in with me."

What? Live with Jack? I'm freefalling at the thought.

I want to say no—I should say no—but a frisson of energy is filtering through me. Hope? Excitement? I wouldn't have felt this way about the prospect of living with Jack Lansen a few weeks ago, but something is different now.

I should never have sung for him.

Living with him would be an inevitable disaster. I know that, and I'm sure he does too. We're combustible. We shouldn't be left in close proximity.

But despite all that, I want to say yes.

"No," I confirm, ignoring the impulse to do the opposite. "I'm not living with you. I bet you snore like a rocket launch."

Jack's brows dip over his blue eyes, which gleam as though my protests amuse him. "You've got damp in the ceiling, a boiler that's always breaking, intermittent hot water and fucking asbestos in the roof, and you're worried about me snoring?"

I glare at him. He must know it's not the snoring I'm worried about. Not really. It's him, the way he flirts, his gorgeous smile... the way my heart is beating out of control just because he's in the same room.

"You can't stay here," he says slowly, as though he thinks I don't understand the issue. He finishes the tea he's making, putting one of the mugs on the table and pushing it towards me. "Strong. Dash of milk. Two sugars," he says, not taking his eyes off me. "The way you like it."

He knows how I take my tea? When did he work that one out?

As he continues staring, making my heart beat fast enough to win one of his damn car races, I realise that he might not feel the same way I do. He flirts with *everyone*. There might be nothing special about me. He did kiss Lydia at the racetrack, after all. And for all I know, he took her home after I left and had wild, sweaty sex with her.

Images of Jack, naked and sweat-covered, ambush me, and heat floods my core. *Fuck.* I can't live with this man. He's not even doing anything, and I'm aroused.

I try my best to anchor my unruly imagination to the real-life version of him, wearing his tailored suit and cashmere overcoat. But it doesn't help because this man is veritable suit-porn.

"You'd be doing me a huge favour," he adds, eyeing me carefully. I suspect he thinks my silence is reluctance. "But if there is someone else you could live with, I can reimburse your rent."

I run through my options and come up short. Even if I wanted to live with my parents, which I don't, I can't because they don't live in London, and I need to be here for work. Maybe I could ask my friend Marie, but her new place only has one bedroom. She used to live here with me and Kate until she moved in with her boyfriend, and I can't see him wanting me hanging around.

A fiery heat rises to my cheeks and worsens with each passing second that I'm not offering an alternative. In my peripheral vision, I can see Jack's brows rising.

"Just come and live with me, El," he says so gently that something inside me turns gooey and warm. "I promise I don't snore."

The only sound in the flat is our tandem breathing. The moment feels potent, as though anything could happen. Jack could shove me against the wall and kiss me, and I wouldn't object.

He picks up the tea he made for me, which I still haven't touched, and holds it out. "You want this?"

I take it from him, cupping it with both hands. "Thank you." He watches my fingers, and I eye him over the rim of the mug. "I'm not living with you," I add.

He flashes that handsome smile. "Come on. You know you want to. Pack your stuff. I'll get you moved in next week."

"What? No. You can't do that. You—"

He hovers his foot over the pedal bin, shooting me a cheeky grin.

Oh, no. "Stop!"

Ignoring my interjection, he presses his foot down, and the bin lid squeals wide, revealing my slippers again, right there on the top. Perfect. Almost new. I cringe at how obvious it is that there's nothing wrong with them. It's like they're screaming all my secrets, revealing that I threw them away in a strop because they prevented me and Jack hooking up.

He picks them out and holds them up. "You might want to bring these though. You know... for when I do want to fuck you."

My mouth opens and closes, but words fail me. *Fucking arsehole.* He tosses the slippers across the room, and they land by my chair.

He's smirking, clearly enjoying my discomfort. "Why did you throw them away? Having regrets about the other night?"

Yes. "No," I spit, but Jack's so amused that he barely takes a breath before he continues.

"Wish we'd fucked instead?"

That's it. That's enough. I slam the tea down on the table, and liquid slops over the edge as I leap from my seat. "You are such an arsehole.

Fuck." I shift from foot to foot, pumped full of nervous energy that I can't control, while Jack keeps grinning at me like he's enjoying the show. "I am not living with you. I refuse. I absolutely refuse."

There's an angry scrape to my words. I bend down, grab the slippers, and hurl them at him in rapid fire, one after the other.

He ducks, hands over his head, as they hit his arms and fall to the floor. He looks like he's desperately trying to contain laughter, his face contorting with the effort. And damn it, it makes me want to laugh too, because this is ridiculous. We're ridiculous. I'm ridiculous.

Everything about this is stupid.

But I don't laugh. Instead, I stalk right over to him and start tugging off my cowboy boots. He watches me, eyes twinkling like I'm the best thing he's ever seen.

Vaguely, through the haze of irritation, I'm aware that I like the feel of his eyes on me. *I don't want him to stop watching.*

I'm hopping on one foot to tug the boot off, then the other, and finally, when I'm free, I slide my feet into the slippers and put my hands on my hips.

"Go on." I jerk my chin at the door, trying to convince him—*to convince myself*—that I'm mad at him, when really, I'm full of a strange, bubbling warmth. "Go and find someone else to play your stupid games with. I'm not interested. Get out."

Jack doesn't move, and the air between us crackles. He takes a small step towards me, his voice soft when he says, "I only want to play with you."

I'm speechless. *What?*

"Three months, El," he whispers. "We can manage that, can't we?"

I frown. It's not *that* long.

He must notice my hesitation because he leans a little closer, and says, "Come and live with me, please."

Please.

I'm undone.

The energy skating between us prickles against my skin, and the sweetness of the tension feels like temptation. *I want to do this.* "I don't want to share a bathroom with you."

He pulls back, his lips tipping up at the corners. "You won't have to."

"Or a bedroom."

Jack's full on smiling at me now, making my heart flutter. "I promise, no shared bedrooms."

"Okay, then."

His smile disappears, and he goes still. *He wasn't expecting me to agree.* "Okay?"

"Yes. I'll move in with you for three months. But I'm assuming we'll never see one another because you'll be off earning all that money, and I'll be working tables. Or at gigs."

"Sounds about right."

"Perfect." I nod at the door. "You can go now."

He performs an elaborate mock bow, making laughter bubble up my throat, and this time I let it out, and he grins at the sound.

This is fun. Being with Jack feels so good.

Jack must agree, because he looks thrilled, and it warms my heart to see it. "I'll send a van for your stuff next week." He pushes open the front door, then pauses, looking back at me. "And, El?"

"Yeah?"

"Don't forget those slippers."

I smile as he turns away, and I can hear him chuckling all the way down the stairs and out onto the street.

9
ELLY

Jack is at work the day I move into his house. His driver delivered a set of keys to my flat last week, wrapped in a package so extravagant it was fit for diamonds.

The house is insane. It's a double-fronted London townhouse with four storeys and an intimidating black lacquered front door at the top of four York stone steps.

It's absolutely massive.

I knew Jack had made a lot of money, but this place must have cost him millions. Literal millions. If I'd known the house was like this, I'd have moved in immediately.

My phone buzzes, and I pull it from the pocket of my sheepskin coat.

Jack: Don't nose in my room.
Me: Wasn't going to.
Jack: Good. You have to wait for an invitation ;)

His message has nerves sparking in my stomach. He is dreadful. You can't stop the man from flirting. It's like his whole personality is just flirting. But it is kind of appealing. This huge great muscly man, who is always smiling, eyes gleaming. He always looks so… *alive*. Like he's aglow with excitement. Everything is a joke to Jack, and there's something sexy as hell about the fact he doesn't take life too seriously.

Maybe, just maybe, I like him. Not to hook up with...but to flirt with? To mess around with? Yeah. I do.

I type a quick response.

Me: Which I would politely decline.

I wait a few moments for a reply, but when one doesn't come, I put my phone away again, trying to ignore the ache of disappointment that follows.

I unlock the front door and let the men inside. The van and removal men were totally unnecessary. I have hardly any stuff—I could have carried it myself—so I'm glad Jack isn't here to see it, but I'm thankful that he sorted everything out for me anyway. He didn't have to do that.

I step into the large entrance hall to find the house is just as impressive inside as it is outside. It's like a boutique hotel, with modern art on the walls and flowers on the hall table. And it smells like... *Jack*. It's as if the wooden floor is oozing his cologne. Waves of arousal begin to pulse through me. *Might as well admit it.* Walking into Jack's delicious-smelling multi-million pound home is a huge turn-on.

I lead the removal men upstairs to the bedroom on the second floor that Jack has designated as mine until my lease ends.

It only takes a few minutes for the guys to bring everything up and disappear. When they're gone, I make my way to the kitchen. It's so clean and tidy in here, like a show home. Everything put away so perfectly. I wipe my finger along the kitchen counter and check the tip for dust. *Not a speck*. And the floor practically sparkles. Jack must have a cleaner, or a housekeeper, because there is no way he gets on his knees and scrubs it himself.

I type Kate a quick message.

Me: I had no idea your brother was such a neat freak.
Kate: He's very particular. Don't touch his stuff.

A laugh snorts out my nose, and I'm glad no one's here to witness it.

A folded piece of paper with my name written on it catches my attention. I snatch it from where it rests on the kitchen island, open it and read.

El,

Welcome to the bachelor pad. Make yourself at home. Help yourself to anything you want from the fridge, but don't lick my cheese.

Jack.

P.S. Always wear slippers.

I laugh at the note, aware of a funny sensation behind my breastbone, like a small, warm kitten is curling up there. If Jack wants me to always wear the slippers, he must mean that if I don't...

I abort the thought. It's Jack. He's joking. Flirting. He wrote 'don't lick my cheese' for goodness' sake. Even though he admitted he wanted me at the racetrack, it was probably a passing desire... he's likely forgotten about it or moved on to someone else. He's not exactly the type to doggedly pursue one woman. He has too many options for that.

Next to the note is an envelope, on top of which is a batch of photographs. I move closer to get a look and fan them out. They're all attractive women. *How weird.*

I tidy them into a pile again and push them away. I shouldn't be looking at Jack's stuff. *But, really, what the hell are they?* I clench my fists in an attempt to resist the temptation to look at them again. *Come on, Elly. Be good.*

My skin itches.

Fuck it. What harm would it do to look?

I pick up the one on top, but as I do, it catches the one beneath and flips it over. My stomach drops as I see the name *Lydia* written in Mrs Lansen's neat script. I recognise her handwriting from the letters she used to send Kate back when we were at boarding school. I quickly flip it to the picture side, revealing Lydia's beautiful face smiling at me. I turn it over again to read Mrs Lansen's annotations.

Lydia Archer. Twenty-nine years old. PR Manager at Archer Consultancy. Very sociable. Academic. Successful. Perfect for Jack. Granddaughter of Sir Marcus Compton. Fine breeding.

Perfect for Jack? These notes are like a window into Mrs Lansen's twisted mind. And... *breeding?* Ha. It's as if she thinks Lydia is some kind of pedigree dog.

Pedigree bitch.

I instantly reprimand myself for the mean thought. I don't know Lydia. Maybe she's not that bad, and she owns her own company, which is impressive. I'll give her that much. She's a high flier. I take out my phone and put her name into Google, and it brings up an array of glamorous photos of her with various celebrity clients. In several of them, she's draped all over that famous actor who Kate and I met in one of Nico's clubs earlier this year. Michael Drayton.

Ugh. A flutter of insecurity explodes in the pit of my stomach. Lydia's beautiful and competent. Maybe she's more suited to Jack than I am.

I scan through the rest of the cards, reading the notes on the back. Mrs Lansen must have put all these together and given them to Jack. *How interfering can a mother be? That woman is crazy.*

I shuffle the pictures back into a pile and push them away.

But wait. Jack took Lydia on a date. Before or after he got these cards? Maybe he's taking these suggestions seriously. *Maybe he's just as crazy as his mother.*

What an awful thought. I dismiss it instantly, because no one is as crazy as Mrs Lansen.

After a day of unpacking and getting familiar with the house and the local area, I'm sitting at the kitchen island on a fancy rotating bar stool, staring at a bowl of Persian chicken and walnut stew I made this afternoon. Jack might have said I could take things from his fridge, but there was nothing in there, apart from twenty half-size cans of Angel Tree tonic water, ten bottles of Dom Pérignon, and a block of cheddar cheese, so I went shopping.

I used to love cooking when I was younger. I did a lot of it with my mum in the school holidays. She was a real foodie, and was happy as long as I was doing exactly what she wanted, and I was happy just to be with her. *So cooking it was.* The thought raises a bitter taste at the back of my tongue, because at the time I didn't realise she only wanted to spend time with me on her terms. As soon as I told my parents I wouldn't be going to law school after uni because I wanted to be a musician, our relationship fell apart. It's not as though they've cut me off exactly, but I get no financial assistance from them, and whenever we do meet, they make sure not to ask a single question about my career, my music, my aspirations, or my life in general. The weather is practically all we have left.

I shove all those thoughts out of my mind. I don't want to think about my parents right now.

I lift my fork and assess the food I've made. It's a veritable feast. Nowadays, I rarely cook anything fancy because I'm alone most of the time and happy to eat a cheese sandwich, which, ironically, I could *almost* have made from the contents of Jack's fridge.

But what better way to say *'thank you for letting me live in your Notting Hill mansion for the same rent as a tiny flat in South London'* than Persian chicken, cumin roast potatoes, a pistachio and feta dip with flatbreads, and tabbouleh? But now that I'm sitting here, with my plate piled high and enough leftovers to feed an army, I feel like an idiot. I should have checked whether Jack had plans. I don't even know when he's coming home, and there is no possible way I can eat it all myself. The ingredients were crazy expensive, too. I had to buy three bottles of pomegranate molasses that I definitely can't afford. *Beans on toast for me for a week after this.*

I don't want to wait all night just so we can eat together either. If Jack walks in and I'm sitting here like I'm about to say grace over a bowl of untouched food, waiting for his delectable arse to walk in, I don't know what he'll think. It'll look like I'm serving him up dinner, like a good little housewife.

That's definitely not what I meant to do. *Is it?*

This is confusing.

I tuck into the food, but I'm not really tasting it. My mind is all over the place, and I keep glancing at the pile of female faces staring up at me from the island. It's like they're watching me. It's unnerving. I push them out of sight behind the fruit bowl.

The sound of the key in the front door makes me sit up straight, and my heart does a little jig. *He's home.*

The door creaks as Jack enters. At least, I assume it's him. I can't see from here.

Footsteps approach, and I spin on my kitchen stool to find him standing in the doorway in a long dark overcoat, leaning on the door frame. He stares at me, and I struggle to take my next breath. *He's gorgeous. And big. Really, really big.*

"Hi, there," he says, brushing a hand through his hair. His voice is all smooth, and the hairs on my forearms stand in slow motion. I wish I was wearing long-sleeves.

I point my fork at him. "Don't '*hi there*' me. I see what you're doing."

One of his devastating smiles breaks over his face, and I briefly wonder if I could fall in love with his smile and remain immune to the rest of him. "What am I doing?"

"Don't pretend you don't know." I spin on the stool so my back is to him, but he's making that amused humming sound in his mouth, and it resonates deep in my core. *Damn it*. He hasn't even fully entered the room, and hidden parts of me are already throbbing.

His footsteps come closer until he's right beside me, and every muscle in my body tenses. I pretend to focus on my food, but really all I'm doing is observing him out of the corner of my eye and growing light-headed because my breathing has become unaccountably shallow.

He takes off his coat and suit jacket, folds them carefully, and drapes them both over a kitchen chair, before he pulls out a stool and sits down next to me. He smells like fresh air and whatever that delicious scent is he wears. I inhale like I'm greedy for it.

He's smiling so wide I can see his perfect white teeth in my periphery. My insides are fizzing as though I'm about to go to a party I've been looking forward to. *This is messed up.*

He stares at my bowl of stew, and his gorgeous smile turns slightly crooked, as though he's both puzzled and amused. "The whole house smells like... whatever that is."

I shrug. *That's not what I was smelling*. "Oops. A girl's gotta eat."

"What is it?"

"Khoresh-e-Fesenjan."

"Which is?"

"It's Persian. Chicken and walnut stew with pomegranate molasses."

Jack's eyebrows fly up. "There's no way you found pomegranate molasses in my cupboards. Or that many walnuts."

I laugh, but it sounds more nervous than amused. *What if he hates this?* "No. I went shopping. Even I couldn't make a meal out of a block of cheddar cheese and a gallon of champagne."

Jack dismisses my comment with an eye-roll. "My housekeeper's away. She normally stocks the fridge."

"I took a tonic water," I say, tapping the small can beside my plate. "Figured you could spare one."

"Best tonic on the market," he replies, nodding at the can.

I vaguely recall Kate telling me Jack was the first investor in Angel Tree tonic water when one of his school friends set up the company. A decade later and the drink is everywhere. Sold out to some huge drinks corporation for nearly a hundred million, and Jack got an enormous payout. Money rains into his life, whereas I seem to be in a permanent state of drought.

He leans over my dish, inspecting it at closer range. My heart flutters at how intimate this is. How *domestic*. Mrs Lansen might have picked out a load of suitable partners for her son, but I'm the one who gets to sit next to him at dinner. *I'm winning.* I shake the bizarre thought away. *I must be losing my mind.*

"That looks kinda disgusting," he says, wrinkling his nose as he inhales. "Smells good though."

Before I can think about it, I've filled a fork and I'm holding it out to him. "Taste it."

He frowns at the lump of stew but opens his mouth wide around my fork, and his lips wrap around the tines. He lets out a low, appreciative moan that vibrates up the fork and into me until it nestles right between my legs. *Oh boy, am I in trouble here.*

The fact that I'm feeding him must occur to both of us at the same time, because Jack's eyes shoot up to mine and lock on, alarm erupting in his gaze, but it vanishes instantly, replaced with a look that says, *'I know what you were thinking, and it was dirty'*.

Heat rages through me, but I force my features into stillness, refusing to acknowledge his expression, which wipes clean in response. He pulls back, an almost respectful look on his face as he chews on the food. "That's surprisingly good," he says after he swallows. "Is there more?"

I nod at the hob, where I've left a big pot full of stew and the other dishes. "Plenty."

He gets up and walks over to the worktop, hesitating as he notices all the pots and bowls of dishes I've made. "Holy fuck, you've made a mess. You hosting a dinner party?"

I blush. "Nope." I want to tell him I did it for him, but for some reason, I can't bring myself to. "I... I like cooking."

Ugh, that sounds pathetic.

He *hmmms* in the back of his throat, but before he can comment on the sheer volume of food I've prepared, the doorbell rings. Jack freezes, his focus shifting inward as if he might be able to determine who's at the door through the use of some inner sense. "You sure you aren't expecting people?"

"No."

His lips turn downward and he heads out into the hall, and I strain to listen. The door opens with a creak and an excited female voice announces, "I brought sushi."

The silence that follows is a beat too long, and my heart drops for the duration of it, plummeting down what feels like a ravine of emotion. I should have known Jack Lansen would have plans. *A date. A woman. Sushi.*

I'm such a fool.

"For me?" Jack replies, surprised, and at the tone of his voice my heart starts the slow climb back up. He's as shocked by this arrival as I am.

"For us. It's from that place you said you liked."

For us. That sounds... *cosy.*

There's a shuffle of feet and the click of heels on the wooden floor. Whoever is out there is coming in, and I'm pretty sure Jack didn't actually invite them inside. Not vocally, at least, but then he's a master of body language...

Jack clears his throat. "I wasn't expecting—"

A breathy giggle cuts him off. "I told you I'd get some for you."

A lengthy pause follows. "Right. Well, maybe you should come in then." Jack sounds incredibly reluctant, but very polite. If it was me out there, I'd be backing right back down the front steps around now.

A moment later, Jack's in the doorway, eyes wide and apologetic, a bag of what I assume is sushi in his hands.

"Hey, Ja-ack," the woman calls, turning his name into two sultry syllables. Jack swings back towards the door, and I follow the motion.

Lydia appears in the doorway, and her trench coat falls open, revealing lacy black underwear that leaves very little to the imagination.

I nearly choke on my mouthful of food just as Lydia catches sight of me, letting out a deafening scream as she quickly pulls the coat closed, but not before I've got an eyeful. She has an absolutely killer body, and she's clearly here for sex.

"Oh, shit," I mutter, ears still ringing on account of Lydia's epic screech.

"You didn't say you had company," she says, addressing Jack as if I'm not here, a pinch of breathless annoyance in her voice.

"You didn't say you were nearly naked under there." Jack covers his mouth with a fist. His expression is hovering somewhere between entertained and appalled. I suspect he's suppressing a smile, and it makes me want to laugh. In fact, the urge to giggle is so intense that I'm not sure I can keep it inside. When mixed with the self-recriminations that it was foolish to cook for Jack on my first night, the sensation is discombobulating, as though I'm a balloon that's being both inflated and deflated at the same time.

"You remember Elly," Jack says, gesturing to me, and I rapidly swallow my amusement.

Lydia nods, her arms tightly crossed over her chest. "The waitress."

Jack tilts his head as though he's contemplating contradicting this. "She's my housemate," he clarifies.

Lydia's eyes widen. "You live together?"

"We do," I confirm, aware I sound like I'm staking a claim. Jack's eyes flash to mine and the delight on his face tells me he hears it too.

"Oh. Gosh, I only bought enough sushi for two." Lydia looks genuinely uncomfortable, and she glances to Jack for help. I get a sudden twinge of guilt. She didn't know I was here, or that I'd cooked. She didn't mean to sabotage my efforts, and she's dared to make a huge play for Jack, in her underwear no less, and here I am, laughing at her.

I'd hate it if someone did that to me.

"Relax." It's an ironic word choice given that my insides are squeezing together like a concertina, but Jack's love life is none of my business, and I don't want to interfere. Maybe later I can source some Tupperware and pack the leftover food away and eat it during the week. I pick up my bowl and walk towards where Lydia is standing in the doorway. "I'll leave you to it."

"Wait, don't go," Jack pleads. There's a panicked look in his eyes that almost makes me pause, but there's no way I'm staying here, knowing Lydia is only wearing her underwear beneath that trench coat.

"No, really, I'll leave," I say quickly. "Enjoy your dinner." As I pass Jack, I lean into him and add, "Sushi is a delicacy, after all."

10
JACK

A clammy sweat breaks out over my skin as I stare at Lydia, who's still standing in the doorway. Elly brushes past her on her way out, a tiny, elegant pixie in comparison to Lydia's statuesque glamour. I've never had a particular preference—I've fucked all sorts of women—but tonight, there's a clear winner. I want to rush after Elly and slide my hand against the dip of her waist to pull her back into the room. *But I can't fucking do that, can I?* For now, I'm resigned to watching her walk away from me. *Again.*

Lydia shoots me a *'thank goodness she's gone'* look, which I don't return. Instead, the urge to call Elly's name swells in my throat.

Lydia steps closer, all black lace panties and bra spilling with soft breasts as she lets the trench coat fall open again. Objectively, she's hot, and this whole scenario is teenage-me's wet dream, but right now it leaves me cold. And weirdly clammy. *Fuck.*

Lydia takes the bag of sushi out of my hands and places it on the island. She sits on the recently vacated seat, where only minutes ago El was feeding me that delicious stew she cooked. The eye contact we made over the fork was way more intense than anything I'm feeling for Lydia in her heels and underwear.

"Nigiri or dragon roll?" Lydia says, making herself at home as she takes the plastic boxes, places them on the counter and opens the lids. I recognise the packaging. It's expensive sushi. She's gone all out.

"You can't turn up here like this—"

Lydia turns from the food to me. "You seem a little tense." She stands and rests her hands on my shoulders, and I immediately want to shrug her off, but I hold still. "Why don't you take a moment. Have a drink. Whatever you need to—"

"I don't need anything." I shift out from under her touch, holding back the impulse to shove her away. "Honestly, it's so generous of you to bring food, but I'm really busy this evening. I've got a load of work to catch up on. You ought to have called first."

Lydia's eyes darken, as though some nasty thought is passing through her mind. "Is it her?" She nods in the direction Elly went. "Are you interested in the waitress?"

"Can you stop calling her a waitress? Her name is Elly."

Lydia stiffens. "Are you interested in her?"

"No. That's not it. Elly's... a friend." My head feels foggy. *What is Elly to me?* She's Kate's friend... *my housemate*. But isn't she something else too? *Something different*. Something that causes a pinching sensation in my heart, like the onset of fucking heartburn. "You're a beautiful woman—"

"Good. That's settled then." *What the hell?* Lydia sheds her coat, throws it on the stool on her other side, and sits back down, crossing her long, bronzed legs. There's a seductive look on her face, and sitting there in her underwear and heels, she looks as though she's sprung to life from a Playboy magazine. "I'm all yours," she purrs. "Do whatever you want with me."

She raises one leg and pushes her aggressively pointed high heel against my crotch and rests it there. For a moment, I don't know what the fuck to do. I could get laid right now, could have my cock inside her in under thirty seconds. I could spend all night fucking this gorgeous woman who's laying herself out for me. The basest part of me is tempted… very fucking tempted if I'm entirely honest, despite the weird alarm bells ringing in the back of my head that nothing about this scenario is good and that Lydia might, in fact, be slightly out of her mind to turn up like this.

But more important than any of that, if anything happens with Lydia tonight, while Elly is upstairs, then I might as well score out the possibility of anything happening between me and Elly with a big black marker. And there is no way I'm going to do that. *Absolutely no fucking way.*

I take Lydia's ankle in one hand and ease her leg off me until she takes the weight of it herself and lowers it to the floor, tossing me a resentful glare. I start packing up the sushi again, pressing the lids into place and thrusting the boxes back into the bag. "That's generous of you. Very generous, and I'm flattered. But no, thank you."

I push the bag at her and then lift her coat, holding it out so she can easily slide her arms into it and get the fuck out of here.

Lydia stares at me for a few long, painful seconds, until she gets up, *very* slowly, and turns her back to me so she can slip her arms into the sleeves of her coat. She draws it tight with the belt and turns to face me. "You're making a mistake, choosing her over me."

"I'm not choosing anyone." *I am.* "I don't think we'd be good together. I'm sorry, but that has nothing to do with anyone else."

She glares at me like she knows I'm lying. "Big mistake, Jack. Big." She snatches the bag of sushi and marches out of the room, hips swaying like a runway model.

The thing is, to me, it doesn't feel like a mistake at all.

11
ELLY

The whole time I'm up in my room, I'm listening for noise downstairs. *Is he going to fuck her? Are they going to keep me up all night?* Lydia looks like a screamer. A grab-the-headboard-and-yell-the-house-down kind of screamer. My stomach churns at the mere idea, and it occurs to me that I hadn't thought this whole housemate thing through. Jack's going to be bringing woman after woman home, and I'll be sitting here alone, listening to the noise.

What a thought. I'm not sure I can eat at all now, and the plate of food is stinking out my room. I open the window, but it doesn't help.

I creak open my door. Downstairs, heels clack out into the hall, and the front door opens and closes. *Has Lydia gone? Has Jack Lansen, the ultimate womanizer, sent her away? Surely they can't have eaten all that sushi already?*

Now I'm curious, and *dammit*, I don't want to sleep in here with a full plate of food.

Taking my plate, I creep downstairs, barely breathing in case Lydia is still here. If she is, she's probably laid out naked on the island with sushi all over her.

The kitchen door is ajar, so I reason that she probably isn't in there. But then again, she and Jack together are probably a pair of exhibitionists. Just in case, I close my eyes as I knock.

"Yeah?" Jack replies.

Keeping my eyes closed, I push the door open and tiptoe into the room, my free hand extended before me. "Is it safe? Are you naked?"

Jack chuckles, and the deep rumble of it makes my previously churning stomach flutter. "No."

I pop my eyes open, only to be greeted by Jack's gorgeous smile, and I can't help but grin back at him as an unreasonable wave of giddiness surges over me. He's sitting at the island, digging into a huge bowl of my stew, with a side of cumin potatoes and tabbouleh.

"Sushi didn't do it for you, then?" I ask.

"I had a more appealing option. Something more to my taste." His tone is so suggestive that a blast of heat sizzles through me.

I arch a brow, keeping my voice casual. "We still talking about food?"

"Were we ever?"

I can't keep the smile off my face as I say, "You're a bad man, Jack Lansen."

"What?" he asks with false innocence. "I'm beginning to wonder if you have a one-track mind."

"Me? If I do, it's because you—"

His eyebrow creeps up again, cutting me off. "I what?"

I don't dignify the question with a response. "She's gone, right?" I ask after a moment. "She's not in the bathroom or something?"

Jack laughs. "She's gone." Then his face turns serious, and he glances at my full plate. "You didn't eat either?"

"Didn't feel like it." He lets that one settle for a moment, the slight frown on his face his only response. "Can I join you?"

He pats the stool next to him, and I drop onto it, and that giddy, happy feeling at being next to Jack washes over me again like it never left. I put my bowl next to his and we eat side by side.

"I can't believe she showed up like that," I say, after swallowing a few mouthfuls.

One edge of Jack's lips tilts up. "Just a regular Friday night for me. Normally, there's a queue all the way down the street."

"Bullshit," I exclaim, and his smile expands. "It's five degrees out there. She must have been freezing."

"Says you in your tiny skirts." He nods at my bare thighs. I press them together, trying to ignore the stirring of heat between them that answers his glance.

"Eyes up, Lansen." The reprimand elicits a short rumble of laughter from him, which delights me. "I'm wearing my skirts for me, not you." We eat together quietly for a few moments. "I thought you weren't interested in Lydia."

Jack side-eyes me. "I'm not. I told her as much at the racetrack, but she evidently chose not to hear me."

I muse over this for a moment. "Definite red flag, right there."

"You got a thing about red flags?" His eyes narrow, but there's a teasing light behind them, which makes my stomach flip. "You're not worried about me, are you?"

"No." The heat of a blush spreads over my cheeks. "But you need to be able to spot the red flags if you have to work your way through all these..." I push the fruit bowl aside, revealing the pile of photos, which are still lying on the island.

Jack's open expression shutters as he reaches out with his free hand and grabs the pile, dragging it closer. "You weren't supposed to nose around." His voice is serious for the first time this evening, and I feel a stab of regret at having caused it.

"You left them out. It's hardly nosing if they're right there in the middle of the island. Lydia's picture is in there, so I assumed you were working your way through them."

He grips his fork a little tighter, and his other hand presses down harder on the photos, as though he wants to make them disappear.

"You gonna pick another one?" I ask.

He holds my gaze, making an uncomfortable heat flare in my chest. "No."

"But she wants you to," I probe. "Your mother."

He gets up, pulls open the cupboard which conceals the bin, and drops the whole pile of pictures in there. He slams the cupboard shut and takes his seat next to me again, rolling his eyes to the ceiling with an audible exhale, as though he's sending a prayer up to heaven. "What my mother wants is irrelevant. I make my own choices."

Heat is still rolling through me, and Jack throwing the pictures away only fanned the flames. My picture is definitely not in that pile his mother chose, which means he could still choose me. But Jack says nothing to indicate that's what he means, and I wish the thought hadn't occurred to me at all.

We sit in silence, but now I feel awkward. I've completely ruined the rapport we had going on. *Nice one, Elly*. I shouldn't have asked him about the pictures. I finish off the last few bites of my food and stand to clear my plate, trying to ignore the fact that Jack's usually cheerful face is fixed into a disgruntled frown. I drop my plate and cutlery on the side of the sink, because the sink itself is full of all the dirty utensils and pans I used earlier.

"Woah, hold up," he says when I reach the door, and his tone is so commanding that I stop.

"What?"

"You can't leave this mess. Look at the place. It's like an Elly-bomb went off in here." He points around the room with his fork. "This is chaos. You gotta tidy this up."

I stare at him, trying to work out if he means it. In the flat, I always left my dirty dishes in the sink. Our kitchen was a tip, until one of us caved and sorted it out. As Jack stares at me, I reflect on how pristine his kitchen looked before I started cooking and then I take in the scene before me.

Shit. I'm a slob, and Jack is... *Jack*. Neat. Tidy. Clean and smart and professional.

I wince in embarrassment, and I have to force myself to raise my eyes from the mess to meet his expectant gaze. "Oh."

"Yes," he says, nodding. "Oh."

The way he's looking at me is scrambling my brain. He's not even coming onto me or leering at me this time. He's just watching me, waiting for me to start cleaning his kitchen.

I'm conflicted. Part of me is so embarrassed that I hadn't thought to tidy up, that I want to get down on my hands and knees and lick the crumbs off the floor, just so Jack will smile at me again. But another part of me wants to shove his handsome face into a bowl of tabbouleh because I cooked all of this *for him*—admittedly I didn't tell him that—and he's sitting there eating it with relish, issuing orders like he owns the place.

But he *does* own the place. This is *his* house, and it's really generous of him to let me stay and to open up his life to me this way. He could have demanded twice the rent to let me stay here. Actually, ten times the rent is more realistic because this house is spectacular.

Once my lease is up, I'll never be able to live somewhere like this again. I don't want to ruin it by refusing to clean a few pans on my first night.

He raises a brow, obviously taking my hesitation as a refusal. "Kate might not have cared that you leave the place a mess, but I do. If you want to stay here, you have to tidy up when you cook. I want to make this very clear right now, because if I don't say anything your mess is going to piss me off too much for us to live together."

Wow. He must really hate mess. Or maybe it's me he doesn't like.

Definitely shouldn't have asked him about those photographs. That's what tipped his mood into this dark spot.

As I stare at him, all handsome and smart in his white shirt, looking more like he's at the boardroom table than the kitchen island, I can't help wondering if he spends his evenings scrubbing pots when he's here by himself. I can't imagine it. "Do you clean up yourself when you're alone?" I ask not because I want to avoid the work, but because I really want to know.

"Not normally, no. My housekeeper takes care of it, but she's away until next week. I told you. And I like my privacy. I keep staff to a minimum, so yes, when I need to, I clean up after myself. But that aside, you leaving the kitchen like this is unacceptable."

I barely hear his last comment because I'm hung up on the fact that he values his privacy, but was willing to let me live here, and that urge to please him flares right up.

I can always shove his handsome face into a bowl of tabbouleh another time.

I roll up my sleeves and get to work.

12
JACK

I sit back to watch Elly clearing away the mess. The food. *Why did she make such a fuck ton of it? Was it an accident?* Maybe she meant to leave some for me. Maybe she was thinking about me coming home from work... *Hmm.*

I like that idea.

Shit. It's her first night and she's already messing with my head.

She begins cleaning the surfaces with a cloth and spray she found under the kitchen sink. As she moves, that little mini-skirt flaps around her thighs. It's so short that I can almost see her underwear as she flounces around, her toned legs flexing with each step. A throb of desire pulses in my groin. *Christ, I shouldn't be staring like this.*

How am I going to endure three months of this temptation?

Better aroused than annoyed, though. What with Lydia showing up, and Elly questioning me about Mum's damned photos and then leaving all her crap all over the kitchen with no intention of clearing up, my mood was on the cusp of souring.

But with a woman as attractive as Elly flitting about my kitchen, making everything tidy again, flicking her mountain of blonde curls off her face as she works, being in a bad mood for long seems impossible.

She bends over to put a pot back in the cupboard, and I catch a glimpse of her underwear. Pink, a little lacy. Heat shoots through me like liquid fire. *Damn, that's a short skirt.* I have to force myself to look away, but a second later my eyes are back on her and that tiny skirt.

I love it. The skirt can stay.

She glances over her shoulder at me, shooting me a look as though she knows *exactly* what I was just thinking. "Are you going to help, or are you just going to watch?"

Just like her to call me out. I take another mouthful of the delicious food and swallow it down, not breaking eye contact as I say, "Watch."

Her frown deepens, and she turns fully to face me, putting aside the pot she was holding. *She's annoyed.* "I'm really grateful that you're letting me live here, but I want to make something very clear too."

"Okay..." I say, inviting her to continue.

"We're housemates," she states in a no nonsense tone that has me sitting a little straighter. "So if I cook, you clean. And vice versa. You're probably not familiar with the arrangement, but that's how it works." She glances at the ceiling, as if she's considering her words. "Although, if you buy the food, and I do the cooking, then we can clear up together. That's fair. We share the load."

It's on the tip of my tongue to make a joke about how much I'd love her to share my load, but I sense it wouldn't go down well. And I don't want to piss her off more, because she's clearly slaved away in this kitchen for hours, and she didn't have to do that. The least I can do is help.

"All right," I concede.

She claps her hands, seemingly satisfied with this outcome. "Good. Because I'm not your slave."

My slave? Why does that sound so good? And also, did she read my fucking mind?

I huff a laugh, but she leans back against the kitchen counter, which makes her breasts pop in that little jumper she's wearing, and suddenly nothing seems funny anymore.

I'm too distracted to give her an answer. There's a fire behind her eyes, and she shakes her head at me, as if to say, *'what are you looking at?'* She's waiting for some response, but I can't remember what she said.

I gather my now-empty plate and approach her at the counter until I'm an arm's length away. Her gaze drifts up my torso, her head tipping back a little to look up at me. When her eyes lock onto mine, electricity sparks through me like she's lightning and I'm made of metal. Every cell in my body brightens, and suddenly, we're a high-voltage circuit. *Connected.*

I know she feels it too because her eyes widen, and she tries to shift back as if she can snap whatever force has us bound, but she's already pressed up against the counter and has nowhere to go.

I reach around her to put my plate in the sink, but the movement brings us even closer until I can smell that citrus scent of hers.

She stiffens, and every scrap of my awareness is focused on that motion, and for some incomprehensible reason, I freeze too.

We're locked in, our faces far too close, my forehead almost tipped to meet hers, our breaths mingling by the sink. Romantic's not the word for it. Fucked up and sexually charged might be somewhere in the right ballpark.

"Jack?" She breathes my name as though she's trying to call my awareness back, but it doesn't work. I'm too busy staring at her, my gaze skimming over her face like I'm taking an inventory. Eyes, light blue. Chin, angular. Delicate. Like a pixie. The cupid's bow on her pink upper lip; her nose, small, pointed; cutest nose I've ever seen, with a little piercing on the side that, on anyone else, I'd fucking hate, but on her it looks *perfect*. And all that curly blonde hair. *I want to tug on it.* I'm taking it all in at a million miles an hour. I must look half-deranged.

She's so pretty. Beautiful, even.

"What are you doing?" Her voice is so soft I can hardly hear it.

The question brings me back. *What am I doing?* Having some kind of dick-and-brain meltdown because we stood a fraction too close?

"Helping you clean up." It sounds like bullshit, but it's why I came over here in the first place.

I take a step back, trying to collect myself, but all I can see are her feet, which are bare. Naked. All ten toes, perfectly fucking naked on my kitchen floor. "Your slippers. Where are they? You need to wear them." This feels crucial, because if Elly doesn't put those damn slippers on her feet, I'm going to shove her against the wall and kiss her, and the fact that I want to makes me mad. Teasing and flirting is fine, but this is something else. This feels compulsive... a raging desire that has me by the balls. I'm not in charge, and I don't like it.

Get your fucking shit together, Lansen.

"What's the obsession with my slippers?" she whispers. "Forget about them. They were a joke."

"I'm not laughing."

Blood pulses through my upper chest and down my arms. My palms start to buzz.

All I'm aware of is her beautiful face staring up at me, and those pink lips. *Fuck, I want to kiss them.*

I am in so much trouble here, and my breathing is all out of whack. I hit the gym a lot... I'm fit. *Athletic.* There is no logical reason why I'm breathing like I just ran a marathon.

Elly cocks her head, looking me up and down, and something about her expression—how alert it is, and the sharpness in her gaze—lets me know she's no longer sharing this out-of-this-world-nothing-exists-but-you moment with me. She's retreated to some place where she can be rational... where she can see what's happening from an objective distance.

"Why are you all riled up? Is this what a messy kitchen does to you? A few dirty dishes and you're losing your shit? Bloody hell." She turns her back to me and starts filling the sink. "Let's clean up before you give yourself a coronary."

A coronary? I'm not that worked up... *Am I?*

I'm about to respond when Elly lets out a squeal.

The bottle of pomegranate molasses slides out of her grip, hits the surface with a bang, and splatters the remaining contents all over my shirt. *Shit.* I need to soak it now, or it'll stain. Without thinking, I start unbuttoning it, undoing the cuffs and pulling the whole thing off.

It takes a second or two for me to notice that the kitchen is very, *very* quiet. I look up to find Elly staring at me, a tea towel dangling from one hand, the almost empty pomegranate molasses bottle, which miraculously didn't smash, in the other. Her eyes are drifting over my pecs, my abs, and I'm suddenly thanking God for all those hours I spend in the gym because I know I look good. It would appear that Elly agrees, because her gaze is all admiration as she pins her bottom lip with her teeth, then lets it roll slowly outward again.

"You all right?" I ask, because I can't let this moment pass without drawing attention to her reaction.

She nods as though she's in a daze. She's still not meeting my eye, keeping her gaze fully trained on my chest instead.

"Okay, then..." I say, letting my words trail off, but still Elly says nothing. I can't remember my bare chest having shocked a woman into silence, especially not one as vivacious as Elly, but I'm feeling pretty proud of myself right now. A little puffed up, even, and it's a bloody good feeling, especially given how out of control I felt only moments ago.

Leaving Elly drooling by the sink, I cross the kitchen and enter the utility room, where I grab the stain remover out of the cupboard and start spraying the sauce splashes on my shirt.

I've nearly got them all when I'm aware of a presence behind me. I put the bottle down, settling both hands on the countertop.

"What?" I ask, without turning around.

"If I have to wear slippers, you have to wear a shirt," she says, so quietly I'm not sure I heard her correctly.

I turn to find her standing in the doorway, looking more unsure than I've ever seen her. Elly's all brash jokes and laughter. But right now, she looks really unnerved. "Why?"

She flaps the tea towel in the air. "Because—"

"Because now you want to fuck me?"

Elly stands a little straighter. "Are you trying to make this the most awkward housemate situation ever?"

Well, that wasn't a *complete* denial.

"No. I'm just saying what I see. You've followed me in here like I have something you want and you've barely looked at my face since I took my shirt off."

Elly hisses dismissively, but two spots of red appear on her cheekbones. "I'm not here to fill the gap in your sex schedule because you sent Lydia away. I have no interest in sleeping with you."

My mind whirrs. Elly's shown more resistance to my advances than any other woman I've come across, and damn if it doesn't make her all the more appealing. But right now, it's clear as fucking daylight that she wants me, and I'm not going to let this opportunity escape. I can't let her walk away without roping her into... *something*. Something that will bring whatever the hell I'm feeling for her under control. Quick as a flash, an idea occurs to me. "You willing to bet on it?"

She tilts away from me. "Huh?"

"Let's scrap the clothes rules. You don't have to wear the slippers, and I don't have to wear a shirt. Wear whatever the hell you want. Let's turn this into a game. A competition, if you will. And then we can see which of us breaks first."

Her brow crinkles as though I've said something incomprehensible. "Breaks?" She breathes the word like it's a dirty secret.

"Yeah. Breaks. Which of us gives in first."

"What are you talking about?"

"You want me, and I want you." Her pretty pink lips part, but either she doesn't know what to say or she's lost the ability to formulate words because she doesn't object, so I keep talking. "The fact that we're going to end up in bed together is as inevitable as the sunrise. So let's make it fun. Who's going to be the last one standing? Who can resist the longest? Who can—"

"No." She rears back, holding both hands up as though she expects me to rush her. "No, no, no. Absolutely not." She clenches her teeth and an aggravated groan escapes between them. "I knew I shouldn't have agreed to live with you."

I assess her annoyance, weighing it up. *Is there still room to play?* "I'll make it worth your while." She halts at this, and I know there's definitely room. "If you can get me to break first, I'll refund all your rental payments. You can live here for free. In fact, I'll reimburse you for all of last year too, at market value. So what's that? Twenty-five thousand?"

A look crosses her face as though she's checking it adds up. "Twenty-five thousand?" she repeats.

Got her. "Yup."

"And all I have to do is resist your advances?"

"You resist *and* seduce. I'll do the same. Whoever caves and begs for sex first, loses. Whoever can hold out, wins."

"That's perverse. I don't want to sleep with you."

I shrug. "Okay, so you'll definitely win. What do you have to lose? If there's really no hope that I can seduce you—"

"There isn't."

"I disagree, but whatever. Let's play the game."

She draws her chin right in, staring at me like I'm a madman. "If I get free rent, what do you win?" She waves her hand at me. "What do you get out of it?"

A smile threatens to break across my face. "I get to see you beg."

She begins to laugh, not in amusement, but in disbelief. "Wow. You're unbelievably arrogant. And fucking crazy."

"Not at all. I've always found that when I want something, the getting of it is that much sweeter if I've had to wait. When we fuck, it'll be better because of the game. It's going to be so good it'll blow your mind."

Elly splutters, her mouth wide, before she collects herself enough to say, "We aren't going to fuck."

"Yeah, we are."

A mask of fury comes down like a shutter. "You are a total arsehole. You know that?"

She backs off into the kitchen, leaving me chuckling to myself in the utility room.

She is definitely going to break. And she definitely wants to fuck me.

"It's a win-win, El," I shout after her. "Even if you lose, you get to have sex with me, because when you beg, I'll say yes."

A crash, as though pots are being slammed together, sounds from the other room, and Elly shouts, "Does your sister know what a douchebag you are?"

"I think she has a fair idea," I shout back.

Elly's clattering noises continue with renewed vigor, and I picture her out there washing up, all worked up and furious. It has me laughing to myself. I'm far more amused by this whole thing than I should be, which is a good result, seeing as I was pretty worked up earlier. I put my shirt in the sink to soak and fill the basin with warm water. When I'm finished, I come back out into the kitchen but Elly is gone, and everything is clean.

In the silence, my phone buzzes against the kitchen counter, Elly's name flashing up.

Elly: 25k is not enough to engage in this dumbass game with you.

Me: What amount would convince you to play?

Elly: 100k.

Me: Done.

Elly: Ha! You're crazy. Prepare to lose, Lansen. I will never beg, and I will never sleep with you.

Me: We'll see about that.

Elly: Game on.

13
ELLY

Jack Lansen is an idiot. If he thinks having sex with him is worth more to me than a hundred thousand pounds, he's going to be sorely disappointed. He's so arrogant, he probably does think that.

Doesn't he know what that much money means to me? I wouldn't have to live paycheck to paycheck anymore, or scrimp every month, struggling to make ends meet. I might even be able to save something, and if I can save then I won't have to go home and live with my parents and give up my dream of making a living from my music.

This game could change my life, and if Jack Lansen is enough of a fool to offer the chance, then I'm grabbing it with both hands. There is absolutely no way in hell I am going to lose. In fact, I'm determined to win as fast as possible. I'll be irresistible, but unattainable. That's my game plan.

Irresistible, but unattainable.

I'm standing in front of the full-length mirror in my bedroom, wearing a pale pink camisole and French knickers, and wondering if it's too much to go down to breakfast in them. They're cute and sexy without being explicit. I could definitely play them off as my regular underwear (although, of course, they aren't. They're for special occasions only).

I shimmy in front of the mirror, fluff my mass of blonde curls, and decide that—*fuck it*—if Jack Lansen wants to play, then we're going to play. And I am going to have fun doing it. Excitement fizzes beneath my skin. Even though this whole scenario is stupid, and I will never, ever, admit I engaged in it to Kate, I want to play with Jack. I might even be grateful for this silly game, because it ties me to him, linking us together in a way I couldn't have achieved otherwise. I'm not just any old housemate; I'm the other half of this game he's concocted.

We're playing with fire.

On my way down the stairs, I realise it's pretty cold. Not cold like Jack hasn't turned the heating on, but cold like it's autumn and there's a chill in the air. My nipples are hardening beneath the silk, and I'm under-dressed and covered in goosebumps.

The gurgle of the coffee machine greets me. *Jack's in there.* Annoyingly, my stomach does a little flip. Or three. *Flip, flip, flip.*

The Commodores, *Easy*, is playing in the background, so softly that I can only hear it if I really concentrate.

As I hit the bottom step, I take a deep breath, ready to swan around Jack's glamorous designer kitchen in my underwear. I turn the corner and stop short, because he's standing by the oven, wearing only a pair of boxers.

He's cooking, and the sight of his muscled back, and the shifting hollow between his shoulder blades as he prods at something in a pan, has my breath catching in my throat and my mouth drying.

He must have heard me come in because he glances back at me, does a brief eye-sweep of my attire, and turns back to the food with a quick, "Morning, El."

Shit. My sexy French undies seem to have had no impact on him, whereas he's effortlessly exuding sex appeal. He doesn't even have to try. Maybe he wears his boxers around the kitchen every weekend. And why wouldn't he? He lives alone, most of the time.

"Eggs?" he says. "There's fresh coffee." He jerks his head towards a pot sitting on the island. He takes the pan he's been prodding off the stove and rests it on the side, then turns fully in my direction. As he does, every word I intend to say disintegrates in my mouth because he is absolutely, spectacularly perfect.

Every muscle is drawn in perfect relief. His pecs are sculpted, and the ridges between his abs are so deep I want to lick them, and the tapering V of muscle that disappears beneath the waistband of his boxers is like a neon arrow pointing at the goods hidden down there.

I can't handle Jack Lansen without a shirt on. If I keep staring, I'll start to drool. I don't know why I thought I could play this game, because if anyone is irresistible right now, it's Jack.

I'm going to lose.

He must have done this deliberately. He saw my reaction when he took off his shirt on my first night here, so he knows exactly what effect his bare skin has on me. But he's being so casual. *Am I attributing the wrong motive to his near nudity?*

"Eggs, El?" Jack repeats, frowning at me.

I gather myself. *I'm a performer. I can do this.*

Be sexy. Sexy, sexy, sexy.

"Yes, please," I say, taking a seat at the island, attempting to slide onto the designer stool as gracefully as possible, but my bare thighs stick to the seat. If I make any sudden movements, they'll squeak against the leather like a fart.

My muscles tense with the strain of staying as still as possible. I can't have my first move in this game be letting out an enormous skin-on-leather squelch. That's definitely not going to bring Jack Lansen to his knees.

"You look a bit uncomfy there, El," Jack says, casting an assessing look over me. "Everything okay?"

I wince as I carefully raise my bare thigh off the leather, praying no noise erupts. *Easy does it.* "Fine. Yeah. I'm good," I tell him, as I shift silently into a new position.

That was a close call. Jack, oblivious to my concerns, flashes a cheeky grin as he plates up some eggs and slides them across to me. He pours me a coffee and pushes that across too.

"You do this for all the girls?" I ask.

He chortles as though my question has surprised him. "Yeah. Nothing like morning-after eggs. When I bring someone home, we tend to work up an appetite."

A flicker of pain slashes through my chest, but I force my smile to hold. "I thought you were supposed to be seducing me, not telling me about all your conquests."

"You asked. I'm not going to lie to you. I'm not going to deceive you into bed."

"You're not playing dirty, you mean?"

Jack laughs heartily, and something deep inside me begins to glow, because the sight of this handsome half-naked man laughing is sexy as sin. Suddenly, it doesn't matter how many other people he's been with because, in this moment, it's just us. "Speaking of playing," he says, "I wrote this out. For clarity."

He puts a cheque on the island, made out to me. I pick it up and inspect it. It's unsigned, but on the back he's written, '*I, Jack Lansen, do solemnly swear to pay Elly Carter One Hundred Thousand Pounds if she can get me to beg for sex.*' His signature is scrawled beneath it.

Despite how amused I am, I fight to keep a straight face and say, "Is it legally binding?"

He reaches over and snatches it back. "I don't know, but I'll sign it if you win. Which you won't."

So arrogant. I'm about to roll my eyes when a little voice pipes up in my head, saying '*rightly so.*'

He paces over to the shelves, which are decorated with glassware that looks like a modern art installation, and lifts down a tiny statue of a man. *Oh, my God.* It's the model of Priapus—the Greek God of fertility—I gave him at his last birthday, complete with an enormous erect cock that's nearly as big as the man it's attached to. It was a stupid joke of a gift, and it's totally out of place in Jack's sleek designer kitchen. *I can't believe he kept it.* Jack slides the cheque between the statue's cock and his torso, displaying it like some kind of lewd certificate, and balances it back on the shelf before turning back to me.

"You kept him," I say, nodding at the tiny Priapus statue.

"Of course," Jack announces, as though he would never have done anything else, and my insides flutter. He comes back towards me and leans against the kitchen worktop opposite. "Eat," he instructs. "Your food will get cold."

The eggs do smell good, but really it's the feel of Jack's eyes on me and the casual command in his deep voice that has me picking up my cutlery and starting to eat.

He watches me, eyes glimmering with amusement. "Nice underwear by the way. I can see your nipples."

A shot of heat bursts through me, and my nipples, if possible, harden even more, like they're trying to poke through the thin silk at him.

"I can see yours too," I say, determined to give as good as I get, and he hums an amused chuckle.

He puts both hands behind him on the counter, making no effort to hide said nipples. I'm not sure I thought man-nipples were hot until right now, but Jack's are perfect, sitting there in the middle of his sculpted pecs.

"What are you doing today, then?" he asks.

It takes me a moment to recalibrate to such a mundane topic, but after a second, I'm there. "Same old. Shift at the Marchmont. I have a set tonight." *Maybe he'll ask if he can come.* Hope flurries like confetti in my stomach, but after a few long seconds of silence, I know he's not going to.

Conversation drifts. He tells me about the renovations they're doing on my old flat, and I tell him about the songs I'm writing.

Just as I'm starting to feel at ease in his company, he rests his forearms on the other side of the island and leans towards me. His blue eyes darken to an even deeper shade, and the weight of his gaze is so intense that I freeze, a forkful of scrambled egg half-way to my mouth. "What?" I ask.

"You look good, El."

The comment is casual—throwaway, almost—but the tone is jam-packed with suggestion. I take a careful breath as he gives me the sexiest closed-lipped smile I've ever seen. The air thickens, locking around my neck, pressing down on my breasts. My lungs shrink to a quarter of their normal size. *Why is it so hard to breathe?*

Jack's eyes are still on me when he says, "Are you turned on right now?"

As though his question broke a dam, arousal floods my body. *Yes, I'm turned on.* My synapses malfunction and all I can manage to say is, "Huh?"

"If I came over there and slid my hand into those tiny little shorts, I'm pretty sure I'd find you wet." My heart catapults around my chest cavity and heat roars through me. *Oh, my God.* "Are you wet for me, El? Because I'd really like to feel that."

My mouth drops open and I'm fairly sure my lungs have teleported to another universe, because I can't breathe at all.

He observes me for a few seconds before his expression cracks like a mirror and he slaps his hand down on the kitchen island, bending double with laughter. "You should see your face," he wheezes. "It's too easy. Too easy..."

Shit. The game. I forgot about the game. "Why, you—" I shoot out of my seat, letting out a rip-roaring leather-skin-fart noise. *Oh, dear Lord. The humiliation*. My cutlery drops from my hands, clattering against my plate, spattering egg over the surface and onto my camisole. I glare at Jack, but he's laughing like he's losing control and this is the funniest thing that's ever happened.

"This game isn't supposed to be funny." My voice is high and squeaky, and I'm not sure if I'm angry or amused or humiliated. Probably all three. "You're not supposed to be laughing at me. That's not how you get me into bed."

His shoulders are shaking. *Hell*, his whole body is shaking. "I'm not sure I want you in my bed if you're going to fart like a troll."

"I did not... I didn't fart. That wasn't a fart. I *never* fart." *Lies*. "Ever. Especially not in bed. If I were in bed with you, I definitely wouldn't fart."

Jack is choking on his own laughter. "Careful El, you sound like you want me to win," he says between bursts.

"I don't... I do not—"

His laughter calms abruptly, and his voice cuts me off. "But you are wet, right?" His eyes are so bright, it's like there's a disco happening inside his head. It's a magnetic look on him, and no matter how annoying he's being, I find myself captivated by his stupid, handsome face. "Because it's only a short walk from wet to begging. I'll win this game in no time."

Fuck's sake. He's infuriating.

I spin to march out of the kitchen, but he calls after me, "You'll have to up your game if you want to play with the pros, El."

I can hear him chuckling, all pleased with himself, and I'm not having that. He can't think it's that easy to mess with me. I turn back around, fuelled by an impetuous irritation I can't control. "Oh, yeah?" I say, and, when I'm sure his attention is on me, I yank up one side of my camisole and flash him a boob.

His eyes nearly pop out of his head, heat firing in his gaze, burning away all traces of amusement.

"Jesus," he curses, his hands tightening on the countertop as my shirt falls back in place.

The air crackles with a new energy, and tension wraps around me, crushing my ribs. *Damn.* Suddenly, my actions don't feel like the stroke of genius they did only seconds ago. Even though my breast is well hidden again, everything feels different. My naked nipple has smashed our current reality into pieces and spun us both out into a different, more awkward one.

"You trying to fucking kill me over here?" Jack half-laughs, half-rasps, desperation weaving through his tone.

I feel a flush of success at his reaction, but I don't want to gloat, and I'm already ashamed at having used such a childish tactic. I school my face into a semblance of dispassion. "No. I'm trying to win."

His jaw tenses, and I can't stand here with his heated, ravenous gaze on me any longer. I turn and leave the room, but as I mount the stairs, my heart is beating so fast it could very well explode.

What the hell was I thinking, flashing Jack Lansen my boob?

14
ELLY

I spend the next week creeping around the house. It's not that I'm not willing to raise my game, or *'play with the pros'* as Jack would have it, but I already exposed a breast, and I don't know where I go from here.

What's the next move?

Whenever I walk past his bedroom, my heart thumps so hard I worry it'll rocket right out of my chest. Sometimes I can hear him showering, and the idea of him naked and soaking wet under running water makes everything worse.

How am I supposed to resist, when I'm constantly bombarded by temptation?

I've been trying to focus on preparing for my interview at the Granville Agency, the most important event of my career so far. That should be dominating my thoughts, not Jack bloody Lansen and this stupid game. *But... fuck. Why does the most annoying man in the world also have to be the most attractive?*

I force thoughts of Jack out of my head, replacing them with Robert Lloyd and my interview. This day has been looming closer, my anxiety spiking with every hour that passes. My fixation on Jack is nothing more than a form of avoidance. *Surely?*

Thinking of him is easier than worrying about this.

I couldn't eat a bite this morning, and I'm still hungry as I make my way to the Granville Agency. It's located within a huge 1930s building, covered in oversize white Metro tiles, in the centre of Soho.

I stand outside in a daze. This is such a big opportunity for me that if I let myself truly appreciate the magnitude of it, I'll turn and run. *Get it together.* I deliberately root my feet to the ground, and suck in a few deep breaths to calm myself, but my heart is having none of it, continuing to beat at a rapid hum.

I'm so nervous that I'm visibly shaking, which is crazy. *I can do this. Can't I?* If I can sing karaoke before a rowdy crowd, I can do this. This is nothing.

Fuck. I can't fool myself. This is far from nothing. This is huge. My music is the most important thing in my life; it exposes my soul to the world.

Doubt swarms my mind like bees, filling my skull with the buzz of negative thoughts. For years, the only place I've performed is the Marchmont. And now I'm here, meeting the agent who represents Amy Moritz.

It's insane. I shouldn't be here.

What if I'm not good enough? What if Robert Lloyd left the card for someone else? Maybe it was a mistake.

I'm spinning out.

Shit.

I summon what remains of my courage and stride into the building, where I register for a visitor's pass at the main desk. They instruct me to take the lift to the fifth floor for the Granville Agency.

When I get there, I check in with reception and take a seat in the waiting area. Next to me, sits a gorgeous redhead who smiles kindly.

"Who are you meeting?" she asks.

I don't want to talk to anyone. I need to concentrate on keeping my arse in this chair, or I'll lose my nerve and run away.

But the redhead is peering at me, and I can't ignore her. I have to respond.

"Robert Lloyd." My voice is so quiet that the girl frowns and leans in. I clear my throat and repeat, "Robert Lloyd."

"Ooh," she coos. "That's a big one. You must be really good."

A contraction occurs in my chest. *Am I?*

Nico deserves the best, and you aren't it.

Why does Jack's comment have to come back to me now? Fuck him and fuck these intrusive thoughts.

My heart thrums like a muted drumroll, and my pulse throbs in my fingertips. They feel both numb and over-sensitive at once. *What if Robert Lloyd asks me to play for him? I won't be able to work my hands.*

The girl reaches into her bag and pulls out a business card, which she holds in my direction. "This is me," she says as I take the card between my trembling fingers.

I stare at it. I don't have anything like this. It's glossy and professional with a logo and her name in the middle. My vision blurs a little. *Shit.* That's a definite sign of rising panic. I blink to clear it, deliberately slowing my breathing. *Come on Elly, you can do this.*

I focus again on the card. The handles for all her social media platforms are listed on the bottom of the card. This girl is a pro.

I don't have an online presence at all. I hate the idea of being seen out there in the world, where I can't control the response. Social media is like an untamed beast, lurking beneath still waters. If you take a dip, it'll pull you down and strangle you. It's easier to stay away entirely.

"I have two hundred thousand followers," the girl says, and I get the sense she doesn't care if I'm listening or not. She's speaking to inform me, and anyone else who happens to be listening, that she belongs here. That she, in fact, deserves her seat in this waiting area. I don't hear a glimmer of insecurity in her tone, which makes me feel even worse.

She continues wittering on about her rapidly expanding fanbase, oblivious to the way I'm shrinking. *Do I deserve my seat?* I have no following... no fans to speak of. I'm a wild card, and if Robert backs me, he'd have to start from scratch.

Why would he take a gamble like that, when he could scoop this girl up in all her readiness? She's a done deal.

And she's beautiful. She takes out her phone and plays me a video, letting me use her headphones to listen to the song. Her voice is spectacular, her sound unique. I tug the headphones out before the piece is over and give her a weak smile. "It's great," I say, but I feel violently sick.

I glance at the clock. *Ten minutes until my meeting.*

My hands start to sweat.

Is it hot in here? It feels fucking hot in here.

I fan my face with my hand, wishing I'd worn my hair up because it's sticking to my neck. I try to distract myself from my discomfort by focusing on the other people waiting. There's a group of men dressed in black with long hair, chatting amongst themselves. They look happy, confident. In the opposite corner sits a gorgeous woman with impossibly long legs, who looks like a model. Perhaps she is one.

I don't fit in here, with my messy hair and my worn out guitar case. And my stupid tryhard cowboy boots. *What does Robert Lloyd want with me?*

"I played at the Shepherd's Bush Empire last month. That was pretty incredible. Where do you play?"

The girl's voice crashes through my internal monologue, and I blank out. I can't tell her I haven't played anywhere other than a tiny pub in Soho, where hardly anyone ever comes to hear me.

I'm a fraud. I can't stay here alongside people who are performing at the Empire, and who have hundreds of thousands of followers online.

The girl is still staring at me, waiting for a response. "A few bars in the West End," I admit, keeping it vague. *A few.* What an exaggeration. A deep blanket of shame covers me.

Why did I think I could do this?

"Oh, yeah? Cool. Where did you record your demos?"

Fuck. "Demos?"

"Yes. Who did you use? Which producer? I went to a studio in Fulham."

My insides are shrivelling, and every organ feels like it's cramping. I don't have demos. All I have are my songs, recorded on my phone and laptop. It's painfully amateur. I've always wanted to get my music professionally recorded and produced, but I've never had the money to do it. I've been too busy trying to make my damn rental payments.

Now, all my financial choices are feeling idiotic. Maybe Kate would have covered my rent for a few months if I'd only told her about wanting to record my music. If I'd told her about this interview, she might have helped me. But I didn't. I've tried to keep it all hidden, not wanting to worry anyone. *Not wanting to fail.*

The pain of striving to hide how hard it's been hits all at once. *I can't do this anymore.*

The girl continues talking about the producer who worked on her songs in the studio he set up in his mother's basement but I'm not really listening. This is possibly the most important moment in my career, the most important moment for my music, and I'm completely unprepared. It's too important to fuck up.

But the realisation is too late. I've already fucked up. Every choice I've made has resulted in this situation. Me, letting myself down. Prioritising the wrong things. Not asking for help when I've so desperately needed it. And now I'm being given a chance, and I'm not ready. I've sabotaged this, just like I've sabotaged everything else in my life.

If I go into this meeting, Robert Lloyd will laugh me half way home. I won't be able to bear the shame of it.

I'll die.

My left knee begins to shake, making my entire leg vibrate, and Jack's words suddenly blast loud in my head, occupying every inch of space in my brain. *If she were any good, she would have made something of herself by now.*

Never have someone else's words felt so excruciatingly true. I can't do this. No microscopic part of me that believes I can.

"Excuse me," I say, lurching from my seat in one swift movement, leaving the girl half-way through a sentence.

I push my way out of the reception area, my vision turning unfocused at the edges again. *It could be tears. Or perhaps my brain is malfunctioning, my optic nerve shutting down.*

I need to get out of here. Now.

I ignore the worried calls of the receptionist as I jab my finger on the button for the lift.

The doors open so fucking slowly. I can't wait. I'm beginning to hyperventilate. I catch sight of a fire exit and head that way instead, clattering down the stairs. I'm barely aware of anything but the violent echo of my footsteps and the thump of my guitar case against my legs.

I don't stop for a second, and in moments I'm out on the street, sticking my hand out into the road, hailing the next cab. It pulls over and I yank the door open. I huddle into my seat, clutching my guitar to stop my hands from shaking. My breaths are coming quick and shallow, and I feel sick. I push the guitar to the seat next to me and lower my head between my knees, riding out the wave of nausea.

"All right, love?" the driver asks, his voice laden with what sounds like genuine concern, but I'm not about to share my shit with a cab driver I don't know.

"Yes, thanks. Notting Hill please," I say, trying not to let my voice break or allow the shame that's beating at my defences to break through. I'm holding it together by a thread.

I breathe in and out. In and out. For a few moments, it's all I can manage, but the relief I'm seeking doesn't come.

Before I can stop myself, I'm beating myself up for what happened. I ran away from the biggest opportunity I've ever had.

Shame and self-loathing roll over me, as thick and dark as tar. I was a fool to think I could handle this.

15
JACK

The moment I open the front door, I know something's wrong. I don't know how I know, I just do, and that eerie sixth sense makes the hairs on the back of my neck stand up.

The house is dark, as though no one's home. It normally smells like exotic cooking, but tonight it smells like furniture polish. It smells the way it used to before Elly moved in and started attacking my kitchen with a flair that I hadn't anticipated.

"El?"

No response.

I flip on the lights in the hall and make my way to the kitchen, and what I see makes my stomach lurch. Elly is slumped over the kitchen counter, arms akimbo, her head lolling to one side.

Fear swoops in my gut. *Fuck. She's dead. She's fucking dead.*

I rush towards her, catching sight of the empty bottle of wine and the half-empty glass with lipstick on the side that sits on the island next to her.

She groans, and the side of her face distorts where it's stuck to the granite, and I get a shot of relief. She's really, *really* drunk, but not dead.

I put a hand on her shoulder and shake her gently. "El?" She groans again. *Responsive, thank God*. I drop down beside her, my legs weak with after-effects of the adrenaline. "I thought you were dead."

"Lansen. You're home," she slurs. "Missed you."

Missed you? The booze must have addled her brain, but I don't care. I'm practically soaring with relief because she hasn't died in my kitchen. If she wasn't so drunk, I'd kiss her.

I keep my hand on hers. "You drank a whole bottle of wine?"

Her eyes flutter open. "Yah." She makes the word long and slow.

I pick up the empty bottle and check the label. *Domaine Leroy. Fuck.* She's polished off a thirty-grand bottle of wine like a teenager downing a litre of peach schnapps, but the hint of irritation I feel dissolves in an instant. There's no way she got this drunk for no reason. "Next time, wait for me to come home before you crack open the good stuff."

She waves her index finger indiscriminately in my direction, as though she can't quite see where I am. She's probably seeing three of me. "You want to get drunk with me?" She gives me drunk eyes that are obviously supposed to be sexy or seductive or something to that effect, but she only succeeds in looking more violently inebriated.

"That would be safer all round. What happened?"

"Not telling you, Mr Perfect." She blows a sloppy raspberry at me, slumps back down, and closes her eyes. "Your life is perfect. You have it all. A perfect fucking life. Money, career, looks…"

Where is this coming from? "What happened? Did someone upset you?" An unprecedented flare of rage bursts through me at the idea that someone caused her to come home and drink herself stupid. "Who was it? What did they say?" She shrugs, but that's not enough of an answer to satisfy me. "Tell me who it was, El. Tell me who hurt you."

Her eyes are still closed when she slurs, "No one. No one hurt me. I did it. Me. I hurt me. I'm *useless.*"

What the hell is she talking about? I'm confused, but at least there isn't another party involved. "No, you aren't. I won't let you think that."

"A perfect body. You have that too," she says, circling back to her previous line of conversation as if we never deviated.

"You think that's all you need for a perfect life?"

She stutters a drunken moan, and tears leak from the corners of her eyes; because of the tilt of her head against the island, they dribble down the side of her nose. She's not sobbing. She's leaking tears. I can't tell if she's really upset, or just incredibly drunk. Probably both.

I wipe the tears away with my thumb, stroking her cheek. Her skin is so soft. I haven't touched her this intimately since that night at the racetrack when we nearly kissed. She doesn't react, but when she exhales it sounds like a small, satisfied purr.

"Love," she whispers. "Love too. Then you'd have everything you need for a perfect life."

A wry laugh seeks to escape my mouth, itching in the back of my throat. *Is that what I need?* I'm not sure love is on the cards for me, because the cards all bear the faces of very specific women, chosen by my mother. I'm not going anywhere near that shit.

"Ah. My life is definitely not perfect then." I wipe another tear from her face, and she stares up at me. If she wasn't so drunk, her eyes half-glazed, the moment would be unbearably intense. In sobriety, it would easily reach a level of intimacy we haven't shared before.

"You're sweet," she drawls, interrupting my thoughts and prodding the island with one finger to anchor herself. "I like you a lot more than I thought I did." She smiles up at me, and the flicker of happiness that ignites in my heart takes me by surprise. "I like it best when you take your shirt off. One day, I'd like to f—"

I press a finger to her lips. "Shhhh. Drunk talk is bad talk. Save it for when you're sober."

Her lips form a sloppy grin against my finger, and she makes that purring sound again. "You're not trying to win the game."

Does she think I'd take advantage of her? Or was she about to beg me for sex?

"You mean because you're drunk? I wouldn't do that."

She glances at me. "You're a good man. Even if you do throw your money around like Mr Monopoly."

Mr Monopoly? I'm about to make a witty comeback when she groans. "I shouldn't have drunk so much."

"Do you want food? Are you going to be sick?"

"Maybe."

I get her a glass of water and an Alka Seltzer, insisting she drinks it, and then I fry some bacon and make her a sandwich, which she eats with inebriated gusto, licking the grease from her fingers. Afterwards, as I'm clearing up, she falls asleep, snoring gently against the counter.

I watch the rise and fall of her shoulders, and the way her hair shifts with each breath. I can't leave her here. She'll fall off the stool and hit her head on the stone floor.

I pick her up, cradling her in my arms, and carry her up to her room. I put her on the bed, and briefly wonder if I ought to take her clothes off, and then immediately reason that I can't possibly do that, so I tuck her under the covers fully clothed instead.

But she's so drunk, I can't leave her alone. What if she throws up? I put the waste-paper basket at the side of the bed in case she vomits, and sit in the chair by the window. I'll sleep right here, and if she's sick, or she needs help, I'll be nearby.

I'm about to lower myself into the chair when I really take a look around the room. *Fuck, it's messy in here. Does she ever hang up her clothes? Put stuff away?* I try to ignore the mess, but everywhere I look, something's out of place. *Damn it.* Quietly, I fold up the clothes strewn about the room and put her shoes back in pairs near the cupboard. When I'm done, I settle into the chair to wait.

"Jack?"

I spring to my feet, rushing towards her before I know what I'm doing. "Yeah?"

"Will you hold me?"

My muscles seize, and I halt halfway across the room. She seriously wants me to get into bed and hold her? *Christ.* "What?"

"Please." Her head is rolled halfway into the pillow, her mouth against it. It's hard to understand what she's saying, but she shifts and her next sentence is clear. "I'm so sad."

Those three words reach inside me, grip on, and start to fucking tug. I hate the idea of her being sad. I knew she was, or at least suspected it after her behaviour tonight, but to hear it spoken so plainly in her own words is haunting.

"Please?" she says again, and a sound like a sob fills the room, making the tension that had taken hold of my shoulders grip harder. I can't leave her here, drunk and miserable. She wants company. That's it. *I can give her that, can't I?* I won't try to win this stupid game I've set in action. We can put all of that aside tonight.

I bend to untie my shoelaces and slip my shoes off. "Okay." At my agreement, she gives a sweet-sounding sigh that gets me hot in places it shouldn't. *Focus, Lansen.* She's drunk. This is not a moment to get aroused; this is me making sure I don't need to take her to A&E to get her stomach pumped. This is me, offering *comfort*.

This isn't something I normally do with women. I like to keep things casual. Sex is fine, but this... whatever *this* is, is not in my repertoire. I don't *snuggle*.

But for some reason, I find myself climbing into the bed next to her and sliding into place like a big fucking spoon in a cutlery drawer. I don't want to disturb her any more than necessary, so I stay quiet and slide my hand around her waist. She's so soft, so warm, so *small* compared to me. I'm barely breathing, but I can smell the citrus scent in her hair, and without thinking I shift a little closer so I'm nuzzling her neck.

What the fuck am I doing?

My heart is thudding, and there's a definite unease in my stomach, like the contents are tidal. Being this close to her is affecting me on some unexpected level. I'm hyper-alert, more so than I am behind the wheel of one of my cars. *Something* is happening here, but I don't know what, and while it's not entirely comfortable, it's not unpleasant, either.

"This okay?" I whisper, my voice rough against her ear.

"Mmm." She slides her hand over the back of mine, where it rests on her waist, and threads our fingers. "Thank you. I don't want to be alone. I'm always alone."

Fucking hell. She's trying to wreck me. She's normally so bold that hearing her talk like this makes it feel as though I'm witnessing something I shouldn't. A peek behind the curtain Elly normally keeps tightly drawn.

"I wanted to be famous," she slurs. "When I was a kid. I wanted to be Taylor Swift."

Her words surprise me, and all I can do is mindlessly repeat them. "Taylor Swift?"

Elly's wild hair shifts. *She's nodding.* "Yeah. Or Amy Moritz. I thought I could be that good." She moans a little, and the sound has my dick giving an unwelcome throb. Elly definitely doesn't mean the noise to be anything near sexual, but being this close to her, my hands on her like this, in a fucking bed, for Christ's sake, has my dick confused. I mentally warn it to keep its head down. "But I'm not sure many people are *that* good. Especially not me."

I shift her hair away from her ear and whisper, "You're as good as you want to be. As good as you let yourself be. You decide, El. No one else."

She makes a little whining noise, and I suspect she's thinking of saying something else, but a moment later her breathing is deep and even, and I know she's fallen asleep.

I intend to get up. I don't need to be here now. I can sleep in the chair, just in case. I'll just give myself one more minute…

When I wake, I'm disoriented. The light from the window is at the wrong angle. The bed is wrong. I'm still wearing a shirt and suit trousers. This isn't my room. The pieces slot together pretty quickly, tessellating even more rapidly when Elly gives a sleepy sigh.

Fuck. I've been here the whole night, Elly tucked in front of me, my arm resting over her hip. I'm far too hot, my skin unpleasantly sticky. And *Christ Almighty*, I have a hard on like nothing else, pressed right against Elly's arse.

For a moment, I wonder if I'm turned on, then immediately dismiss it. Morning wood. That's all. It would be wrong to be genuinely aroused. She was drunk last night. Probably still is. And here I am with my dick straining in my trousers while she's completely unaware of my presence. But I can't deny there's something that feels so right about being here with her in my arms. If there hadn't been, I would never have been able to fall asleep like this, so close to another person. I like my space at night.

I shift backwards, so my hips aren't pressed into hers. I try to move as little as I can. She's still asleep; I can tell from the breathy exhales sounding at regular intervals and her lack of movement. I don't want to wake her.

I'm like a fucking ninja, the way I'm raising my arm, allowing it to levitate over her hip before I snatch it away once I'm clear of skin, and rolling backwards off the bed.

When my feet silently hit the floor, I check the time: 6.05 am. I stand and stretch, then walk around to the other side of the bed so I can see her face. She's so peaceful like this. *What on earth could have driven her to come home and get so fucked up? To sit alone and drink an entire bottle of wine?* I push a strand of hair off her face, and she murmurs in her sleep. *So beautiful.*

I should go. I'm drifting into creepy territory here. She's made it through the night and has a full glass of water for when she wakes up, so she doesn't need me anymore.

And I have to go and handle my morning glory before my dick busts a hole in my trousers.

I let myself out of the room, wondering if I'm annoyed or relieved that Elly is still asleep and will likely never know that she slept all night in my arms.

16
ELLY

Drinking an entire bottle of wine by oneself is never a good idea, even if it is to numb the pain of having crashed and burned at the biggest career opportunity of one's life.

I vow that it will never happen again. Neither the wine nor the running away. I can't keep fucking things up for myself. I can't bear to think about the Granville Agency or Robert Lloyd, and I'm almost thankful for the hangover that's bursting my skull like a thousand tiny men are in there battering sledgehammers against my brain, because it means I can avoid thinking about everything that happened yesterday.

I'd rather throw up my insides than replay that shitshow in my mind.

I have no idea how I got myself to bed, and I have weird blurry memories of Jack making food for me. And him lying in bed with me, but that must have been a dream because I woke up alone. He must have sent the housekeeper into my room at some point too because it was unusually tidy when I sobered up enough to notice.

I apologised about drinking his wine this morning, but he didn't seem bothered and made some joke about my expensive hangover. He was a little weird and awkward about it though, which is unusual for Jack, so I figure I need to at least try to replace it.

When I googled the wine, I nearly wet myself. It costs over thirty thousand pounds. *Crazy.* I'm eaten up with guilt over it. I can't afford to replace it, but I figure I have to do *something* to pay him back, so I'm at the supermarket, searching for ingredients to cook a feast that says, 'sorry I helped myself to your extremely fine wine and nearly threw it all back up again'.

When I have everything I need, I head to the wine aisle. *Ugh, I don't even want to think of alcohol today, let alone peruse the offerings, but I'll stomach it for Jack.*

I'm inspecting the bottles, searching for a replacement, when I become aware that someone is approaching me with more direct purpose than is usual in the supermarket.

I look up to find Lydia Archer striding towards me, and my stomach does a nervous flap. *What is she doing here?*

Blind panic races through me, and in my head I can hear the words *red flag red flag red flag* over and over again.

Did she follow me in here?

No. That would be weird. A little crazy. It's got to be a coincidence.

Other shoppers turn to watch her as she passes them in the aisle. She's tall and beautiful—*intimidatingly so*—with that long dark hair flowing down her back and heavy eye makeup. She's wearing a pale silk shirt and loose navy suit trousers beneath a long coat. She has a Kate Middleton look about her.

"I thought that was you," she says, not sounding entirely friendly. "The waitress."

"Elly," I correct. My voice sounds dead.

She stands right next to me, surveying the wines as though they're what she came in for, but she has neither a trolley nor a basket. Maybe she really did come in here just for me. A shiver trips down my spine at the thought.

"What are you looking for?" Lydia asks.

I don't really want to talk to her, but I don't know what else to do. "I drank a bottle of Jack's red. I want to replace it."

She picks one off the shelf, inspects the label, and replaces it. "What was it?"

"Domaine Leroy something."

She barks a laugh, sneering as she turns to me. "You thought you'd find something like that in the supermarket?"

My stomach drops. I might not be a connoisseur, but I have Google and a phone, and I know damn well that I'm not going to find a bottle of Domaine Leroy at Tesco. But I can't afford to buy one *anywhere*, so this was the next best thing. It's the thought that counts, right?

Lydia's thick eyelashes flutter on an eye roll, and the condescension in her expression makes me grind my teeth. "Clearly, you have no idea what you're doing." She runs her finger along the row of red wines before settling on one of the more expensive ones and tapping the label with a perfectly painted crimson nail. "This is the best you'll get in here."

She lifts it from the shelf and hands it to me. I take it from her, but I have no intention of buying it. I'm not going to let her make me feel like an idiot.

"No, thanks." I slot the wine back in its place. "I'm cooking dinner for Jack tonight, so I'm going to choose something to pair with it."

It's barely perceptible, but I don't miss the way her body tightens as she straightens up.

She gives me a look that sinks to my bones, all dark and cold, and before I can wonder what she's doing, she leans so close that for a second I think she means to kiss me, but she shifts her mouth to the side and presses it against the shell of my ear. Her voice is full of quiet vitriol when she whispers, "Keep your hands off Jack Lansen. Don't. Fucking. Touch. Him."

It's as if someone opened a trapdoor, and my insides tumbled out. *Did she really say that?*

My mind spins as I try to work out what's happening. I freeze, and Lydia steps away, smugness twisting her lips as if she's pleased by my reaction. Thrilled that she's shocked me into stillness.

Before I've gathered my senses, Lydia turns and strolls towards the exit without picking up a single item to buy.

My heart is beating in every cell of my body, thumping through me, and the shock turns to anger. *How dare she lay claim to him like that? Who the hell does she think she is?* Just because her face was on one of Mrs Lansen's cards, it doesn't give her the right to order me about.

I spring into motion, pacing after her, my basket banging against my hip. "Hey, Lydia." She turns, surprise etching her face at the sight of me fast-walking in her direction. "You don't make the rules." My voice sounds far off, as though the angry tone belongs to someone else.

She casts me that condescending look again. "Maybe not. But I'd advise you to follow them."

With a final sneer in my direction, she turns and leaves, and I feel remarkably foolish, standing in the middle of the supermarket, breathing heavily as though I've just been attacked.

But haven't I?

I take a few moments to resettle my breathing. *It's okay. I'm okay.* What could Lydia possibly do to me?

And how dare she tell me what to do?

She can't. *I will damn well touch Jack Lansen if I want to.* The thought brings with it a wave of inspiration, and I decide right then and there what my next move is in this game I'm playing with Jack, and how I'm going to bring him to his knees.

All I need is a costume.

"That bitch does not get to decide what I can and cannot do." I pick up a bra that has holes where the nipples ought to be. It's possible I'm taking this thing with Jack a bit far, but seeing as he's unmoved by pretty pink silk and lace, I'm upping my game. I hold the bra up against my chest. "What do you think?"

I'm standing in the middle of a Soho sex shop with my ex-flatmate, Marie, and because I can't share what's going on with me and Jack with Kate, Marie is the next best thing. I reached a tipping point where I could no longer keep all of this inside. I needed to share.

Marie was so surprised by my news that she didn't ask a single question about my career. I haven't revealed anything about the way I imploded at the Granville Agency, and Marie, thank goodness, hasn't asked. Not that I'd tell her anyway; she's a hard-nosed career woman through and through, and I'd never get any sympathy from her. *Do I even want sympathy?*

Fuck it. What I want is to forget about it completely.

Marie screws up her face. "Lydia will never know if you dress up for Jack or not." She waves a limp finger towards the nipple holes in the bra cups. "You don't need to do this."

"Yeah, but *I'll* know, and I'm not having my actions dictated by a beautiful woman with fake eyelashes." But the nipple holes are a bit excessive, even for me. I put the bra back and keep searching.

Marie tuts as she flicks through a rack of crotchless panties, then abruptly abandons her perusal and pins me with a pointed stare. "I'm going to put it out there. You need to put an end to this game." I pull a *'how dare you tell me what to do'* face, but Marie keeps going. "This is Jack Lansen we're talking about. Slept with half of London.

Dreadful flirt. Ego the size of a small planet. Not to mention he's your best friend's brother. Don't get involved. And definitely don't do it to spite some woman who assaulted you in the supermarket."

"I'm doing it for the cash," I say matter-of-factly, although the words don't have the heft of truth, and I wonder if Marie will pick up on it. "A hundred thousand pounds. It would take years for me to earn that much."

I hold up a black corset with purple trim and a matching suspender belt. Marie rolls her eyes, but I like it, so I keep hold of it and lead the way to the changing rooms. Marie takes a seat outside my cubicle as I hurriedly undress.

"That man has more money than sense," Marie muses. "You must've really got under his skin."

God, I hope so, because he's already so deep under mine that I'm not sure I can get him out. I haul on the corset, striving to keep my voice calm. "Maybe. I guess."

I check out my reflection. This outfit is hot. I might be in flats and no make-up, but my breasts are falling out of the corset in the best way, making me feel ridiculously sexy for a Friday morning. It's so much better than Lydia's underwear and trench coat affair.

The curtain to my cubicle opens and my hands fly to cover me in the scant underwear. "Hey!"

Marie pays my outburst no heed as she stands there with her mouth open, her eyes darting all over my face. "You like him. I can hear it in your voice. Fuck, Elly." Her hands slap against her cheeks, and I'm desperately trying not to react, even though my heart is rampaging around my chest like *Phil Collins* on the drums. "You're into Jack Lansen."

"I'm not... I don't... this is just about the money." I blink like I'm using my eyelashes to fend off a swarm of mosquitos that are set upon draining all the blood from my eyeballs. "I don't actually want to sleep with him." A strange tightening sensation corkscrews through my chest. *What's that about?*

"You sure about that?"

"Yes. I do not fancy Jack Lansen." *Ugh*, that corkscrew sensation again. This time, a brief flicker of illumination comes with it. *I'm lying.*

I fancy Jack Lansen, and I absolutely want to fuck him.

I'm mildly shocked by the clarity of the realisation, despite having known it for weeks.

"Wow," Marie says, interrupting my thoughts. Her gaze is fixed on my body for the first time since she pulled back the curtain. "What are you going to do in this getup?"

"Dance in it." I wiggle my hips. "I used to work as a stripper at uni. Paid a fortune. I was the richest student on campus."

Marie's eyebrows shoot up. "I didn't know that. Well, you look great. I'd get on my knees for you in this outfit."

"Thanks. Could you give me a moment?" I say, and Marie steps back so I can close the curtain again and get changed.

When I come out, Marie has a thoughtful look on her face. "Is Jack sleeping with anyone else?"

The question catches me off-guard. I hadn't considered it. I'm not sleeping with anyone, so I'd kind of assumed, while we were locked in this bizarre agreement, that Jack wouldn't be either.

Marie gives me a sympathetic look. "Use a condom. That's all I'm saying."

"I'm not going to have sex with Jack."

But I totally want to.

Marie shakes her head dismissively, like I'm a lost cause. It's clear she knows I'm lying. "What are you going to tell Kate?"

"Nothing. She was fine with me and Jack living together, but she definitely wouldn't be okay with this, so I'm not going to mention it."

Marie looks at me like this is my stupidest idea yet, but thankfully she doesn't call me out on it. Although, to be fair, the look is enough to have ants squirming beneath my skin.

We spend a while longer flicking through the clothes and examining a bizarre array of sex toys. When we've finished, I take everything I've chosen to the till—a corset that pushes my boobs up so much they might fall out, a suspender belt and stockings, and a pair of platform PVC heels. It's not tasteful, but it's certainly a look. The cashier rings it all up.

Marie's eyebrows shoot up at the total. "Fuck, that's expensive."

Holy fuck, it is. "It's an investment," I quip. "The return on this is going to be huge."

17
ELLY

A week passes before I put the next stage of my plan into action. When I get back from my Friday afternoon shift at the Marchmont, I have a quick supper and go up to my room. I've paid attention to Jack's schedule, and I know for a fact he gets home earlier on Fridays.

I do my makeup heavier than normal, and then get dressed in the outfit I bought from the Soho shop. I buckle into the platform heels. Shit, they're high. I haven't worn shoes like this for years, but walking in them comes back to me quickly, like riding a bike.

I prance in front of the mirror, and I'm suddenly filled with a sense of excitement. I haven't dressed up like this for a man since I worked at the strip club, and it feels a lot like reclaiming something I've lost. *When did I give up on all this stuff?* I never took all my clothes off back then, but near enough, and I know a thing or two about using my body to drive men wild. And I look crazy hot in this outfit, even if I do say so myself.

Jack is going to lose his mind.

I head downstairs, lingering at the front door. Right on time, I hear the beep of his car in the drive as he locks it.

I'm about to open the front door when I hear voices.

Shit. He's not alone. I hadn't planned for this. I run back to my room and throw a skirt and jumper over the corset and suspender belt. The outfit looks ridiculous paired with these enormous platform heels, but they make my legs look amazing, so I keep them on.

My heart is racing as I take the stairs down to the front door. I force myself to appear calm just as Jack unlocks it and steps inside with Seb and Matt Hawkston in tow.

Jack stares at me, blinking a few times like he's got a floater in his vision. *Is it the make-up that's causing the double-take? Perhaps it's the shoes.* Either way, I've got his attention, and my skin starts to heat under his gaze.

"Hey. Elly, isn't it?" Seb says, grinning at me and stepping in front of Jack, who has clearly lost his ability to form words. *Did I do that?* "We met at the racetrack. That's some voice you have. You can really sing."

"Thanks." I smile, immediately feeling more at ease on account of the warmth in Seb's greeting.

Matt, Nico's other brother, stares between me and Jack as though he's trying to run a calculation in his head and can't make the numbers work. And no wonder, because Jack, who's usually so together, appears to have been blindsided by my appearance.

"Good to see you again," Matt says to me, gruff and low.

"What are you doing here?" Seb asks.

I explain that I'm living with Jack until my lease ends, which Seb accepts, although I don't miss the querying glances he directs at Jack, who cocks his head slightly in response, as though none of this is his fault.

"Are you joining us for poker?" Seb asks me.

Jack hasn't stopped staring, and his gaze is like a laser beam that's stripping away my skin. I have no idea if he wants me to join them or not, but if I'm going to win this game, I need to be where Jack is.

"I'd love to."

"You'd love to," Jack repeats like his brain is only semi-engaged with the thought-to-word process. Then his full concentration appears behind his eyes and he says, "It's high stakes. I don't think you'll be able to—"

Seb's arm is suddenly around my shoulder, and the action completely cuts through whatever Jack is about to say.

"I'll cover her stake." Seb winks at me. "Let's give Lansen a run for his money, shall we?"

Jack frowns, his brows drawing so low that he looks almost like he's scowling. Is it because he doesn't want me to join them, or because he doesn't like the fact that Seb is touching me? I hope it's the latter.

"Yes, please," I say, smiling up at Seb.

Jack huffs. "Fine." He nods his head in the direction of the dining room. "You two go and make yourselves comfortable," he instructs the Hawkston brothers. "Elly and I will get drinks."

As Matt and Seb walk away, I make my way to the kitchen, Jack pacing right behind me. There's a strange tension in the air, and I wonder if Jack can feel it too. It's as though we both know *something* is going to happen tonight.

Jack closes the door behind us, and a strange pressure squeezes in my heart. I turn to find him standing behind me, every inch the boss man in his suit and coat, and it occurs to me that if he were to give me an order right now, I'd obey in an instant.

His blue eyes are hard and scrutinizing as he takes me in, but his gaze drifts up and down my body, lingering over my legs. "You look different." His tone reveals nothing.

"So?"

His eyelids flicker as if to dismiss my question. "Do you know how to play poker?"

"Yes."

He nods. "Okay." He blows out a breath, his shoulders sink, and his features take on a new softness. "You look good. Your eyes..."

So it is the make-up.

His voice is full of admiration. It coats me like warm honey, and I let out a small laugh as I step towards him. In my ridiculous heels I'm much nearer his height than I am normally, and I can't help glancing at his lips. As if he knows what I'm thinking, his tongue slips out and wets the bottom one.

"El?" he breathes, and the sound ripples all the way down my body. *I want to kiss him, and he knows it.* But that's not how to win the game, is it?

"Shh," I say, reaching up for his tie. He doesn't stop me, and I undo it, easing it out from under the collar of his shirt. A burst of his cologne wafts towards me, unravelling a little coil of arousal low in my hips, which I ignore. "Just remember," I whisper into his ear. "I play to win."

I pull back to see his blue eyes a shade darker, his jaw tight, a muscle standing out along the edge.

"So do I." He takes his tie from me, rolls it up neatly and tucks it into the pocket of his coat. For a few seconds we stand there, a fraction too close, holding eye contact that scorches in ways it shouldn't, before he says, "Let's get those drinks then, shall we?"

The rest of the night passes without a hitch. I play some fantastic poker, and although I don't win much, I don't lose either, which is just as well seeing as I'm playing with Seb Hawkston's money.

Seb is so much fun. He's a joker, making us laugh, teasing me about my cards, pretending to lean over and see my hand. Not to mention he's gorgeous, but so is Matt. All the Hawkston brothers are freakishly good-looking, but I've no interest in either of them that way. Next to Jack, they're nothing.

We've been drinking Scotch all night, and I feel mellow and happy.

Every so often, Seb's arm creeps onto the back of my chair. He's not coming onto me. I don't get that vibe at all, but each time he leans towards me, Jack's eyes flash over at us like a spark of gunfire, setting off a fission of sexual energy deep in my core.

He hasn't spoken much, and as the game goes on, his expression fixes into a furious frown. He's losing. Badly.

Part of me wonders if that has anything to do with the way Seb is being with me. If Jack and I weren't playing the game, and if Jack was seriously interested in me, I'd think what I was doing was cruel. Teasing him this way. Making him jealous. But none of it's real. I might be flirting with Seb, but it's Jack's attention I crave. *And even that's only for the game. Right?*

The money, think of the money. A hundred thousand pounds.

Finally, the poker game ends, and the men say their goodbyes. Jack merely grunts from his seat at the table. He's lost a shit load of cash. But if he will play poker with billionaires...

Seb stands and looks at me. "Grumps might need a shoulder to cry on." He indicates Jack.

"Fuck off," Jack mumbles.

Seb tips his chin. "Sleep well, Lansen."

"I'll see you out," I say, rising to my feet to escort Seb and Matt to the door. We head into the hall, where Matt bids me goodnight and lets himself out, but Seb lingers a moment until we're alone.

"I had fun tonight," he says, and my heart skips a beat. I've been so fixated on Jack that I hadn't stopped to worry about Seb, other than to assume he couldn't possibly be truly interested in me. *Have I led him on?* He pulls a business card from his wallet and hands it to me. "I'd like to take you out sometime. Call me."

My blood turns cold. "Oh." I stare at the card, but don't take it. "I don't...I..."

Seb gauges my reaction, his eyes narrowing slightly. He flicks the card back into his wallet, but he doesn't look annoyed. "You and Lansen, eh?" He chuckles. "Thought so."

My chest tightens. Jack and I barely spoke to one another all night. *How did Seb know?* "There's nothing going on."

The smile that curls his lips is all scepticism. "Not yet, maybe. But Jack never loses at poker." He leans in to kiss my cheek. "Thanks for helping me distract him. Don't stay up too late." He turns and trots down the steps, waving the back of his hand at me as he goes.

I linger in the hall for several minutes after they've left, but Jack doesn't emerge.

I could go upstairs, call it a night, but nervous energy is pumping through me, especially after what Seb just said. *Did Jack really lose tonight because of me?* The idea that I affect him that way is thrilling. Guilt tussles with the thrill, but I'm not going to let it stop me focusing on our game and what I set out to achieve this evening. I spent a fortune on the outfit still concealed beneath my regular clothes, and I'm damned if I'm going to let it go to waste. Plus, if I don't do this now, I'll lose my nerve.

Swallowing down my hesitation, I totter down the hall on my heels and enter the dining room, where the debris from the poker is still laid out on the table. I hadn't noticed how low the lights are in here, and the room is almost smoky, as if we'd been indulging in cigars. But there's no smell of smoke, and only the scent of Jack's cologne hangs in the air.

He's seated at the head of the table, hunched over, a furious energy emanating from him, penetrating every inch of the shadowed room.

"How much did you lose?" I ask in a hushed voice.

"Enough." He stands and starts putting all the chips away. Shuffling the cards, he spares me a glance. "You're a fucking nightmare, you know that?"

For a second, I contemplate turning around and going to bed, but I dismiss it as momentary weakness and forge on with my plan. "Is you losing my fault?"

A dark laugh rumbles from him, and he begins shuffling the cards faster, fanning them out, letting them fly from hand to hand. It's mesmerizing. "Couldn't fucking concentrate with you here."

A little buzz shoots through me. Maybe Seb was right, and if Jack's prepared to make an admission like that, then this might be the moment to strike.

"Sorry." I pout my bottom lip, but Jack doesn't look amused. "Let me make it up to you."

"How do you plan on doing that?"

"I'll dance."

Jack stops shuffling the cards, and without the flickering noise of them the room is deathly quiet. "Dance?"

I give him what I hope is an enticing, but seductive smile, acting as if I have this all under control, even though butterflies are swarming through my insides. I must be crazy. But I'm committed to this plan. Committed to winning.

I haul my jumper over my head and toss it to the ground.

Jack squints as though he's looking into a light that's too bright, but I don't miss the moment his eyes widen as he takes me in. *He likes what he sees*. He looks like he wants to question me on my actions, but the expression vanishes, replaced with one of liquid heat. *Perfect*. His lips form what looks like an overawed '*fuck*', and the heat in his eyes flows through me as though he's funnelling it right to my core.

I need to make a move. One that's not me running away from the explosive scenario I've set in motion. I can handle Jack Lansen and the way he's looking at me. *Can't I?*

I've already linked my phone to the sound system, and the music starts playing. I start to move, slow and sensual, and then I undo my skirt and let it fall to the floor, revealing the stockings and suspender belt.

Jack's body goes taut. He doesn't take his eyes off me, but he's holding himself back, as though he's expecting me to scream '*Gotcha!*' in his face. But this isn't a joke, and I need him to get involved.

I walk over and pull out the chair he was sitting on, turning it around and gesturing for him to take a seat.

"What are you doing, El?" Jack's body is preternaturally still, but his eyes roam hungrily over me as I move.

"Playing with the pros."

He tilts his head, contemplating my response. "Okay," he says, putting the pack of cards on the table and dropping into the chair. "Show me what you've got."

"No touching," I confirm.

Jack swallows, and his Adam's apple bobs up and down. *God, he's got a sexy throat*. The column of it, the dark stubble peppering it. "You're the boss," he replies gruffly.

A pulse thumps between my legs at his words. *Maybe this is too much*. But—*fuck it*—I'm not running away again. "No talking."

He makes that little humming sound and sinks back in the chair, his thick thighs spread, and his shirt sleeves rolled to the elbow. His energy beats against my skin so dense and potent I can almost taste it.

I run over in my head what I'm doing here. Get him hard. Walk away. *Irresistible, but unattainable.* Hopefully, everything I've already done tonight has primed the path.

The music makes everything easier, filling the room with its sensual beat. I move to the rhythm, letting instinct take over, stroking my body as I dance, running my hands over my hips... my breasts. Jack's mouth is drawn into a tense line, but his eyes are blue fire. As he drags his gaze over me, paths of scorching awareness steal over my skin. I have every scrap of his attention, and it feeds me like I haven't eaten for a week. I'm gorging on the sensation of being admired by Jack Lansen, and I'm not sure anything has ever felt this good.

As I move my hips, letting the music guide me, heat builds low in my core. A dangerous, simmering heat that could boil over at any moment. I'm in my body, following its impulses like a slave, but simultaneously heady with the knowledge that I have this huge, gorgeous man at my mercy. His fingers tighten around the arms of the chair, like he needs to cling on to prevent himself from reaching out to grab me.

My clit is throbbing, desperate for friction. Begging me to get a little closer. I wonder if Jack knows what dancing for him is doing to me, or if he thinks this is all part of the game.

Unable to resist, I slide onto his lap, straddling him, my arms around his neck. His warm breath hits the exposed part of my breasts, and I tremble with pleasure. In response, a low moan rumbles in his chest, and he releases the arms of the chair, letting his hands hover over my thighs, but he pulls them back, remembering he's not supposed to touch. His eyes flicker shut, and he groans as if this is absolute torment to him, and the sound sends a bolt of white-hot arousal through me.

We're playing with fire.

The music builds, the low bass thump of it echoing the beat of my pulse. I writhe and grind against him, and with each rotation of my hips, the pressure hits my clit, climbing steadily to the inevitable end.

I gasp as I feel him. The long, hard length of him pressed right against my core.

Oh. My. God.

This is dangerous. I should get up. Get off his lap. Walk away. I've done exactly what I meant to do. Achieved the goal. And yet I don't stop, because feeling Jack beneath me like this is *so fucking hot*. I keep moving against him, and he lets his head fall back and moans again. His arms hang limp at his sides, but his hands are clenched so tightly that his knuckles whiten.

"El…"

The way he says my name, a low vibration that ripples right through me, does nothing to quell the rising arousal between my legs. Maybe he's about to give in and admit he wants to quit the game and fuck. If I push a little harder, I could win. I put my hands on his shoulders and lean into him, pressing my lips right up to his ear. "Open your eyes. I want you to look at me."

His broad chest expands, and at my command those blue eyes stare right at me, and the expression is so fierce, so primal, so *predatory*, that I have to force myself not to jump off him and run. And yet it's also so attractive, so compulsive, that I couldn't walk away. *Talk about a headfuck.*

I rotate my hips, pressing down against him more deliberately, aware my breathing is little more than shallow pants. I'm getting light-headed, and a delicious, lust-filled delirium consumes me with each thrust of my sex against him.

I don't think I'm winning anymore. Hell, I'm not even playing, and I don't care. We're inches away from one another, and Jack still hasn't touched me, although our hips are locked together.

"Keep doing that," he grits out. "This is... *fuck*."

A breathy moan slips from my open mouth. If he keeps talking in that deep voice of his, sounding like he's about to lose it, I'll explode. "Shhh," I remind him. "Only I get to talk."

His answering groan is a begrudging agreement.

"I can feel you," I whisper, shifting against him, the steady pulse in my clit driving me to rub harder. His gaze doesn't leave mine when he nods. "You feel so... fucking... good," I murmur, and I'm not pretending, but even as the words slip from my mouth, I know I could play this off as part of the act.

"God, El." His jaw tightens, his throat tensing. "*Fuck*. Don't stop..."

I love the sound of his voice, all desperate and wrung out. I want to kiss his mouth, eat up his words. I don't give a fuck that he's ignoring my instructions.

The familiar tingles of an impending orgasm zap through me. I should stop. I should pull back. But, fuck, if this doesn't feel good, I don't know what does.

Jack jerks a little against me, meeting my movements. I'm not even dancing anymore. I'm just grinding on him like a teenager, dry-humping him, but I'm so far gone I don't care.

"Fuck," I breathe.

"I know, I fucking know," he says on a moan, and I don't think I've ever been this turned on before. My blood whooshes in my ears, blocking out even the sound of the music playing, and Jack is meeting me halfway, the two of us a mess, tangled up, pressing ourselves as tight to one another as we can manage, without him actually laying a hand on me.

I close my eyes, head falling back as waves of increasing pleasure ripple through me. I let out a whimper that's so distorted by lust, I can't believe I made the sound.

"Open your eyes," Jack grits out.

"What?" I gasp.

"Look at me when you come."

His words spark something in me, and when I open my eyes, he's there. *Right fucking there*. Staring at me. His eyes never leave mine, and as if his gaze is the flame that lights the fuse, I explode. Pleasure rips through me, powerful surges of it blasting through my body.

I cling to him, more unfamiliar noises tumbling from my lips. Wild, passionate sounds driven by the force of the orgasm that seems to go on and on and on, eking itself out as I rub myself against his hard cock. "Oh, fuck, fuck, *fuck*..."

I shudder with each rising crest, finally collapsing against him, my body radiating heat and slick between the thighs. Beneath me, Jack's chest moves like bellows, sucking in huge breaths.

He hasn't come. He's still hard, right between my legs. *Fuck*.

A vibration emanates from his chest and it takes me a split second to realise he's chuckling. Not a loud, ridiculing laugh, but a desperate, disbelieving peel of laughter, as though he has no idea how any of this came to pass. My guts tighten and my body stiffens, regret rapidly flushing through me, stronger with each roll of Jack's laugh.

"You may be the best housemate I've ever had," he pants.

Oh, shit. How did I let this happen? I can't speak. Can't form a single word. This was not the way this was supposed to go.

Jack must see something in my expression that kills his laughter, because it dies the moment we make eye contact. His erratic breaths are warm against my face, and in a twisted moment of connection, he presses his forehead to mine. "Thank you for the dance." The whispered words are painfully sincere, making inexplicable tears prick my eyes. I let my hands slide from their resting position on his shoulders down his chest, settling where I can feel the racing of his heart. We sit like that, neither of us moving, as if what's happened has left us both shell-shocked. Finally, Jack says, "Do you want to come upstairs?"

The question strikes like a lightning bolt and I snatch my hands back, curling them into fists. *I've massively fucked up.* He thinks he's won the game, and now he's expecting me to jump into bed with him. It's no wonder he thinks that. I totally lost control. Didn't stick to the plan. In fact, I veered so far off the plan that I can't even see it anymore.

I fucking failed.

Until now, I'd managed to avoid thinking about my dreadful interview with Robert Lloyd. I'd managed to put it out of my mind, distracting myself with makeup and shoes and poker and *Jack fucking Lansen,* but now, in the face of this new humiliation, it all comes flooding back in bright technicolour.

This is what I do, isn't it? Fuck stuff up. Self-sabotage. *I am fucking useless. I fail at everything I try*. Not only did I screw up the biggest opportunity of my career, but I can't even get Jack Lansen, London's biggest playboy, to beg me for sex without suffering a mind-blowing orgasm of my own. *How pathetic is that?*

Without looking at him, I slide off his lap. He eyes me cautiously, like I'm a bomb that might go off at any moment, as he stands and adjusts himself. He's still hard—*rock-fucking solid*—and from the way his trousers are straining, his dick must be enormous.

I'd be lying if I said part of me wasn't screaming, *yes*. *Yes, I want to come upstairs with you*. But not tonight. I won't let myself down again. I refuse to be like all those other women he persuades into his bed, losing their heads when he's around. *Even though I am, and I already have*. But right now, I have a chance to regain at least the semblance of control.

I stand taller and meet his gaze head on. "I didn't beg."

"Huh?"

"You haven't won. I didn't beg you for sex. Those were the rules. And I won't beg. Ever. I don't want to come upstairs and I don't want to sleep with you." I'm being too emphatic, speaking too loud and fast, desperately over-compensating for the orgasm, which is just another of my failures, none of which Jack could never understand.

A bemused look crosses his face. "You just came on m—"

"It wasn't real. I faked it," I lie.

Tension zaps between us, and Jack's eyes narrow. "Okay." He stretches the word and it drips with an unspoken air of disbelief, but he doesn't push me on it.

My eyes drift down to his crotch, where a dark patch spreads across the fabric, clear evidence of my orgasm. *Oh, shit*. I panic internally. I can't handle the depravity of it, right there on his fucking trousers.

I dare a glance at him, which only makes his gaze dip to where I've been focusing, and I see the flash of awareness when he notices it too. "You've made a mess of me," he purrs.

The shame that flushes through me is so intense, I can't bear it. I need to get rid of the proof that this ever happened, right fucking now.

"I'll clean it," I gush, stepping up to him. "I'll take them to the dry-cleaners." My sense of self-preservation must have clicked off-line, because my hands drift towards his waistband as though I mean to strip him right here and now. "Please, let—"

"El." He says my name like a warning as he moves back. "If you don't want to see this over the finish line, then you need to step away from the trousers. My dick is on a hair trigger here."

I retract my wandering hands and he waits as if expecting me to say something, but I'm so caught up in my own head, plagued by self-recriminations, that I can't speak.

Jack quietly assesses me, and although his gaze is gentle, we can't connect on any real level while this game is in play. When I say nothing, he raises a brow and says softly, "I can recognise a real orgasm, El."

The arrogance. But he's probably seen a million of them. *Given a million.* Regret swirls like a snowstorm, threatening to bury me. I'm just another number to him.

I'm too humiliated to speak. My throat swells, a great sob keen to leak out. *Fuck.* It's the orgasm messing with my head, raising all sorts of shitty emotions. I want to cry, but I will not let him see it. *Damn him and damn this stupid fucking game. Why did I ever agree to play?*

His stance softens as he rubs at the back of his neck, and somehow I know he registers everything I'm feeling, despite my best attempts to conceal it. *God, I'm a fool.* A deep, cramping ache runs from my belly to my throat. *If he so much as touches me right now, I'll burst into tears.* "I'm sorry," he murmurs, closing the distance between us, reaching out as if to draw me into a hug.

I hold up a hand to block his approach. "Don't touch me," I snap, my breaths coming fast. "I said no touching."

Jack retreats, a frown marring his forehead, and I understand his obvious confusion, because one second I'm trying to undo his trousers, and the next I'm telling him to keep his distance. I'm past the limits of rational behaviour. "All right," he says slowly, his palms open and raised, padding the air as though I'm a bull who might charge him and he wants to back the fuck away, little by little. "I don't want to upset you." He glances at his watch. "It's late. We should go to bed. Separately." He dips his chin in farewell, and when I don't respond, he strides from the room.

Fuck, fuck, fuck.

Before I can question it, I'm following him, each step blasting pain through the balls of my feet in these damn stupid heels, anger burning through me like lit petrol.

"Even if I wanted to come upstairs with you, which I don't, I wouldn't." I spit the words.

Jack halts in the hall, then turns back to me slowly, and as he does, I stiffen, bracing for some kind of showdown. My hands rest on my hips. I'm on the offensive and I can't hold back any longer.

"I don't want to be the person you come home to, when you're out there"—my hand flails so violently towards the front door that I wonder if it could actually come off my wrist—"doing whatever you want with whoever you want. I refuse to be another woman on your list of conquests." I almost scream this last part, and somewhere in the back of my mind a little voice is whispering, '*Stop it. Why are you acting like a crazy woman? This is supposed to be a game*'. But I'm so embarrassed, so angry, so filled with shame, that I'm powerless to act any other way.

An amused smirk has crept its way over Jack's face while I've been talking, and it completely knocks me off. But when I don't smile back, his amusement vanishes, and he tilts towards me, like he's eager to hear whatever I'm *not* saying. Like the fact I'm standing here in his hall, staring at him, matters to him.

"El, what's going on in that pretty head of yours? Because what I'm hearing isn't making sense."

Anger fizzes right below my skin, but even so, part of me is leaping at the fact Jack Lansen called me pretty. The collision of both sensations renders me speechless.

Jack's still peering at me, concern etched into the slant of his mouth and the tight corners of his eyes. "Is there something you want to know?" His voice is gentle and laden with concern. "Because it feels like you're trying to ask me a question."

Something stutters in my chest like a car being jump started. I want to latch onto his offer of kindness, but I can't because if I do, I'll break. "No. I don't have anything to ask you. I don't care how many people you're sleeping with, because I won't be one of them."

He pins his lips together like he's deciding to hold back the first thought that crosses his mind. *Crap.* He's too smart not to see beyond my bitchy comeback. I've given myself away, caring so much about who this stupid, gorgeous, irritating man is sleeping with, but then I've already done that tonight in the most explicit way, so what does it matter?

Thankfully, Jack lets it slide. "Fair enough." He sighs, and if I didn't know better, I'd think he looked a little dejected. "That was one hell of a performance tonight. I'm impressed. Truly. I'd tip my hat to you if I had one." He turns to head up the stairs, but then he pauses.

He runs a hand through his hair, brushing the thick dark locks of it off his face. Under his scrutinizing gaze, I feel ridiculous, dressed up like this, breathless and shameful, having orgasmed on his lap like nothing else in the world mattered, which at the time, it didn't.

"Do you want to quit?" he whispers. "We can stop playing, if you want to. If this is too much, we can ditch the whole thing." At his words, the urge to cry swells in my throat and burns behind my eyes again, and all I want is for him to put his arms around me. I thought this game would bring us closer, but right now it feels like all it has done is drive a wedge between us. *It's a mess.*

I clench my teeth, biting down so hard on my molars I can feel the beginnings of a headache. "You could have put me up in one of your hotels. I never needed to move in with you."

He runs a finger around the back of his collar, tugging at it. He looks a little unsure, but then his hand falls away, and when he speaks, there isn't a hint of uncertainty in his voice. "I could have. Didn't want to. I like you being here. As I said, you're the best housemate I've ever had."

I let his comment hang for a moment. *He likes me being here.* Despite my emotional turmoil, the thought makes me feel good. "Even though I'm messy?"

He smiles, but it's a small, careful smile, as if he knows it might upset me and he doesn't want to do that. "*Because* you're messy." His eyes dart to the stain on his trousers for a second, and he adds, "You make the best fucking mess, El. I'd take it a million times over if it meant I'd get to spend time with you, even if you never let me touch you." My heart does a curious somersault in my chest. How is it so easy for this man to manipulate my moods, guiding me through them like they're nothing but a gentle breeze? "And if you don't want to play anymore, then I don't want to either."

What happens if we don't play? What happens to us then? Is there even an 'us' without the game? "We didn't ever have to play. You could have..." *asked me out. Taken me to dinner. Done something fucking normal.*

He cocks a brow. "I could have what?"

I heave a breath, intending to share my thoughts, but every word lodges in my throat. *Maybe he never wanted to do any of those things.* "Nothing. It doesn't matter."

He pins his bottom lip with his teeth, examining me as though he's not entirely satisfied with what I've just said. "All right. If you're sure." An awkward beat passes. "So… are we still playing?"

The question sounds tentative, but his eyes blister with a heat that roasts me on the inside. A smug little smile tugs at his lips, like he knows I don't have it in me to say no. To say I'm not playing. To deny him the pleasure of this game. To deny myself.

Say no. Say no. "Yes."

He fists a hand, and for a second I think he's going to pump the air and congratulate himself on the result he wanted. But instead he lifts it to his lips, concealing his smile before he says, "The climax of this game is going to be better than the one you just had. I guarantee it."

Oh, my God. This man is a fucking nightmare. And yet I can't resist, but I don't want him to think he's got me already. "It wasn't just me. You got hard," I bite back, nodding at his dick. "I can still see it."

His eyes are shining with amusement, with *life*, and it's so endearing that even though I want to be annoyed at him, I'm failing. "Yup. The sexiest woman I've ever met just came on my lap. Of course I'm hard."

And with that, he turns and walks up the stairs, leaving me gawking at his perfect muscled arse in his tailored suit trousers, annoyed that his words have my body gearing up for round two, and wishing I could follow him all the way into bed.

Winning this game is going to be harder than I thought, and tonight was a close call. If he'd said the right things in my ear, at exactly the right moment, he could have got me to admit that I want to fuck him. Want it *bad*. But he didn't. I'm still in the game, and the money's still there to play for.

But is it worth it?

18
JACK

I don't know what to make of Elly. We've always had this slightly antagonistic flirtatious relationship, but in spite of all my claims to the contrary, I never knew whether it was one that would definitely go anywhere until she orgasmed in my lap last night. Brought herself off right there on my crotch.

Fuck me, that was one of the hottest things I've ever experienced, and it took an extraordinary force of will not to touch her. If she'd lasted a moment longer, I'd have come right there with her. I was pretty pleased I didn't, to be honest, because it gives me the edge. The upper hand. *I'm winning*.

And yet, I don't feel good about it. I'm not sure how I feel, especially given Elly's reaction when it was all over. She was a fireball of frustration, on the verge of tears, yelling that she'd never sleep with me. If she'd said she wanted to quit, I'd have let her walk away, no questions asked. But she didn't, and her refusal gives me hope that I'm still in with a chance.

Only when she finally gives in, sinking to her knees and begging me to satisfy the need that only I can satisfy, will I truly feel like I've won. But fuck me, I want that woman so much, I'm not sure how long I'll be able to hold back from doing it first.

Images of her opening her eyes, staring right at me as she came, burst across my mental screen like fireworks.

My dick stirs at the memory, and I'm mildly surprised, given I've already jerked off thinking about it twice this morning and it's only 11 am. If I wasn't in the office, I'd beat another one out, because these thoughts are distracting. I can't focus.

I haven't seen her today. She didn't come down for breakfast. We didn't even pass one another in the hall before I left for work. Perhaps she's embarrassed. There's no reason to be. I'm not judging her. As far as I'm concerned, the whole thing was bloody brilliant, until the end, which was confusing as fuck.

Have we taken this game too far? Did I push too hard? Do we need to talk about it?

I sit back in my chair, strumming my fingers on the desk. I'm itching to call her. Send a text. Check she's all right. But we haven't had that sort of contact since we agreed to play the game. Feels like a boundary I'm not sure I should cross.

But I want to because I'm pretty sure we could have a really good time together for the next couple of months. And—*fuck*—seeing her let loose on me, hearing those noises she made as she came, feeling the way her body twitched with pleasure... I'd be a liar if I said I didn't want to see her do that again. Preferably naked and sitting on my dick.

A knock on my office door rips me from my thoughts. "Come in," I call.

Seb Hawkston blasts into my office, a massive grin on his face. "Great night last night. Thanks so much. I feel a bit rotten today though." He taps his head, letting me know he's got a hangover.

"Glad you enjoyed it."

"Listen, about Elly," Seb begins, and I immediately tense up. "Can I get her number?"

Images of Elly, arms latched around my neck, moaning in my ear, assault my brain again. "Err, no."

Seb's mouth twitches, eyes alert. "Why not?"

I mentally fumble for a reason but come up short.

Seb laughs, and the sound makes me grit my teeth. I'm not sure there's ever been a more annoying noise. "I've never seen you so distracted by a woman before," he says.

I push my chair back from my desk and stare at him. "You came in here to laugh at me?"

Seb slides both hands into his trouser pockets. "Not exactly. I wanted to double-check. I can normally get a good read on a room and the people in it. I offered her my card last night and told her to call, but she didn't take it."

A traitorous heat simmers through me. If she had taken his card, I would have been crushed. Completely flattened. "She didn't?"

"Nah. She's into you."

I drop my forehead into my hand. I don't know what the fuck I'm doing with Elly. The game is fun, but it has put limits on what we can be. What she thinks I can offer her. And clearly, after her reaction last night, it's more complicated than it should be. Maybe it was a mistake, but I can hardly back out now, can I?

I don't fucking know what I want from her, but Seb's right. She *is* distracting. She fills my thoughts like no one else ever has.

"But if I'm wrong, and you aren't keen, let me know," Seb continues, his words tearing me from my thoughts. "I'd still like to take her out."

I respond without thinking. "Don't fucking touch her. Don't even try, and if you do, I'll—"

Seb laughs again, cutting me off, but when I glare at him, he compresses a smile as though he finds my sudden protectiveness amusing. "You are keen, then. That's all I needed to know." He pauses to observe me, then shakes his head. "*Fuck*. I've never seen you like this."

He doesn't say another word and saunters out of my office. For a few minutes, I sit staring into space. *Am I really that different this time?*

A montage of Elly begins playing in my mind. Damn Seb, coming in here and making me think of her. *Fuck it, who am I kidding?* All I've done is think about her. Might as well plunge right in. *Indulge myself.* I pull my phone out of my pocket and, without pausing to question it, I bring up TikTok and search Elly's name.

A bunch of Ellies come up, but none of them are right.

I do the same with Instagram. Facebook. I even try X, but there is nothing anywhere. She has no social media presence at all.

An unexpected annoyance flares. How does she expect anyone to find her music if she's not putting it out there? I send Kate a message.

Me: Is Elly on social media? For her music?

Kate: Nope. You still trying to work out if she's good enough for Nico's party? Because she is.

I type a response. Delete it. Type another and delete it, then Kate sends one.

Kate: Should I be worried that you're sitting at your desk stalking Elly when you should be working?

Me: I'm not stalking. Just interested.

Kate: Don't believe you for a second. Elly's not a dish to be tasted at the buffet. Leave her alone and get back to work.

When I get home, Elly's playing the guitar and singing in her room, and something in my stomach flutters. The word *'butterflies'* springs to mind. I roll my eyes at myself, but in spite of whatever reaction I'm having to the sound of her voice, I take off my coat and jacket, hang them up, and take the stairs to her room. There is no way I am letting her ignore me, or what happened last night.

She might be able to pretend that orgasm didn't happen, but I can't. She's given me the sweetest taste of what it might be like to have her, and I am desperate for more.

I stand outside her room, holding my breath, listening to her sing. The melody, the sweet cascade of notes, elicits an emotional response that I've never felt from any music other than Elly's. I could stay here all night, letting her songs drift into my subconscious and carry me away to some other world. She's a siren. A witch, casting a spell with music that floods my veins like a drug.

She's really good. I have no idea why she hasn't made it yet, whatever that looks like. She should be putting this stuff out in the world. Sharing her gift. That annoyance flares again, but at the same time something stirs in my chest, as though her song is tugging on my heart. Maybe even my soul...

Reality check. I'm lurking outside my housemate's room, listening to her sing, hoping I get to witness her orgasm again. This is not sustainable behaviour.

I knock on the door, and the noise stops.

"Go away."

Hmm. Maybe she's not as up for this game as I thought she was. I knock again, more gently this time, and lean right against the door when I say, "Are you avoiding me?" The guitar begins strumming again, but she's no longer singing. I knock again. "Come on, El. Open up."

Silence is followed by soft footsteps pacing towards the door, and my chest tightens.

The door swings open, revealing Elly in her pyjamas and those pink fluffy slippers back on her feet. I note them, but say nothing.

"What do you want?" She cocks a hip, one fine-fingered hand resting on it. Her eyes blaze like she wants to raze me to the ground. Everything I meant to say withers and dies in my mouth. *What the fuck was I going to do? Give her a winning smile and say, 'Hey, El, how about some more orgasms?'* Even I'm not enough of a dick to realise that, based on the look on her face, she's not going to take me up on it.

"If you don't have anything to say, then go away," she quips. "I don't want to play with you right now. This is my practise time. It's important. Don't interrupt me when I'm playing."

Frustration crackles through me. *Why is she being like this?* Elly goes to shut the door, but I stick out my hand to stop it. She might be mad, but she doesn't have the strength to shut me out.

"If you take it so seriously, why don't you have any social media?"

She backs up a step, the anger draining from her face. My question has obviously knocked the wind out of her sails.

"Yeah," I say, nodding. "I looked you up, and there's nothing. Can't find your music anywhere. How do you expect to make it if you won't let anyone hear it?"

"I do let people hear it," she mutters.

"At the Marchmont Arms? That dive in the West End? Who the fuck do you think is going to hear you down there? Are you that naïve?" With each question, the harshness in my tone increases.

Elly's shrinking before me, wilting like I'm stealing all her nutrients. An inner voice warns me to stop, trying to remind me that this isn't what I meant to say when I came up here. Not even close, but her defensiveness has me on the attack. And if there's one thing I know how to do, it's spot other people's weaknesses. I've been doing it ever since I was a kid, so I could know what they were and make sure I didn't fucking have any.

"Fuck you," she snarls. "My career is none of your business. How dare—"

"No." The word erupts from my mouth, and Elly tries to push the door closed again, but I'm still holding it open. "Don't shut me out. This is important. You want to know what I think?"

"No. No, I don't."

"I think you're frightened, and that's why you're stuck in this hopeless rut of waitressing and gigs. Do you want to spend your life waiting tables and singing in that shithole? Why aren't you out there looking for a manager? An agent? Something?"

These words jolt her, as though they're charged with a force that runs right through her body. I've hit a nerve; by the looks of it, a fucking big one.

She lunges towards me, hands striking my chest, but the impact is negligible, like moths batting the underside of a lampshade. "Get out. Get out of my room."

I catch her wrists, holding her still. She's breathing unevenly, snorting exhalations through flared nostrils. I've never seen her look so angry. Not that I'm surprised, because I've gone for the jugular tonight, and I really don't know why, but now that I've started, I can't stop.

"You can dance for me like you did last night, all dressed up and playing a role, and that causes you no issues. You can come on my lap, for fuck's sake. But putting your music out there? Letting people see something that actually means something to you? Where you're not pretending? You can't fucking do it."

She wrenches her hands out of my grip and thrusts her chin forward. "You have no idea what you're talking about. You don't understand—" She lets out an angry groan. "I don't know why I'm even bothering to explain myself to you. Get the fuck out of my room. Get out. Get out," she repeats through gritted teeth, eyes burning with rage. But I'm not listening to her, because—for reasons I don't even understand—I'm pretty fucking pissed off about this.

"Not until you hear me. You're good. You're really fucking good, and if you don't put yourself out there, no one will find you. The world doesn't owe you anything. No one is coming to get you, to drag you out of obscurity. Fame and fortune aren't going to appear on a silver fucking platter, no matter how much time you spend practising."

Her eyes well up as she stares at me. *Shit*. I didn't mean to make her cry, and all I want to do now is put my arms around her and comfort her, tell her I'm sorry and I don't mean any of it, but I can't lie to her. I do mean it. I mean every fucking word, even if I didn't mean to say any of it.

"Save your pep talk for your employees. I don't need your help. I can do this on my own." Her voice breaks, and I feel the pain of it right in my chest.

This time, when she goes to slam the door, I step out of the way and let it happen. I cup my hands around the back of my head and let out a frustrated groan.

What the fuck just happened here?

19
ELLY

I'm pretty sure I hate Jack Lansen. Ninety-nine per cent sure. Barging into my room like he was coming to a boardroom meeting to lecture me about what I'm doing wrong... *Arrogant fucking bastard.*

Just because he's marching around the West End in shoes that cost more than a month's rent, he thinks he knows what I need? What's best for my career? What the fuck does Jack Lansen know about music?

He knows about success, a small voice whispers in my head.

Well, fuck him. I don't need his advice. Interfering git. He didn't even ask what I wanted, he just assumed that what I have isn't good enough. That I *must* be dissatisfied. I don't know what I did to drive him to say those things either. Before he started yelling at me to take my career seriously, I hadn't seen him since I orgasmed on his lap, and he asked if I want to keep playing our stupid game. If I'd known what he was going to say before he knocked on my door, I never would have opened it. But I did, and now the atmosphere in the house is... *toxic*.

I've managed to avoid him for almost a week. I haven't officially quit the game, but I might as well have, given how I've taken to creeping in and out of the house when I know he's busy or away. It's not a great action plan, but for now it's working. I'm so furious that not even the thought of the money can keep me on track.

"I told you the game was stupid," Marie says, and I bring my attention back to her, realising she's been talking to me and I haven't been listening. She's in the Marchmont Arms to hear me perform, and I'm sitting in a dark corner of the pub with her. I finished my bartending shift twenty minutes ago, so I had a bit of time to catch up with her and I've filled her in on everything that's happened recently with Jack.

"It's not the game. It's him," I say, although I know it doesn't make sense. Without Jack, there is no game.

Marie presses her lips together. "What are you going to do now?"

"Hide."

She gives me a pitying look and takes a sip of her wine. "Can't believe you orgasmed on his lap."

Marie's statement hits like a punch to the gut. If Jack hadn't balled me out about my career, then maybe I could have made my peace with what happened the night I danced for him. But now, in hindsight, it feels awful. I don't know how I got so carried away. It must be the way he smells. His face. Those deep blue eyes and his long, dark eyelashes. Or maybe it's an invisible army of pheromones marching across the house from his room to mine, infecting me whilst I sleep.

Even recalling it now—the way he closed his eyes, the movement of his throat, the rigidity in his jaw that told me he was struggling to hold himself together—I'm turned on. And as much as I hate the effect he has on me... I also don't. It was great. I loved it. I loved every second of it until it was over, and I realised exactly what I'd done.

I can hardly think of it without wanting to die. I got myself off by grinding my crotch on his erection. And then, because I was too fucking turned on not to, I went up to my room and gave myself two more orgasms whilst thinking of the expression on his face when he'd watched me come. *Horrendous*. And as if that wasn't humiliating enough, the next time he saw me, he got aggressive about my music.

Maybe I invited it by telling him to go away, but the gear switch was so abrupt, it sent me into a tailspin. It was as though he couldn't understand how someone could be so *useless* when it comes to their career, and felt compelled to let me know.

He might not have used that exact word, but he was so furious, that's how it felt. And damn it, after my disastrous panic attack at the Granville Agency, I think he might be right. That's what made it so much harder to hear what he had to say.

Jack Lansen, businessman extraordinaire. Everything he touches turns to gold, whereas everything I touch turns to shit.

We're completely incompatible.

It's confusing to feel all these conflicting things for one man. My head feels like it's exploding.

"You realise that for as long as you're friends with Kate, he's going to be a feature in your life. Parties, weddings, christenings..." Marie's voice brings me back and I find her shaking her head at me, forcing me to contemplate all those future events, where a mere glimpse of Jack will bring the humiliation booming back in surround sound. My cheeks start to burn. "And now he knows you're into him because you rubbed one out on him."

"I'm not into him. I got carried away. And he was hard too."

"But he's a guy. They're more physiological than we are. You could have been anyone, and he'd have been hard."

My body feels like it's being wrung out like a wet towel, and when the sensation reaches my head, I slam my eyes shut. *Is that true?* He said I was the sexiest woman he'd ever met... but then, he's Jack. All smooth words and easy charm. I let out a pitiful whimper-groan.

"You two look positively conspiratorial."

At the sound of Kate's voice, shock radiates through my body so hard I nearly shoot forward in my chair and hit my head on the table.

Somehow, I manage to keep myself in check and calmly turn to find her standing behind me, beaming at the two of us, a glass of wine in hand. *Please say she didn't hear us discussing me dry-humping her brother.*

"Your brother laid into Elly about the state of her career," Marie says quickly. "Banged on her door to tell her she's wasting her life singing down here."

Kate sits at the table, a concerned expression on her face. "Oh, no. I'm so sorry. That's very Jack though. He likes to get the best out of everything... always wants to maximize his employees' potential and their performance." She sips on her wine, scrunching her face at the taste. The wine here is like battery acid. "It's actually one of his strengths. He's an excellent boss."

Of course he is. The perfect boss, the perfect man. *Fuck him.* "He's not my boss." Even to my ears, I sound remarkably bitter, and Kate's eyebrows draw together as though she suspects there's something else going on, but before she can query it Marie downs the rest of her wine and asks, "What's new with you? Give us some good news."

Kate glances at me like she wants to check it's really okay for us to move off this topic so fast. I give a tiny shrug to let her know I don't care.

"I've booked the venue for Nico's party. It's going to be amazing. You're still up for performing, right?" Kate eyes me over the rim of her glass as she takes another sip of her wine, winces, puts the glass down, and pushes it aside.

"Are you sure you want me to?" I ask.

She reaches over and grips my hand. "Stop doubting yourself. I know how good you are. You know it too. It's time to get you out of here." She nods around the dingy Marchmont basement. "And onto a bigger stage."

"I completely agree," Marie states, as though her proclaiming it is the thing that's going to make it happen.

Deep inside, a note of sadness rings out, the tone of it settling in my heart. It's not just Jack who thinks I need to sort out my career. It's my friends too.

How do they all know that I want fame and fortune? That I want to be discovered? How do they know I'm not happy right here, doing exactly what I'm doing? None of them asked me. Then again, I haven't exactly been keeping them up to date on my feelings. I still haven't shared the details of my non-interview with Robert Lloyd. I'm ashamed of myself.

Pathetic.

A lump rises in my throat, and I pull out of Kate's grip.

She frowns at me. "You okay? I know the party would be different. A big step up. There would be five hundred people there."

I take a steadying breath. *Nico's party.* "Five hundred?" I query.

"Nothing compared to when you're playing for ninety thousand people at Wembley Stadium," Marie says, nudging me with her elbow and winking. I'm not sure if it's meant to be a joke or an encouragement, so I ignore it.

"Exactly," Kate says. "You can definitely do this."

"Thanks." I strive to keep my voice calm, but my heart is racing. I want this, *I do*, but fear is threading its way through my veins. How can I admit to wanting something that feels impossible? Every time I try to take a step forward with my career, it bites me in the arse. If I had told Kate what happened at my interview, how I totally lost my nerve and ran away, there's no way she'd ask me to sing for Nico. "Of course I want to do it. I'm honoured you asked me. Really."

I can do this.

"Elly." Marcia's harsh voice cuts across our conversation, and her index finger slices from me to the stage area. *Crap.* It's my set, and I'd been so distracted that I lost track of time.

"Break a leg," Kate says, toasting me with her glass of cheap white.

Marie slaps me on the bum as I get up and walk away. "Show us what you're made of," she says, and winks again.

"Boooo."

My heart jerks at the sound, fingers stalling on the strings. No one has booed me while I've been performing since I started. Back then, I was so nervous I kept halting and forgetting the lyrics. That doesn't happen now, and you have to have a pretty thick skin to get up on stage every night, even if it is only at the Marchmont Arms. But for some reason, the noise slides right into a weakened crevice, knocking me off.

My fingers stumble, but I resume the chords so fast that maybe no one noticed.

"Get your tits out, love."

Who is heckling me like that?

I blink into the light that's shining right in my face. I can only see the people right at the front, and it's not them. A few people are glancing over their shoulders, trying to work out where the disturbance is coming from.

Marcia, stony-faced, is striding through the bar, heading towards whoever is shouting. They sound drunk.

"Sing something happy. This is shit," comes another voice.

The numbness I felt at first morphs to heat, sweat beading on my forehead and the back of my neck. *This is horrible, but I can handle it. Can't I?* There aren't that many people here, but I wish Marie and Kate weren't witnessing it. They're both so together... so accomplished. Kate's a businesswoman to her core, and Marie will probably become a consultant at the hospital before she's forty. *And me... what good am I? What have I done? What will I ever achieve?*

Why are these doubts running through my head right now? I'm on stage, my fingers strumming. I'm still singing, but even I can hear how bad it sounds. I can't perform when my head is a mess. I'm not in the moment. Not present. My heart is racing and I'm overwhelmed with doubt and fear, and the awareness of those people out there in the bar, shadows I can't make out, waiting to jeer at me.

"Get off," comes a voice.

And then, even through the light hitting my eyes, I see something careen through the air towards me. It slaps hard against my shoulder, bursting like a water balloon. I gasp, fear sparking through me like a million needles. My mind erupts with panic. *What's happening?*

The remains of whatever hit me slops to the floor by my feet. A slice of tomato.

A slice of fucking tomato, all greasy and covered in ketchup like it had been nestled inside a burger before it was launched across the room.

For a few moments, I'm stunned. My cream shirt is spattered with a mixture of ketchup, tomato juice and burger grease. Some is in my hair. On my face.

The thoughts come like a torrent. How did this happen? How am I here, singing in dive bars where no one is listening, and if they are listening, they're abusing me?

The bar is quiet, but whispers and jeers begin quickly, rising like a tide of discontent. An impulsive anger jerks me out of my seat, and I stand, guitar hanging around my neck by the strap. "Hey," I call out. "Who did that?"

I look around, catching sight of Marcia standing before a table in the corner, three burly blokes sitting at it. I can't see their faces from here, but I would guess they're maybe around my age.

Rage rises through me like a storm. *How fucking dare they!*

I'm out of my mind. This isn't me. But anger is firing like rockets, propelling my limbs as I storm off the platform, through the tables, ignoring the punters staring at me.

I haven't progressed far from the stage when one of the bouncers grabs my shoulder. "We've got this." He pins me in place, moving around me to join Marcia and another bouncer as they escort the men out. They stumble and yell as they are jostled towards the exit. They're definitely drunk, but one of them catches my eye as he's being manhandled from the table and there's a nasty leer in it.

I don't know what I did to deserve this tonight, but just as the thought passes through my head, the man yanks his arm from the bouncer and throws something.

A split-second view tells me it's another slice of tomato, but before the thought is even fully formed it hits me right in the face. The slam of it stings, and I yelp, blinking away the splash of seeds and juice from my eyelashes, wiping it with my fingertips. And suddenly my anger vanishes, subsumed by a powerful wave of sadness, and for a moment I worry that I'm going to break down in the middle of the Marchmont, weeping in front of everyone.

Marie is on her feet, storming after the receding figures of the men, pointing her finger and screaming at them.

Kate swoops out of nowhere, her arms circling me. "Let me take you home," she says, and all I want is to fall apart in her hug, to weep and cry from the shame and humiliation, crumbling beneath the weight of the frustration that after all these years and all the songs and the hours of playing, *this* is where I am. But I don't. I take a shaking breath and nod, then walk out of the bar with my head held high.

Kate's hand rests gently on my shoulder and Marie, face like thunder, is pushing through the bar to join us, but even so, the only thing I'm really aware of is the echo of Jack's words again. *If she were any good, she'd have made something of herself by now.*

20
JACK

I haven't seen Elly since I interrupted her practising and we ended up yelling at each other last week. I've been in the office or out for drinks most nights, and her hours are so random I never know when she's going to appear. I've heard her practising the guitar in her room, but I haven't wanted to disturb her.

It's been a heavy week at work. We've had tenders out with developers for three new sites across the UK, and on a fourth site, where development is already underway, they've uncovered a fucking Roman burial ground, which is going to delay construction for God knows how long while the archaeologists go in and investigate.

I unlock my front door earlier than normal. I've had enough. I'm ready to relax. But more than that, I want to see Elly. I want to get things back on a more friendly footing... back to normal. If we even have a normal to return to. I suspect we don't.

Maybe we're done. Maybe that lap-dance orgasm incident was too much. Or maybe it was the fight. She's probably still avoiding me. I guess she could be thinking the same of me, but I haven't been doing it deliberately. Either way, that changes tonight because our game is nowhere near complete, and I'd much rather play with her than fight with her.

I hang up my overcoat and march into the kitchen, rolling my sleeves up as I go. I have no idea what time Elly is coming back, but if I'm going to break down her resistance, or at least have a little fun after this shitty week, then I might as well get started.

I don't cook often, but when I do, I make it count. There's rarely anything in my fridge to cook with, but today I gave the housekeeper instructions to stock up and leave the cooking to me. She bought everything to make coq au vin. If I want to win this game and have Elly begging me to sleep with her—*God, what a fucking delightful thought*—then I need to crack out the big guns.

I grab down an apron from the back of the door. It's one Seb Hawkston gave me as a joke, and it's printed with a man-sized image of Michaelangelo's David. Full frontal marble nude, dick and balls and all. Somehow, it seems appropriate.

I open a bottle of wine and pour myself a glass as I cook, and put on some music.

An hour later, and there's no sign of Elly, but the coq au vin is simmering and I've polished off half a bottle of wine.

She probably has a gig. This was idiotic. God knows how long I'm going to have to wait. I sit on the sofa and pull out my phone, typing Elly's name into all the social media channels again.

Still nothing.

She's had a week to take action on my advice, but she hasn't. I was probably way too harsh on her. But how can someone so talented be so reluctant to share their ability? If it were me, I'd have been singing from the rooftops for years. Revelling in the groupies and fans or whatever the fuck women I'd have following me around on account of my guitar playing and kick-arse vocal skills.

Perhaps I ought to apologise... but then, *why*? I'm right. She needs to get a grip and suck up the pain of putting herself out in the world, unless she wants to stay stuck right where she is for the rest of her life.

A noise outside startles me. *Shit*. Elly could be back any minute. I rush to light the candles on the kitchen table, but, seeing the flickering light illuminate the kitchen, nerves cascade over me as forceful as the downpour that night I picked Elly up in my car.

What the hell am I doing? This looks like I'm seriously trying to seduce her rather than mess around and have a little fun. This doesn't look like a game, this looks... *romantic*. *Fuck*... it looks like I *care*. Not that I don't care... but... *shit*...do I?

I'm questioning everything I've done this evening, but I don't have time to make sense of it because a key sounds in the lock.

How do I make this look less like a date and more like... a game? Less *'I've been an arse so I've cooked dinner for you'* and more, *'I'm ready to forgive and forget, if you're prepared to play'*?

I catch sight of the apron featuring Michaelangelo's David, which I slung over the back of a kitchen chair when I finished cooking. It's just the thing to take the edge off... but I need to be pretty fucking quick.

21
ELLY

The memory of everything that happened at the Marchmont Arms this evening is occupying my thoughts like a lump of old meat, foetid and penetrating every inch of space with its stench. On top of that, my inner critic has been beating me up like a twenty-stone man armed with a cat-o'-nine-tails. I'm flayed raw inside. The chants are stuck on repeat. *I'm wasting my time, I'll never make it, I'm no good, I'm a joke, I'll never get out of the Marchmont, and maybe they won't even want me there anymore.*

A black cloud of doom is swirling around me, smothering all my enthusiasm for life. For music. For the guitar and my songs and performing.

Maybe Jack was right. If I was going to come to anything, it would have happened already. Maybe he only made out that he thought I was any good that night in the flat because he wanted to sleep with me, which is exactly what I'd expect of him. Or at least I would have before I moved in here. Now, I'm not so sure anymore. Maybe he just likes the game. The chase. He wants to win.

An unhealthy rage, directed at Jack, surges through me. Somewhere, buried deep, I'm aware that what happened at the Marchmont tonight wasn't his fault... that it has nothing to do with him. But as I unlock the door to his great big fancy house, I want to lay all the blame at his feet. His big stupid rich-man feet, in his big stupid rich-man shoes.

The lights are on in the kitchen, which surprises me. I really hope I'm not about to come face to face with Jack. I might bite his balls off, and I wouldn't be fucking sorry about it.

I contemplate tiptoeing up to my room but I haven't eaten and something smells really, *really* good... I poke my head into the kitchen, but there's no sign of him, so I walk in. There is, however, a giant pot on the hob. He's been cooking. *Weird*. He hasn't cooked since I moved in here.

There's also an open bottle of wine on the island next to an empty glass. Jack must have finished up earlier and left it out. Which is also a bit weird, seeing as he's such a neat freak. I shrug and help myself to a clean glass and pour myself some. I shouldn't drink, especially not after last time, because I'm using the booze to numb my pain and that's a slippery slope, but I don't care enough to restrain myself.

I sit quietly sipping, letting the alcohol soothe the anger boiling in my blood. The lights go off. My heart leaps. *What the hell? A power cut?*

It's only then I notice that there are candles flickering on the table behind me. It's set for two people.

Crap. Jack must have a date. Just what I fucking need right now... to have to deal with him and one of his women. Something curdles in my stomach at the thought, and I wince. *Awful*. Maybe the noise of them having sex will keep me up all night.

Now that I come to think of it, I haven't seen Jack with anyone since I moved in. He hasn't brought a date back here at all. It was bound to happen eventually, and it would be tonight when I'm feeling super shit about myself. She's probably gorgeous and sexy and—

Music starts, interrupting my thoughts. It's low, but loud enough that I know exactly what it is. Barry White. *You're the First, The last, My everything*. It's coming through the inbuilt speaker system in the ceiling. *God, that's cheesy*. So Jack.

What a fucking arsehole. A low burn smolders beneath my ribcage, a red hot coal of rage sitting behind the bone, waiting to burst into flame. Jack Lansen has life all sorted. Women falling at his feet, more money than he knows what to do with, a promotion to the Hawkston Board by the age of thirty-five. And he looks insanely good in those suits he wears. And in only his boxers, he's even better.

Ugh. I definitely hate him. One hundred per cent sure.

I knock back a full glass of wine in one go and get to my feet. If Jack's going to be getting it on with some random woman, I better get out of here quick. Take my misery upstairs to my room. I don't want to see him right now, not after what happened at the Marchmont.

"Well, hello there."

Jack's deep voice sounds from somewhere behind me, and I spin to find him leaning against the door to the utility room, the darting light from the candles making him look almost spectral. For a second, I think he's entirely naked, but then I realise he's wearing an apron printed with Michaelangelo's David. But every visible part of Jack, his feet, his ankles, his calves, his arms, his shoulders, are bare.

Is he naked under there?

He smiles, flashing his great big cheeky grin that would make other women melt. That would normally make me melt, but today, after everything I've been through... his smile *breaks* me, and, staring at him in his stupid apron, Barry White pulsing through the speakers, candlelight flickering over the room, I start to cry.

And I don't mean my eyes get watery. I mean, a great big sob cracks right through my chest and erupts out my lips like it's trying to break the sound barrier. Out of fucking nowhere.

Jack's smile vanishes. "Shit. El. What the... Alexa. Stop." But Barry White doesn't stop. It gets louder. "Stop! Alexa!"

Alexa isn't listening. And I'm crying, grateful that the booming voice of Barry White is concealing the ragged sobs leaking from my body like I've been storing them up for this exact moment. I sink back onto the stool, dropping my head into my hands.

The slapping of bare feet on the tiles tells me that Jack is moving around the room, opening cupboards, slamming things around. Finally, the music dies and we're left in silence.

His footsteps approach. Closer and closer, his proximity compressing the air in my lungs, which does nothing to help my gasping, sobbing breaths. Any moment now, I'll asphyxiate myself.

I'm a mess. A complete wreck.

"What's going on?" He's so close that I can smell him. My body prickles at his nearness, even though I'm mostly absorbed with my own pain. My tears. So much sadness I can't keep it locked down anymore. "Is it David?"

I peek up at him, and the inches between us are lit only by the glow from the candles, giving the impression we're alone in a shadowed world. "What?"

He's staring at me with this tentative little smile on his face, concern flashing in his eyes. He gestures to the apron. "David. Is he too much?"

I laugh, a helpless wheezing noise. "I can take him off, but I should warn you, I'm completely bollock naked under here. And David is a lot... *less* than me."

He is *naked*.

More laughter bubbles up—although it could be tears, I don't really know anymore—and I cover my face with my hands. "Why? Why are you naked?"

Please say it's not because there's a woman in the other room.

"Because you said 'Game on'," he deadpans, and, even through the tears, my stomach starts doing little flips. He's naked except for that stupid apron *because of me*. I wipe the tears from my eyes with my fingertips.

"But now I'm thinking my timing is really fucking bad," he continues, "because me being naked doesn't normally reduce women to tears. Well"—he cocks his head like he's reassessing this claim—"good tears maybe. Tears of 'that was the best fucking orgasm I've ever had in my life' but not"—he waves a finger at my face, indicating the state of me—"this kind."

"Sorry," I sniffle, and Jack grabs a tissue from the front pocket of his apron and hands it to me, and I snort another laugh through my snotty tears. Only Jack Lansen would have tissues in his apron pocket. "Got anything else in there?"

His lips tilt up at the corners, and he fixes those insanely blue eyes on me. My heart thumps, and I really hope he can't tell that he's affecting me this way. "You're deflecting. What's wrong?"

"Are you really naked behind that apron?"

His eyebrow arches. "I can't believe you doubt me. Stop avoiding the question."

I wipe my nose and stuff the tissue in my pocket. "I don't want to talk about it."

Jack says nothing, crossing his arms over the apron. His bare, incredibly large arms. His biceps bulge. *His skin is so tan.* And the definition in his forearms is spectacular... *I want to stroke them...*

"My face is up here, El," he says.

I close my eyes. "You're a prick."

I expect a snappy retort, but none comes, so I open my eyes again. Jack's staring at my top, right where the tomato hit. "What's on your shirt?"

I glance down at the stain on my cream shirt and the memories of the Marchmont Arms—the heckling and the tomatoes and Marie yelling and Kate trying her best not to make a big deal of it while she handed me tissues to wipe the mess off my face—invade my mind. This has been a shit night. I burst into tears again.

Before I know what's happening, Jack's great big bare arms are surrounding me and my face is smashed against that stupid apron and I'm sobbing so hard I can hardly breathe.

I fist my fingers into the apron. I want to get closer to him so I slide my hands around his back and his skin is bare and warm. I want him to hold me forever so I can cry and cry and never feel sad again.

And then, louder than ever, the memory of his words crashes through my skull. *If she were any good, she'd have made something of herself by now.* The recollection unleashes a flood of other thoughts, bursting through my psyche so fast I can't stop them. *He thinks I'm shit too. He could have thrown that tomato himself. He's just as bad as they are.*

I shove my palms against the rough fabric of the apron. "Fuck off, Jack. Get off me." I'm wiping my nose, my eyes, toppling off the stool and gripping the island to stand up straight.

Jack backs off, eyes wide with alarm, hands raised in the air. "What did I do? What happened to you tonight?" The sight of his handsome face contorted with confusion, and the desperation in his eyes, penetrates my fury for just long enough that I give him a partial answer.

"I had a gig."

Jack's brows pull low over his eyes, making the blue of his irises darken. "Okay." He stretches the syllables, as though he's struggling to make sense of the connection, and might be a little afraid that whatever he says might set me off again. "What happened at this gig?"

A choking stone of sadness blocks my throat. *I can't do it. I'm not good enough.* That's what this gorgeous man believes, and fuck it, if tonight is anything to go by, he's right, and I hate him for being right.

He said it from the get-go. *Nico deserves the best, and you aren't it.*

The words explode from my mouth. "You bastard. You absolute prick."

Jack flips his palms upward. "What the fuck? What's happening? What's going on? I am so fucking confused right now." His voice is raw, and part of me longs to explain, longs to tell him how I'm feeling, but I'm cresting on a wave of irrational rage and there's no way of getting back to solid ground. "Everything's a joke to you, isn't it? You just want to play your stupid game." My voice is breaking, even as I wave one hand up and down his body to indicate the ridiculous apron he's wearing.

His eyes are wild, scanning all over my face like the rapid movement will help him make sense of me. He's doomed because not even I know what I'm doing.

"I don't want to play anymore." The words tear at my throat. "Not with someone like you."

He stiffens. "What does that mean?"

"You're an arrogant, judgmental arsehole."

We glare at one another, neither of us moving. Jack draws breaths in through flared nostrils, and my breathing is all over the place. The tension filling the space between us has sky-rocketed, and the kitchen feels like it could go up in flames at any moment.

"You can be fucking rude, you know that?" he grits out. "I don't know where this is coming from. How am I supposed to know what's going on if you won't tell me?"

"You want to know? Last week, when you barged into my room, you didn't ask if I want to sing in the Marchmont. You didn't ask if I was happy there. You never asked what *I* wanted. You just came to my room and told me what to do. What to want. You never asked."

His chest rises and falls a few times before he speaks, as though he needs to calm himself. "Tell me then. I'm right here. I'm listening. If you can tell me you're happy, I'll never mention it again."

I'm so obviously not happy that answering his question seems pointless. "Fuck this. Fuck you. If you just want sex, go and find it somewhere else. I'm never going to sleep with you." I spit the words out with such vehemence that Jack steps away from me, and I'm bracing for him to swear at me or yell and tell me to pack my bags and get the fuck out of his house.

For a few elongated moments, neither of us does anything. Then, to my absolute amazement, Jack unties his apron, unloops it from his neck and chucks it on the floor like the damn thing did something wrong. Like all of his rage is crumpled up into that ball of fabric lying on the tiles.

And then he's there, entirely naked in the middle of his kitchen, staring at me. I've seen him topless plenty of times, but like this, without a scrap to cover him, he's breathtaking. The lines of his body are illuminated by the light from the two candles still flickering on the table, casting his muscles in high relief. He's like a model in a photoshoot, where nudity is art. The broad shoulders, the defined pecs, the abs... all of it is perfect. But it's the muscles tapering down in that perfect V to his groin that draws my attention, and I follow them right to his dick which, although not erect, is big. Really fucking big, even hanging there.

Jack Lansen's dick.

My heart swings around unanchored in my chest. I can't breathe. Not one tiny gasp of air. I've never seen a body like his in real life. I'm almost dizzy before I manage my next inhalation.

"Why... why... *shit*. You're naked. Why?" The voice doesn't sound like mine. I think my soul has left my body. *I can't believe this is happening.*

"Had to make you stop talking somehow. You weren't making any sense." His voice is calm, as though we haven't just been fighting and he hasn't exposed himself in the kitchen. As though this is an average night, and we're having a totally normal conversation.

"You're naked," I repeat, and my voice is almost a squeak.

"Well observed."

"Fuck." The word hisses out between my lips, a sound that settles somewhere between a curse and a sigh, and my jaw hangs loose as awe and anger spiral through me like a tornado. "You can't get naked and think it's going to fix everything. You're not taking this seriously. You're not taking *me* seriously."

He fixes his attention on me, and the energy in the room changes, as though he flicked an invisible switch, turning all the anger in the air sexual. "Believe me, I take you very seriously."

His voice is low and seductive and it makes heat simmer in my core, but my stomach swirls with anxiety. I'm simultaneously so attracted to him, and so annoyed, and so fucking nervous about the fact he's naked and where this might go and what it means, that I might throw up.

"Put your clothes on. I just told you I wouldn't sleep with you." I'm impressed with how calm I sound, all things considered.

Jack rubs his hand over his jaw. He's so casual in his nakedness, like he has absolutely no body shame. Like it has never occurred to him that his body might not be universally appealing.

To be fair, he might be right.

"Final answer?" he asks.

I want to tell him yes, but the word stalls on the tip of my tongue. Teetering right on the edge, not daring to take the plunge.

He waits, but when an answer doesn't come, he dips his head and runs a hand through his hair. "Right, then. Guess I'll head to bed."

He starts walking towards me. He'll have to pass me to get to the door. The tension between us is crushing my chest with each step he takes and my heart is beating like a hummingbird's wings... *so fucking fast.*

I can't stop staring. His body is honed for strength, like an animal. A lion prowling towards me. I want to dig my nails into those muscles, feel how hard they are. *His quads are huge...*

An intense ball of need swells between my thighs and I cover my eyes with my hands. *It's too much. This man is way too fucking much for me.*

He stops right in front of me. I can sense him there. *What the hell is he doing?*

Warm, heavy hands cup my shoulders. "If I get dressed, will you have dinner with me?" His voice is so soft that if I could, I'd wrap it around me and lie down in it.

What game is he playing now? I shake my head.

"El, look at me. Don't play coy. I know you've seen your share of naked men before."

I swallow. *His hands are so big. So hot.* His touch is burning me up. I'm sweating. I pop open one eye. "None who look like you," I mutter.

A rumble of delighted amusement sounds from deep in Jack's chest. "I don't want to fight with you. Have dinner with me."

I open my other eye, forcing myself to keep my gaze above his jawline. He holds my stare like it's something precious, his face eager and pleading. "No. I just told you I wouldn't sleep with you."

"Dinner, El. Not sex. I'll put my dick away."

I huff the tiniest laugh. "You're ridiculous."

"But you like me."

It's not a question, and I swallow back the reflexive '*yes*' that springs to the space behind my teeth. Regardless, Jack hums as if he heard me speak it and liked the sound.

"I'm going to tell you something," he whispers. "Just one time. So listen carefully."

"Okay." The word is little more than an exhalation. I'm pretty sure I haven't taken a full breath for minutes now. It's making me lightheaded.

"I don't want to play anymore either." His voice is strangely soothing, and my breathing settles into a more regular rhythm. "Because I like you. I like you a lot. Way more than the game. Way more than wanting to win. I can't stop thinking about you, and I don't want to find sex elsewhere. I only want you. So let's start over. Have dinner with me. Now. Tonight. Tell me what's wrong. Tell me what made you cry."

I drop my head into my hands again, pressing my fingers into my eye sockets, then drag them down my face and look back up at Jack. "Are you fucking with me? Is this a play? A move?"

"No." He slides a hand from my shoulder to my neck, grazing the bare skin. His thumb rests on the divot at the base of my throat. My body fizzes, everything going tight and then loosening, over and over, in a pulsing rhythm.

"I don't believe you. You're naked. You took the apron off. That's a move if ever I saw one. You're still playing the game."

He chuckles lightly, and the sound dusts my skin like glitter. "Okay, get ready, because I'm about to be really fucking honest." He takes a breath and it feels like he's stolen all my oxygen with it. "I'm done playing. No more games. I don't want you to come in my lap again, El. I want you to come on my dick. Naked. I want to see you fucking bounce on it."

My loins burst into flame like dry kindling. *Wow.* Jack Lansen is a dirty-talker, and he wants *me*. Right now, nothing else in the whole world matters.

"Have sex with me," he rasps.

"Really?" I whisper, a hint of neediness in my tone as though I'm asking a favourite teacher if their praise is genuine. "Are you begging?"

"I am. I'm begging you. Please."

Oh, my heart. I've never heard him sound so earnest. If he's begging, then I've won the game, but I don't even care anymore because Jack Lansen is all but on his knees for me, and that's worth so much more than money.

I want to laugh. I want to dissolve into fits of giggles. I want to scream at the top of my lungs and jump up and down. I don't know what the fuck I want because my brain has short-circuited, and all the nerve endings in my body are shooting through me like a meteor shower across the night sky.

"I want to come inside you," he continues. "I want to feel how wet you are for me right now." My pussy gives a responding throb and I clench my thighs. *Very wet.* Suddenly, the only thought in my head is that his dirty talk totally turns me on. As though he knows, Jack shifts a little closer and whispers in my ear. "I want to hear you scream my name as I make you come apart." He pulls away again, and I lean towards him like he's controlling my movement. He lets out a tiny chuckle, little more than a gust of air, and his breath hits my skin, sending a pleasurable shiver through me. "Fantasising about it with only my right hand for company isn't going to cut it anymore."

"You thought about me?"

"Many times. You're all I've thought of for weeks," he purrs, making more slickness gather between my legs. "Have you..." He pauses, and everything in me tightens. *Please don't ask.* "Thought about me?"

His question ignites nuclear fission inside my torso, and an explosive wave of heat assaults me. "Yes," I breathe.

"Did you touch yourself?"

Oh, fuck. "Maybe." He raises a brow that demands the truth, and I surrender it. "Yes," I croak.

"Did you come?" he whispers.

I think I'm going to faint. All I can do is nod and mumble, "Uh-huh."

"Good." His smile turns almost wicked. "At least we know we're on the same page."

My cheeks must be fire-engine red, whereas Jack looks as handsome and relaxed as ever. Is this conversation affecting him at all? I glance down because I really need to know if he's hard.

Fuck. His dick is huge and rock solid. *Definitely affecting him, then.* I can see every vein on his shaft. The flared tip is so swollen it shines. It's *spectacular*. The urge to open my mouth and take it down my throat beats through me so hard that I nearly drop to my knees right then and there.

"Hey," he says, and when I look up, the wicked edge to his smile is gone. "I don't want to jump the gun though. I'll get dressed, and we can have dinner. We can start there. Okay? And you can tell me what the hell happened to you tonight."

How dare he turn me on like this and then pull it all away. "No."

He quirks his head. "No?"

And then, because I'm done playing too, I reach out and slide my fingers around the hard length of him, gripping his glorious cock at the base, right there in the kitchen.

22
JACK

*F*uuuuuck.

I hiss as Elly drags her hand up my shaft, and a heady wave of desire whips through me so fast that I get dizzy.

She did not just do that... did she?

The room is still lit by candlelight, and she's so fucking perfect, so pretty, her curly hair all wild, her breaths coming in little puffs as she works me.

"Are you drunk?" I ask, because I have to know.

"No." Her hand doesn't stop gliding up and down my dick. "Are you?"

I grit my teeth. *This feels so fucking good.* I groan as Elly runs her thumb over my slit, massaging a bead of pre-cum across the head. "Not really. Had a couple of glasses while I was waiting for you to come home."

"You were waiting for me?" The arousal in her voice sends a jolt of the same through me.

"Yeah," I rasp, my eyes shutting as Elly's fingers cup my balls briefly before returning to my shaft.

"This wasn't for someone else?" She nods her head at the candles on the table and the pot of coq au vin on the hob. "No date?"

My back arches. *Fuck, I didn't know a hand job could feel this good.*

"No date," I stutter through a groan of pleasure, and her hand gently squeezes my cock as though she's rewarding me for it. I suck in a breath, and stars appear in my peripheral vision. "I haven't been on a date since I heard you sing."

"Oh, wow," she says, all breathy, and the sound is such a turn on that my blood runs hot. I don't want to stop her doing what she's doing, but I also need to know she wants this. She was yelling and crying only a few minutes ago. I can't keep up.

"You don't have to do this." My voice is full of need, and it's obvious that what I really mean is, '*Please don't stop*'.

She steps closer, her clothes bristling against my bare skin, her hand rhythmically pulsing up and down my length, which is suddenly so fucking hard I can't think of anything but her touch. She stands on tiptoe, her lips brushing my ear. "I want to." That husky voice again.

"You sure?"

She pauses to spit in her hand, and the wave of desire that hits me is scorching. I'll be nothing but a pile of ash when she's done. "You trying to get me to stop?"

"Fuck, no." My voice is all gravel.

She starts again, the motion slick with her saliva. *God, this woman.* Pleasure swirls, building right at the base of my spine, making the tip of my dick tingle. This isn't going to take long. *Shit*. How embarrassing. A few weeks of obsessing over her and she only has to touch me for a minute before I'm close to exploding.

I inhale deep, Elly's scent filling my nostrils. *So good*. Clean, sweet. A hint of citrus.

I pull her closer, my legs bracing to hold me up as my orgasm approaches. I clench my jaw, grind my teeth. Her hair is against my mouth as I speak. "That's so good, El. Fuck. You're good at that. Don't stop."

She nestles right against me, her hand still moving furiously between us as she looks up. Those blue eyes, those pretty pink lips... that little pixie nose...

Oh, fuck me. I'm going to lose it.

I throw my head back, eyes shuttering as a blast of pleasure tightens my thighs, tugs on my abs, and tenses every muscle in my fucking body. All sensation pools in my groin as I rock my hips towards her, my cock eager for that final push. I'm teetering right on the edge, approaching the summit of what's going to be a fucking amazing orgasm. "I'm close..."

She stops, and her hand leaves my dick, the crest of pleasure instantly receding, only to be instantly replaced by a gut-churning wave of disappointment as my balls clench. *What the fuck?* I open my eyes to see her take a step back and stare at me, arms crossed. "I won."

"Huh?"

"Admit that I won."

We're talking about the game? How the fuck are we talking about the game when I'm about to blow my load? I don't give a flying fuck about the game.

Wait. *Does she care about the game?* My heart dives off a cliff, even as my oh-so-close orgasm recedes. *What the fuck is happening?*

"Now?" I've never sounded more unhinged in my life.

She nods. "You said the game ended when one of us said they want to fuck more than they want to play." She pokes her sternum with two fingers. "I won."

I start nodding, aware I look desperate. "Yeah. You won. You won. You won the fucking game."

"Okay. Good." She spins away from me and starts to walk out of the room. "I'll send you my bank details."

"Are you fucking kidding me right now?" I call after her.

She glances over her shoulder at me, then at my cock which is still hard and throbbing like an angry motherfucker. "I just wanted to hear you say it." She pauses, and I'm so sure she's going to leave me standing here like an idiot, that when she steps back towards me and drops to her knees instead, shock radiates through me so forcefully that I wonder if I'm going to pass out. *Fucking hell.* She opens those beautiful pink lips and runs them over the head, skimming it lightly.

I'm going to wake up any second. This can't be fucking real.

A rough groan leaves me. "What the—"

Her tongue darts out and licks over my tip, and before I can finish my question she swallows my cock, and the sight of it disappearing between those pretty pink lips is almost more than I can handle. Arousal consumes me, blowing my mind. *If this is a dream, then bring it the fuck on.*

Her mouth is soft and warm, and the suction is perfect. She slides her fingers around to grip my arse, pinning me in place. I let out a rumbling moan of appreciation as my hands come to the back of her head, fingers sliding into her hair as she works me, one of her hands fisting the base of my shaft. Her head bobs up and down, her tongue curling around the tip, flicking it, slopping back and forth over it to lick up the beads of pre-cum before she swallows down the length again.

Need gathers in my hips, hard and unrelenting. I want to thrust down her throat, fuck her mouth until I come, but seeing as she started this, I let her set the pace.

"Fuck, El. You're so good at this. Shit," I groan, gripping her head. "Look at you taking my cock like a good girl." She gives an answering moan and the vibrations shoot up into my hips, adding fire to the burning ball of heat in my groin. "I'm going to come," I grit out, and she nods like it's okay and *I can't fucking believe it* and then the orgasm hits like a hurricane.

My toes curl, my head tipping back as a deluge of sensation destroys the last of my restraint. "Fuuuck, El," I roar as hot reams of cum spurt into her mouth.

She takes it all while I'm groaning and shuddering and losing my fucking shit in the middle of the kitchen. I rest my hands on the back of her head, fingers tangling in her curls, as she sucks me dry, swallowing every last drop, and the pleasure is so intense it's almost painful. "Fuck, fuck, fuck…" I gasp with each final zap that shoots through me. It's like she's torturing me, eking out every last spark with her sweet mouth.

Then she sucks right up to my tip, and her mouth pops off, a string of saliva briefly connecting us. She sits back on her heels, her tongue swiping over her lips, which are puffy and swollen.

My legs are weak, and my head is swimming. *What the fuck just happened here?*

I want to collapse to the floor right in front of her, but I don't think she'll appreciate that, and I'm still confused as fuck, so I say, "Hungry? I made coq au vin."

She frowns up at me, holding my gaze for a few seconds before the expression on her face crumples and, even before it happens, I know what's coming.

She starts to cry, and the bottom falls out of my stomach.

Fuck.

She drops her head in her hands and her shoulders shudder, all that blonde hair spilling like gold across them.

Panic cascades through me at break-neck speed. *Did I get her consent? Did she want this? Shit, shit, shit.*

Talk about a rough comedown. I sink to my knees opposite her, my heart beating so fucking hard that when I reach out and touch her shoulder, my hand is shaking. I expect her to jerk away from me, but when she doesn't a little of the tension I'm carrying melts away.

"El, what's going on?" I whisper.

She takes a couple of hitching breaths, struggling to breathe through the tears. "Tomato."

What?

I lean a little closer, but she's still got her head down, not looking at me. "What?"

Her head snaps up. "Tomato."

Tomato? I seriously hope I'm about to wake up, because this is one bad fucking dream. "I'm sorry... what? I have no idea what's going on, and it sounded like you said 'tomato'."

She sniffles, wiping her nose with the back of her hand. "That's what's on my shirt."

I glance at the stain, but it doesn't clarify anything. My mind is still recovering from that orgasm, and my thoughts are diving around like pinballs.

"They threw it at me. At the Marchmont."

The pieces start to fall into place. "Oh, my... *fuck*. Who did?"

"Some drunk guys." A sob, louder than the others, breaks out. I am not equipped for this. Women coming apart on my dick, I can handle. Women generally falling apart... *fuck, no.*

"I need to get dressed. Don't move. Let me put my clothes on." I jump up and dash to the utility room, where I pull on my boxers and trousers and then shove my arms through the sleeves of my shirt.

When I come out, fingers fumbling to do up my buttons, Elly's still kneeling on the floor and something about the sight of her there breaks my heart a little. *She didn't move.*

I help her up, ushering her over to the sofa. She sits down, and I take a seat next to her. Little by little, between pitiful sobs, I get the full story out of her.

"Those arseholes," I say when she finishes. *What kind of jackasses do that to a woman singing on stage? Especially one as beautiful and talented as Elly.* "I'll fucking—"

"I thought of you when they started throwing stuff at me."

I pin my mouth shut, holding back the threats. *That doesn't sound good.* This feels... precarious, as though anything I do or say might make her yell at me, or run away. But I have to ask. "Why?"

Elly screws her eyes shut like she's staving off tears, then she takes a deep breath and opens them. "Because of everything you said at the flat when you were talking to Kate. You said that if I was any good, I would have made it by now."

Her words crush my insides into a tiny, uncomfortable ball, regret flooding my veins like I'm hooked up to a drip of the stuff. *I'm an arse. How could I have been so unthinkingly cruel? Am I any better than the dickheads who threw stuff at her?* I rub a hand over my eyes. "God, I'm so sorry. That was ignorant. I made an assumption without hearing you. You know I think you're great."

"Do I?" she whispers.

"Don't fish."

She sniffles a giggle. *Progress.*

I want to reach out and hold her, but I feel like I can't. *Christ.* Moments ago, she had my dick in her mouth, and now I don't know if she'd accept a hug.

She sighs loudly, wringing her hands in her lap. "We fucked this up."

My heart jolts back and forth like an ice cube in an empty glass. "Can you be more specific?"

She gestures between us. "This game. We fucked up. We shouldn't have played at all. Now, every time I see you, for the rest of our lives, I'll just remember you coming down my throat. When Kate gets engaged, or married, or has a baby or there's a party and you're there, I'll be seeing you naked in the kitchen all over again."

I snort. *Can't fucking help it.* "Is that so bad?"

She dips her head and presses her palms to her cheeks. "Awful."

I wince. "My ego is taking a pounding tonight. But at least you'll have your winnings to make you feel better."

A mirthless chuckle escapes her. "I can't take it. It'll feel like you paid me for a blow job."

It's my turn to laugh. "Most expensive blow job ever." We share a quiet moment, then I add, "The money was yours before that."

Elly sniffles again, wiping her eyes with her hands. "What now? Do you want me to move out?"

My muscles tense. "Why would I want that?"

"Because this'll be awkward."

I hold her gaze, but she looks away. I hook a finger under her chin, forcing her to look at me. "I don't want you to move out. This doesn't have to be awkward. This isn't some one-night stand where we have to do the walk of shame back to our respective bedrooms."

"Then what is it?"

I release her chin. "I don't know. But I really hope it's the start and not the end. But we did fuck up a little."

"How so?"

"There's something we should have done first."

"What?"

Elly's pupils dilate, and the air thickens around us. My gaze drops to her mouth, and her lips part just a fraction. I can't resist any longer.

I cup the back of her neck, intending to ease her towards me, but Elly's already moving, our mouths drawing together like magnets.

Our lips meet, and the energy of the contact runs through me like electricity. As if it shocks us both, our movements become hurried, desperate, our kiss furious. It's wet and hot and Elly's fingers press into the back of my neck and tug my hair as she pulls me into her. I can still taste me on her and it only serves to increase the heat sizzling through me. I don't know how I'm going to resist carrying her up to my room and fucking her all night.

She finally pulls away from me, her lips all red and slick and puffy. *Gorgeous.* We rest our foreheads together as our breathing returns to normal.

"We definitely fucked up," she whispers, breathless, as she leans into me.

"Don't overthink it. We might not be playing a game anymore, but we can still have fun."

"Fun," she confirms, although I suspect there's a note of disappointment in her voice that causes a twinge of discomfort in my chest.

"Exactly. Fun," I repeat. "Shall we start now?"

23
ELLY

Jack stares at me with a hungry look in his eye. How bad would it be to go through with this? We've already crossed the line—I've already won—and that kiss has left me eager for another round and my clit is throbbing forcefully between my legs, demanding that I take action. I want to fuck him. *I do.*

But if we do this now, it's still part of the game. It's not real. And as much as I hate to admit it, I don't want to be another woman Jack Lansen fools around with.

And to add to that, I'm not entirely convinced that everything I've done with him tonight wasn't an attempt to make myself feel better, to give me something else to focus on, to drive out the crippling self-doubt after being assailed on stage with the leftover shit from the inside of someone's burger. Those fuckers might not have wanted me, but Jack certainly does, and I'd rather keep it that way. If I give him everything right now, he might lose interest.

I'm overthinking it, even though Jack warned me not to. But I don't want this to become some casual fling I'm indulging in with my housemate. Wouldn't it be better—*wouldn't I prefer it*—if there was a possibility this thing with Jack might really go somewhere?

I make the decision right there on the spot, even though I have no idea what it would entail or what it might look like. *Definitely.* But if so, this surely isn't the way to start it.

Finally, I speak. "The winner decides whether we have sex or not, right?"

"Right." He elongates the word, cautious, as though he's anticipating he won't like what I'm about to say. "It's your choice."

"I don't think that's a good idea."

Surprise flashes in his gaze, and he looks hesitant when he asks, "Do I want to know why?"

I stand and shrug, affecting a nonchalance I don't feel. I'm tied in knots over this. I want him, but not like this. Not this way. "Because your dick is far too fucking big," I deadpan.

He drops his face into his palm and begins to laugh so hard that his shoulders shake, which in turn makes me smile. "You were managing just fine," he says, looking up when his laughter eases.

My heart trips up a little, and my cheeks heat at the memory of sucking him off. Confusion and arousal tangle inside me and I can't for the life of me remember what I was going to say.

"What's going through that pretty head of yours, El?" *I love how he says that. It sounds as though he cares.*

"I haven't had sex in six months," I blurt. *That's not what I meant to say.*

He draws back the tiniest bit, a teasing look on his face. "Six months? You remember how it's done, right?"

"Fuck you," I say, but there's no edge in my voice. He's so close to wearing me down, and I force a serious expression onto my face so he can't tell. "But we shouldn't get involved. At least, not any more than we have done already, because we have to live together for the next two months."

"See, to me, that sounds like a reason to do it. Two months of uninterrupted good times." There's that sexy smile again. *Damn, he's hard to resist.* "And I owe you an orgasm. I don't like being in debt."

I don't know what it is about hearing him say the word 'orgasm', but it has my attraction to him running wild all over again. I can feel it writhing like a separate being inside me, wanting to take control of my body and launch it at him.

"Willing to pay you back with interest," he adds, reaching out and hooking his fingertips against mine, making my hand tingle. It's a surprisingly gentle gesture. "I'm very good at it."

I roll my eyes. "I'm sure you are. But the answer is still no." I turn to leave, desperately trying to ignore the little voice in my head screaming '*you idiot*', when—

"El, wait." I swing to face him and he springs off the sofa, pacing to the shelves and reaching for the cheque that's still balanced between Priapus' cock and his torso. He slides it out, takes a pen from his trouser pocket and signs it, and hands it to me. "This is yours, fair and square."

"I can't."

"Fuck's sake. Of course you can." He grabs my hand and presses it into my palm until my fingers clutch around it. "And thank you. I'd rather play with you than anyone else."

For some reason, his comment makes me want to cry again, but I blink it away before he can see it, and even with my winnings in my hand, I feel like I've lost.

I rip the cheque in half. "I'm not taking your money."

He raises his brows. "You don't get to refuse your winnings." He pulls his wallet from his pocket, flips it open and eases out a black card. "Take this," he instructs, holding it out. "And if you see something you want, you can buy it."

I shake my head, refusing to take the credit card. "You're mad."

"No. I'm fair." In one swift movement, he slides the piece of plastic into my bra before he taps me on the shoulder as he walks past on his way out. "PIN is my birthday. Month and date."

A flush of irritation has me calling out, "What makes you think I know your birthday?"

He flips the back of his hand at me over his shoulder, casually waving away my objection. "Don't pretend you don't know."

I can hear the smile in his voice, but I shake my head at his audacity anyway. *So fucking arrogant.* But the thing is, I do know. I've known the date of his birthday for *years*.

24
ELLY

I can't think of a single thing I'd want to buy with Jack Lansen's black card. It sits on my dressing room table, glaring at me every morning.

Mr fucking Moneybags.

The thing is, I don't want his money. I want *him*.

"Penny for your thoughts?"

I look up to find Jack staring at me across the kitchen island. It's Saturday morning, and he's heading to the gym and is wearing shorts and a t-shirt, muscular arms and legs on display. It's a good look on him, and I can't decide if I prefer this version of him to the suited one. They're both yummy.

Over the last couple of weeks, we've slid into this semi-awkward but friendly rapport. He hasn't given up making suggestive comments, but he's also sweet and kind and thoughtful, and he leaves little notes for me in the kitchen on the mornings I'm not awake before he leaves for work.

He stares at me, waiting for an explanation for my unfocused expression. But I can't tell him that all I'm thinking of is him, and how I'm wishing I hadn't turned him down on that offer to have more 'fun'.

What am I frightened of? Would being one of Jack Lansen's many women really be that bad?

I'm all too aware of his reputation, but for some reason, he feels like a safe space. Somewhere I could let loose sexually. Like he could hold it all, and let me be what I'm meant to be. And I'd love it. I know I would.

I'd get invested.

I would fall for him, and he'd walk away like it was nothing more than sex. Good old physical fun times. I'd end up with a broken heart and he'd move on to the next woman on his list.

I can move on from a blow job in the kitchen, but not from heartbreak.

Jack brings his coffee over and sits next to me at the kitchen island. "Well?"

Shit. Sitting next to him has my nerve endings blasting off like a firing squad. *Lethal*.

Just have sex with him. You know you want to.

He's still waiting for my explanation. I have to give him something else.

"Lydia told me not to touch you." The comment is out before I can stop it.

Jack's lips pucker as he tries to restrain what I assume is a smirk. "Before or after you took my dick in your mouth?"

My face immediately gets hot. "Can you please not throw that into casual conversation?" He chuckles, low. "Are you sleeping with her?"

Jack tenses and everything feels awkward. "No. And I haven't slept with her." *Fuck*. This is a definite reminder that I should not get involved with someone like Jack Lansen. Too many women, too much baggage. "When were you talking to Lydia?"

"I bumped into her at the supermarket, and she told me to 'keep my hands off Jack Lansen'. In fact, she said, 'Don't. Fucking. Touch. Him'. She looked like she might kill me if I disobeyed."

He barks a laugh. "You didn't listen, did you?"

"This is serious."

Jack shrugs, his eyes halfway to rolling. "I was joking. I agree, it's a bit odd. But so what? She can't touch us here. We can do whatever we want."

"I guess so."

"But you don't want to do what I want to do, so..." He raises a suggestive eyebrow. "We'll have to do something else."

My skin prickles. *What is he up to?* "Oh, yeah?"

"You're performing for Nico's party, right?"

"Yes."

"Are you ready for it?"

I wince, recalling how I wept in Jack's arms about the Marchmont and being pelted with tomatoes. I've been back to the bar since then, but my performances have been shaky and subpar. And without fail, my mediocrity raises the memory of my disastrous non-interview with Robert Lloyd, like a vampire clambering from a coffin I thought I'd locked, seeking to suck the fucking life out of me...

"I want to help you," he says when I don't reply.

I cock a brow. "Another pep talk?"

Jack huffs and rubs a hand over the scruff on his jaw. "The last one went down so well, thought I'd try again. What can I say? I'm a glutton for punishment."

I don't know why, but the word *punishment* has my veins steaming. The effect he has on me is unprecedented. I'm spinning from annoyed to aroused and back again like I'm in orbit, and the effort it takes to pretend I'm unmoved is leeching my energy. "What's your agenda? Is this so you can get in my pants?"

He chuckles. "No. Well, not entirely."

"Why, then?"

"Because you're ridiculously talented, but you aren't positioning yourself for success. You're underperforming."

My spine straightens. *How dare he.*

Jack scans my face. "You think I've just insulted you, don't you?"

Fuck. The man is a mind reader. "Sort of."

He points a finger at me. "That right there is where you're going wrong. Your mind is primed for insults. You're expecting them. You have to flip the script." He sighs. "If you won't have dinner with me as a date, then let me take you out to talk about your career instead."

"We can talk about my career right here."

"Out is more fun." I tut and shake my head—*always after the fun*—but Jack is undeterred. "I might not be a musician, but I do know a thing or two about getting ahead."

I pause, trying to sink into my body and work out how I feel about this. But all I come up with is, *this sounds like another game.* And no matter how much I'm pretending I don't want to play with Jack Lansen, I absolutely do.

"Sure," I agree, and Jack grins so wide it makes me want to kiss that fantastic mouth of his again, and thoughts of all the wonderful things he could do with it drop into my mind in a slideshow of temptation.

He taps the kitchen work surface with one hand, snapping me out of my fantasies. "Great. Tonight."

His decisiveness has nervous laughter spilling from my mouth. "You don't waste time. What if I have plans?"

"Do you?"

"No," I concede.

"Then let me take you out."

I want to disagree because seeing him get his own way and look so smug about it is infuriating. But instead, I blurt, "No blow jobs. No kissing."

My heart thrums, and the realisation hits me all at once. *I don't want him to think I'm just another slut who'll get on her knees for him.* I'm trying to claw my way back to some idealistic version of chastity, as if that would make him want me more. There's me thinking I could be all sexually liberated with Jack, but social conditioning has done a fucking number on me.

Jack's brows shoot up at the same time as his lips tug up at the edges. He places his hands on his heart and says, "You're crushing my dreams here, El."

My stomach dips like the damn thing is swooning. "Let's keep it to my career," I say calmly, as if kissing and blow jobs, and the idea that they might feature in Jack's dreams, doesn't turn me on.

"Sure. But just so you know, I still want to kiss you."

All the air in my lungs escapes in a gasp, making Jack bite his lip with his perfect teeth.

"You're not making this easy," I mutter. "We need rules so this thing doesn't go off the rails."

"I love that you think we're still on the rails." He reaches out, and before I can stop him, his thumb grazes my cheek as he runs his hand down my face, leaving a trail of blazing heat.

He knows exactly what he's doing, and my boundaries are so flimsy, he can push right past them. I'm tilting towards him, leaning into his hand. *Hopeless.*

His fingers fall away, but his eyes are trained on me, and amusement flits across his gaze. As it almost always does. "We'll leave at seven," he instructs. "Be ready."

25
ELLY

I definitely have demons urging me to the dark side because I'm not wearing any underwear. *Nothing*. Just a knee-length maroon jersey dress that hugs my breasts and flares from the waist, paired with my trusty cowboy boots and sheepskin coat.

There's a war going on inside me, because as much as I don't think this thing with Jack should go any further than it already has, I prepared for tonight as though it definitely will and I can't help wondering if he has too.

"El, the car's outside," Jack yells from downstairs.

I smooth down the dress, press a hand to my chaotic curls in a vain effort to tame them, and sling my handbag over my shoulder. "Coming."

The sight of Jack standing at the bottom of the stairs in chinos and a long navy overcoat, collar popped, has my heart thumping. It's unnerving how much this feels like a real date, even though I know it's not.

"You look..." A little divot forms between his brows. "You look like..." He gives up and ruffles his hair with one hand.

"Very eloquent," I tease, hopping down off the bottom step.

Jack snorts a little and averts his gaze, but I get the impression it's directed at himself rather than me. He grabs his keys and phone from the hall table. "This is business. It doesn't matter how you look." A dark sensation plunges through me, but just as I worry it's going to sink my mood entirely and possibly ruin the evening, he adds, "but you look fantastic. I'd fuck you in a heartbeat."

"I hope you don't say that at your other business meetings," I say, unable to contain the smile that's spreading over my face as I skip to catch up to him.

"Only when I really have to push a deal over the line." I let out a laugh, and he holds his hand out to me. "Come on. The driver's waiting."

I put my hand in his and static sparks, zinging up my arm and somehow landing right between my legs, where my bare pussy suddenly feels incredibly vulnerable.

Damn. I should've worn underwear because we're only five minutes into the evening and already my pussy is getting ideas of her own, and I'm really not sure I have the willpower to stop her. Or even want to...

Dinner is delicious, and we share more wine than we ought to. I laugh, a lot. Hanging out with Jack feels so good. Fun. A *lot* of fun.

This is the best date I've had in years.

"You've got to record all the songs. Studio quality." He takes a sip from his wineglass. "Tell me you've done that?"

I shake my head, and Jack lets out a low groan. "All this fucking talent...What's the deal with that?"

"What?"

"Hiding."

I cringe. Everything in me wants to shrink at the discomfort of being made to face my own failings, and I fidget uneasily to reduce the sensation. "I'm not hiding."

He leans towards me across the table, pinning me with a serious look. "You're this incredibly confident, sexy woman. And yet..." He spreads his hands like he has no idea how to finish the sentence. "You're the whole package. And somewhere along the line, you've forgotten it." A fierce blush rages over my skin, and I twist a ringlet of hair around my finger. "It's a good thing I'm here to remind you."

His features settle into the familiar cocky expression, and a flare of heat bursts in my chest like he lit a fire under my ribs. I'm suddenly so hot, I feel sweaty, and my thoughts run wild. *This is business. Business.*

This man is confusing me.

I'm not wearing any underwear.

I cross my legs, trying to ignore the slickness gathering between my thighs. This is a disaster.

"We'll film you. You gotta put the songs out. TikTok, Instagram. Spotify. Whatever the hell people are using these days." He strokes his chin. "Actually, you should probably just pick one place to focus and grow that. Otherwise it'll be overwhelming."

I nod like I'm listening, but really I'm just staring at him. At his gorgeous face, that square jaw... those fucking eyelashes.

"Sound good?" he queries.

I nod frantically, although I'm not even sure what he just said. Something about social media. I'm not ready for that shit. My whole body revolts when I even think about it, so Jack might as well be talking to a brick wall.

"Great." He signals for the bill, and a few minutes later we're out on the street. It's cold, our breaths fogging like smoke. I pull my coat around me, wishing I'd put on tights. My legs are freezing.

"Home?" I ask.

Jack shakes his head. "There's one more thing we have to do before we go back." He grabs my hand and tugs me along the darkened Mayfair street.

"Where are we going?"

"Just around here," he says, his long strides clipping along the pavement, me tottering behind him.

He stops outside a large church that's nestled between terraced buildings. Letting go of my hand, he pushes open the huge wooden door. "Come on," he says, tipping his head inside.

I hesitate. "Are we praying?"

"No." He shrugs one shoulder. "You can if you want to. But I know what I'm worshipping." He looks me up and down deliberately, and my heart stutters. "That's a killer dress, by the way. Did I mention that?"

"You did not. You said it didn't matter what I looked like."

"And that I'd fuck you in a heartbeat." He grins. "Get inside. It's cold. Your nipples look freezing."

So he has noticed my lack of underwear. And he's right. They're hard as bullets, but I'm not sure it's on account of the temperature. "Such a gentleman."

"Always."

I shake my head at him as I pass into the church. It's empty, but there are dim wall lights glowing and displays of battery-operated candles in alcoves, and the air smells of wax polish and some kind of incense. Frankincense, perhaps.

"We shouldn't be in here," I whisper.

"They leave the door open for a reason."

I bite back the urge to tell him that I'm pretty sure his reason isn't the same as that of the church, but he snakes an arm around my shoulders and whisks me up towards the front, taking a sharp right turn before the altar.

He pushes through a side door and leads me down another corridor. There's a warren of passages back here, and we pass down several of them before Jack stops in front of a door, pulling a key from his pocket.

What the hell? "Don't tell me you're moonlighting as a priest?"

He slides the key in and unlocks the door. "No. But I know the owner."

"God?"

His laugh is dark and ripe, and far too sensuous for a church. The two of us here, so close together in the semi-darkness, has sinful thoughts racing through my mind. Jack's scent fills the air, and my hormones begin to buzz. That naughty part of me—*the slutty part*—wants him to stop what he's doing and take me right here, against the wall.

He pushes the door open and flicks a light switch, turning on more of those dim wall lights that lit the church. He ushers me inside, locking the door behind us. Before me is a large hall full of velvet upholstered chairs set out in rows, and the walls are painted a tasteful gold, faux marble pilasters lining the room. We've entered from the side, and at one end there's a large door that looks like the main entrance. At the back, there's a raised stage with a grand piano.

I stare for a moment, taking it all in, and it hits me like an electric shock when I realise where we are: Stanmore Hall, one of the most famous classical music performance venues in London.

"Is this part of the church?" I ask in awe.

"No. I mean, maybe it was once, but not anymore. The regular entrance is locked tonight." Jack points over at the main door, which I assume must open out onto the street.

Locked? I turn to him. "Hold on. Isn't Andrei Orlov supposed to be playing here?" The information filters through my mind, dredged up from my subconscious. The world famous concert pianist was definitely scheduled to play this week. "Yes, he is. Kate and Nico were talking about coming to see him. This is a sold out show. Where is everyone?"

Jack slides a hand into his pocket, his eyes bright. "It is sold out. I bought every ticket."

Shocked laughter explodes from me. "What? How? You only asked me out this morning. Jesus. All those people. Andrei..."

"Don't worry. Everyone was well compensated for their tickets. And Andrei is fine; he's giving Kate and Nico a private performance instead, and I'd far rather watch you than a classical pianist. So, tonight, the stage is yours."

My legs feel weak. "Stanmore hall," I whisper. "You're crazy."

"You have to stop calling me crazy. I'll develop a complex."

I shake my head, unable to process what he's done. *He is crazy*. He must be to do this for me. "I can't believe this. I can't play here, I can't..."

"Of course you can. Get up there," he says, nodding at the stage. "You can play the piano, can't you?"

"Yes. But..." I'm so overwhelmed that Jack would even think to do something like this, that he'd think I was worthy of performing in a space like this, that I struggle to find the words. Finally, I settle on, "I'm not wearing my slippers."

"I know." His seductive tone trickles over my skin like melted butter, then he switches it off, turning matter-of-fact. "But performing is part of who you are, and I like being around you, so I'll have to get used to you being irresistible when you do." My breath stutters, but Jack barely pauses. "This is practice. Performing somewhere different."

"I've performed in other places."

"Oh, yeah? When? And karaoke doesn't count."

I screw up my face, hating that he's pushing me on this. It's been a long time since I performed anywhere other than my bedroom or the Marchmont. To rocket from there to here seems like a dream come true, but I steel myself to do as he's asking. "Fine."

I stride through the rows of chairs and trot up the short flight of steps to the stage. Jack follows me, meandering slowly through the rows as I remove my coat, drop it to the floor and prop my handbag on top before I take my seat at the grand piano. I never, *ever*, thought I'd perform somewhere like this. *I shouldn't be here*.

Jack settles into a chair in the front row and takes his phone from his coat pocket, deliberately pointing it at me.

"Are you filming?" I ask.

"Yes. We need the footage for those videos you'll be making."

I dismiss his comment with a sideways glance and begin to play a few bars of *I Vow to Thee My Country*, which seems appropriate seeing as we came through a church.

"Nope," Jack calls.

I lift my fingers from the keys. "Why not?"

"I want to hear *your* songs. Not a bloody hymn. Anyone can play those."

Fine. I shuffle on the stool, getting more comfortable as I decide which of my songs to play.

As I strike the opening chords, I sense the shift in the room. I've chosen one of my more melancholic songs, about heartbreak and loneliness, and the notes prickle over me, raising the tiny hairs on my arms. The acoustics in here are phenomenal and I play right through to the end, lost in the song, the lyrics, allowing the pain of the words to flow through my voice.

I get so caught up that I completely forget that Jack is watching me until he starts slowly applauding, each booming clap making the air tremble.

He gets up from his seat and removes his coat, throwing it over the chair next to him before he mounts the steps and comes to stand closer to me. My body strains at his approach, as if a mere touch from him would reinforce the idea that I've done something good here.

"Play something else," he says as he straddles the piano stool next to me. It's a duet stool, so we both fit, but only just. In this position, his thigh muscles stretch against his trousers. *He's huge.* I'm pretty sure I can see his dick through the fabric.

I avert my gaze, my body turning rigid at his sudden proximity. *Why is it that with Jack, everything feels like foreplay?*

Because it is, comes the answer.

He brushes some of my hair away from my face, tucking it behind my ear. Such a tender gesture, and somehow possessive... as though he has rights over my body. And I have absolutely no objection.

I begin a second song, but the rhythmic rise and fall of Jack's chest in my periphery is soaking up nearly all my attention. His knee grazes my thigh, and I gulp, missing my cue. I can't play like this.

I stop, and for a moment neither of us speaks, and I let my hands fall into my lap. The static crackling between us is so intense, I'm pretty sure we could power half of London with it.

"El?"

I swallow, keeping my gaze on the piano keys. "Yes?"

"I think you're wonderful."

His words nestle right inside my chest, where they swell and bloom like budding flowers. "Please..." I plead, not knowing whether I'm asking him to stop or keep going.

His hand comes to my cheek, and with gentle pressure, he turns me to look at him. "Please what?"

My breathing turns shallow and rapid. "I can't..."

"Why not?" he purrs. "We'd be so good together. You know we would. Here, turn around." He ushers my body into position, and I have to lift a leg to straddle the piano stool opposite him.

He rests a hand on one of my thighs. *I'm not wearing any underwear.* He might be making the moves, but I plotted for a situation exactly like this to arise, and now, under Jack's darkened gaze, wetness gathers between my legs.

As though he knows, he teases at the fabric of my dress, easing it up until his hand rests on my bare thigh. "Can I see?"

"See what?" My voice is so faint I can barely hear the words myself.

"You know exactly what," he rasps as his hand slides higher, stopping only a few inches from the top of my thigh. "Your bare cunt." I moan, and he huffs the slightest of laughs. "Did you think I didn't know?"

My blood sizzles beneath my skin, but I can't summon words to respond. *Just a little higher. He needs to shift his hand a little higher...*

"Can I?" he asks again, and this time I nod, remembering that both doors are locked. *It's just us in here. Safe.*

His hand slides up my dress, blistering heat rising across my skin, and my hips lift off the stool a little, trying to meet his touch.

His fingertips tickle as he slows his approach to the apex of my thighs, stretching each second out until I don't think I can stand it any longer.

Touch me.

And then his fingers are over my clit, and all the blood in my body drains to that one point, my pulse beating hard and heavy under his hand. He pushes lower, seeking out my wetness with his thumb. He closes his eyes as he pushes inside me, finding me soaked.

"Oh, shit," he mutters. "You want this so bad." My cheeks heat at being called out, but Jack trails his thumb from my entrance, through my lips, and over my clit, rubbing it in circles, making me whimper and forget my embarrassment. "Why would you fight this?" The low whisper of his voice stokes my arousal. *I'm so turned on, I can't think.*

"I don't know," I stammer, my hips rising again to give him more space. "I don't—"

"Let me give you what you want, El."

I swallow, nod. "Yes, yes... please..."

Jack removes his hand and flips up the loose skirt of my dress, leaving me entirely bare and exposed. His hooded gaze is fixed between my legs, and to see him so aroused has coils of desire snaking through me.

"I need to fucking see this," he growls, and before I know it, he slams the lid of the piano and lifts me onto it, using his hands to spread my thighs and positioning himself between them. "We are going to have so much fucking fun," he says under his breath, keeping his gaze anchored between my legs as if he's talking to my pussy and not to me. Then his gaze flicks up to where I'm propped on my elbows, staring down at him. "Tell me you want this. I need you to say it. I need to hear it."

"I want this."

"What do you want?"

"Everything. All of it."

There's a glimmer of satisfaction in his gaze as he lowers to kiss my thigh, licking his way up. But just as he reaches the place I want him, he stops. "Take off the dress."

I glance around the room, and even though there's no one here, I can't help worrying.

Recognising my fear, Jack's expression softens. "The doors are locked. No one can get in."

"Okay," I murmur, trusting him implicitly. *We're safe.*

His gaze heats. "I want you naked. Spread out right here." He knocks a knuckle on the piano. "Just for me."

"This is a Steinway," I whisper. "We can't."

Jack emits a low rumble of laughter. "Anything happens to the piano, I'll replace it." *So typical.* "Relax."

He sweeps his hands up my thighs and tugs the dress over my head, and suddenly all my fear is forgotten and I'm shuffling out of the dress, almost as eager to remove it as he is.

I throw it to the floor and rest back on the piano, entirely naked except for the cowboy boots. *This is it. This is what I've been waiting for.* Jack stands back and surveys me. He blinks, eyebrows shooting upwards like he can't believe his eyes. "This is... you are..."

I smile, a sense of power surging through me at having rendered him speechless.

"I want to take a photo of you like this." His voice is so full of awe that he sounds dizzy with it, making a rush of arousal blast from my hips to my extremities. The idea of letting him do something so reckless has me almost shaking with desire. With need. I feel so wanted right now that the sensation is too much for my body to contain. It makes me lightheaded.

"Do it," I whisper.

Jack's eyes widen. "Really?"

I nod, my body little more than a quivering mess of needy desire as Jack takes his phone from his pocket. *Fuck, this is dangerous.* He pushes my legs apart a little more, and I feel the slickness between them increase as he takes a picture. He comes in close, then steps back to get all of me in the frame, taking more photos as he moves around the piano. I must look absolutely wanton, and I fucking love it. *This is me reclaiming my sexuality.* Each time his phone makes the little shuttering noise a jerk of arousal sparks at my clit.

"Fucking hell," he mutters as he finally puts the phone back in his pocket. He settles himself between my legs and places a hand on each thigh. "I've wanted to do this for so long," he purrs, and his eyes darken, smouldering with a deadly heat before he dives between my legs.

He slides his hands under my bum, tilting my hips up. His tongue swipes eagerly from my arse all the way up to my clit, and energy sizzles through me. *Oh, my God, Jack Lansen is eating me out.* The thought makes my libido spike and my head falls back on a moan, collapsing against the piano as he devours me, his tongue dipping between my folds and spearing into my entrance, sucking and licking, sending need spiralling through my body faster than he can satisfy it, driving me to a frenzy that makes my legs spasm and my toes curl.

As though he knows I need more, he hauls me deeper into his mouth, sliding me closer to him, curling two fingers into me, creating pressure inside whilst working ravenously with his tongue on the outside, playing my body like a musical instrument. It feels incredible. *So fucking worth it. Worth every game and more because this man knows exactly what he's doing.*

"Don't stop. Don't stop. Don't ever... *oh*—" The warning tingle of an orgasm grows low in my hips, expanding and pulsing. I rock into his chin, forcing myself against him harder, deeper, driving my clit into his mouth as his fingers pump inside me.

"You taste... so fucking sweet..." The low growl of his words vibrates against me, sending frissons of pleasure into my hips.

"Oh... oh..." I moan and grab his hair, forcing his face into me, riding him, shifting to get the pressure just right... working myself against him. Pleasure rises and falls, flows and ebbs with each shift of my body, and I chase it desperately. Jack eats me more vigorously, bringing me right to the edge of my orgasm.

My thighs tense, clamping around his ears, and he hums against me, not letting up as he continues to lick and suck.

"I'm close," I whine, my voice thin and desperate. "So close—"

He pulls away, and I squeal his name. "Jack!"

"Wait. Wait for me," he says, and I push up to see him fumbling at his trousers, undoing them.

We're going to have sex? Here?

My hips rise off the piano, straining towards him. I'm so eager for him... to feel him inside me. I've dreamed of this moment, brought myself off to this moment, and now that it's really happening, it can't come fast enough. *Hurry up.*

He fishes a condom from his pocket and at least four more fall to the floor.

"How many people were you planning on fucking tonight?" I ask, attempting to mock him, but instead sounding hopelessly breathless.

He kisses me roughly, each swipe of his tongue slaking my desire, before he pulls away to tear the packet open with his teeth. "Just you." He doesn't look at me as he releases his dick from his boxers. God, it's beautiful. The slit on the flared tip is practically gaping, and there's pre-cum glistening in the hole.

"How many times?" I say with amazement, and as his gaze locks onto mine, a lopsided grin haunts his lips.

"As many times as you'll let me." He rolls the condom on and shuffles towards me, his trousers still around his ankles.

He drags me closer to him, my legs dangling off the piano, and slides the tip of his dick up and down my slit, making me ache with need.

Seeing him there, standing between my legs, watching the way his dick moves over me with rapt admiration, only makes it worse. I've never needed to be filled so badly. I could scream.

"You are so fucking wet," he rasps, nudging his tip inside me. I wince as he slowly sinks deeper, stretching me. *He's so big.* "All right?" he queries.

"Uh-huh. I'm okay," I breathe.

"Can you take a little more?"

God, yes. "Please," I beg.

His voice is rough with desire when he asks, "Can you take it all?"

The question sets me alight. If he doesn't fuck me properly, I'll combust. "Mmm," I moan.

He lets out an equally lusty groan as he plunges in, and the burn of the stretch shifts to a fullness that completes me, sating that aching, driving need as Jack fuses our hips.

Oh, my God. He's inside me. I want to savour this moment forever.

Like the same thought has occurred to him, he stays there, fully within me, without moving. Just staring at me.

"I can't believe we're doing this," I whisper.

"I can," he says, hauling me up towards him. I wrap my arms around his neck as our mouths meet in a desperate collision, his tongue slipping between my lips and feeling like velvet as it strokes mine. My hands find his nape and my fingers weave into his thick hair. I deepen the kiss, our tongues tangling like dancers who won't let go.

When we separate, he's breathing hard. His pupils are dark and dilated, the evidence of his arousal all over his face. "You're more wonderful than I ever imagined," he pants, his voice all awe.

"You... you..." I begin, meaning to tell him I feel the same, but words completely escape me as his hands find my hips, and he begins to pump into me, his handsome face a vision of concentration. I grind against him, meeting each of his thrusts with my own. To be handled like this, entirely naked apart from my boots, with Jack almost fully clothed, only heightens the experience. I'm totally vulnerable to him and I love it. Every fucking second of being spread out for him, seeing him eat me up with his eyes, and now thrusting into me with such focus, as though there's nowhere else he'd rather be... *it's perfect.*

"Take this off," I murmur, fumbling with the buttons on his shirt, and once I've undone a couple he tugs the whole thing over his head and throws it to the floor, kissing me again. My hands slide over his shoulders, down his chest, where his muscles are firm beneath the warmth of his skin. I'm touching him everywhere, eager to press as much of my body against his as possible.

He shifts a thumb over my clit, which is swollen and ready to explode at the slightest touch. Shocks of pleasure zing from that point, and he continues to thrust, making my pussy pulse with an impending climax way before I'm ready. I mewl helplessly, digging my nails into his skin. "Oh, oh, Jack—"

"Come for me," he rasps, and my orgasm detonates, harder than ever before, bursting through me like a shower of glitter, tingling and sparkling in every cell. I tip my head back and scream his name up into the domed roof of the concert hall. "Jack, Jack, Jack..." The sound reverberates, carried by the acoustics, filling every corner of the hall and ringing in my ears. "I'm yours. Take me, *please.*" And he does, pumping into me through the rise and fall of my orgasm, stringing out every last drop of pleasure my body has to give, until his thrusts grow erratic and his dick pulses inside me.

"Fuuuuck," he groans, and every tendon in his neck is visible as the tension of his orgasm tears through him.

Each jerk of his cock feels like a secret I've earned, and as our breathing returns to normal, hormones flood my body, opening me up to the feelings I'm trying to hold at bay. I stave them off, shutting the door, locking them up. *I will not fall for this man.*

He sinks against me, and I hold him close, his face pressed against my bare breasts. He teases my nipple with his fingers and sparks of ecstasy ricochet through my boneless body. His fingers still, but I don't let go of him. We stay like that for what feels like a long time, but is probably no longer than a minute. We're so close... so *intimate*. More so, even, than what we've just done.

"Don't freak out on me," he whispers.

"Huh?"

"Don't cry. I don't think I could handle it right now."

I push him off my chest. "I'm not crying."

He nods. "Great. Because this is supposed to be fun."

"It was. It was..." I trail off, not knowing *what* it was, exactly.

Inside me, his cock softens and he pulls out. I lie back on the piano, breathing deeply as he ties up the condom, wraps it in a tissue from his pocket, and throws it in the bin. He fixes his trousers, picks up his shirt and puts it on, making quick work of the buttons. "It was amazing. You're amazing," he says, pulling me off the piano so I'm standing. His gaze rakes over me and I burn up beneath it. "This is what you should wear at home. Just the boots. Unbelievable." His smile widens. "Can I kiss you?"

I splutter a laugh. "You just fucked me like a porn star, but now you're asking permission for a kiss?"

He scrapes a hand through his hair, looking awkward for the briefest of moments before he says, "I don't want to take anything you don't want to give."

Seeing the way he's looking at me, as though he'd do anything to make me happy, but isn't quite comfortable with the desire to do so, has my heart expanding and my answer spilling out before I can stop it. "I want to give you everything. All of it. It's yours."

When I spoke them earlier, the words could have been passed off as meaningless utterances, released in the throes of passion. The verbal equivalent of ejaculation. A sexual sweet nothing. But now, in the aftermath, they feel heavier, and the meaning they convey is much more than I'd intended to share.

Jack's mouth opens a little, his eyes widening as he stares at me for an extended beat.

Was it too much? Too soon?

I thought what I was feeling was mutual, but maybe I was wrong. I'm immediately uncomfortable. I glance around for my dress and grab it from the floor, hauling it over my head like it'll protect me from whatever the fuck is going on between me and Jack right now. If he's going to let me down easy, tell me this can only ever be casual, I'd rather not hear it. I'd prefer to pretend I never said anything.

He steps towards me, his blue eyes serious for once. "Can you stop faffing?"

I give him the barest of glances as I tug at the sleeves of my dress, the hem, as if the damn thing won't sit right, even though it's perfectly comfortable. "I'm not faffing. I'm getting dressed."

He comes to stand beside me. "Okay. Stop that then."

I roll my eyes, forcing a lightness into my tone despite the fact that my heart is rioting and a black cloud of *something* hovers just out of sight. "You just want me to stay naked."

"I'd love that." Grabbing my hand, he tugs on it until I face him. "But not right now." He exhales heavily, waiting until he has my full attention before he speaks. "I want to give you everything too, El."

My next breath doesn't come easily. We're treading uncharted ground, and nervous tension has me vomiting my thoughts. "Really? Because this was supposed to be business. Tonight was supposed to be dinner and my career and we turned it into sex on a piano, and it feels really intense and you keep mentioning 'fun' as though anything other than 'fun' might kill you. And that's okay. I get it. You want to have fun. You want to play. Nothing is serious. Nothing is—"

"El, stop." I halt at his command, anxiety winding through me as I await whatever he's about to decree. "I have the most fun with you. More than I've ever had with anyone." One side of his mouth tilts into a smile. "I'd be happy to have fun with only you."

My chest is tight, my heart strangled off its beat. *Does he mean what I think he does?* I don't want to make assumptions. I can't take that risk. He's still talking in terms of 'fun', after all. I narrow my eyes at him. "What are you saying?"

He breaks into a smile. "What are *you* saying?"

We stare at one another for a few long moments, neither one of us ready to break. Finally, I give in. "I don't know." I shake my head, twisting my fingers into my curls. "Fuck, I don't know," I say, half-laughing, half-dying inside.

He arches a brow, a smile still teasing his lips. "You do know..."

"All right." I heave an enormous breath, filling my lungs until they're fit to burst. "I'm not prepared to do this fuck-buddy thing. Not with you. I'm not going to torment myself over it. I'm not going to have amazing sex with you and then pretend it's just fun and that I'm not moved by—"

"You like me, huh?" His eyes sparkle. He's loving this. *Bastard.*

I'm hot; constricted. *Exposed*. I shrug, trying to backtrack from my emotional explosion. "Not that much. A bit. I could take you or leave—"

His kiss cuts me off, tongue sliding into my mouth, and the passion in it conveys more than any words. I feel everything reciprocated a thousand times over.

By the time he pulls away, I'm spinning with want. I can barely focus when he flashes a smile and whispers, "It's my massive dick, isn't it?"

I thwack a playful hand against his pecs, and he chuckles, pulling me tight against him. I relax in his embrace, my body softening against his strength.

He rests his chin on the crown of my head, speaking hushed words against it. All hint of joking vanished from his voice. "You know what?"

"What?" I whisper, hope fluttering in my veins.

"I really like you too."

My heart leaps. "You do?"

"Yup."

I nuzzle against him, relishing the relief that's soaking my soul. "Can it just be us? No one else? No other women?" He *hmms*, and the sound vibrates through me. I ease my head out from under his chin and look up at him. "You're thinking about making a joke about threesomes, aren't you?"

He laughs, loud, which is all the confirmation I need to know it's *exactly* what went through his mind.

When his laughter fades, he looks at me seriously. "You want to be exclusive?" I hold back my nod for a second or two, but when I release it, something like satisfaction flickers across his face. "What makes you think we weren't before?"

"I need you to be explicit."

He squeezes me tighter. "Okay." He pauses, and for every millisecond of the hiatus, my heart thumps at triple speed. "I haven't thought about anyone else since the night you sang for me back in the flat. I don't want to be with anyone else. I only want you. Exclusively. No games. No fucking about. I'm pretty obsessed with you already, and if you say no, then I'll sit up in my bedroom and wank to all the pictures I took of you tonight until the day I die."

"Oh, God," I wail, the idea of Jack masturbating over the photos distracting me from everything else he said.

"Too much?" Laughter ripples through his tone.

"No."

"Good. Because I'm not done. If I'm exclusive, you're exclusive. If you so much as look at another guy, I'll kill him."

My eyes flutter shut briefly. "I won't be looking anywhere else."

"Great. Because I want you all to myself. Every last inch of you. You're mine." He cups my arse and squeezes, and I let out a tiny yelp. "No threesomes. Got it?"

My face splits in a smile. "Yes."

"Then let's go home and fuck until dawn. Sound good?"

"Sounds fucking brilliant."

When I wake the following morning, wrapped up in Jack's luxurious sheets, he's lying beside me, watching me.

"Hey there," he says, his voice low, and his face a vision of happiness.

In the beam of his admiration, a pleasant, tingling warmth fills my body. I've never felt like this with anyone before. It's as if there is no other place in the world I fit as well as I do here, in Jack Lansen's bed. He strokes a fingertip over my shoulder and down my arm, and the sensation only increases.

"You've brushed your teeth," I whisper. "You're all minty fresh."

"Obviously." He kisses me again.

"But I'm not," I say, pulling away.

"I don't give a fuck. Come here." He pulls me against him, and he's hard and warm and *fuck me,* I think I love him.

But before I get carried away, there's a matter that does need attention. "About those photos..."

He smiles, and I feel it against my mouth. "You want to see how hot you are?" he mumbles against my lips.

He reaches for his phone on the bedside table, opens the screen and orients it so we can both see the images as he scrolls. *Woah.* They're explicit. Some of them are porn-worthy, but others are tasteful. Some of them are beautiful. The light, the piano, my skin, my hair, my boots.

"We should probably delete these," I tell him, even as arousal trickles through me, seeing myself as Jack must have seen me. I flick to the next one, which is a photo he took between my legs. "We should definitely delete them."

"Yeah. Sure," Jack says, but his focus is on the photos, as if he wants to soak them up before he agrees to get rid of them.

"I'm serious. Promise me you'll delete them."

He groans. "I like them." He leans in and runs his tongue up the side of my neck. "But okay."

All of a sudden, the memories of last night hit hard, and my clit is beating an incessant rhythm and I can't wait anymore. *I need him.*

I tease the phone from his hands and put it on the bedside table, wanting him to focus on me. The real, present moment, me.

"Fuck me," I order. "Right now."

He props himself up on his elbow, his eyes flashing fire, and I know I have his full attention. "Again?"

"Again," I confirm, and as he slides his hand between my legs, I forget about the photos.

26
JACK

"What's our story?" Elly asks. She's trying for casual, but I can see right through the act. "Are we telling people?"

She sounds nervous and refuses to look at me as she busies herself in the kitchen, making some strange concoction for breakfast. I suspect it's pancakes, although I'm pretty sure I saw some chickpeas get mixed in there, so I'm a bit dubious, but she's wearing that pretty pink silk underwear set, so I'm happy to watch.

We've been fucking, almost constantly, for ten days. It's been glorious, and I can't get home from the office soon enough. I'm definitely sleep deprived, but it's worth it. "You mean, are we going to announce ourselves as a couple at the charity fundraiser for my dad?"

Elly frowns. "Not appropriate?" I smile at her because I can't help it. She's licking a wooden spoon in long swipes with the flat of her tongue and it has all sorts of inappropriate thoughts racing through my head. "We're arriving together," she continues, "so I thought maybe we'd have to explain it."

"We live together. We don't have to explain anything. It makes total sense that we'd arrive together."

Elly stirs the batter she's making more vigorously, and I know she disagrees.

"I like it just being us," I state. "Do we need to say anything?"

She stops stirring. "No. I guess not. I just figured maybe—"

"You know what my mother is like. I can't spring something like that on her."

She puts down the wooden spoon and places both hands flat on the island on either side of the bowl and stares at me. "Is it because I'm not on her list of approved partners?"

I wince. *That fucking list.* My mother stepped over the line there. Who I date is none of her business, and I intend to keep my feelings for Elly from her for as long as I can. Otherwise, she'll rip her apart. "She can be difficult, and she'll be emotional tonight as it is. It's better if I tell her another time, in private. Not at the party. And as for Kate... I'm not ready to tell her. Are you?"

Elly considers this. "No."

She looks a tad perturbed, so I walk over and put my arms around her from behind. I nuzzle into her neck and kiss her, and she makes a low humming sound. If chocolate made a noise when it melted, it would be *that* sound. "I want to fuck you when you make that noise," I rasp against her throat.

She repeats the noise, dipping her finger into the batter and bringing it up to my mouth over her shoulder. "Try this."

"What is it?"

"Try it," she urges, but when I refuse to suck the batter off, she smears it on my cheek. It's cold and wet and thick.

"Hey," I cry, grabbing her wrist and spinning her so she's facing me. "Seriously, what is this stuff?"

"It's chocolate chip pancake batter."

I tug her towards me, so her chin is against my bare chest. She's peering up at me, and her breathing is heavy. "Liar," I growl.

She grins, and then, in a flash, she sticks her hand in the bowl, scoops up a handful of mixture, and smears it in my hair and down the side of my face.

"What the fuck?" I splutter.

She writhes, trying to escape my grip, staring up at me with those big blue come-fuck-me eyes.

"You shouldn't have done that." I hoist her up on the island, my hands rising up her thighs. "I'm going to punish you for it."

She draws back a little, but her eyes darken. "Jack..." she warns.

"You've been bad. Very bad," I say slowly, relishing how aroused Elly suddenly looks, sitting there with her legs apart, her flesh hot beneath my fingers. I ease my hands under her top, pulling it off and she wriggles out of it to help me. *She has beautiful breasts.* I throw her top on the floor and suck one of her nipples into my mouth, flicking it with my tongue. She tips her head back and moans, and it's then I know I have her.

I release her nipple with a pop, grab the bowl of batter, and tip the whole thing over her bare chest. The milky batter slops over her, and her head jerks up and she shrieks. Her eyes flash with annoyance, and she swipes at me, but I move out of reach.

I'm fighting back laughter, but somehow Elly still looks gorgeous, like a nude model painted in batter. It's hilarious, and disgusting, and I still fancy the pants off her.

"You bastard," she yelps, but she's laughing and her eyes are alight with a bright vivacity that's irresistible. She jumps off the island and runs at me, the batter dripping down her naked torso.

"Fuck, you look hot," I say between gasps of laughter as Elly chases me around the kitchen. "Like a sexy pancake." I'm losing it now, laughing uncontrollably, and she is too.

I slow down, raw bursts of laughter still exploding from my mouth, and Elly leaps at me, jumping on my back, one arm around my throat, the other thumping my shoulder, but it barely hurts. I hold her there, reaching behind me to keep her safe in this piggy-back position, until our laughter eases and she slumps against me, the batter slick between us.

"Who's going to clean up?" I ask as we recover from the hilarity.

She leans forward, curling herself over my spine so her mouth is next to my ear, and whispers, "I was cooking, so it's your turn."

I let her slide down my back until her feet hit the floor, and then I turn to her. "How about we shower together?"

She pretends to ponder this and then flashes me an excited smile. "Okay."

"And then we can have sex."

"Wait, you mean you don't want me covered in batter?"

"Am I allowed to say no?" She lets out a puff of outrage and swipes at me again, but I dodge the blow and pull her into my arms, kissing her hard, and she melts into me. I break off and whisper against her lips. "I want you any way you come. Always."

"I know," she breathes.

Outside the door to Nico's flat, Elly grabs my hand and squeezes. "Last time I touch you tonight, I promise," she says, letting go.

"I sincerely hope not. All I want is your hands all over me."

She giggles, then frowns. "I thought you never noticed me."

My heart clenches as memories ambush me... moments over the years when I noticed Elly, but refused to acknowledge how I felt because she was off-limits. My little sister's friend. Now, they return, hard and fast, like images passing through an old-school projector. *Click, click, click-fucking-click.* All those times she accompanied Kate to one of my parties, when her mere presence set off tiny energetic shocks through my body that I brushed off like lint from my sleeve. Or when she gifted me that stupid little statue of Priapus, complete with an erection that reached to his forehead, claiming it meant nothing, even though I was convinced it meant *something*. But even that memory I locked away, another occurrence I never allowed myself to examine too closely. Now, with the clarity of hindsight, I know that each one of those moments burrowed deep into my psyche, waiting to be recognised. *I always liked her. Christ.* What a revelation.

It's fucking intense, but I blink to clear my head, making light of it as I say, "You? You're impossible to ignore. Annoying as hell, but completely captivating." *You always have been.* I lean in. "And now that I've had a taste, I'm addicted. I'm never giving you up."

She smiles that little private smile, and at the same time the door swings open, and Mum is standing there in an evening dress that falls all the way to the floor. It's black, sleek, and elegant. She's draped in gold and diamonds, and her face is packed with makeup. Her eyelashes are so thick with mascara that they look rigid, like miniature train tracks. But even so, there's no denying that Mum looks good. Impressively glamorous, by any standard.

"Jack," she exclaims. She leans in to kiss me on both cheeks and I get a whiff of heavy patchouli perfume.

"You look wonderful, Mum."

"I do, don't I?" she says, which has been my mother's response to comments on how good she looks for as long as I can remember.

She pulls away from me and looks down at Elly, who is at least five inches shorter. "Eleanor." She glances between us. "Kate did tell me you two were living together. What a bizarre arrangement." Mum frowns and rolls her eyes before pushing the door wide. "I suppose you'd better come in. Didn't you get the memo about the dress code?"

Elly's wearing a white lace dress paired with her cowboy boots and sheepskin coat, which is smart for Elly, but not up to Mum's standards. Elly blushes, her brow creasing.

"Mum," I reprimand, but Mum only rolls her eyes more elaborately. Elly scowls, and I nearly reach out for her hand but resist. It's not worth my while having Mum suspect anything is going on. Not yet, anyway.

But I needn't have worried about trying to reassure her, because Elly stands a little taller and meets Mum head-on. "Hi, Mrs Lansen. I wasn't aware it was a fancy dress party. You make an excellent Morticia Addams. She's very sexy, for a monster."

I stifle a laugh, holding it in my throat. Mum gasps, and Elly flashes her an '*Is there a problem?*' smile, and when Mum merely stares at her, she wanders into the party, telling us she's going to find Kate. I have the strangest urge to run after her and give her a high-five. Not that I love her disrespecting my mother, but sometimes she fucking deserves it.

Mum links her arm through mine, and I escort her through the party. "That girl is so rude. I honestly don't know why Kate is friends with her. It must be a nightmare living with her. I do feel for you, darling. Really, I do."

"Turns out, she's a wonderful housemate." I lean closer to Mum, as if I'm about to impart a juicy piece of gossip. "I rather like her."

Mum draws back and stares at me. "You've changed your tune. I distinctly remember you telling me how useless you thought she was, and how irritating you found her."

I fist my free hand at my side, reminding myself to keep my mouth shut despite the desperate urge to count the fucking ways I've changed my mind and spill it all at Mum's feet; how wonderful Elly is, how fucking glorious the sex is, how I like her more than I've ever liked anyone and how absolutely elated I am that she came to live with me in the first place. Mum has *no idea,* and I intend to keep it that way. When I offer nothing further, she ushers me over to a group of women, all draped in high fashion and glistening with jewels like the window displays of Burlington Arcade.

Mum announces our arrival with the words, "You remember Lydia, don't you?"

Lydia? What the hell is she doing here?

A full-body shudder threatens to overtake me as Lydia beams at me, before kissing me right on the lips. *Jesus.* I glance at Mum, who looks delighted by this.

"Jack, your mother is absolutely fabulous. Like Joanna Lumley." Lydia gives me a huge false smile that has me clenching my teeth. "We've been spending some time together."

They have?

I hold up a finger, and Lydia looks taken aback that I'm halting her flow. "I'm sorry. I need a moment to speak to my mother." I pull Mum away from the group of women, who stare and then continue their huddled conversation. Mum, with an expression on her face as though she has absolutely no idea what I could possibly want to talk to her about, follows me.

When I'm out of earshot of the group, my voice is sharp when I ask, "What is Lydia doing here? I ended things with her. I was very clear about it." *Wasn't I?*

"Don't pull that face," Mum whispers. "I've been spending a little time with her, and she's a delight. We've had tea at Fortnum's twice since we met at the racetrack. Did you know she knows the Weston family? They gave us complimentary champagne." Mum gives a lovesick sigh that has me feeling bilious. "I can absolutely imagine her as my daughter-in-law."

"That is fucking ridiculous," I spit with vehemence.

Mum gasps. "Jack. I'm shocked." She recovers instantly, suggesting she's not only *not* shocked, but also not bothered by my reaction and may, in fact, have anticipated it. "You never came back to me on which of the women you preferred. I told you I'd arrange a date for tonight."

Our conversation in the car after the race comes back to me. I'd pretty much forgotten about it. Over Mum's shoulder, I can see Elly talking to Kate, and the urge to go over there and grab her is almost all-consuming. I have to force myself to finish this conversation with Mum. "I don't want to have a date with any of them."

"I thought you'd say that." She gives my arm a reassuring squeeze. "Enjoy yourself tonight, won't you? Mingle. Chat. Make some new friends." She blows me a kiss and leaves me wondering what on earth has gotten into her.

Without Elly by my side, the time passes agonisingly slowly. Another fucking event where I can't touch her, only this time we're a legitimate couple, and pining has been replaced by compulsive need, at least on my part. Somehow, that only makes it harder to endure the temporary separation, and jealousy burns through me whenever any other guy talks to her. She's so friendly and flirtatious that I'm sure they'd get the wrong idea in no time. *She's mine.*

Maybe she was right. Perhaps I should be telling my family. Perhaps I need to stake my claim. At least then I'd be able to hold her hand in public. But, God, is it worth it with Mum? She wouldn't like it, that's for sure, and I'd rather spare us both the pain of Mum's condemnation for as long as possible.

I've had a few drinks and caught up with some of my father's friends by the time Elly reappears at my side, her expression so concerned that my stomach drops. Her hands latch onto my arm. "Jack. They're all here," she hisses.

"Who is?"

"The women from the cards. Every single one of them your mum picked out." An unsettling shiver rolls down my spine and settles in my gut. Elly takes note of my alarm and says, "Didn't you notice?"

"No. To be honest, you're the only woman I notice."

Elly waves away the compliment. "I'm serious. I counted them. All of them. Even Princess Astrid." She points over to the window, where Astrid is talking to Nico and Matt Hawkston.

"Oh, fuck me."

"Yeah," she nods emphatically. "This is like some crazy speed-dating event for you, disguised as a charity event in memory of your dad."

I scan the room, noting more familiar faces. There's the woman who might be getting divorced, dressed in a floor-length silk gown, her hair twirled up on her head. She's talking to two other women I recognise from Mum's cards. One is the daughter of a Yorkshire baronet who I know has never worked a day in her life, and the other runs her own hedge fund. Mum has all bases covered with these women.

All bases but the one I'm interested in.

"Shit," I mutter.

"Yeah. Shit," Elly says, wide-eyed.

We turn to look at one another, and, after a moment of heavy silence, we nearly burst out laughing, and as I'm standing there in the middle of the event, my hand smothering inappropriate laughter, Elly leaning into me to hide her own, I'm hit by the realisation that she isn't only a gorgeous woman I'm sleeping with, she's also a friend, and I don't know exactly when it happened, but it has, and I fucking love it.

An idea pops into my head, and I feel compelled to act upon it. "You know what you're going to do?" I curl my arm around her waist. "You're going to show everyone in this room how talented you are."

Elly doesn't have a moment to object before I haul her up towards the band, who are just finishing a song.

"Jack, no," she hisses, resisting my pull, but it's a token effort. She's mostly following me, and I'm confident I can ignore her empty protests as I lead her through the party.

When we reach the band, I step up to the guitarist. "Would you mind if my friend here..." I indicate Elly. "Performed a song quickly?"

He's young, maybe in his early twenties, and he looks like a startled rabbit. "I can't do that."

"Nonsense," I say, one hand reaching for his guitar. "Just one song. I'm Jack Lansen. This event is in memory of my father. My mother and sister hired you. They won't mind."

The poor young bloke looks utterly confused, but he hands me the guitar, which I pass to Elly, who looks as stricken as the guitarist.

I step up to the microphone. "Good Evening," I begin, my voice booming through Nico's enormous flat. "I'd like to thank you all for coming tonight. My father would have been delighted to see so many familiar faces and new friends." Someone claps, and I note Lydia near the front, gazing at me. *I wish she'd fuck off.* "I'd like to take this moment to introduce an extraordinary new talent. Miss Elly Carter."

I stick out my arm in Elly's direction. She rises to the occasion perfectly, stepping up to the microphone, whispering to me as she passes, "You'll pay for this later. Putting me on the spot like this."

"Play with the pros, El," I whisper back. "I know you can do it." My fingers trail over her lower back as she moves past me. I return to the crowd, letting her hold the stage alone.

Everyone begins to clap, and Kate is grinning, grabbing Nico's arm and hauling him closer to us. Mum is over to my left, gesticulating angrily at me as though she's about to fly off the handle, but I don't give a fuck. If she's going to surprise me with a load of unsolicited dates, then she ought to be prepared for a return shot.

"Well, this is unexpected," Elly begins, adjusting the guitar. "But I'm honoured to sing something while we're all gathered to remember Mr Lansen."

She begins to sing, and she's barely got a few bars in, her sultry voice floating over the crowd, before a voice beside me says, "Holy fuck, she is smoking."

I turn to find Seb Hawkston grinning, eyes pinned on Elly. "Jesus, Seb," I mutter, shaking my head. "Let it go."

"Oh, come on, Jacko. Tell me you're fucking her, because if you aren't, you're missing a fucking trick."

"Leave it," I say, without taking my eyes off Elly.

"Of course he's not sleeping with her. She's the waitress from the Marchmont." Lydia has appeared at my side. I swear the woman is following me. "When are we going on another date, Jack? I haven't heard from you for a while."

"We're not," I snap. "I'm seeing someone."

"Oh. Oh, gosh." Shock reverberates in her tone. "Really? Are you?"

I turn fully to Lydia, though I loathe to take my attention off Elly. But this needs to be done. I need to make it clear for this woman to get it through her thick skull. "I'm seeing someone else, and it's serious. I really like her, so I'm sorry, but we won't be going on another date. I'm sure you'll find someone more suited to you than I am."

Lydia's face blanches. "Oh. Jack." Her eyes flash to Elly, who's still singing her heart out. "Is it the waitress?" Her voice is thick with disdain.

"Fuck's sake, Lydia. Her name is Elly. And yes, it's her."

Fury emanates from Lydia's eyeballs like jets of hydrochloric acid, but before she can respond, Seb's hand slaps my back.

"Yes, mate. I fucking knew it." He sounds so delighted, you'd think he was the one sleeping with Elly. It's strangely endearing that he's so enthused. "Well done."

I ignore him, turning back to the only person who matters. Elly's song is finishing, and all I want to do is rush up to her, take her in my arms and kiss her. I can't seem to hear her sing without being nearly overwhelmed with desire.

Elly's taking a bow, but she catches my eye, and I tilt my head in the direction of the cloakroom, and I know she'll follow me when she can. I make my excuses, leaving Lydia with Seb, and Lydia's glare is so vicious that I feel it searing into my shoulder blades even after I've walked away.

27
ELLY

My heart is racing after that performance. Jack is constantly pushing me to do things I'd never do, but when it goes as well as that did, I don't mind. If only I could have channelled a little of that confidence when I went to meet Robert Lloyd.

If Jack had been at my side then, would I have managed to hold it together?

Before I can worry that Jack is somehow integral to me taking these steps, Kate, teary-eyed, rushes over to ask me if Jack and I had planned that performance because it was brilliant. I tell her we hadn't, but I'm thrilled to have been able to contribute to an evening like this for her dad. I give her a hug and tell her I love her, and she clutches me tight before she excuses herself so she can go and socialise with her dad's old friends before they leave.

As soon as she's gone, I rush off in the direction Jack went. I'm keen to find him. That subtle nod of his head was enough to have my pussy clenching. He said we wouldn't tell anyone about us, but it's clear he wants something to happen.

I turn a corner in Nico's enormous flat, and there he is, leaning against the wall, scrolling on his phone. I watch him for a moment, taking him in. As though he senses my presence, he looks up, an almost startled expression on his face that dissolves into a sexy smile when he registers me.

"You prick," I say, walking towards him. "You totally sprung that on me."

He's still grinning when I lace my arms around his neck, and he pulls me close, but I can tell he's a little tense. I assume he's worried his mother or Kate might find us here.

"You were brilliant," he says, his voice hot and low against my cheek. "I bet everyone in the room wanted to fuck you."

"Did you want to?"

"Yes." He leans into me and I can feel how hard he is. "Obviously."

Arousal blasts through me, faster than lightning. "Shit, Jack," I whisper, but before he can respond, his phone buzzes where he's holding it against my hip. I lean back. "Am I interrupting? You weren't working, were you?"

He nods. *Of course he was working.* "Checking emails."

"Hmm." I kiss him on the lips as I take the phone from him and put it on the table. "Can we not work right now?"

He groans, but it's lusty, not exasperated. "What do you want to do?"

I want to ride him until I ache, but I pause, assessing him. "Are you okay?" I think of Kate's teary expression. "Given this is an event for your dad, I was wondering—"

"No. We're not talking about my dad now. I'm fine." He kisses me again, tilting his hips towards me. *Fuck. He's so hard.* "Tell me what you want to do," he whispers.

Encouraged, I slide my hand over his crotch. "What do you think I want to do?"

He gives me a sly look. "Here? In the corridor?"

I tilt my head. "Not into public sex?"

He smirks. "Not when my mother is in the building." He grabs my arse with both hands. "We should go in here." He takes my hand and opens the nearest door, leading me into a large bathroom.

He locks the door behind us, and we're on one another in seconds, hands grabbing, fingers tearing at clothes. He's kissing me ravenously, his fingers in my hair. I can't get enough of him. I need to merge right into him, to become one with him. The wanting is at levels I've never experienced before. The kiss feels like it lasts forever and no time at all; everything distorts when I'm with Jack.

I break off, whispering, "I'm wet for you."

He groans and tips his head back, exposing his throat, peppered with stubble. "Fucking hell. You're worse than me." He says it like I'm wearing him thin, but he smiles like he loves it. His hands are greedy as they rush to pull up my skirt. He shifts my panties to one side and slides a finger inside me, his eyes going wide at how slick I am. "You're so filthy. You know that?" he murmurs against my ear as he pumps his finger in and out of me, and I moan as I grind against his hand. "Anyone could find us here."

"Exactly," I say, all breathless. "So make it quick. I've waited all day, and I know you have a ton of condoms in your pocket."

Jack mutters under his breath as he removes his finger from me and tugs a condom out while I wriggle out of my panties. I make fast work of his trousers, releasing his stiff cock, and he rips the packet open with his teeth and sheaths himself quicker than I've ever seen it done.

He presses me against the wall and lines himself up at my entrance, a look of intense focus coming over him as he plunges into me. The sudden sensation of fullness goes some way to satisfy the empty ache low in my core. I hook my legs around his hips and he drives into me, over and over, pinning me in place.

I can see us in the mirror, him fucking me hard, thrusting into me. His muscled arse is perfection, moving that way. I begin to whimper, and Jack grunts in my ear. Suddenly, he shifts us, lifting me onto the counter.

It takes a moment to settle into our new position, but when we do he nods at where our bodies meet and says, "Look at you. Look at how you take me." I lean back and he slows down, sliding in and out as we both watch, transfixed. It's unbelievably hot, seeing my body swallow his cock inch by inch, the cream of my juices streaking the condom.

With one hand I find my swollen clit and begin to move my fingers over it in circles, and Jack latches onto the motion, pupils dilated until they're little more than black pits of desire. "That's it," he coaxes. "Faster."

I obey, my fingers flicking over my clit at a pace that sends electric currents spinning out from the bundle of nerves. My climax approaches like the swell of a wave, inevitable and inescapable. I want to drown in it and pull him under with me. "Oh, God, so good...it's so good," I call out, delirious with pleasure.

"I love how much you love this," he murmurs. "Let me hear you scream."

And I do. The noises coming from my lips are loud and unreserved, driven by arousal so fierce that I don't care who hears me.

"Fuck, oh, fuck, Jack." I'm frantically rubbing at myself, lust turning my movements frenzied as the buzz of my approaching orgasm grows.

"Hold it," he rasps. "Don't come without me."

"I can't, I can't..." I wail as my orgasm rips through me, leaving me shuddering in Jack's arms.

This is my safe space. Here, with him.

"Wow, El," Jack breathes. "No one fucks me like you do." I know he's close too as his relentless pounding slows, his thrusts growing irregular, until he jerks into me, panting and holding me close. "Fuuuuuck," he groans, as he empties himself inside me.

I go limp, linking my arms around his neck to stop myself from slumping in a heap, and we breathe in each other's breaths. There's a tension to the moment of our comedown, as though we ought to fill the silence with those three tiny words. They're practically knocking behind my teeth.

I love you, I love you, I love you.

"I love the way you fuck me," I whisper instead, and he kisses me deep, and I disappear into the warmth of his tongue, the feel of his lips on mine.

A bang on the door shocks us both. Someone is outside.

And I was being *so loud.*

"I'm waiting out here," comes a woman's voice. She sounds annoyed.

Shit. How long have we been in here?

The door handle rattles. Thank goodness we locked it.

Jack rests his forehead against mine, his breaths still coming rapidly. "Damn it." We stay like that for a few moments, until our breathing settles.

"We have to come out," I hiss. "We can't stay in here now."

Jack groans and pulls out of me, discarding the condom and tucking himself away. I hop off the counter.

There's another bang on the door, and Jack emits a low Jack curse. "Sniff. Rub your nose. Make it look like we were doing coke."

I bristle. "You'd prefer whoever is out there to think we're doing drugs rather than hooking up?"

He shrugs, and half a laugh escapes him. "Maybe."

"Should I be insulted?"

He grabs me and pulls me to him. "God no," he growls, and he kisses me again, rougher this time. "You're wonderful. Perfect. I'd fuck you again right now if I could. But whoever is out there doesn't need to know what we were doing in here."

I push off him to fix my dress and smooth my hair—as much as my curls can be smoothed—in the mirror. "Okay. Let's go."

He unlocks the door, and the two of us walk out, shameless, right into Lydia.

Awkward.

Jack looks so shocked that he completely forgets to touch his nose or pretend he's been snorting cocaine. "Lydia. Hi." He sounds robotic; there isn't an ounce of genuine greeting in his words.

She looks us both up and down, her face a parody of revulsion. I glance at Jack, taking in the way his thick, dark hair is all mussed. It couldn't be more obvious that I just hand my hands in it. But maybe, *maybe*, she hasn't noticed.

We push past her and just as I think we're safe—

"It's disrespectful, doing that in someone else's house."

My heart races and Jack mutters another curse. Together we turn to face her where she's standing, one hand on her hip, glaring at us.

Jack plants his feet to the floor, pulling himself up taller. "I don't know what you think we were—"

Lydia cuts him off. "I know exactly what you were doing. I could hear you. They could probably hear you in the main room. And at your father's memorial event. It's shameful."

Jack's mouth opens, but his jaw is tight, his expression full of regret.

Lydia pulls a disgusted face at him, then at me. "I'll find another bathroom to use." She turns and strides away from us, and we stand in silence, watching her go.

"Fuck." Jack's head jerks once as he utters the word. "That was unfortunate."

My heart is still hammering, and it's not because we were caught having sex. It's because we were caught by *Lydia*. She might have no rights over Jack, but the memory of her warning me not to touch him hangs in the air like a whiteout on a mountain. *Dangerous*. "She'll tell your mum, won't she?"

Jack nods. "Likely. Let's go and have fun while we can."

28
JACK

The later it gets, the more the party loosens up. This is what Dad would have wanted. He always loved a party, and if he could see us enjoying ourselves, I know it would please him. Mum and others of her generation—Dad's old friends—have mostly gone home. The band has called it a night, but Elly has been singing a cappella, filling the room with the sensual sound of her voice.

It makes me want to fuck her all over again. And again. And again.

It blows my mind that she can be so talented, so unbelievably sexy, and yet be content to waste her talent in the Marchmont Arms. There's no way I'm letting that happen.

At one point, I lead Elly to a darkened corner and we begin to dance, my hands straying over her shoulders and down her spine until I have her arse cupped in both hands. My mouth is on her neck, my lips touching the skin, my nose inhaling her citrus scent. I want to fucking eat her, swallow her right down so she can never leave me.

I've never felt anything like this before.

"Get a room, Lansen," Seb calls out as he approaches us. He's wielding a bottle of tequila, doling out shots to everyone he passes as though we're still at university.

We break apart, and Seb pours us each a shot. When he moves away Elly says, "We're not being very subtle. Maybe we should hold off. Wait until we get home. We've already been caught once."

"I never want to wait with you."

Her face lights up with a smile, and she taps the end of my nose with her fingertip. "Me neither. But what was it you said? Something about it being sweeter if you have to wait."

"Did I say that?"

"Yes."

I give her a dubious look. "I'd like to formally retract that statement. I'm all about instant gratification now."

She laughs, giving me a disapproving glance as she returns to the main party area again, and when she's gone I feel oddly bereft.

She's the only person I want to spend my time with. The thought unnerves me a little. It feels serious, and I'm not sure I'm ready for that, even though it's what I said to Lydia to get her to back off.

But fuck, if I don't love being with her.

It's after midnight by the time Elly strolls towards me again. Everyone who's still here is drunk or high and draped over the furniture like yesterday's clothes.

"Let's go home," she says when she reaches me. "I'm ready to call it a night."

"Me too." I reach for my phone, and my stomach plunges. I don't have it. I slap my other pockets, trying to hide my concern from Elly.

I quickly run through my memories of when I last had it. I was using it outside the bathroom to look at the photos I took of Elly. The photos I promised her I would delete, but never did. I'm pretty sure she'd be pissed if she knew, so when she asked what I was doing, I lied.

"Can you tell the driver we're coming? He's waiting outside," I say, forcing myself to sound calm. "I'll get our coats."

Elly nods, and I dash back down the corridor to the bathroom. I know I had my phone in my hand, but then Elly wanted to fuck and I have no idea what I did with it after that. She's a total distraction.

Heart thudding, I approach the table I was standing beside when Elly propositioned me, but even from here I can see the phone's not there. I crouch down, checking beneath the table. It's not there either. *Shit. Did I really leave it here? Or did I take it into the bathroom? Did I leave it somewhere else?*

I can't remember. I've had too much champagne.

I check the bathroom, but it's not there either. Lydia was waiting out here, right next to the table, when we came out. Maybe she picked it up. Gave it to Kate. I grab our coats from the cloakroom and head back to the party.

When I find Kate, she's lounging on the sofa, her bare feet resting in Nico's lap. "Have you seen Lydia?" I ask.

She raises an unfocused gaze to mine. She looks physically and emotionally exhausted, and more drunk than I am. Not that I blame her; losing dad was tough for both of us, but it hit Kate especially hard. Even after all this time, she still struggles with his absence. "No," she slurs.

"She was with Seb last time I saw her," Nico says. He doesn't sound drunk, but he's not fully concentrating. He's too concerned with Kate. "You know what he's like. They're probably going at it in a spare bedroom." He eyes me for a moment. "I thought she was into you, mate. No hard feelings, eh?"

"None at all." I lean over the sofa, trying to get my sister's attention. "Look, Kate, I can't find my phone. But it's here. It's somewhere in the flat. I had it earlier. I've got to head home, but can you look for it? If you find it, call Elly and ask to speak to me. Okay?"

Kate mumbles something, and I know she's possibly too drunk to listen, but Nico says, "Sure. Where did you last have it?"

"Outside the cloakroom." I rake a hand through my hair. "I think. I can't remember."

Nico nods. "Don't worry. It'll be safe here. I'll get my driver to bring it to you when we find it tomorrow."

Thank fuck someone's listening. "Thanks. It's important."

He rolls his eyes. "You'll survive one night without it."

29
JACK

The morning after the party, a lurch of guilt rouses me. *My phone. Where the fuck is it?*

But then, almost immediately, I notice Elly sleeping next to me, and the guilt calms. If Elly is here, everything is all right. The rest can wait.

A strip of light between the curtains falls over the bed, leaving her in the spotlight. Which is exactly where she should be, and where I'll make sure she is once we've got her over whatever block is holding her back from owning her talent.

She's sleeping on her front, her mass of curls spilling over my pillow, her back rising and falling in a relaxed rhythm. I can't believe she's here. It's the same feeling every morning, as though I'm drifting through a dream. After all the years of barbs and teasing and ridiculous banter... and how many times she's pissed me off in the past... I've known her for a decade, more or less, but never like this. Never soft and vulnerable and *mine*.

I stroke a fingertip down her spine, and she murmurs into the pillow. "Let me sleep. You've exhausted me."

Her grumpy voice brings a smile to my lips and warms my heart. *Fuck, I'm in too deep with this woman, but I don't care.* I kiss her shoulder blade. "You have to get up, El."

"Why? It's Sunday."

"Because I booked you into a mate's studio. Recording time."

She jolts up to sitting, eyes wide and pinned on me, but I'm staring at her perfect breasts because she's just exposed them and it's been a good couple of hours since I last saw them. I reach for one, needing to run my finger over that small pink nipple. Elly slaps my hand away. "You did what?"

I shift back, surveying her, trying to get a read on this reaction. "Are you mad?"

"No." She squeals and throws her arms around my neck, kissing me full on the mouth. It only takes a second for what was an excited slam of her lips to mine to turn into something else entirely, and I break off before I get too aroused. "We have to stop..."

"Do we?"

"Today, yes."

She shoots me a sly look before she jumps out of bed, and I get a tantalising glimpse of her naked form before she disappears into the bathroom. *My bathroom.* I hear the water turn on and a blissful satisfaction rolls over me. *She's showering in my shower.*

I must be far gone for her if the fact she's making herself at home in my space makes me feel like this... all warm and contented.

The doorbell rings, hauling me from my thoughts. *Who is here this early on a Sunday?*

I push back the covers, pull on a hoody and boxers, and head downstairs. As I approach the door, the bell rings again. Whoever is out there is impatient. Maybe even irate.

When I open the door, Kate is standing on the doorstep, wrapped up in a coat and scarf. She has a furious expression on her face and at first she doesn't acknowledge me, instead tilting her head and peering over my shoulder as though she's looking for someone else, but, seeing no one, she fixes her gaze on me and holds out my phone without a word.

I have no idea what she's thinking, or why she's decided to deliver my phone in person despite the fact she must have a cracking hangover after last night. Cautiously, I take it from her. "Thanks. Where was it?"

"The table outside the bathroom. Exactly where you said you left it. I found it this morning."

"That's weird. I swear I check—"

"Are you sleeping with Elly?"

The question cracks out like an accusation, and my heart rolls like a die. "You looked at my phone?" I squeeze the handset tighter, panic setting in that Kate has been riffling through my photos.

Kate draws back, her upper lip curling. "Of course I didn't look at your phone." She says it with such disdain, as though it's insulting that I'm asking whether she would invade my privacy like that, and I know in a flash of clarity that she never would.

Still standing on the doorstep, Kate stamps her feet one after the other, not in irritation, but because it's so cold out here. I'm being rude, not letting her in, so I back up against the front door, opening it wider, and she brushes past me towards the kitchen. I follow behind, aware of a prickling sensation inside my body, as though it's preparing for a fight.

In the kitchen, Kate paces back and forth, twisting one of the buttons on her coat. I stand still, watching her until she halts and brings her attention to me. "Is it true? Are you sleeping with her?"

"Why are you asking?"

"Mum told me you were. She's freaking out because apparently you and Elly were going at it in the bathroom of Nico's flat last night."

"Mum? But how—"

"She phoned me this morning at the crack of dawn to ask for confirmation, and I couldn't give it to her. And you know what I thought? I thought, there's no way Jack would screw around with my best friend." The look on Kate's face is one of desperation, and her voice is thin. She's speaking fast and it feels like my brain has to do cartwheels to catch up. "There's just no way you'd do that, right? Especially not in Nico's flat. That's my *home*. I thought, surely he wouldn't fuck my best friend in the bathroo—"

"Shit. Kate, hold on a sec." I hold up a hand to stave her off. "I just woke up."

Kate pauses. "Is it true? Did you fuck Elly in—"

I let out a groan, and in response Kate lets out a little gasp, one hand rising to cup her mouth. "You did. Oh, my God. How could you? She's my best friend and I love her and if you are using her because it's convenient, I swear I will—"

"I'm not. That's not what this is. Fuck's sake. Is your opinion of me that low?"

The silence that follows is so onerous I wonder if it could crush us. Kate's eyes look watery, and my breathing turns shallow. "There's no evidence to the contrary," she admits, although she looks heartbroken to say it. "You've never been serious about anyone. I guess I didn't think you could do it, and when I heard it was Elly this time, I panicked. I don't want her to get hurt."

An uncomfortable squeeze occurs in my chest. "Fuck, Kate." The words come out low and deep, and I rub a hand down my face. Kate winces in response, as though she knows I've taken a hit.

We stare at one another, and I can't get mad at her because, as much as I wish she wasn't, she's right. I'm not sure I thought I had it in me to have a serious relationship, or if I even wanted to, either. This thing with Elly, and how gloriously fucking happy it makes me, has come as a surprise.

Kate puts a hand to her forehead. "Can I get a glass of water? I feel like crap."

I get a glass, fill it, and hand it to her. She gulps half of it before setting it down on the table. She leans her hand next to it, as though she might fall over without the support.

I wait a few moments in case Kate has anything else to say, but when she doesn't speak, I do. "Did Mum say how she knew?" A nasty sensation ripples through me, bringing with it a certainty I don't need to voice, but I do anyway. "It was Lydia, wasn't it?"

"Yeah. She told Mum she caught you coming out of the bathroom. Said the two of you looked guilty as sin, and the noises…" Kate presses two fingers between her brows and shuts her eyes, while I cringe because it makes me sound like a teenager who can't keep his dick in his pants. She clears her throat, making eye contact when she continues. "Lydia was very upset about it. She really likes you. And Mum *loves* her. I think the two of them had plans to see you going down the aisle before Easter, and now you've gone and messed it all up for the sake of a 'quick fuck in the loo'." Kate uses her fingers as quotation marks. *Are those the words Mum used? Jesus.*

"That's nonsense."

"Not to Mum, it isn't. She's been screaming at me over the phone, saying you're a deviant and she's on her way back to London to rescue you from the clutches of 'that harlot'."

I cover my face with my hands. "Oh, fuck."

"Fuck is right. And you know she's always thought Elly's a loose cannon. Can't get her head around the 'wants to be a musician' thing. Thinks she's a wastrel." Kate fills her cheeks with air and blows it out. "Didn't help that you were always complaining about how she never paid her rent on time." Filled with regret, I let my eyes flicker shut for a moment. "And now she's convinced Elly's a she-devil who's dead set on seducing her perfect son. She's coming to stage an intervention."

"She can't do that."

Kate lets out a sharp burst of laughter that sounds anything but amused. "This is Mum we're talking about. She can do anything she wants. She left half an hour ago so if you don't want her smashing your door down and carving Elly's insides out, then you need to get out of the house." Kate picks up her water and finishes the rest. "You've put Elly right in the firing line. Don't fuck with her. She's important to me, and if you break her heart, I will skewer yours and cook it on the barbecue."

There's something adorable about just how hard Kate is willing to fight for Elly, but it still annoys me. "I'm not fucking with her, but that's all I'm giving you because this is none of your business. In fact, you're nearly as bad as Mum, coming round here to ask me about this. It's interfering and—"

"Totally different. Mum's coming because she doesn't like Elly. I'm here because I love her."

Kate's words make my heart hurt, for a variety of reasons. "Neither of you trust me, though." She bites into her bottom lip, shame washing over her face, and when it's apparent she's not going to contradict me, I check my watch. "Elly and I have to head out soon. We're going to a recording studio."

"You're what?" Kate asks, eyes wide.

"I booked her studio time, so she can record her—"

"You did that for her?" Kate sputters.

"Yeah, at Elmwood Studios."

Kate's lips part in a soundless '*wow*.' And it *is* impressive; there's no better place to record than Elmwood.

"I've set up all her social media channels too, so she can stream the music and make the videos. I've roped in one of the guys from the marketing team at work. Derek. Do you know him?" I continue, and Kate nods. "He does freelance for creatives, so he knows what he's doing in terms of positioning her." Excitement is burning through me, destroying my previous annoyance. The feeling is exactly the same as when I'm at work on a project that's definitely going to come off. It's a buzz... a high, and I know Kate can feel it emanating from me.

"Okay, wow," she says, in little more than a whisper. "You're invested."

"Hey."

The two of us turn to the sound of Elly's voice. She's standing there in the doorway, looking beautiful and happy and like she's been fucked all night, and at the sight of her I want to do it all over again. I have to hold myself back from pushing my sister out of the house so I can get on with it.

Elly's smile falters, taking in whatever it is she can see on our faces. She looks from Kate to me, then back to Kate. "What's going on?"

"I came to return Jack's phone. He left it at Nico's last night."

Under Kate's gaze, Elly's cheeks turn a little red. "Oh." There's a long, uncomfortable silence, only broken when Elly whispers, "You know." Kate quirks a brow, inviting clarification. "About us," Elly adds sheepishly.

"Yeah," Kate says. "I do. Can we talk?"

The two of them seem to have forgotten I'm there, so I announce that I'm going for a shower, and walk towards Elly. If we were alone I'd kiss her or pull her against me, but with Kate staring at my back, I can't do any of that. I'm about to keep walking past when Elly grabs my hand.

"You lost your phone?" she hisses, quiet enough that Kate won't be able to hear.

I shrug one shoulder. "Last night. But it was only at Nico's. I knew it was safe."

Her brow creases, and her blue eyes are pools of worry. "The photos. You deleted them, right?"

My pulse beats in my ears. *Would it be wrong to lie, if it soothes her concern?* Without thinking it through, I commit to the falsehood. "Yes." It's only a white lie. I'll delete them as soon as I have a moment.

Elly sags with relief. "Okay." She puts her hands on either side of my face and kisses me, brief and soft, and when it's over I don't hang around to hear whatever Kate has to say about it. I need to shower and get the fuck out of the house before Mum decides to show her face.

I'm halfway up the stairs when I take my phone from the pocket of my hoody and select every one of Elly's beautiful photos, intending to delete them. But right as my thumb hovers over the button, I can't press it. She's so beautiful, the photos so sexy, and what if this thing between us doesn't work out? What if Kate warns her off, and all I have left at the end are these pictures?

I can't delete them. *I can't.*

30
ELLY

When Jack has left the kitchen, Kate paces towards me, and my heart thuds like a bass drum. I have no idea what she wants to say about this, or what she thinks of it. I feel both guilty and defensive, and she hasn't said a word yet.

"I thought you didn't like my brother."

I brace at her statement, even though I'm not sure if she's accusing me of lying, or if she's genuinely curious.

My first impulse is to reply, "I don't," but even as the words rise, popping against my tongue, I wonder why. Why has that been my stance all these years? *I don't like Jack Lansen.* It's been a mantra I've lived with since the first time I met him at Kate's house when I was sixteen. I'd happily flirt with him and tease him, but I always maintained that I didn't like him.

Now that I think about it, I have no fucking clue why. Was it all the women? All the money? Am I really that judgmental?

If I dismiss those objections, I have nothing to back up my dislike. All this time, I've been fooling myself; trying to convince myself that I didn't like him. But I can't do that anymore.

Not only do I definitely like him, there's a chance that what I feel for him is more than that.

"I was wrong," I admit.

Kate's face is very still, and then she smiles. "God, you two," she says, as though we're kids who've exasperated her, and she can't believe the antics we've got up to while she's had her back turned. A tinge of worry creases her brow. "I hope you know what you're doing."

"I don't."

Kate tips her head back to look at the ceiling and lets out a sad-sounding sigh. "If it doesn't work out, promise me it won't affect our friendship. I won't have Jack messing this up for us." Her concern unsettles me. I don't want to consider how this could all go wrong. I'm not sure I feel secure enough to handle that yet. Kate must read all this on my face, because she hugs me and whispers, "I love you too, you know."

"Oh, I don't think he loves me," I choke out.

Kate doesn't reply, but she squeezes me a little tighter.

The studio owned by Jack's mate is none other than Elmwood Studios, owned by Dan Elmwood himself, where Amy Moritz recorded her first album, when she was only seventeen, which hit the top 50 in the US charts. She went from being unknown to world-famous almost overnight.

I'm completely overwhelmed. Walking into the building earlier, I wanted to grab Jack's hand and never let go; the excitement was almost too much to bear. The walls were plastered with Platinum records in sleek black frames and signed images of famous pop stars and rock bands.

Never in all my life did I really think I'd get to record in a place like this, let alone with Dan himself, who is one of Jack's old friends from school. He made time for us on a Sunday. He said it's a favour, but I'm sure Jack must have paid for the time, and it can't have been cheap.

We've been here all day, and Jack has taken photos of me the entire time. He must have hundreds by now. It's been hard to concentrate, with him simmering in the corner, taking more photos, reminding me of how he took pictures of me on the piano... I'm blushing at the memory.

"You won't have any storage left if you keep clicking like that," I say to him.

"I'll shift you to my hard drive." He raises a suggestive eyebrow, and my responding giggle sounds ridiculous.

When I've finished, we gather our things and say thanks to Dan, who waves us off with a profusion of kind words about my work, looking as exhausted as I feel.

I shoulder my guitar as we make our way out onto the street. I need to go home and put my feet up.

"Shall we get dinner?" Jack says, as he takes my guitar from me without a word.

"I'd rather head home. I'm knackered."

A flinch skates across his face. *What's that about?* "We should eat out. I don't want to cook and I haven't stocked the fridge."

"I don't care. I'll have a slice of toast. I'm not hungry. I can't face eating out now. Let's just go home and be together."

There's that flinch again. A bolt of worry races up my spine.

"Okay," he says, but the tension in his voice suggests he's very much not okay at all, and he leads me back to his car without a word. I can sense there's something wrong, and for the duration of the drive back to his house, he's on edge. I can feel his energy scraping up against me. I figure he'll tell me what's wrong when he's ready, but I don't like it.

He parks up outside the house, a grim look on his face. And when he gets out of the car, he scans the surrounding area, peering into the shadows like he expects to be pounced on as we walk up to the front door.

"What the hell is wrong with you?" I ask. "You were moody in the car, and now we're here, you're all jumpy, like you think the bogeyman's going to spring out of the bushes."

He sighs. "Kate said Mum was coming up to see me."

Ah, that explains it. "God, I hate your mum. No offense. She's always so prickly and judgy. I think she hates me."

That grim expression fixes itself back on Jack's face. "She can be tough work," he concedes, but the tight set of his shoulders has sirens ringing in my head. His mum might be a dragon, but he's unnecessarily tense about the prospect of her being here.

"She doesn't have keys, does she? Is she gonna be in there?" I nod at the house, dreading the idea of having to deal with Mrs Lansen right now.

"She does not have keys to my house," Jack confirms.

"Then what are you worried about? It's late. She's not going to turn up now, is she? She probably came while we were out and went home again. Come on. Let's go have a cup of tea."

Jack presses his lips into a line and forges to the front door, but before he opens it, he turns back to me. "About last night, and Kate finding out about us—"

"Oh yeah, I was thinking about that too. How did she know? Did you tell her?"

"I didn't." He sighs and moves his hair from his forehead with one hand, surveying me for a moment. "You're beautiful."

His words slide inside and unravel me, and before he can say anything else, I pull him in for a kiss, and in seconds, his mouth is melting into mine. Kissing someone has never felt as intense as it does with Jack. One touch of his tongue against mine, and my whole body is on fire.

"We don't have to stop now, do we?" I whisper, recalling how he said we didn't have time to fool around this morning.

He frowns like he thinks it's a bad idea, and takes his keys from his pocket to open the front door, but I put my hand on his arm to stop him.

He throws me a questioning look. "Two seconds and we'll be inside," he says.

"I'm serious. I want you now."

He draws back, a smirk on his face. "Really? In the porch?" He hasn't opened the front door yet, and he glances to the street beyond his front garden and the low wall that separates us from the pavement. There's a street lamp a little way away, but here, in the shadows, no one can see us and the street is empty. There's no one around.

"Right here," I confirm.

He puts down my guitar and pulls me into him, kissing me again, one of his hands tangling in my hair, cupping the back of my head.

And then, again, those words come to mind.

I love you.

I kiss him deeper to drive them away. *I cannot fall for this man.* His hand runs up my thigh and I hike my leg onto his hip. He shifts us so my back is pressed against the wall.

We're going to have sex, right here on the doorstep.

"Well, this is just lovely."

Jack's body goes rigid, and my heart seizes, panic raging through me. Someone else is here. *Close.* Far too close.

"Shit, Mum. What the hell?" Jack blurts as he releases me and I totter a moment, unsteady on my feet. I smooth out my dress, my heart racing as I studiously avoid looking at Mrs Lansen, standing on the garden path only a few feet away.

Jack turns away to rearrange himself, and his breath fogs out into the cold night air. I hadn't noticed how cold it was when Jack's body was pressed against me...

Finally, Jack turns back to his mother. "You can't show up here like this."

"Well, here I am." Mrs Lansen spreads her hands like her appearance is a party trick. "Are you going to invite me in?"

"No. Fuck. No. Not right now." Jack rubs the heel of his hand over his forehead. His eyes are darting all over the place. "We've had a long day—"

"You don't appear to be lacking energy," Mrs Lansen says, her voice all clipped and displeased.

Jack glares at his mother, but there's something shifty in the way he's standing. The way his gaze is so unanchored, and the sight of him unnerved like this strikes fear into a deep part of me. "Whatever you're here to say, please come back tomorrow. Or we can talk on the phone."

"No." Mrs Lansen steps closer, wagging a finger at Jack. "Your behaviour is unacceptable. We have to talk about this now. I heard a rumour that you were having sex in the bathroom at your father's charity fundraiser, so I came to find out if it was true. And now that I'm here, I see it is."

Jack grits his teeth, but makes no objection. And I can see why. What we did, repeated in Mrs Lansen's clipped voice, sounds awful.

"Do you realise the damage that does to our reputation? Our family name? Clearly, Eleanor is leading you astray."

I suck in a sharp breath, her words sweeping away my ability to speak. But then a voice in my head pipes up that maybe she's right. *It was my idea to have sex at the memorial event. I wanted it. And now, here on the doorstep... that was my idea too.* Shame curdles my insides, and bile burns the back of my throat.

"She isn't. I can make my own decisions," Jack snaps.

But Mrs Lansen isn't looking at him. Her angry gaze is fixed on me. "I know what you're doing, trying to ensnare my son. Are you trying to get pregnant? So he'll have to support you? So you can live off his money—"

"Mum. Fuck," Jack yells. "Shut up."

Mrs Lansen turns to him. "Tell me you're using condoms. Tell me she's not going to be the accidental mother of my grandchildren."

I can't move. I can't process. *Accidental mother? Grandchildren?* "You think I want his money?" I ask, even though it's not the most pressing question I have, but I can't get my head straight to work out exactly what is.

Mrs Lansen's lips pucker, and she eyes me like I'm nothing but dirt. "It's not as if you have any of your own, or are capable of making any. I won't let you exploit him."

I'm freezing up, unsure what to do in the face of this attack. My brain is swirling with thoughts, trying to make this situation make sense. Does she know about the game? Does she know Jack was going to pay me? "I haven't touched the money."

Mrs Lansen draws herself up tall. "What money?"

Jack storms down the steps and yanks his mother's arm. "Go home. You shouldn't be here."

She tugs out of his grip. "What money is she talking about? Are you paying her? Are you? Is she a whore?"

"Jesus, no." Jack's furious voice cracks through the night air. "Please, leave."

His mother's face becomes determined. "You mark my words. She'll get herself pregnant, and you'll be saddled with her for the rest of your life. Anchored to a little slut. If you're not paying her now, you'll be paying her a fortune then."

That's it. That's enough. My frozen shell shatters and I trip down the steps after Jack, calling to his mother. "How can you be so vicious? We haven't done anything wrong."

"Oh, I beg to differ. This is all wrong." Her finger wags again, waving between me and Jack like a windshield wiper. "I will not let you lure my son into your trap. He'll never take you seriously. Never."

My stomach drops. *Is that true?* I knew this woman hated me, but I'd never been on the receiving end of her vitriol this way before.

"Mum, stop," Jack orders.

Mrs Lansen focuses on Jack. "I will not. At some point, this behaviour of yours will catch up to you, and one of these women will get pregnant. Dear Lord, let it not be this one." She points at me without looking at me, then adds. "She's a waitress, Jack, and she'll never be anything more than that. You must have told me a million times how useless she was. Never paying her rent, making excuses, trying to scrape the pennies together every month from her ridiculous attempts at being a serious musician. You said so yourself, and now here you are, doing what you usually do, hooking up with whoever is nearest and easiest, even though they'll never be good enough. I'm putting a stop to it for your own good."

A lump rises in my throat, so large that it feels like my gullet might explode, bringing with it the urge to cry. I don't need to look over at Jack to know everything his mother said is true, because I can feel it in the way he's gone completely still, as though he's sensing the approach of the end of the world and knows he can't do anything about it.

But I ask anyway, my voice weak. "Did you? Did you say those things?"

The blank expression on his face gives way to one of distress and hopelessness, and I know, I *know*, he said it all. He thought it all. He might want to be with me now, but Jack Lansen—perfect, handsome, kind Jack Lansen, with his expensive shoes and his multimillion pound home—doesn't think I'm good enough. He didn't choose me. He chose the nearest woman. The *easiest* woman. And it's right there on his face for his mother to see.

It's humiliating. I feel so betrayed by this one beat of hesitation, so foolish to think this man might stick by my side, that I can't bear it.

He moves towards me. "El, this is bullshit. It doesn't matter what I said before. What matters is now. And now..." He pauses, and my heart feels like it's dangling on a thread.

"Now, what?" I whisper.

His gaze slides to his mother, who's standing there listening to every word. My heart pounds through each moment of silence, willing him to speak.

Whether it's two seconds or ten that I wait, I don't know, but Jack says nothing, and suddenly I can't stand another moment of it. I know what I want, and it's this man, but if he won't claim me in front of his mother, then maybe she's right. "Fuck you."

Jack stares at me like he can't believe this is happening, as though perhaps I'm the one whose behaviour is incomprehensible.

"Fuck you," I say again, and I turn and storm back up to the front door. Jack's key still dangles in the lock where he left it when he stopped to kiss me. I grab my guitar from where it's propped against the wall, twist the key, and force the door open.

Behind me, Jack is shouting obscenities at his mother that I can't make out. His voice is angry, rumbling with barely contained violence, but I shut out the sound. I step inside and turn to close the door, catching a glimpse of Jack striding towards me up the steps.

And then I slam the door and turn the lock.

31
JACK

I halt when Elly closes the door, a dark sense of doom spreading through me. This is so fucked up, and I have no idea how to put it right.

I spin back to my mother, who is still standing on the garden path, handbag clutched in front of her, wearing a twinset and pearls as though she's on her way to church, rather than to destroy my life.

"Why are you here?" I yell. "What possible reason could you have for showing up here and saying things that are so fucking cruel?"

Mum pulls back a fraction. "I'm protecting you. I've seen plenty of women like that girl in my life." She flaps a hand dismissively towards my front door. "I've been around long enough to know the type. Using their bodies and their pretty faces to catch a man. You might think you like her now, but it's a temporary madness. A hormonal melee."

I drag my hands down my face and let out a frustrated roar. "You need to leave. Right now."

"But darling, I only have your best interests at heart. She's not right for you. This is exactly why I made that list of potential wives. So that you wouldn't find yourself in—"

I hold up a palm. "I'm not having this conversation. What I do and who I see is none of your business. It hasn't been for a long time."

She folds her arms over her chest. "Well, yes. I would have thought that too, but if you will be having sex at your father's memorial event, or out here where anyone could see, then I'm forced to make it mine. You're quite clearly losing your head. You need someone to help you see that. Your behaviour is completely unacceptable, and if I can't set you straight as your mother, no one else will. No one cares about you the way I care, darling."

I step right up to her, looking down my nose. She doesn't even flinch at the way I'm crowding her. "Go home," I grit out. "You've made your point. Get off my property before I physically force you off. And I really don't want to have to do that."

Mum huffs. "You could have had Lydia Archer, and you chose this." She bats the back of her hand towards my front door again. "When you come to your senses, I'll be waiting." Her mouth puckers like an arsehole as she glares at me, but I don't give her an inch. She can fuck off right to hell for all I care.

She turns and lets herself out of the gate, and when she's out of sight I rush to the front door and try the handle.

Locked.

"El? Open the door. Let me in."

I press my ear to the wood, but hear nothing. I slam my hand against the door, making my palm sting. "You there? Come on, El. Please."

"Did you say that stuff about me?" Her voice is small.

The answer swells my throat, as though I'm allergic to it. "Not all of it." The silence that follows is like a vacuum, sucking out my insides. *Fuck.* "I'm sorry. It was before I knew you. Before we—"

"Go away."

I feel my heartbeat, anxious and rapid, in every cell in my body. "Can you open the door?"

The silence is broken only by the sound of Elly crying.

"Please, El. I'm so sorry. I don't think any of that stuff about you now. I think you're wonderful."

"Why didn't you say so? Why didn't you..." She fades out, sounding like she's choking on her words. *Why didn't I what?* My mind can't process shit right now.

"Please, let me in. This is what Mum wants. She's trying to drive us apart. Who cares what she thinks? I don't—"

"Don't what? Think any less of me? Because I'm a slut? A whore? A useless waitress who can't pay her rent? Fucking say it, Jack."

"Don't try and put words in my mouth. I don't think that. You're not." I sigh and lean against the wood. "I love the way you are. I fucking love it. I love everything about you. I love your voice and your music and your songs. I love the way you sing. The way you laugh. I love your eyes, and your hair, and that fucking nose piercing. And I love that you spread yourself on that fucking piano and let me take those photos. I love that you writhed on my lap and made yourself come. I love that you got on your knees in the kitchen and took me down your throat. Don't make it wrong. Don't let what my mother said make it wrong. It's not."

"She thinks I'm a gold digger. A slut."

"I don't give a shit what my mother thinks, and neither should you." I hang my head, fisting my hands so hard they hurt. "El... please, you're *my* slut, and I fucking love you for it."

A crushing pain grips my entire chest as the words leave my mouth, but it's the silence from the other side of the door that breaks me.

Nothing. She has nothing to say to me.

"Let me in," I murmur.

"Not tonight," she replies.

I hold my breath, and the pump of my blood whooshes through me so hard I can feel it in my fingertips. The wrenching sound of Elly's sobbing ekes through the door... she's breaking her heart just inches away from me, and I can't make it better. I can't fix it. I want to scoop her up in my arms and take away her pain. I want it so much that my body aches with it.

"Damn it, Elly. Open the door." The words grate against the inside of my throat, leaving it raw.

She doesn't respond, and I hear her move away, her footsteps fading as she retreats deeper into the house. I stay there, sitting on the top step outside the house for far too long, waiting for her to change her mind. I stay there so long that the cold numbs my fingers and toes.

I send message after message

Me: Sorry, sorry, sorry.
Me: What can I do to make it up to you?
Me: What do you need?
Me: Please, El. Let me inside. We can talk about this.

I lose count of how many times I say I'm sorry, but all my messages remain unread.

And then, after Elly's bedroom light goes on, and finally switches off again, signalling she's going to sleep, I send Kate a message.

Me: Can I crash at yours tonight?

The typing dots appear and disappear, but when she finally responds all it says is, ***Of course.***

Kate stares at me over the breakfast table in Nico's flat. "Mum turned up to save your soul, right?"

I let out a sigh that sounds like a groan. I don't want to have this conversation at all. "Yes. In all her glory, scratching her claws like a tiger."

Kate presses her lips together, and I know she's trying to contain the urge to say, '*I told you so*'.

Nico strides into the room. He's sharply dressed for work, whereas I'm completely dishevelled. I hardly slept. He hands me a fresh suit, shirt, and tie. "You'll be too broad for it, but it'll do for a day."

"Assuming she lets him back in," Kate says.

Nico chuckles, but I can hear the disapproval in it. "I'm going in early. You two take your time." He drains the rest of his tea, then gives Kate a peck on the lips before letting himself out.

When he's gone, Kate resumes her aggressive death stare.

"What?" I snap.

"You're crap at this relationship stuff."

I roll my eyes. I'm not going to let her lay into me about this, because I already know I'm shit at it. I don't need reminding. "I've never done this before."

Kate sighs. "Well, first—"

My phone rings. It's the bank. I signal to Kate to be quiet and answer it.

"Mr Lansen?" comes the voice on the other end.

"Speaking."

"There's been some unusual activity on your account. There's a large transaction pending, and I need your authorisation to clear it."

Low-level panic sets in. I'm not buying anything right now. *Jesus*. Fraud is not something I have time for. The hassle is a royal pain in the arse.

"It's your black card," the voice says.

I jerk upright in my chair, causing Kate to frown, gesturing at me with her hands and mouthing, "*What?*", as though it's crucial to her existence that she knows what's going on too.

The black card is the one I gave to Elly. The one I forced on her when she ripped up the cheque. The one I slid into her bra when she won the game. *Is she using it now, or has she lost it? Has it been stolen? Wouldn't she have mentioned that?*

"What's the transaction?" I ask.

The speaker clears his throat. "A car."

"A car?" I blurt, and Kate looks at me in alarm. "What kind of car?"

"The card is being used at the Lamborghini showroom in South Kensington."

I let the words beat around my skull for a moment, as if that might help me make sense of them. "Are you fucking kidding me?"

"Erm, no, sir. This is not a joke. Do I need to cancel the transaction?"

Kate is leaning right across the table, trying to hear what's happening.

I stand and cover the handset, then hiss at Kate. "Call Elly. Now." Kate doesn't move, so I repeat, angrily this time, "Now. Get her to tell you where she is, right fucking now. I think she's trying to use my credit card." Kate frowns, then looks alarmed for about half a second before she grins.

I shoo her away, aggressively mouthing, 'Now,' at which she dashes for her phone as though I've stung her with a cattle prod.

She swipes on the phone and puts it to her ear. The buzz of a ring sounds a few times before the line goes dead. Kate curses under her breath and tries again. She has to do it twice more before Elly's small and tinny voice says, 'Hello?'

Kate makes eyes at me and then walks away to the window, and proceeds to talk to Elly where I can't eavesdrop. I tug on my bottom lip as I wait, my mouth drying up.

"Sir? Are you still there?" says the voice at the end of my phone. I'd forgotten he was still on the line. "What do you want me to do about this transaction?"

"Leave it pending. I need to check something. I'll call you back."

"So I'm not authorising this purchase, sir?"

Fuck. "Not yet."

I hang up the call and wait for Kate to get off the phone. It feels like she's taking ages, so I start getting dressed in the suit Nico left for me, shoving my arms through the sleeves of the shirt, pulling on the trousers.

It's tight, but it'll have to do.

Kate hangs up and paces towards me. "Elly's angry and humiliated. She doesn't want to see you."

"Fuck that. Where is she?" I bark out.

Kate sighs, and I get the sense she never intended to keep this information from me. "South Kensington. In the Lamborghini show room."

I leave the flat so fast, I can't even make out what Kate is yelling after me.

32
ELLY

I don't know what propelled me here first thing in the morning. Maybe it was the aftereffects of Mrs Lansen's cruelty, or the upset that Jack wouldn't own his feelings in front of her.

Either way, when I woke up and saw Jack's black card sitting on my dresser, I knew I was going to use it. And now I'm sitting in the driver's seat of an orange Lamborghini. It's beautiful. The most amazing car I've ever been inside. I might be a little in love.

But apparently, you can't swan into the showroom and buy a Lamborghini off the shop floor like you're picking up groceries. Especially if your name isn't on the card you try to pay for it with. *Who knew?*

It's annoying because Jack deserved to wake up to me having spent hundreds of thousands on a flashy car that he would never buy. He's all class and subdued colours and sophistication. A sleek Bentley with soft leather and walnut interiors.

Not an orange Lamborghini. Because *Who the fuck buys an orange car?*

I snort at the memory of the night he picked me up in the rain, the two of us soaked by the water sprayed up by that orange car. I clasp my hands around the steering wheel, imagining driving this bad boy around town with the roof down, throwing my middle finger up to all the well-dressed arseholes in West London, of which Jack is one.

I'd race through a puddle if he was standing at the side of the road, and soak him to the bone. I'd fucking delight in it.

I try my best to look calm and collected, as if checking out expensive cars is something I do every day, rather than an impulsive petty action I've taken to piss off my boyfriend.

Is he my boyfriend?

Movement by the door snares my attention. Jack's here, striding towards me with an expression on his face like he wants to strangle me. My breath catches in my throat and my stomach flips—*good flips*—making me wonder if my fight-or-flight response is messed up.

Anyone else would be running from a man who looked like *that*. But here I am, buzzing with excited anticipation. *He came.*

I focus on the car salesman, smiling at him as though he's the most interesting man in the room, despite the fact my heart is hammering because of the furious man striding towards me.

"What the hell, Elly? A Lamborghini?" Jack says when he reaches me.

The salesman takes one look at Jack and scurries away to hide in the corner. *Coward.*

I try not to be affected by Jack's frustration. He's the one who messed up, not me. This—me being here, sitting in this car—is totally justified.

Isn't it?

"I like it." I flick my curls off one shoulder in an affected attempt at nonchalance. "It's very me, don't you think? Much better than that Bentley you're driving around in."

Jack mutters under his breath, then opens the driver's door. "Get out."

I stare at him. The air crackles. I say nothing, but my knuckles tighten on the steering wheel. I'm not following his orders. Not today.

When he realises I'm not going to move, he leans in and says, "Are we going to talk about last night, or are you just going to sit there, pretending you didn't try to spend nearly a million quid on my credit card? It's extremely passive-aggressive and potentially illegal."

"Arrest me then." I hold out both wrists and give him puppy-dog eyes.

His expression melts for a second, exposing a touch of amusement, but then he catches himself, forcing the anger to hold. "You're being very immature."

I laugh, one shrill burst that sounds unhinged. "Immature? I'm not the one who's too scared to tell his mummy how he feels."

He drags a hand through his hair, shifting it off his forehead. "Fuck's sake." It's a low curse, more exhalation than speech. "It's none of her business how I feel about you."

How does he feel about me? I keep gripping the steering wheel and refuse to look at him. I'm angry... *I am.* But coming here, trying to buy the car... it *is* immature. But I want his attention more than anything else. I want him to care...

The words spill from my mouth, almost without permission. "So you don't care what your mum thinks of me? About the stuff she said?"

Damn it. I was doing so well at playing the role of the scorned woman who doesn't give a rat's arse about all that nonsense, and now I've given it all away.

He puts a hand on the car door and leans towards me. "Am I going to have to get this tattooed on my forehead? No, I don't give a shit what my mother thinks, and I should never have let her speak to you that way. I'm deeply sorry about that. I swear I'll never let anyone say a bad thing about you, ever again. Now, get out of the car."

The words are what I wanted to hear, but the tone is wrong. Harsh. Exasperated.

"Nope."

"Nope?" He holds my gaze for a few seconds, like he's waiting for me to say more, but when I don't, he huffs. "You locked me out my fucking house. And now this?" He gestures to the showroom, the car.

"I was annoyed."

"Well, so am I." He storms towards the desk. He's probably going to get me kicked out. Maybe even arrested. I sit back, cross my arms over my chest, watching him, waiting for someone to come and drag me out of here by the hair.

I don't know how long I wait... long enough to get so bored that I end up scrolling on my phone. I only look up when I sense Jack coming back. He doesn't look angry anymore. He looks pleased with himself. As he gets closer, he throws something at me.

I drop my phone to my lap and catch the missile.

Keys.

I'm speechless. For a moment I stare at them, then up at him, but he's not where he was a second ago. He's opening the passenger door and getting in beside me.

"You do have a license, right?" he asks as he slams the door. "I hope you're a good driver because driving a car with an engine like this is not the same as a regular vehicle. It'll shoot off like a rocket. You'll probably need lessons to learn how to handle it properly."

My jaw hangs slack. "What?"

Jack sits back, that devilish smile back on his face. "She's yours." He tips his chin to indicate the car.

My stomach sinks to my tailbone. *What the actual fuck?* I rotate in my seat, so I'm facing him. "You bought it?"

He smirks. "You looked so good in it."

My heart begins to thump a panicked beat, and the sensation swells until it feels like my heart is the only organ in my body. *No way.* "You bought the car because *I look good in it*?"

"Yup."

I sit back, hands raised, but not touching the wheel. "No. Oh, no," I bleat.

Jack scratches the scruff on his jaw. *So casual.* "You'd filled in most of the paperwork anyway. If you'd told me before, we could have planned this. Customised it. Personalised this beast." He taps the dashboard. "We could have put one on order." He flashes me that cheeky smirk again, but I'm so stunned, that it doesn't affect me as it normally would. "Very amateur to buy whatever's on the shop floor."

Amateur.

"You're kidding me." My fingers are tingling. "You bought this?"

"You wanted it, didn't you?"

My brain is misfiring, and everything I thought I wanted crumbles. I didn't really want this car at all. I wanted to piss Jack off. I wanted him to say he loved me. How I could have wanted both those things, and expected one stupid action to achieve them simultaneously, I have no idea. I wasn't thinking straight. But one thing is clear: I never expected him to *actually* buy the fucking car.

I feel faint. "Oh, no. No way. You have to return it. Take it back."

Jack starts to laugh, his sexy smile exposing dazzling white teeth.

"What?" I gasp. "Why are you laughing? Is this a joke? Are you joking? Please say you're joking."

"It's not a joke." He points to where the staff are opening the glass doors so I can drive the car out of the showroom. "Let's get out of here."

"No. No way. I could buy a flat with this car. A house. I could move to the countryside and retire for the rest of my life. It's insane to spend this much on a vehicle. *Insane*. I can't let you do this."

He chortles. "You *can't let me do this*? You're the reason I'm here." He slaps the dashboard. "Let's go."

Oh, my God, what have I done? I'm an idiot. "Shit. No. No, no..." I open the door and stumble backwards out of the car.

I'm freaking out. My hands are flapping like I can shake out the adrenaline. *This is crazy.*

Jack gets out of the car, looking wary now rather than amused. He approaches me with his arms outstretched, as though I'm a cornered animal liable to run. "Give me the keys. I'll drive." His voice rings with a decisive authority, but I'm too spun out to appreciate it.

"No, no, no..."

All eyes are on us. We're a spectacle, and being watched makes my panic rise further. Jack, on the other hand, looks totally calm. He holds eye contact, grounding me, and my heart rate slows. He takes a cautious step closer and clasps my hands in his, stilling their motion. His touch is so warm. *Safe.* "Money aside, do you like the car?" he whispers.

I screw my eyes shut, feeling him tease the keys from my grip. I let him take them.

"El, do you like the car?" he repeats.

How does he make the question sound both seductive and calming? My resistance disintegrates. I suck in a breath, and on the exhale admit, "Yes. I love the car."

"Then it's yours. I want to give you everything, El." He pulls me into his embrace, holding me tight against him. I'm in a cloud of his scent, his body heat, the soft fabric of his suit, and the tension slides off me. But, wait...

"You smell different," I state.

"It's Nico's suit," he says, his voice rumbling against me.

"Oh." *That's my fault.* "Sorry."

He squeezes me tighter, acknowledging my apology, and whispers into my hair, "I'm sorry too. Let me drive you home."

I let him guide me back to the car, and he opens the passenger door to help me inside. He leans across me to buckle me in as I sit in a daze, overwhelmed by his sudden proximity. One night apart, and I missed him so, *so* much.

I want to pull him against me, kiss him, maybe even force his head between my legs, but he's gone again before I've collected my thoughts.

He gets into the driver's seat and starts the engine, which revs like nothing I've ever heard. I slam my hands over my ears. "Shit."

Jack side-eyes me, breaking out into another one of those breathtaking smiles. And then he drives the ridiculous orange Lamborghini off the forecourt.

"I fucking hate orange," he mutters, glancing across at me. "But I love you."

33
ELLY

I'm ecstatic. Floating. Buckled into an orange car.

I watch Jack drive for a few moments, relishing the concentration that washes over his handsome features as he focuses on the road. He looks huge in this car, and we're so low to the ground.

He loves me.

I want to say it back. Want to scream it. *I love you. I love you. I love you.* Instead, I say, "You're crazy."

He smiles, keeping his eyes on the road. "Nothing says I'm sorry like a Lamborghini, right?"

"I thought it said I love you."

He chuckles. "Yeah, that too." He reaches one hand towards me and I thread my fingers through his large, warm ones. He squeezes my hand. "Are we okay?"

I make him wait for it, just a little while. "Yeah. Your mum is a bitch, though."

He glances at me. "You know I'm not her, right?"

A strange darkness settles in me. "I do, but a mother's influence is like a virus. It can linger, dormant, for a really long time until something triggers it. We think we're all free and independent, but we're not."

Jack shudders. "Sounds horrific." He's quiet for a moment. "What did your mother say, then? What did she infect you with? What's gonna spring out at me when I'm not expecting it?"

I snort. "You don't want to know."

"I do, actually. I want to know everything about you."

I roll my bottom lip through my teeth, pinching it until it hurts. "It's more what she didn't say. She's not vocal like your mum. She's quietly disapproving. Both my parents are. The silent treatment was a big punishment at home." I let out a sigh. "They're both straight-laced corporate lawyers."

Jack scratches his forehead. "Oh, yeah. There was that big case last year—"

"There's always a case. It's their whole life. When I refused to go to law school, they stopped my allowance. Said if I wanted to pursue music that much, then the music should be able to pay my way. And if it couldn't, then..."

"Then what?"

"Then I'll be exactly what they think I am. An embarrassment. A failure."

"They said that?"

"No. But I know they think it, and it's really hard not to believe it's true when it's what your parents think about you." I sigh, and Jack's worried gaze darts from the windscreen to me, and he gives me a small smile as if to say, *'it's okay. I'm here for you now'*. "We don't really talk much anymore. Mum always wanted me to be more like Kate."

"Kate, my sister?"

"Yeah. She's Mum's ideal daughter. Ambitious, hard-working, corporate. Earns a fortune. Gorgeous. Wears respectable clothes. Kate wouldn't be seen dead in cowboy boots, unless it was fancy dress, maybe. And she has straight hair and no facial piercings."

Jack huffs as though this is ridiculous. "Well, I'm glad you're nothing like Kate, because this situation"—he waves a hand between us—"would be a fucked-up Freudian shitfest." I laugh. "You're perfect, just as you are. Uniquely you. Unbelievably talented, and if your parents can't see that, then that's on them."

Warmth spreads through my upper body, burning fiercely around my heart. *I think I love him.* No one has ever supported my career the way Jack has. But there's still something I need to know before I can completely relax with him again. "Did you hook up with me because I was the 'nearest and easiest' woman?"

He grunts dismissively. "No. I hooked up with you because I wanted to. A lot. A hell of a lot, actually." He pauses, and I wait, barely breathing. "You weren't the easiest, anyway. Lydia was right there offering herself to me in underwear and a trench coat."

True.

He sighs and taps the steering wheel with his index finger. "Look, El. I've been with a lot of women. That's no secret, but you... you're something else." The awe in his voice has butterflies springing to life in my stomach. "Watching you wander about my house, playing all our games, seeing you dress up and strut about... and getting to know you... *all of it.* I love it. I love *you.* I love how funny you are, and how you make me laugh. I haven't laughed so much with anyone else, ever. I love being around you, and even if you didn't want me, I'd still be here, waiting for you to notice me." He glances over at me. "The sex, too. Can't forget that. The feel of your skin"—he reaches over and strokes my thigh briefly—"the taste of your mouth. The taste of *you.*" He bites his bottom lip, his gaze dipping downwards, making heat flare between my legs. "All of it has been wonderful, and I love you so much..." A little line appears between his brows, and when he speaks again, there is the slightest tremor in his voice. "If this doesn't work out between us, it's gonna really fucking hurt, so can we try not to let that happen?"

No one has ever said anything like this to me. My body aches from how much I want to tell him I feel exactly the same, but I can't. Not yet. It takes all my concentration to say, "We can definitely try."

"Good. Because I'm not buying another one of these ridiculous cars, unless it's one I can race on the track." He winks. "And I'm not keen on this either." He thumps his fist to his chest, almost the way a smoker might shift phlegm from their lungs. "It's deeply uncomfortable, this love bollocks."

A series of gasps pop off my tongue. "Love *bollocks*? You are so romantic," I say, sounding as sarcastic as I can manage.

He chuckles. "Hey. This is new for me. The worst I've had to endure in the past is heartburn."

I gape at him. "Wait, no one broke your heart? All those women and you never cried?"

He snorts, as though this suggestion is completely ludicrous. "No."

This feels surprising and yet not surprising all at once. "You didn't love a single one of them?"

He pauses, his cheek distorting like he's rubbing his tongue on his molars as he thinks. "No. It was all good fun, but no."

"So you never lost someone you loved?"

His reaction is subtle but intense; eyes flickering, fingers squeezing the wheel. "Yeah, I did. My dad."

Guilt sears me. Of course, he knows what loss feels like. Perhaps not in a romantic way, but his father died suddenly of a heart attack less than a decade ago. Jack watches my reaction in glances he steals from the road.

He flicks the indicator and turns into our street. He parks the car outside the house, switches off the engine, and turns towards me. In the silence that follows, the air turns heavy. "If anyone's going to break my heart, it'll be you."

The anticipation of pain in his voice shoots across the space between us, embedding itself into my heart like a bullet. "I won't, if you won't," I say quietly.

"Deal." He leans across the car and kisses me, and his tongue is soft and warm and the scruff on his jaw scrapes my face.

Sitting in the passenger seat of this ridiculous car, Jack's tongue in my mouth, it occurs to me that life is perfect.

This, right here, is perfection.

The days following Jack's confession pass in a blur of sex and kisses. I've never felt so loved. So completely safe. Long may it continue.

I love you, I love you, I love you. He's said it so many times that I find myself wondering if I'm dreaming. It feels too soon, too fast, and yet not at all. It's as if this state of affairs was always there, like a pool of water I could have dived into at any time, but I chose to stand at the edge instead, convinced it was too dangerous to take a swim.

I'm fully submerged now, and the water is blissful.

This morning, Jack is wandering about the kitchen in just his boxers. I'm not sure I'll ever get used to seeing him bare-chested and up close this way. He's jaw-droppingly ripped, and I can't believe it's me who gets to be here when he takes his suit off.

"Hey," he says to grab my attention. *As if he doesn't already have it.* "Your album came back from the studio. Listen to this."

He holds his phone to his mouth and instructs, "Play Elly's Album."

He smiles and tips his head at the speakers in the ceiling, wordlessly instructing me to listen as the chords of my first song ring out.

"Elly's Album?" I ask.

"I didn't know what you wanted to call it, so for now, it's just Elly's Album. Do you have a title in mind?"

"Nope." I hadn't let my imagination go to the place where I had a full album, let alone a name for it. I was accumulating songs without a fixed goal, as if they might magically coalesce into something worthy.

Yet again, Jack has pushed me where I couldn't go alone.

He stands still and we listen for a few seconds until my voice trails over a high note at the emotional climax of the song. I've sung it a million times, but it still gives me shivers to hear it. "That, right there. That is fucking genius," Jack says, pointing upwards, as if my song is a visible item in the air around us.

He sways to the melody. "You have a gift. Not many people can take feelings out of the ether and turn them into something other people can understand. You're translating a language that has no words, but that everyone recognises. It's like magic."

My heart soars, but Jack instantly goes back to the phone, completely unaware that he's just doused me with the best compliment ever. He swipes his phone screen, and the music reverts to the first track on my album. He points both index fingers at the speakers in the ceiling. "You're gonna be big. You have to start believing it."

He's always saying these things to me. Little sound bites, telling me how good I am. How talented. How beautiful. He's re-writing my script, day by day, and I love him for it.

"You haven't posted anything on social media for three days," he says, still scrolling through his phone. "Why not?"

Jack set up my social media channels a few weeks ago, while I sat by his side, and although it made it easier to face the writhing fear in my gut when he was there, as soon as he wasn't, I ran away from it again. If I put myself out there, people can laugh. People can say I'm crap. I can fail.

"It's embarrassing."

"You believe this is good?" He gestures once more to the speakers.

"Sure." I can hear the hesitation in my tone, so I've no doubt Jack can too.

He comes towards me, right up close until he puts his palm right between my breasts and my breathing shallows. "In here. Do you believe it in here?"

I look deliberately at his fingers. "It's hard to think with your hand on my tits." Looking chastened, he removes his hand, but he cups my cheek with it instead and I rest my face there for a moment.

"You've got to start believing, because that impacts every single action you take." His words are a tender whisper that nestles in my heart. "If you believe, you'll go the extra mile. You'll make that extra post, write another song, make the last song even better. If you don't believe, you won't bother. All those choices are cumulative, and they have ripple effects you can't anticipate. And I'm telling you, it's good."

He strokes my cheek with his thumb, and I hope he can't read the doubtful thoughts running through my mind, not only about me and my ability, but about him. Jack Lansen isn't exactly the arbiter of taste when it comes to music. "Thank you," I say.

Jack tips his chin in acknowledgment of my thanks. "We can get Derek to step up the posts he's doing for you, shunt more of the burden to him, if that would make it easier. He's been doing a good job, right? He's great at the marketing for creative types."

"Creative types?"

He lifts his hand from my face and rubs at his jaw, his tongue swiping over his bottom lip as he assesses me. "That's what you are, isn't it? All the feelings and the lyrics and the music."

"And what are you?"

"Not that." He nods his head up at the speaker in the ceiling, changing the subject. "This song. Start with this one. Put it out there over and over again until it goes viral."

Fear splices my insides. *Viral?* Millions and millions of people hearing me? *Seeing me?* "I'm not ready."

"You are."

I fidget, shuffling in my seat, tearing the croissant in front of me into tiny pieces. "The idea of it is terrifying."

He's staring at me with such a serious expression that I almost cower before him. "What's the fear? Because fear is bullshit. If you know what it is, you can disprove it and move on."

That sounds ridiculously simple, and I can't believe it would ever work. Could I have done that when I was sitting in that reception area, waiting for my interview with Robert Lloyd, panic rising through my veins like a tsunami?

Could I have rationalised away all my fear?

Under Jack's watchful gaze, my thoughts begin to churn and anxiety claws at me, but I don't want him to see how frightening this is for me. Everything comes so easily to him. He's so competent, so capable, so confident in his own ability.

"You know what?" I say. "I know I'm good at what I do. The music, the song-writing. The singing. I do *know* that, but..." I fade off, struggling to complete the thought.

Jack eyes me, as though he's weighing me in some way, then he blows out a breath in a gust. "Seriously, if I find the prick who made you this afraid of putting yourself out there, I'll destroy him." He pauses, his eyes widening into an expression of appalled revelation. "Oh, shit. Am I gonna have to kill your mum and dad?"

I let out the tiniest laugh in response. "No. Maybe. There is no one person. It's the whole thing. Music is precious to me. It's my creative outlet... it's intimate. Private, almost. I gave up a lot to do this, and once things are out in the online world, they're no longer mine. I can't control what people think of me or my music. If it's not perfect, everyone will tear me apart." The fear grows as I put it into words, rising like a cobra up my throat, preparing to strike. "If I put myself out there... Shit happens. I let it in. I *cause* it. Like your mum turning up and screaming at me. Or the tomatoes at the Marchmont. And those are small scale. What happens when something goes viral? If I don't—"

"If you don't do anything, nothing can hurt you?"

His words burn right through me, exposing a truckload of excruciating pain behind them as though they're dragging every bad memory through my torso. *I'm trapped by my own fear.* I can't look at him. Tears are throbbing behind my eyeballs, waiting to spill.

"El," he says, his voice soft. "No one is perfect. If that's what you need to be to move forward, you're going to be sitting in the Marchmont strumming that guitar for the rest of your life. There will always be people who don't like you. There will be critics. There will be people who are rude and obnoxious and say fucking nasty shit. But if you don't let the shit stick... if you don't let it get inside your head... you win."

"I get it. I can hear you, but..."

I can't. I can't do it.

Jack's large, warm hands come to rest on my shoulders. "All you need to do—all you *ever* need to do—is get up and try again. You keep fucking trying until you get where you want to go, and you make sure you're letting the shit slide off on the way there. You have to be bigger than what people throw at you, or it will crush you. And I really don't want that to happen because I like having you around." My insides begin to fizz, releasing tension I wasn't even aware of. How is it possible for a few kind words to dispel pain I've endured for years?

But it's not just the words. *It's him*. Knowing I have Jack Lansen's support means more than I could ever have guessed it would. It's a balm that soothes all my wounds.

His piercing blue eyes fix on me. "I love you. And you're brilliant. Get out there and shine."

"Okay."

He kisses me gently, but when he pulls back he's still frowning as though he's not convinced I've taken the advice on board. He dips his head to make sure he has my full attention. "I've got a meeting at nine, so I have to go get dressed. I'll get Derek to call you. You're wonderful. Don't forget it." He releases me and turns away.

"Do you have five minutes?"

He stops, glancing back over his shoulder, a dark eyebrow rising. "What do you want to do in five minutes?"

"Fuck me before you go."

He sighs like I'm asking for the world, pretending it's such a hardship when we both know it isn't, and says, "Only because I love you." The words make me swoon, and when he lifts a bunch of bananas from the fruit bowl and reveals a pile of condoms beneath, I'm too turned on to even laugh.

He rips one open and sheaths himself, taking me there on the counter. Quick and hot and sweaty, and we come together, groaning, screaming and gasping as though there isn't enough oxygen in the room.

Afterwards, Jack rests his head on my shoulder, and I whisper into his ear. "I love you too."

He chuckles. "It was the condoms in the fruit bowl that finally did it, wasn't it?"

I've never felt this happy. "Yes. Absolutely. That's what it was."

34
JACK

Kate and I are standing at the back of Nico's party venue. The enormous ballroom is empty, aside from the band and Elly, up on the stage. There are a couple of lighting and sound technicians flitting around, making sure everything is perfect for tonight.

"You know, I never thought you and Elly would be a thing that worked." Kate doesn't look up at me as she runs a pen down the side of a clipboard, ticking off items on her party to-do list. She taps the pen twice when she reaches the bottom and finally looks at me. "Is she going to stay with you after her lease ends?"

Unease wriggles up my spine. *I haven't thought about what happens after.* "Are you going to bring this up every time you see me? We've been together for a month and I'm already sick of hearing it."

"Maybe. It blows my mind." She sighs and glances at Elly, who's dominating the stage, singing her heart out during her sound check. *I can't believe I'm sleeping with that goddess.* "She sounds really good. How's she getting on with all the other stuff?"

"She's been putting out social media content consistently, which is a step in the right direction. Derek's helping her out and people are actually listening to her music. The reception has been good so far. I think that helps, but she's nervous about tonight."

"She'll be fine," Kate announces confidently.

I really hope so.

"Those videos are really good, by the way. One of them is getting loads of views," Kate says, tucking her clipboard under one arm and pulling her phone from her pocket to bring up one of Elly's videos. It's simple; just her strumming the guitar and singing, but Derek's done some clever editing which adds an edge of glamour to it.

"Shit, that is loads," I say, noticing the viewer count in the corner. It's nearly fifty thousand. I refresh it and the number jumps. "Derek's uploading the best ones tonight. They might catch the momentum."

"Good idea. People love her sound too. Look." Kate scrolls to the comments then frowns.

"What? What is it?"

Kate's frowns deepens. "Trolls."

I snatch the phone and look myself. There are loads of great comments, but there's a barrage calling Elly a slut. An ugly whore. And others saying she can't sing, which is patently untrue. "Has Elly seen this?"

Kate flips one hand palm upwards. "I have no idea."

"Shit." I hand Kate back her phone, pull my own from my pocket, and dial Derek. "Mate, quick favour," I say when he answers. Kate's quietly watching me. Potentially judging, but I ignore her. "Can you log into Elly's account and delete those comments? Yeah? About halfway down. Block the users. You're supposed to be watching this shit." I wait as Derek tells me he's doing it.

"That's all done," he says, when he finishes, "But there is something odd about some of this stuff coming through."

"Oh yeah?" A chill prickles its way down my spine. Kate's still watching me, intrigued.

"It looks like a lot of it is the same person, or a group of people. Deliberately going after her account."

Bizarre. Who would do that? "Block them all. Look, I've got to go. Can you keep your eye on it? Tonight is a big night for Elly. I don't want any distractions."

Derek agrees, and I hang up, although there's an unpleasant feeling lingering in my gut.

Kate squints at me. "You've got him censoring the comments? I can't work out if that's fucked up or thoughtful. How long has he been doing that?"

"A few weeks. He has all her login details. He posts most of the videos and all that shit. I don't think she'd do it otherwise."

Kate levels a serious look my way. "You can't fix everything for her. You won't be able to protect her from that stuff forever. And you're going behind her back to hide it."

"I don't want her to be discouraged. Not yet, anyway. It's early days." I look over to where Elly is strutting across the stage. "She makes it look easy, but this is a big deal for her."

I think of Elly in the kitchen that day, so upset at the idea of people attacking her online. *If it's not perfect, everyone will tear me apart.*

Kate frowns, and her lips part as though she's about to say something else when her phone rings. She stares at it for a second before turning it so I can see. 'Mum' is visible on the screen. I reach out and swipe my finger to decline the call.

Kate shakes her head and puts the phone away. "She keeps calling. Says you still won't answer."

"I'm not interested in speaking to her."

"She won't stop. She thinks she's losing you. It's breaking her heart, and she's holding Elly accountable."

What a nightmare. "She needs to apologise. Is she calling to apologise?"

Kate's lips draw tight. *That's a no, then.*

I curse under my breath. "Mum has all these ideas about who's right for me and who's wrong, but it's a load of bullshit." We stare at one another for a moment, and the understanding in Kate's gaze is so palpable I can't ignore it. I dip my head to run a hand through my hair. "Fuck. I had no idea what it was like to be on the receiving end of Mum's crap." Her brow crumples as though I've hit a nerve. "You've put up with so much over the years, and I wasn't there for you—"

"You were."

"No. Not really. Not enough. I want you to know I'm sorry. I get it now. I didn't before."

Kate clutches her clipboard to her chest. "That's because you're the Golden Child. You've always done everything she needed you to do. Made her look good. But for some inexplicable reason, you dating Elly isn't what she wants."

"I don't care what Mum thinks. I like Elly. Really fucking like her. In fact, I—"

"I know."

I eye my sister with suspicion. "What do you know?"

"I know this is different for you. You wouldn't be culling the comments on her social media channels if you didn't care. You wouldn't have Derek working on her stuff, and you wouldn't have sorted out her recording all her songs. And you've never cut Mum out before. You've called her every Sunday night since you were at boarding school, but she's mean to Elly, and you bring the shutters down." Kate swipes a hand through the air as though this is all plain as day. "But you'll have to talk to her eventually."

"Why?"

"Because she's our mum. And she'll be at Nico's party tonight."

"Oh, for fuck's sake."

Kate shrugs. "Just a heads up. You'll have to face her then. But don't expect an apology."

Elly's singing stops, and there's a booming sound as she taps the microphone. "I need a break," she announces.

She speaks to the band, then hops off the stage and comes towards us, and my heart swells with every step she takes towards me.

"You're sounding fab," Kate says, pulling Elly into a side-hug.

Elly looks ecstatic, but a little insecure as she asks, "It's good, right?"

The hesitation in her question makes me want to hug her too. "It's good," I confirm.

We chat for a few moments longer and then Kate excuses herself, running her pen down her clipboard as she walks away from us.

"I'm so nervous," Elly says, wringing her hands.

I put my hand over hers to stop them moving. "You don't look it." I take my phone from my pocket with my other hand and pass it to her. "You're taking off. Some of your videos are getting loads of hits."

Elly pushes my phone away. "I don't want to see. I can't take it. All those comments… all those people out there. I don't need to know."

I slip my phone back into my pocket. "I know what will help you relax." I pull her against me, giving a gentle thrust of my hips so there's no doubt what I'm talking about.

She leans into me and moans against my chest. "I can't have sex now," she mumbles. "I'm too stressed."

"You sure I can't tempt you?"

She shifts against me, and heat pools in my groin. It takes so little with Elly to turn me on.

"Not now. After. When I've finished my set."

I tuck a wayward curl behind her ear. "Fine. I'll wait. But I'm coming to find you as soon as you're done."

I slide my hand down the waistband of her skirt and cup her arse, giving it a hard squeeze that makes her squeal. She pushes me off, laughing, and a contented warmth floods my heart.

But then, almost instantly, it cools as I recall the comments on her social media.

She stiffens in my arms, tilting her head back to catch my eye. "What?"

I don't want to scare her, or make this into a bigger deal than it is. After all, it could be nothing. And if she's going to keep growing her presence online, this stuff is only going to get worse. She'll have to get used to it.

But I want to know if she has any idea who might be behind the comments. Perhaps there's some bitter ex in her past, or some girlfriend she fell out with. Or maybe it's normal, in terms of social media and celebrity. Maybe I don't need to worry, but even if that is the case, I don't feel good about it.

I inhale deeply through my nose. "There isn't anyone who'd want to... you know..."

"Want to what?"

Fuck. I can't do this to her right before her big performance. "Nothing." I sigh. "I'm just checking I have all your attention."

"You do." She presses a kiss to my lips. "I'm entirely yours."

And even though it's exactly what I need to hear, I don't feel any better.

35
ELLY

The venue of Nico's party is lush. I know Kate said she didn't have the money to pay for Amy Moritz to perform, but she certainly has a lot of cash if the free-flowing champagne and delicious canapes are anything to go by. All the guests are gorgeous and well-dressed, and so freaking glamorous. I caught sight of Erica Lefroy chatting to Seb Hawkston by the bar; she's one of the UK's top models, and she's unbearably beautiful in real life.

I haven't had anything to drink because I don't want to perform without being completely in control. Plus, I had such a bad hangover after I drank the bottle of Jack's wine, that I've stayed off the booze ever since.

He hugs me moments before my set. "Go show them how talented you are," he whispers, just as the MC is announcing me. He kisses me full on the lips while the spotlight is turned on us, and people begin squealing and clapping. I feel myself blushing, but I break away and take to the stage.

The set goes by in a blur. The audience is excited and cheers like crazy for me, and when I hear loud whistling between songs, I glance down to find Nico with his fingers in his mouth, and Kate beside him yelling for me.

This feels so good. *Incredible*. My heart is pounding and I'm high off the audience, my songs, and the performance; euphoric almost. And there isn't a tomato in sight.

When I finish, I give thanks, and take a bow, before I descend the stage back into the party.

"That was amazing," Kate says, rushing up to me. She's so excited, she's nearly breathless. "You totally stole the show."

"Absolutely," Nico agrees. "In fact, there's someone who wants to meet you."

"Oh?"

I brush my hair off my face. The stage was hot and I'm sweaty from being under the lights. My heart is racing. The set went better than I could ever have imagined.

"Yeah," Nico says, grabbing someone from behind him. "This is Amy."

I very nearly sink to my knees, because standing right there between Nico and Kate is Amy Moritz, one of the biggest music stars in the world. I'm so stunned that I can't speak. I think I let out a squeak.

Amy smiles her big Americanised white smile. Her hair is shaved on one side and pink on the other. It looks ridiculously cool. I begin to sweat a bit more.

"I am such a huge fan," I begin.

"Oh, no you don't," Amy interrupts. "Thanks, but we're not talking about me. We're talking about you. You've got some serious talent, lady. You wrote those songs?"

I nod, still finding it difficult to speak.

"Wow. Where the hell have you been hiding? What have you been doing for the last decade?"

I stand with my mouth hanging open, and Kate throws an arm around my shoulders. "She's been practising. Isn't she great?"

"Fabulous," Amy agrees. She turns away, and I figure that's it, that's all I'm getting—and I tell myself it's enough to be not only acknowledged by one of the biggest stars, but complimented—when Amy calls out to a tall, dark-haired man nearby. "Robert, come here."

The man turns, and a sickening panic coils in my stomach. It's Robert Lloyd, Amy's Manager. *Shit.*

He frowns, and his stare penetrates my skin, then he breaks into a smile and comes over to join us.

"Wasn't she great?" Amy says to Robert. He agrees and congratulates me on the performance. "Reckon we can help get her career off the ground?"

Robert muses this for a moment, his dark eyes assessing me. He looks to Amy. "That depends on whether she shows up to any meetings."

Amy quirks a brow, and Robert explains that I didn't show up for our meeting at the Granville Agency.

"I assumed you didn't want representation," he says, turning his attention to me. "Thought you must have found something better."

Better? What's better than Robert Lloyd? "No..." I'm sure the regret is scrawled across my face. He gives me a kind smile, and the knot of anxiety in my stomach unwinds a fraction.

"I don't usually give people second chances, Elly. But when they're as good as you, I'm open to it. We can do more than get you off the ground. We can get you flying right to the top."

"Oh. Oh." *Words, Elly.* "That would be... I don't know what to say." I press my palms to my cheeks, finding them warm. "Thank you. I'd love to work with you."

Amy squints as she looks at me, as though she's processing something. "I wonder if we could sing together. How can we make that happen?" *Oh, my God.* I'm dead. I must have died. "Can we do that, Robert?"

"Absolutely," he says, and his enthusiasm matches Amy's. "I haven't heard anyone with as unique a sound as you in a long time. Raw talent, that's what you've got. I'd love to have a chat about your aspirations, because, whatever they are, we can make them happen. Hell, we can exceed them. Can you come in for a meeting? Show up this time." He digs into his pocket and hands me his card. "Take this, in case you lost the other one."

I feel faint holding that little piece of card. *A second chance.* This time, I won't freak out. I'll see it through.

"I'll get your number from Nico," Amy says, before kissing me on the cheek and squeezing my hand. "Actually, wait." Her eyes flash with inspiration. "Let's do it now. Let's sing together. You ready for an encore?"

Adrenaline floods me, my knees threatening to buckle.

"Go," Kate urges, waving me back towards the stage with both hands. Amy, buoyant with enthusiasm, grabs me, the metal of all her rings hard against my hand. She tugs me to the stage again, and leans into the microphone, me standing awkwardly beside her.

"Wasn't that performance amazing? Give it up for Elly Carter everyone," Amy yells, and instantly the attention of the room is back on us and everyone roars. *No, screams.* I don't think anyone expected to see Amy Moritz on stage tonight.

The place goes wild as people get their phones out and start filming and snapping pictures. Amy waves her arms in the air and her sequin-covered dress sparkles. "I'm going to make a prediction. This time next year, this woman is going to be huge." Again, the party clamors, and I can hear Kate squealing. She's bouncing on her toes and clapping, and beside her Nico is grinning widely.

I can't believe this is happening.

"You know, 'Beat Me'?" Amy asks me, referencing one of her massive summer hits. I nod. *Of course, I know it.* "Let's do that." She winks at me and whispers away from the microphone, "Next time, I'll sing one of yours." And I feel like I'm going to explode.

The band begins and Amy sings the opening phrase, her soulful voice filling the room, and then she lets me take over, and *holy shit* it's unreal, standing here next to one of the industry's biggest stars. My feet might be on the ground, but internally I'm soaring.

I make it through the track, and at the end, the applause is greater than I've ever experienced. *It's deafening.* Amy throws an arm around me and we leave the stage together, pushing through the enthusiastic crowd. She promises to be in touch and excuses herself as she's swarmed with people.

"Oh, my God, oh, my God, you were wonderful." If Kate was breathless before, she's hyperventilating now. "And also"—she pulls her phone out of her handbag—"You're trending."

I don't like that word. "What?"

"Yeah. The latest videos went totally viral. Millions of views. A few big influencers have used your sound too. It's all over the place. And Amy posted a selfie when your set started, with you performing in the background. She tagged you. And after that performance"—she nods at the stage as though we're both still singing up there—"you'll be everywhere."

Shit, shit, shit.

I grab Kate's phone, my hands trembling, and check the stats. She's right. Millions of views. And a few hundred people have used the sound already. I refresh and the numbers jump. Leap. Sky-rocket. And Amy has millions of followers and her video already has thousands of views too.

My heart starts beating so hard and fast it feels like it's quivering. I can't handle this. It's too much all at once. *I'm not ready.*

Just as I'm about to start panicking, I catch sight of Jack pacing towards me. I thrust Kate's phone back at her just as he reaches us. He barges right between Kate and Nico, ignoring the way they share an amused glance at his rudeness, and slides his arms around me. "Excuse us," he says to them. "We have a deal I have to see through."

Before I know it, he's tugging me through the crowd, barely allowing me to stop to thank everyone who wants to compliment the set and congratulate me. He draws me close and whispers in my ear, "My dick is so fucking hard after watching you up there. I cannot wait another second to have you."

Tingles of anticipation spread through me. I'm already buzzing, and Jack's mention of his dick sends me into overdrive. "Where are we going?"

We leave the main room and head down a corridor, Jack's large, warm hand cradling mine. He opens doors, poking his head in and then retreating as though he's not finding whatever he's looking for.

"Here," he says, finally, and leads me into a room not far from the main bar. It's decorated in a similar style. White floors, black seats, glowing lights from beneath the banquette that lines the walls of the tiny space. It's a small private space, but there's no lock on the door.

Before I can object, Jack slams the door and pulls me against him. Heat rages through me at every moving point of contact as he skims his hands over my shoulders, my upper arms, my neck.

His kisses are hard and desperate, bruising against my lips, but I meet him with equal vigor. "You are amazing," he says between kisses. "I got hard watching you. And you know what I thought?"

"What? What did you think?" I ask breathlessly.

He bites on my bottom lip and sucks it. "I thought, I am the luckiest man here because I am going to fuck that woman. I'm going to slide my fingers in"—he glides a hand up my bare thigh, teasing the fabric of my underwear which is getting wetter by the second—"and find her soaked for me."

I gasp as he pushes in, raising my thigh over his hip to give him better access. He tips his head back and groans. "Fuuuuck. No matter how many times I imagine this, it's never as good as the real thing."

I grind against him, and his breath heats my neck as he pants while he undoes his trousers. "Please," I beg, already desperate to feel him inside me.

"Shit." Jack's movements cease abruptly. "No condoms."

My pussy pulses, that empty ache inside me calling to be filled. "I don't care. I'm on the pill. I've been checked." My heart cinches as I recall his 'a lot of women' comment. "What about you?"

"I'm good. I got tested before you moved in. And you've seen my house. I keep everything neat. And I mean, *everything*." He draws back so he can see me, and his eyes look darker than ever. "I've never fucked a woman bare before."

Wow.

My heart starts leaping at the idea that I can be one of Jack Lansen's firsts. I didn't think he'd have any left to give. Arousal surges at the thought of feeling him coming inside me. "Really?"

"Yes." He frowns as though he thinks I'm judging him, which I am, but... *holy shit*. I get to be the first woman he's been with without a condom. *Bare*. "Are we doing this or not?" he asks, and the brusque defensiveness in his voice endears him to me even more.

I nod, and I've barely finished the motion before Jack has shifted me to the banquette and hiked my skirt up around my hips. He takes one look at my underwear before he grabs it roughly, and the sound of tearing fabric greets my ears.

"Shit, you ripped them," I mutter, outraged, but Jack only pulls the fabric out of the way and tosses it to the floor, far too focused on the task he's set himself to care. His trousers are still around his thighs, and he's so eager that his desire leeches into me, escalating my racing pulse.

He spreads my thighs and lines himself up, then pauses, his tip right at the entrance, staring down at it. "Fuck. Look at you, so ready to take me. So pink and perfect, and fucking wet." He groans, and the lusty noise makes heat blaze through my veins. He raises his gaze to mine as he enters, pushing every last inch of him inside me, and an overwhelming rush of hormones floods me, drowning me with need and desire, and love for this man.

"This feels so good. Just being inside you." He moans again and I can't bear him being inside me without actually fucking me for a second longer. The fullness is exquisite, but I need more. I lower a hand to touch my clit, but Jack flicks my hand away and works me himself, bringing me to orgasm without thrusting once. My pussy walls clench around his dick, my thighs locked around his hips.

I moan and writhe as the blistering pleasure shoots through me.

"Fuck me, you're gorgeous," he pants when I'm done. "I felt all of that. Every last tremor of your cunt."

He looks beside himself with desire as he thrusts, slow at first, then hard and fast, and in moments a second orgasm begins to bloom, sending blasts of energy pulsing through me.

This time, we come together, my arms wrapped around him, fingers gripping his shirt. When he stiffens, letting out an almighty groan, I feel my heart teetering on the edge. *This is it.* His eyes lock onto mine, and in them, I read a million emotions; fear, vulnerability, love, ecstasy… it's all there on his face—*he's giving me everything*—as his climax spills into me in warm throbs while I tremble around him.

"I love you," he breathes.

"I love you, I love you too," I repeat, as my orgasm wrings me out, binding me to him, body and soul, leaving me boneless and blissfully happy. "God, I love you."

When our breathing returns to normal he says, "I want to wrap you up and keep you forever," and I don't object to the idea.

He pulls out, staring between my legs as I feel the warmth of his seed trickling down my thigh. "Seeing my cum drip out of you is so fucking hot," he says. "Makes me want to take you again right away."

He wipes up the mess on my thigh with his fingers and then slides them right back inside me, as though he wants to push his cum back where it belongs. There's something so primal about the move that heat filters through my body. *That's exactly where it belongs. I wish I could keep it all inside me.* He rubs my clit with his thumb and expertly works that precious spot inside me. It takes him less than a minute to have me climaxing again, clenching around his fingers and spilling more of his cum down his hand and onto his wrist. "Wow," he breathes.

"Wow," I repeat, breathless and exhausted. "You tore my underwear, and I'm going to be leaking your cum for the rest of the night."

"Sounds good to me."

I mock-scowl at him. "Maybe we could go home?"

He laughs. "Can't do that, I'm afraid. You have to go show your face. Work the room." He pulls tissues out of his pocket and hands some to me and we wipe ourselves clean. I watch as he tucks himself in and buttons up. He's too fucking much, this man. His hair is bedroom-tousled and his cheeks flushed, and it looks so good on him. I can't believe I'm this lucky.

"I'm going to burn all my remaining condoms," he says, kissing me as I'm pulling my skirt back down. "I can't go back after that."

I wholeheartedly agree. I'm positively buoyant; this feels like the evening my entire life changes, and I'm so ready for it.

36
JACK

As soon as we re-enter the party, Elly gets dragged away by some new fans who can't wait to talk to her and have pictures taken. She gives me a confused little glance then allows herself to be pulled away into the crowd. I watch her pert arse swaying in that little skirt, her full head of blond curls disappearing into the throng.

Nico appears at my side a moment later. "You like her, don't you?"

"Yeah." I sigh, sounding lovesick, even to my ears.

Nico smiles, but then his expression shifts to one of concern, and my stomach plunges.

"What?" I ask.

"Derek called me. Said he needs to talk to you and you haven't been answering. Something to do with Elly's social media. Can you call him?"

My gut contracts. *Please say nothing is wrong.* "Now?"

"Yeah, he said it was urgent."

I pull my phone from my pocket and excuse myself, heading out of the main bar area so I can make the call where it's less noisy.

"Derek," I say when the call connects. "What's going on?"

"It's not good."

"What? What isn't? I thought the videos were going viral?"

"Yeah, they are. She's getting loads of attention. A ton of it, but there's something else. I wanted to call you before Elly sees. I don't know where the fuck it's coming from, but it's going to hit hard. Gaining traction already."

My heart races, and—*fuck*—my palms are sweating. I lean against the wall in the narrow corridor to steady myself. "What? Fucking tell me already. How bad is it?"

"There are photos of Elly out there. Circulating. They're taking them down, because they're basically porn, but they're popping up again almost as quick. She's being tagged in them. They're everywhere."

My blood runs cold. "Photos?"

"Yeah. I'll send you the screenshots. People are making videos and montaging them. I'm blocking the users sharing the pics from her pages, but I can't keep this back. It's a fucking tidal wave of internet gossip. People love this shit. And they're coming up alongside pictures of Amy Moritz, and she has ninety million followers. It's carnage. I'm sending it now."

My mind scrambles. Surely it's not *the* photos? My photos? *Could I have accidentally sent them? Pressed some button and shared them?* I have to check. Have to know what I'm dealing with here. Maybe I'm panicking for no reason.

Maybe Elly posed for other men. Maybe it's not my photos. My stomach lurches. Would that be better, or worse?

"What do they look like? The pictures?" I ask Derek, and my panic bleeds down the phone.

He whistles. "Fuck, man. They're hot. Explicit. She's on a piano." He chuckles. "It's on brand, I guess. That's a definite pro."

Sweat pearls on my forehead. The back of my neck. My torso. I'm so fucking hot right now, I might expire.

My phone pings as Derek's message pops up, and my fingers shake as I go to open it.

"Jack."

My name might as well be a gunshot fired in a library for the shock it gives me. My phone tumbles to the floor with a crack, and I look up to see my mother staring at me. She's elegant as ever, dripping in jewellery. She stalks towards me like she's on a mission.

I sink to pick up the phone. The screen is cracked, but I find Derek is still on the line as I put the phone back to my ear. "Derek, I've got to go. I'll come back to you." I hang up and slide my phone into my pocket, trying to push down my panic about the photos being out in the world.

"You haven't answered my calls," Mum says, her voice accusatory.

I force myself to focus on her, but inside I'm dying a slow death. "I'm aware."

"You can't ignore me forever." She paces a little closer. "Elly was good out there. She can really sing."

"You re-evaluating her?"

Mum snorts dismissively. "It makes her slightly less useless, I suppose."

Fuck this. I stride towards her, waiting for her to move aside, but she doesn't. Instead, she remains firmly where she is. Immovable. "You deserve the best, Jack. And Elly isn't it." I hear the echo of my own words in my mother's, and it makes me feel sick. Elly's comment rings in my head. *A mother's influence is like a virus...* "Look at Kate with Nico. Now, he's a catch."

"Unfortunately, Nico's taken," I deadpan. Mum's severe expression doesn't crack.

"I'm thinking about the future. My baby boy, locked down by an unworthy woman."

"Oh, fuck off. I'm done with this. If you don't have anything good to say, then keep your mouth shut." I push past her, heading back into the party.

"Don't you dare walk away from me, young man."

I don't stop.

"You'll live to regret this," Mum calls after me, and for some reason this is the thing that hooks me. I swing back to face her.

"Regret what?" I stalk back towards her, eating up the distance between us. "Falling in love? Because I love Elly. She means more to me than anyone else ever has, and if you can't support that, then I don't see that we can have a relationship at all. If you want me in your life, you have to accept my choice. And Elly is it. I'm thinking about the future too, and there is no version that doesn't involve her. You, on the other hand... I'm not sure I see you there."

Even as the words leave my mouth, I know they're true. I'd choose Elly over Mum. I'd choose her over everyone. I love Elly in a way I've never loved anyone before.

Mum must know it too, because her face crumples into a vision of misery, and she lets out a keening wail. It should move me in some way, but I feel *nothing* as I watch my mother weep. She glances at me through the tears, and when she realises I'm not reacting, that I'm not going to hug her or put my arm around her, or attempt to make this better in any way, she says, her voice weak and breaking, "How can you speak to me like this? How can you?"

I grit my teeth, holding back the urge to fix this whole scenario. To apologise and keep the peace and add this to the list of other crap I've ignored over the years. But this time it's too much. How can she accuse me of speaking badly to her, after the things she said to Elly? But then again, Mum's always been one for double standards.

"If you'd rather I didn't speak at all, I'm okay with that too," I say.

Mum heaves breaths like she's having an asthma attack, but the fact that I'm not going to change my mind must be seeping into her awareness, because her odd breathing ceases and she wipes the tears off her face, being careful not to ruin her makeup. *How much of that display was even real?* She ducks her head without another word, hurrying past me back into the party.

Fury is biting through me, tearing at my organs. If this is the type of shit Kate has dealt with for years, then I'm not sure how Mum and Kate have a functional relationship at all. Maybe they don't.

I pace back and forth across the narrow corridor, trying to calm myself, willing the anger to fade, but it doesn't until I remember why I came out here in the first place. *The photos.* At the recollection, fear sweeps in to take its place, and every thought of Mum vanishes.

I take out my phone and open the message Derek sent, fumbling to bring up the images, and what I see nearly brings me to my knees.

No, no, no.

Elly, draped over the piano. The hair, the cowboy boots, her skin, her legs, her breasts... fucking *everything*.

No one had those photos except me. *No one.*

I scroll through them, faster and faster, as if the speed might make them disappear. Might take this all away. But they keep coming, one after the other, more and more of them... every single shot I took.

My legs feel weak, and I slide down the wall, crouching near the floor. I feel sick. Really, truly, violently sick.

What am I supposed to do about this? There are pictures of Elly with her legs spread for me—*for me*—out there in the world. Guilt burns every inch of my insides like I've swallowed a bottle of bleach. My mouth gapes and I cover it with one hand, trying to buckle down the rising panic.

Another message comes through from Derek, containing a link to an existing video.

Derek: *This one is gaining traction. Nearly a million views already.*

With trepidation, I open the attached link to a video. It's by *User5498*, and it's a slideshow of the photos, blurred in all the appropriate places, but still horribly obvious. An AI voiceover is reeling off comments about Elly. "Elly Carter is a slut. A whore. A toxic disgrace—"

"What's that?"

My heart crashes so hard against my ribs, it could almost break the bones. *Elly*. I shut the phone down and look up to see her standing in the doorway, her beautiful face creased with consternation.

"I heard my name. What is it?" she queries.

Fuck, fuck, fuck. "Nothing."

"Don't lie." She paces towards me and sticks her hand out as though she expects me to put my phone in it. "Show me."

"It's just internet crap. Social media. It's not worth—"

"Why are you out here alone watching it, then? And with that look on your face."

An uncomfortable tightness rises up my throat. I have no good explanation for it, so I opt for the truth. "Derek sent it."

"He told you to watch a video describing me as toxic? A disgrace? A slut?" *Shit.* How long was she standing there watching me listen to this fucking video? "Why? To warn you off? To make sure you knew what you were getting involved with?"

"Fuck, no. Nothing like that. He was worried because it might impact your marketing."

"Let me see it. If you don't let me see it right now, I swear—"

"No."

She comes towards me, and I slide back up the wall to standing. My heart is pounding. There is no good conclusion to this. However this pans out, on some level, it's my fault.

She grabs at the phone, but I hold it out of reach.

"Jack, what the fuck is going on? Let me see it."

I shake my head, but Elly is tearing at me, jumping up, and I get the cruelest flash of her trying to reach her guitar that very first night I came back to the flat and she sang for me. I wish I could go back to that moment instead of being here on the precipice of everything going to shit.

I can't hide this from her forever, but I can damn well try for now. *Why did this have to happen tonight, when everything was going so well?*

She gives up, knowing she can't reach my phone and I won't relent. "I'll just look it up myself," she says, tugging her own phone from her pocket.

"No. Don't do it," I rasp, my hand covering hers. "Please don't. Not now."

She raises worried eyes to mine, and somehow the severity of the situation seems to become truly apparent. She backs away from me, still holding her phone, her fingers moving rapidly over the screen, scrolling, typing. I hold my breath.

Her hands begin to shake as she swipes over the screen again and again. It doesn't take long for small whimpering noises to slip from her lips, increasing in frequency until, finally, she sucks in air in one enormous gasp. "Oh, God," she cries, her phone tumbling to the ground before she grasps her stomach with both hands as if she's going to throw up. She bends over, repeating over and over, "Oh, God. How? How? *How?*"

She totters on the spot like she's drunk, and when I try to steady her, she pushes me away. Her head snaps up. "You said you deleted them. Did you? Did you delete the photos?"

"I..."

"Jack." Her voice is sharp and desperate, and she's still bent nearly double. "Did you delete them or not?"

Panic rages through me. I can't think. Can't fucking work out how to fix this. Every good thing in my life hinges on the answer to this question, and I don't have the right fucking one. "No," I admit, and she wails, tremors running through her body, my heart clenching at the sight. "El, please. I don't know how this happened. I would never have shared them. Never. You have to believe me."

I reach out, wanting nothing more than to take her in my arms and ease her distress, but she backs away, waving me off with thrusts of her hands.

"Don't fucking touch me," she spits.

"El, please," I beg, and my voice sounds like it's breaking.

"Jesus, Jack. The photos. All the photos." She covers her face. "Oh, my God."

Her terror spears me, searing pain following in its wake, which I do my best to ignore. "It's okay. It's going to be okay," I promise, even though I don't know that it is. "We can manage this. We can—"

"We can what? What can we do? Shut down the fucking internet?" Her words tremble in the air, hopeless.

"Shit," I mutter.

She lets out a pitiful whimper. "I knew it. I knew getting involved with someone like you was a mistake. I knew it."

Someone like me. What does that mean? "I did not do this... I didn't... I have no idea how they got out."

"You made me do it." For a second I think she means I made her pose for the photos and I'm about to object, but she continues. "You made me start the social media crap. You put those videos up. You pressured me to put myself out there. To open myself up to this kind of scrutiny. This is your fault." Her voice is high and screechy. She doesn't sound like herself.

"El..." *Shit*. I can't calm her, can't bring her down this time. "I swear I didn't share the photos with anyone. And I didn't make that video."

She slams her hands against my chest. "I don't care if you made the fucking video or not. This is your fault. Those pictures are out there because of you. You lied to me. You said you deleted them." She staggers back and scrapes her nails down her cheeks, leaving angry welts. "You fucking bastard."

"El, please. Shit." I don't know what to do, what to say to stop her spiralling. "I didn't do this. I swear."

She continues as though she hasn't heard me, driven forward on a wave of anger as she fists her hands and thrashes them down at her sides. "I would have stayed at the Marchmont. That was enough for me... but it wasn't enough for you, was it? You wanted me to be more than I was. You needed it. You needed it so I would be good enough for your fucking mother."

"Fuck. No." I rake my hands through my hair. *How the fuck did this get so twisted up?* "That's not what—"

"Yes, it was. I wasn't good enough. Special enough. Because God knows, Jack Lansen couldn't possibly date a waitress, could he? Fuck you." She presses her hands to either side of her head like she means to crush her skull between them. *Desperate*. "And now... it's all out there. All of me. All over the fucking internet, proving your mother right."

"Fuck, El. No. Don't do this. You have to be bigger than this shit. Do not let that"—I point at her phone, still lying where she dropped it—"ruin this. This is your moment. Fucking seize it. You're on the cusp of changing your whole life."

She shakes her head. "I don't want it." Her eyes glimmer with unshed tears as she bends to pick up her phone and shakes it at me. "I don't want any of it. I can't handle it. This feels like *shit*, and you fucking led me here. I knew… I *knew* I didn't want to do this, and you came along trying to fix me, telling me how great I was and turning me into some kind of product—"

"Product?" I cover my face with my hands and groan. "What the fuck are you talking about? No one cares about the photos. Not really. You're a beautiful, naked woman, and that's it. No one will care. It'll be forgotten about tomorrow."

She puffs a quivering breath, her face shifting into a mask of devastation, and I know I've said the wrong thing. "Not by me it won't. I care. I fucking care," she spits, her cheeks turning a fiery red. "This is my life. My reputation. Those pictures… those are you and me, Jack. That's what I gave to you, and I was a fool to do it."

Guilt rakes through me, tearing my insides into shreds.

"And the videos are horrendous. The things they're saying about me…" She slams one hand over her heart, still clutching her phone in the other. "I'm deleting my profile. I'm taking it all down."

"Don't do that." I hold my hands out as though I'm trying to stop her jumping off a ledge. "You can't let them win. You're this fucking close to breaking out, El. The photos might even help—"

Slam. Her palm hits my cheek with a brutal sting, making my eyes water. *Jesus*. This shit is out of control.

"Fuck you, Jack. Fuck you. Did you do it? Did you release them as PR? Is this another game for you? Another fucking play?"

Her words sting more than her slap. "God, no. How can you think that?"

"I know what men like you will do for success. I know how hard you push for it. How fucking ruthless you are. You don't care what it might do to me, do you?" My head is spinning, but Elly's thoughts seem to have taken a dark path, and I don't know how to guide her off it. "And you dare to stand there and tell me it's a good thing—"

"I'm sorry. Fuck, I don't think that. But it is what it is. It's done. We have to make the best of it."

"The best? There is no 'best' here." Her face turns hard. "Everything's ruined. The damage is done. I'm a slut and the whole world knows it."

"A million people is not the whole world," I blurt in a clumsy attempt to ease her concern, but she lets out a sob of a laugh, and I wish I'd contradicted the slut part of her statement instead. I scramble for something to say that will calm her down. If she'd only take a decent breath, she'd see that this really isn't as disastrous as she thinks it is.

"You pushed me too fucking far and then threw me to the dogs." She clenches her jaw, but the rest of her body shakes. She turns to walk away, but I'm not going to let her.

I grab her elbow. My heart is racing so hard I can barely think. "That was the best night of my life. Finally being with you... *fuck*. Those pictures are precious to me. I'm sorry I kept them. I am... *so fucking sorry*. If I could go back in time, I'd never have taken them. Having you in my life is worth a million pictures, and I'm an idiot not to have known it. But I didn't share them. I didn't do it. Tell me you believe me. You know I wouldn't do that. You *know* it."

I want to hold her, to soothe her, but there's too much resistance. She'll only push me away.

She tugs her elbow out of my grip. "It doesn't matter if you did or you didn't. They were *your* photos. And now that they're out there, you dare to say it might be a good thing? Fuck you." She breathes heavily, then repeats, "Fuck you," in a tone that makes my stomach feel like it's been slit open with a knife.

"Damn it, El." My voice comes out full of pain. "Everything I did was for you. I only wanted to help."

She's quiet, her chest rising and falling aggressively with each breath. "Well, thanks. You've helped me. You've made your fucking mark on my life, Jack Lansen, and I really, *really* wish I could delete it. I wish I'd never listened to you. I wish I'd never let you in."

My throat feels clogged. *Is she ending this?* "What does that mean?"

Her chin trembles as she turns away from me, but I march after her and spin her back to face me. Tears are falling freely down her blotchy cheeks, and the sight of them causes my stomach to cramp and a dull ache to spread through my torso. "What does that mean?" I repeat, my voice low and hoarse.

She swallows as though there's a great fucking lump in her throat too. "I can't..." she stammers and breaks off, shaking her curls at me. "I can't do this. I can't be who you want me to be."

The ache spreading through me threatens to send me to my knees. *Don't fucking leave me.* I reach for her hand, hooking my fingertips onto hers. "I don't want you to *be* anything. I just want you to be you. Exactly as you are."

She holds my gaze, her eyes watery and bloodshot, and for a second, I think she's going to relent. Then she snatches her hand from mine and says, "I don't believe you." She throws the words up like a barricade, and I know to my core that even if I held her down and yelled in her ear, nothing I said would get through to her.

37
ELLY

Nothing has ever felt this bad. I'm clutching my chest as I hurry away. My entire world is falling apart, and I deserve it. I brought this on myself, falling for someone like Jack Lansen, losing my mind for him, trusting him. And worse than that, I let him influence my career. I let him set me on this upwards trajectory... I gave him *control*.

He hooked me with hope, making me believe it was possible to be greater than I was, and that maybe I deserved more. *So fucking cruel*. I thought this time it would be different. I thought Jack would be there for me, to help me.... To *save* me.

How could I have been so foolish?

I feel sick. Those photos, out in the world, for everyone to see. Me, my body, strewn across the piano. My legs spread... the most intimate parts of me exposed and shared a million times over.

How is this possible?

My mind goes into overdrive, thoughts racing like drunk drivers on a motorway. I can't get a handle on them until one thought booms louder than all the rest: *Jack must have shared the pictures.* He said he didn't, but there's no other way they could have got out. He's the only one who had them.

I can't contain the agony that's splitting me open. Jack's cum is still leaking out of me as I push through the party. It strikes me as unbelievably cruel... I'm trying to escape him, and part of him is still inside me...

I hate him for putting me in this situation. How dare he come into my life with his 'fix this, do that, make this happen' attitude. He can shove that shit up his perfect arse.

I catch sight of Kate in the crowd, smiling at me, but when she sees me—I must look a mess—her face falls. I push past her. I can't do this. I can't talk to her. Not now...

She runs after me, calling my name. "Elly, stop. What's wrong?"

Her features are creased with concern and seeing her staring at me like that makes my heart break all over again. I try to explain, but the words won't come. She'll discover soon enough; everyone will. I need to get out of here.

Kate grips my shoulders. "What is it?"

I start to sob. "I want to go home."

She puts her arms around me. "I'll get Jack. He can take you."

Jack's name lances through me like a laser beam, and I pull out of her embrace, almost doubling over with the impact. "No. Not Jack." The tears well up, choking me. "I can't see him. Not now."

As if my words have summoned him, I catch sight of him coming through the door I just left. He looks distraught, and seeing him like that, as devastated as I am by our fight, wrenches my guts into a tight knot. I grip Kate's arm, and she turns to see what I'm looking at before quickly turning back to me, eyes popping wide as she says, "What happened?"

I squeeze her arm tighter. "Let's go. Please."

Kate hesitates, and then I remember it's Nico's party. She can't ditch her boyfriend's party for me. Jack is getting closer to us with every second that passes, and I can't face him now. *This is his fault. It's all his fault...*

I tug away from Kate and run for the exit. *Where the fuck am I going to go?* I can't go back to the house. Jack will follow me, and I can't lock him out this time.

I hurry out onto the street and call Marie.

"Hey," she answers.

"Can I stay with you?"

There's a brief silence, and in the background, I hear her boyfriend's voice. "She's seen that video, hasn't she?"

Fuck. Everyone knows.

Marie's voice cuts through my panic. "I'll buzz you in. See you soon, babe."

I spill my heart out to Marie, and she sits and takes it all in without judgement. Her boyfriend, Kevin, goes out for a walk so we can be alone. We sit together on her tiny sofa, and I tell her everything I did with Jack, although she knows most of it already.

"He took those photos?" she interjects at one point. "Shit."

I tell her that yes, he took them, and yes, I let him, and yes, I'm an idiot and yes, somehow they're all over the internet now. I tell her that Jack lied about deleting them, but claims he has no idea how they got out.

I don't know what to believe, and I don't know what to think. Marie says very little, and although it's good to talk, it feels like I'm speaking to a wall. She's never been my first choice of a shoulder to cry on, but she's here, listening, and I love her anyway. But the pressure to hold it together in front of her, even though inside I feel like I'm dying, is immense.

The doorbell rings, and Marie glances up, then back at me, before she shrugs and gets up to open the door.

"Oh, Elly," Kate's plaintive voice fills the room as she stands in the doorway, taking in the sight of me. I'm a tear-stained wreck.

I stand to greet her but immediately cover my face with my hands. *Could this get any worse?* My heart is galloping, trying to escape the prison that is my ribcage. If I could, I'd run. Kate is my best friend, and I share everything with her... but *this*... this is next-level humiliation. If she's here, she must have seen those photos... photos her brother took. She's seen... *everything*.

I want to disappear. Barricade myself into a cupboard and hide, but I can't because she's here, staring at me.

I drop my hands, and her eyes lock onto mine. Her face crumples as a slideshow of emotion passes over her face, and sadness crawls right up my throat until my vision blurs and my eyelids prick.

She closes the distance between us, throwing her arms around me. "I'm so sorry," she says. The sympathy destroys my defences, and I burst into tears, and Kate only holds me tighter. "Oh, don't cry. Please don't cry. You're so amazing and wonderful and I wish I could be more like you, posing for pictures like that. You're free and gorgeous and owning your sexuality and proud of it and I love you. Please don't be embarrassed. Not in front of me."

I cry harder, wishing her words were true, but I'm not free and owning my sexuality. I'm dying of shame and hating myself for being an idiot. *Maybe Mrs Lansen was right. I'm nothing but a stupid slut.*

"You left the party," I croak when my weeping eases.

"Of course I did."

"But Nico—"

"He's fine. I'll go back, but I couldn't let you leave without checking you're okay." She rubs a hand over my back. "Jack told me what happened."

The mention of Jack's name burns like a flame, and I physically recoil. Kate's arms snap off me and she steps back, eyes wary.

"Sorry," I mutter. "I can't think about him now. I'm so angry."

Kate nods. "Okay. That's okay. We'll work this out."

She sounds like Jack, wanting to fix everything. A lump rises in my throat and I worry I'm going to cry again, because how on earth can anyone fix this?

I wake the following morning when a weight drops onto the end of the sofa. I slept here all night, curled up with a blanket draped over me. I open my eyes to see Marie sitting by my feet, a guitar in her lap.

"Kevin's guitar," she says, tapping the instrument.

"Okay," I say, not understanding, my mind still whirring with everything that happened last night. Kate stayed for an hour or so before leaving me to go back to Nico's party. She tried not to talk about Jack, but inevitably he came up, and Kate staunchly defended his position, claiming he would never have shared the pictures. It still doesn't answer the question of how it happened, but Kate had no explanation for that one.

"Yours until you get your stuff from Jack," Marie continues, still tapping the guitar. "You might as well make the most of all this heartache." She waves at my face, which I didn't even wash last night. There must be mascara all over me. "Get the creative juices flowing."

A lump rises up my throat and I swallow around it. "I can't..."

"Course you can. It's what any self-respecting musician would do. Use the pain. Plus, I'm not going to sit around comforting you. I don't have time, for one. And for two... it makes me uncomfortable. I'm not Kate. And three, I agree with Jack so I don't have any sympathy. You have to let this shit slide right off. If it were up to me, I'd send you right back to him."

The mention of Jack's name crushes me. *Will I ever be able to hear it without that happening?* "You don't get it."

"Oh, I do. I get that having naked photos leaked really, *really* sucks. But you look smoking hot in those pictures." I cringe, and Marie raises her eyebrows. "Sorry. But I couldn't not check them out, could I? And maybe Jack's right, they might actually work in your favour. You don't know that this is all bad. I also don't believe he did it deliberately. Accidentally, maybe."

"He lied. He said he'd deleted them." I sigh, more to stifle the onset of tears than for any other reason. "If it weren't for him, none of this would ever have happened."

Marie has the decency not to deny this, and we sit in silence, letting the comment hang in the air.

"He's done good stuff too, though, hasn't he?" Marie argues. "I watched the video of you singing with Amy. I mean, fuck, you sang with one of the world's biggest music stars. Without Jack, would you have done that?"

The inside of my nose begins to sting. "Yes. I was going to sing at Nico's anyway. I was always going to do that."

Marie arches a brow that's been dipped in scepticism, and I slump under its weight. I only agreed to sing at Nico's because of Jack. Because I'd overheard him insulting me.

"But you wouldn't have put it online, would you?" Marie asks. "There would be no way for anyone to identify the singer as you if not for Jack setting up all your social media crap. Now you can be tagged whenever someone films you."

I grunt in acceptance. That much is true, but it doesn't feel like a good thing. I'd rather be unknown, unavailable, unsearchable. No hashtags here, thank you very much.

Marie nods like she thinks she's made a very valid point. "I get that you're pissed he pushed you outside your comfort zone, but you should be thanking him. There's no growth in the comfort zone. You could spend your whole life there and convince yourself you're okay because it doesn't feel too bad. It's 'comfy'." She twitches her fingers in air quotes. "But really... part of you is dying in the comfort zone. It's where dreams go to die."

"I thought that was the Marchmont," I grumble.

"That's where they bury the bodies," she says with a chuckle.

But I can't share her amusement. I press a hand to my heart, attempting to soothe the ache of all these *fucking people* telling me how to run my life. "I preferred you last night when you said nothing." I groan. "This isn't growth. This is painful. It feels like part of me is dying right now. Maybe you should bury *me* in the Marchmont."

Marie lets out an extended breath. "I'm not trying to say this isn't horrible... being exposed that way sucks, and people slut-shaming you is shitty. It's always shitty, but publicly, on that scale..." She shakes her body as though she's trying to rid herself of the contamination. "If we find out how the pictures got leaked, I'll kill the perpetrator, but I do not believe it was Jack. And there is no way he made videos sharing them all over the internet, did he? He didn't make slideshows of your photos or videos calling you a slut and whore and all the rest. That was someone else. User 5498, whoever the hell they are. That was the initial video that got over a million hits, wasn't it? And that had nothing to do with Jack. We can establish that?"

"Can we?"

Marie's expression morphs into one of disbelief. "Yes! Even I know Jack wouldn't have done that."

I rub the heels of my hands into my eye sockets, wishing Marie would fuck off and give up her attempts to make me see reason. Now is not the moment for reason. Now is the moment for tears and rage and excruciating, heartrending pain. "Okay," I concede. "It's unlikely he did it."

"Good. And on the plus side, no one would have bothered making videos with your photos if things weren't changing for you. You wouldn't be interesting. No one would care. But you are and they do, and you've worked for that. People are paying attention, and you deserve it. This is a good thing."

I press my fingers into my scalp and groan. "I wanted attention for my music, not for getting indecently naked."

"How is it different from the stripping?"

My head jerks up. I can't believe she's gone there. "Seriously? That was in a tiny club in the backstreets of Newcastle. No one knew who I was. It was completely separate from *me*, Elly Carter. Whereas the music... that is *me*. That's who I am. That's my *soul*. It's personal, and to have these pictures associated with my music... it's unbearable."

A muscle contorts along Marie's jaw. "It sucks. I get it. But you can't blame Jack—"

Of course I fucking can. "Stop talking about him."

Marie leans away from me, her lips pressed tightly together, and we sit in silence for a few moments before she speaks again. "I called Kate. She and Nico can have you to stay. I'd let you crash here, but the place is too small. And Kevin—"

"You're throwing me out?" I sit up, uncurling from my foetal position on the sofa, an intrusive memory shunting to the forefront of my mind of me asking Jack the same thing about my old flat, right before he asked me to move in with him. His gorgeous smile appears in my mind's eye, bringing with it a pain that feels like Wolverine just raked his talons across my internal organs. *Fuck this shit.*

Marie raises an eyebrow. "Sorry, babe. It's all the crying. I can't do it."

I blow air out over loose lips, trying to hide the hurt pounding through my veins. "Shitty night sleep anyway. Your sofa sucks." I fist a hand and thwack the nearest cushion.

"Woah. Easy there." Marie shifts the guitar onto the sofa next to me, taps her hands on her thighs, and stands. "I've got to get to the hospital, and you need to channel all these feelings into the music. You won't be sorry. Every great artist needs to have their heart broken. The more times the better."

"You sadist," I spit.

"Go on." She nods at the guitar. "Make the most out of this. Write a hit song. And whatever you do, don't delete your profile. You're just getting started." Marie blows me a kiss and adds, "Love you, babe."

It's on the tip of my tongue to tell her I don't believe her, when the memories of saying that exact thing to Jack last night swarm at me, stinging every inch of my body. Christ, I can't do anything, can't think anything, without him invading my mind.

As Marie leaves, closing the door behind her, the stinging shifts to blistering, scorching agony. It's burning me up, engulfing me, and I don't know how I'll ever get through it. I might die right here on Marie's sofa. The pain rages through me, splitting me open and I hinge at the hip, my breasts grazing my thighs, hands clawing at my chest and shoulders as I desperately try to contain it.

I wish Jack was here. I wish he could hold me and let me cry and *fuck... I hate him.* I wouldn't be crying like this if it weren't for him and all that pressure he put on me. If it weren't for the photos and the fact that somehow, *somehow*, he let them get out into the world.

I weep until my face is soaked with tears, and my sleeves too, from the vain attempts of wiping them away.

Eventually, the incessant flow of sobbing begins to ebb, and it's then I notice the guitar. All I want to do is snatch up the damn thing and smash it against the wall. But seeing as it's not mine, I don't. I pick it up, check the tuning, and begin to riff.

The next few days pass in a blur of tears. I don't remember ever being this miserable. I can't sleep. I can't eat. I'm a nervous wreck. I can't stop thinking about Jack and what happened between us, and the look on his face after we fought. It's destroying me.

I've been living with Nico and Kate. They're sweet to be around, if a tad sickening, but I'm pretty sure they're being careful not to rub their happiness in my face. Not that I'd notice because I'm completely preoccupied. Those photos are everywhere. I've received so many messages about them from people I haven't seen for years, people I thought I'd never hear from again, and a string of old boyfriends. Even my parents called, but I didn't answer. The last thing I need is a reprimand from them.

If they were ashamed of me before, they'll be furious now. Maybe even blame me for tarnishing their professional reputation. Well, that's their shit to deal with. Not mine.

But in spite of all the messages, it's not enough to distract from the pain of losing Jack.

I've been going over everything in my mind, trying to make sense of it. How much of this is his fault? He didn't delete the pictures, but not because he wanted to use them against me, and he didn't force me to pose for them. He didn't force me to do anything... But they were private, and he failed to keep them that way. How can I forgive that?

"Can you tell your brother to control himself?" Nico's voice blasts from the living area just as I'm coming to breakfast. He doesn't sound angry. In fact, I'm pretty sure he's laughing. "This is madness."

"This has absolutely nothing to do with me," Kate says. "Plus, I think they're beautiful."

I turn into the kitchen to see the entire place is full of flowers. Every inch of floor space is covered. It's as though I've walked into a field of blooms, and every one of them is a different shade of orange. It's the most spectacular floral array I've ever seen. My throat tightens immediately, as Jack's voice rings in my head. *I fucking hate orange, but I love you.* Both Kate and Nico turn to me with strange, guilty expressions on their faces.

"What's this?" I croak out, speaking around the lump that has formed in my throat as I make my way through the bouquets that litter the floor. The scent of roses and lilies fills the air.

"This is Jack," Kate says, spreading her arms to encompass all the flowers. "I think you've sent him crazy. These are all for you."

"No one needs this many flowers," Nico mutters. "Orange, too. It's like fucking Halloween in here."

"It's more like a stunning sunset," Kate says.

Nico throws her a disapproving glare, gesturing at the flowers. "They can't stay here."

I swallow, hoping the lump in my throat will disappear, but it doesn't. "Oh."

Nico waits a moment as if to see whether I'm going to say anything else, and when I don't he adds, "I'm going to call him."

Tears prick behind my eyes, and Kate, noticing the emotion on my face, turns to Nico, one palm up in a stop sign. "Don't call him. We can redistribute the flowers." She steps carefully through the bouquets and puts her arms around me. "You okay?"

I moan a laugh into her shoulder. "Yes. No. I don't know." I take a shuddering breath. "Sorry. I'm not ready to talk to him."

She rubs my back. "Sure. Take your time. I don't think he's going anywhere."

"I love him," I murmur. Kate pulls back from me, her hands still on my shoulders, a curious look on her face as though she's trying to work out how serious I am. Behind her, Nico has gone very still, watching. "I love him," I repeat. "I'm in love with your arse of a brother. And I hate him. *I fucking hate him.* And it's driving me mad because I don't know which one I feel more strongly."

Nico's eyes go wide, and when he moves, he creeps through the flowers as though he's trying to leave without me noticing he's there.

"It's going to be all right," Kate says. "Nico probably has a hitman he can call."

Nico straightens, shooting an alarmed look at us. "I'm not knocking off my best friend because he sent flowers."

Kate laughs. "I meant for *User5498*."

For a second, everything is very quiet. "You're joking, right?" I say, glancing between her and Nico.

"Of course she's joking," Nico says. "I'm in hotels. Not... that shit." He waves his hand as though the suggestion is insanely farfetched, and although I laugh through my sniffles, part of me wonders if it really is that crazy... what would Nico do if someone had done this to Kate?

Before I can ponder it more, Kate pulls me into a hug again. "Don't worry. Karma is a bitch. Whoever did this will get what's coming to them, whatever happens. You spread bad shit in the world, it comes back to bite you. Always. Jack, on the other hand, is only spreading flowers. So... I'm hoping maybe you'll talk to him?"

I give a brief nod. "When I'm ready, yes. Don't pressure me."

She gives me a sad smile. "Okay. Now..." She claps her hands together. "I'm going to see what we can do with all these bouquets."

I bend down to inspect some roses, inhaling their scent.

"Jack also left these for you with the concierge downstairs," Nico calls out to me.

I look over to see him dangling the Lamborghini keys from his fingers. Kate inhales a sharp gasp.

"Apparently you forgot your car," he says, his voice as smooth as silk and his focus all on me, despite the fact that Kate is clearly exploding with questions. "It's parked in the basement."

Kate's mouth goes wide before her hand flaps to cover it. "He bought you that car? The one you tried to buy?"

I scrunch my eyes closed for a second. "I can't keep it, obviously. I can't afford the insurance, and driving it terrifies me. I only have to tap it and it shoots off like a bullet." An idea occurs to me, and I look back at Nico. "You don't want to buy it, do you?"

He laughs. "That orange thing? God, no." The amusement slides from his face as a thought occurs to him. "I know someone who would though."

38
JACK

I'm sitting in my car, parked outside Nico's apartment building. I know Elly's up there, but Kate won't let me inside.

She came over the day after Nico's party to collect Elly's things from my house. I hadn't realised how little Elly owned, but the absence of it is painful. Everything is so fucking neat now. Aggressively tidy and organised. That would have calmed me in the past, but now it's horribly jarring. Neat little reminders that Elly is gone.

I hate being at home when she isn't there, which is why I'm here, waiting for any glimmer of hope that I'll be forgiven. Elly hasn't acknowledged the flowers or the car, and won't answer any of my calls, all because of those damn photos. I wish I'd never taken them.

I scroll through my phone, searching for traces of the pictures. I loathe that the memories of the first time we made love have been ruined by them being blasted far and wide. I've got a team of people on it, hiding the links, reporting the users. With everything I'm doing, they're getting harder to find, but they're still there if you search hard enough, springing up like a game of Whac-A-Mole.

The profile of User5498 has been taken down, but not before the video montage of Elly's photos gained millions of views. There was nothing to identify the profile at all. It's as though it was created with the sole purpose of attacking Elly. I'm determined to find the culprit, whoever they are.

There's a tapping on the window, and I look up to find Kate staring in at me, gesturing with a rolling forefinger that I should unlock the doors, and when I do she gets in the passenger side.

She turns to me, her gaze at once hard and soft, as though she wants to tell me off and hug me at the same time. "You can't stay out here." She looks around the car, noticing my crumpled spare clothes in the back, the empty crisp packets and plastic water bottles littering the seats. "How long have you been in here?"

"Three days."

"You're sleeping in the car?" I shrug and Kate's eyes fill with compassion. "Go home. Elly's not coming down. She doesn't want to see you. And I'm not letting you up."

"I need to talk to her. Please."

Kate sighs. "I should have known the two of you living together was a disaster waiting to happen. The photos, Jack. What were you thinking?"

I can't listen to more recriminations about this. As if I haven't spent every second beating myself up for this royal cock up. "I never meant—"

"Stop. I don't actually want an explanation. I don't care whose fault it was. Clearly, you were both losing your minds if you'd take photos like that on a mobile phone." Kate covers her face briefly with her hands, as though this is all too much for her, and lets out a tiny, exasperated groan before she speaks again. "How did they get out? How did it happen? I've had your back on this. I've been telling Elly there's no way you'd have done that to her on purpose. That you might be a ruthless businessman, but this isn't some PR stunt where you've sacrificed her like a lamb to the slaughter in the name of her career. Please tell me you didn't do that."

"Jesus, no." I've gone over this a million times in my head. I stared at those photos so many fucking times. Could I have accidentally sent them somewhere? Pressed some button, and shared them? No, I don't think so. But how else could it have happened? Could someone have hacked my phone? But why would they bother? I'm not exactly up there on the UK's most-wanted list. "I didn't. I wouldn't do that to her. It's killing me that she thinks I could have done that."

Kate inhales through her nose, staring out the windscreen, her nostrils flaring. After a few moments of silence, she says, "Have you heard from Mum?"

"No. I bet she's loving this. Is she?"

Kate picks at her nails. "I don't know. I'm not answering her calls either. I've no interest in hearing her say 'I told you so' about my best friend. Not when Elly's as upset as she is." Kate stares at me. "She's distraught. You fucked up. Big time."

My heart aches at the thought of Elly upstairs and me down here, the two of us separated by an insurmountable fuck up and my bulldog of a sister. "Is it just the photos?"

"Just the photos?" Kate retorts, clearly horrified that I'd diminish the severity of this scenario with such a question.

"I mean, is it the messaging that's going alongside the photos, more than the photos themselves? All those videos talking shit about her. It's as though whoever made them knows her, or has some personal vendetta. Is there something I don't know?"

Kate shrugs. "I have no idea. Why?"

"I need to know what I'm dealing with."

Kate fixes me with a hard stare. "You're dealing with the fact that you lied about a bunch of explicit photos. You're dealing with the fact that they're out there in the world and it's your fault."

My fault. Hearing those words is never not going to hurt. "I'm doing everything I can to wipe those photos out of existence." I cup the back of my head with both hands, a noise of pure frustration ravaging the back of my throat. "If I did it, if I *caused* this, it was an accident. I would never, *ever*, have done anything to deliberately hurt Elly. *Ever.*"

"Doesn't matter. No woman lets a guy take pictures like that unless..."

"Unless what?"

Kate shakes her head. "She must have decided to trust you. God knows why. And you betrayed that trust."

"Fuck, I know. I *know.*" I can't stand the idea that I did this; that the woman I love is *distraught* because of something I did. "What if someone else leaked the photos? What if it wasn't me? Remember, I lost my phone at Nico's, the night of Dad's fundraiser? Maybe—"

"Jack." She cuts me off, and I know I'm clutching at straws, looking for excuses that don't exist. "Your phone was exactly where you said you left it. Right there. No one had even touched it."

I drop my head into my hands. *Shit.* "I don't see how I could have done it. There's no record of it on my phone. I didn't send them anywhere. I don't—" I break off, groaning into my cupped hands, and Kate squeezes my shoulder.

"If it wasn't you, who was it?" she asks, her voice soft.

My hands fall to my thighs. "I don't know. Lydia? She was there, outside the bathroom. That was the last place I remember having my phone."

Kate splutters. "Okay, that *is* mad." All the softness in her voice falls away, replaced by dismissal. "I know Lydia was a bit disturbed by finding you and Elly together, but what you're suggesting is bordering on Machiavellian. Besides, I'm pretty sure Lydia was off hooking up with someone else. Seb Hawkston, maybe. I bet she wasn't even thinking about you. Either way, you're the one who had such incriminating photos on your phone, and who kept them there even after Elly asked you to delete them. You have to accept culpability here. You fucked up. That's all. You have to take responsibility for that and all its consequences."

The silence prickles.

"Am I going to lose Elly over this?"

Kate is quiet for far too long. "Maybe."

I bang furiously on Seb Hawkston's office door. I am determined to find out what happened to those photos if it's the last thing I do. If someone is out there trying to harm Elly, I need to fucking know about it. Ever since I mentioned it to Kate, I haven't been able to give up on the idea that Lydia had a hand in it, but for the life of me, I can't work out how. The determination to find out who's responsible has driven me here, to Seb's office, a fog of rage clinging to me.

"Quit the fucking noise and come in," he yells.

I enter and close the door behind me. Seb's sitting behind his desk, looking all immaculate in a perfect suit and pale blue tie. Even his light brown hair is perfectly coiffed. I must look deranged in comparison.

Seb raises a brow and unsubtly gives me the once over. "What can I do for—"

"Did you fuck Lydia?"

Seb gives me a bemused smirk and steeples his hands, leaning back in his chair. "A gentleman never tells."

His calm demeanor irritates the fuck out of me. "The night of Dad's fundraiser. Did you, or did you not, fuck Lydia Archer?"

He leans forward, peering at me. "You're serious?"

"I am."

"All right..." he says after a moment. "No, I did not."

My heart is racing. Maybe this is going to get me nowhere. But I have this feeling that maybe, just *maybe*, there's something here.

Seb must read the relief on my face, but misinterpret it, because he says, "You moving on from Elly already? Because I think Lydia would be keen."

"God, no. I need to know anything you can remember about Lydia that night."

Seb strokes his lips with two fingers. "I was drunk. I haven't thought about it, to be honest. It wasn't a big deal."

"Is that it? That's all you've got for me? This is important." I sound frenzied, and Seb leans away from me, his brows drawing together.

"I thought at one point we might hook up," he says. "She's gorgeous, but she wouldn't stop talking about you. The whole time I was with her, she was going on about how you and her are meant to be and she wants to fucking marry you. And I'm like, what the fuck? This woman could be hooking up with me, and instead, she's chewing my ear off about some other bloke. So yeah, no. I didn't hook up with her."

I don't know what to make of this. Seb Hawkston is what my mother would term 'a catch', and I had Lydia pegged as a woman out to hook someone. *Anyone*. But it sounds like that's not the case; it's only me who's the target. "Okay. Nothing else? Nothing weird?"

His gaze drifts, but a second later, he's back with me. "Actually, there is something. She was on her phone the whole time. Obsessively looking at it. Talking about you, scrolling. Jack this, Jack that. It was fucking rude, and so I looked over to see what had her attention, and it was... you know... this naked picture of a woman. No face, the image cut off at the neck. I saw it for a second before she yelled at me to mind my own business. She was really touchy about it."

For the first time in days, hope tingles along the surface of my skin, sinking in and expanding as though I'm being pumped full of air. *We're getting somewhere.* "Do you remember anything else?"

"Yeah. The naked woman in the picture was wearing cowboy boots. I remember specifically, because I said, 'You into cowgirl porn? That's niche, but I can work with it'."

"Really?" I ask, my voice full of palpable excitement.

"Yeah. She got mad at me, gave me an absolute bollocking. Said, 'Jack Lansen would never say something like that'." Seb makes his voice all high and whiny as he impersonates Lydia. "So I walked out. I wasn't going to take crap from a woman who had no interest in me. Anyway, I kinda forgot about it. That evening was a bit of a blur."

Damn it. He's had this piece of information the whole fucking time. "You didn't think to tell me before?"

Seb scratches his chin. "No. Why would I? It was so random. It didn't mean anything. It...." He trails off, his eyes widening. "Woah. No," he says, dragging out the syllable in a parody of shock. "You don't think Lydia took your photos?"

"That's exactly what I think. My phone went missing that night. I reckon she copied them, or airdropped them to herself. Something like that." I feel so buoyant that I want to vault over Seb's desk and kiss him. "And you've confirmed it for me."

Seb grins, making his one-sided dimple appear. "Glad to help, mate. If you need me to testify or some shit, let me know."

I barely take another breath before I'm out of the office and heading down to Soho to Lydia's offices. I don't have a plan. All I have is hope and anger and the desire to do whatever it takes to confirm that Lydia is culpable so I can clear my name, and tell Elly I didn't do it.

Less than thirty minutes later, I'm hanging over the reception desk at Lydia's PR company, demanding to see her. The receptionist is staring at me like I'm an escapee from the nearest prison, who she expects to pull a knife on her.

"Sir, if you don't calm down, I'll have to call security."

"Buzz her. Lydia Archer. Tell her it's Jack Lansen. Tell her I need to see her. She'll want to see me."

The receptionist doesn't take her eyes off me as she calls through to Lydia. "Yes," she says. "There's a Jack Lansen here to see you." Her eyes widen. "Okay. All right. I'll send him through." She hangs up, her energy crackling with surprise and disapproval all at once. "Door on the right at the end of the corridor. She'll see you now."

I blow out a breath and push myself off the desk. *Fuck*. What am I going to say? Standing in Seb's office, I felt so certain, *so fucking sure* that Lydia was guilty, that there was no room for doubt. But now, knowing Lydia's in her office at the other end of the corridor, I'm suddenly not sure. What the hell am I going to do? But whatever goes down, I'm recording it.

I switch my phone to voice memos and slide it into the inside pocket of my suit jacket. I take a deep breath and head to her office.

I open the door to find Lydia sitting behind her desk. "Hey, Jack." She looks calm, but one of her hands strokes agitatedly up and down her throat. She's dressed in a silk shirt, her hair perfectly blow-dried. *Professional*.

Doubt consumes me. Can I come out and directly accuse her of stealing photos and sabotaging Elly's budding career? Is that an accusation that makes sense? It's too bleak, too twisted. What if I'm wrong? Maybe I'm deluded to think someone might be that into me, that they'd do something like this to hurt the person I love... I might need to take another route to get the answers I want.

"Hey, Lydia." I steel myself for what I'm about to say. "I'd like to take you out for dinner."

She looks visibly taken aback. "Oh. Really? That would be great. I'd love that."

"Friday?"

"Sure."

Fuck. What am I doing? "I'll call you."

I turn to leave, when Lydia says, "Changed your mind about the waitress, then? Because last time I saw you, you were buried deep." She laughs at her own joke, and it's such a mocking sound that anger flares in me like a forest fire, and I have to clench my jaw to hold it back. "Yeah. It didn't work out. We had some... issues."

"Oh. I'm sorry. Nothing to do with all those photos that got released, I suppose?" I tilt my head to indicate that maybe that had something to do with it, but really I'm giving her an opening to expose herself. "Such a shame," Lydia continues. "The timing was so bad, just when all her music was taking off. I saw the video of her singing with Amy Moritz at Nico's party. That was good. Really good. Apparently, Robert Lloyd wanted to meet with her to discuss representing her." Lydia breaks off to lick her lips. "That won't happen now. Too much scandal. That shit will never wash." She places her palm flat against her sternum. "Gosh, some of those photos were extraordinary. Like someone got right between her legs with a camera—"

"Cut the crap." Rage is burning through me, and I can't pretend any longer. I don't know why I'm so sure that Lydia did this, planned it, fucked it all up for Elly deliberately, but I am.

"What?" Lydia asks, and her innocence strikes me as fake.

I stalk towards her, slamming my hand down on her desk. She jerks in her seat. "I know you did this. I fucking know you did it. You stole the photos from my phone, then you released them the night of Nico's party. User5498. It's you, isn't it?"

A wicked smile curves Lydia's lips. "Why on earth would you think that?"

I'm rising and sinking on the hope of getting somewhere. Of some of this shit starting to make sense, and her denial isn't about to make me give up

"I know you took my photos." My voice vibrates with barely restrained fury that's turning my body into a fucking furnace. "I know you did. Seb Hawkston saw them on your phone."

Lydia stills. "Ah." She pauses, and I barely dare to breathe. "You were terribly stupid to leave your phone open, with those pictures on the screen. I hardly stole them. They were right there. So careless. I didn't even have to look for them."

"Fuck." I drag both my hands into my hair. "Why? Why would you do that?"

"They were so pretty. A perfect body. Might even be better than mine." She laughs, and chills spread over my skin.

I begin to pace, nervous energy beating through me like stormy waves. "This is insane. You're fucking crazy, you know that?"

She gives me a pitying look. "Some people deserve what comes to them."

Outrage fires through me like a missile. "Elly didn't do anything to you," I bite out.

"Didn't she? You were mine, Jack. She stole you from me. We were so good together. *So good.*" Lydia sighs, releasing a sound like an off key musical note. "She's a heartless slut. Honestly, losing her now is saving you the pain that would inevitably come. You can't trust a woman like that."

I'm struggling to make sense of what Lydia's saying, or how it pertains to me or the photos. *Is this some perverse kind of punishment?*

"She didn't steal me. You never had me. We were never even together. You're deluded. I love Elly. I'm in love with her. There's no one else in the world I want to be with. Especially not you. I feel nothing for you. Worse than nothing. I will never forgive you for what you've done. *Never.*"

Lydia closes her eyes on an eyeroll, and flutters them open again. When she speaks, her voice is so calm, but the words so mad, that she seems unhinged. "Please. You don't love her. She's bewitched you. I'm the one who loves you. She came out of nowhere and swept you away. I couldn't let that go unpunished, so I took your photos. Pushed them out into the world. But really, I'm blameless. She's the one who posed for them. She's more culpable than I am in this scenario, and if you can't see that, perhaps you're the one who's deluded."

What the fuck? "I can't listen to this crap. What's wrong with you? Can you hear yourself? None of this makes any sense."

"It makes perfect sense to me."

I'm starting to think I'm standing before someone on the verge of mental breakdown, and yet it's eerie how sane she appears, how cool her tone is. By contrast, I'm breathing hard, pistons of rage pulsing through me. I can't stay here. I'll fucking kill this woman. One more word from her, and I'll be out of control. I turn to leave.

"I guess we're not having that dinner then?" Lydia calls.

I snap, spinning back towards her, the words exploding out my mouth. "What you've done is illegal. If you think I'm going to stand by and do nothing... let you sit here all fucking smug and pleased with yourself, while the woman I love has been publicly humiliated, then you really are insane."

She gives me a coy little smile. "So... I'll be hearing from you soon then?"

Un-fucking-believeable. It takes all my willpower not to grab her desk and turn the whole thing upside down. I pace away from her without answering, slamming the door on my way out. When I'm back on the street, I stop the recording on my phone and call Elly.

No answer. *Fuck, Elly, pick up. Pick up.*

I call three more times, with the same result, so I send the voice memo I've just recorded, and hope Elly listens to it.

And then I make one more call. "Nico," I say when he answers.

The line crackles, but his response comes through loud and clear. "Tell me what you need."

39
ELLY

My phone buzzes and I flip the screen to view the caller. Jack. Again. He's rung me ten times since yesterday afternoon. I have no idea why the number of calls suddenly increased, but I'm trying to put him out of mind. He can wait until I'm ready to talk. Might as well let him sweat it out while I get my head together.

"You sure you want to sell?" Seb Hawkston's voice pulls me back to the moment, and I put my phone away.

"Yup. I have no use for a car like this. Hardly any miles on her." I tap the bonnet of the Lamborghini, trying to be casual about the fact I'm selling the only thing Jack bought me. *God, I love this car.*

But I need to get rid of it so I can pay Jack back and wash my hands of the whole stupid affair. Having this thing sitting here is a cruel reminder of our relationship, and how perfect it felt when he bought the car and told me he loved me.

Seb Hawkston stands eyeing the car, one hand in his pocket, the other at his jaw. This is the first interaction I've had with anyone outside of Nico and Kate's flat since the photos came out, and I've hardly moved far. We're in the basement car park, and it took a great effort of will to come down here because I'm existing in this unpleasant place where I assume everyone I meet has seen me naked.

I had to force myself to look Seb in the eye when I said hello. I know enough of him to guess he's looked up the pictures. Maybe even studied them. But he has made no mention of them. He's been nothing but a gentleman, and I'm so thankful.

When he smiles, his dimple deepens and his pale blue eyes appear to glimmer. It's cute. I bet a lot of women would drop their underwear for him in a flash, purely for the dimple. *How had I not noticed it before?*

The answer hits even harder. Because Jack was always there, taking up every scrap of my attention. Absorbing the very essence of me.

It doesn't matter how attractive another man is, or how deep his dimple is, I only want Jack.

My heart breaks a little at the thought.

I really need to get rid of this car, so I don't have to keep thinking of him, feeling guilty, remembering how he'd sat in the driver's seat and glanced over at me and said, *I fucking hate orange, but I love you.*

But I can't push Jack out of my head. He lives in there.

Standing here with Seb, while he contemplates buying this damn stupid car, an ache builds within me. *I miss Jack.*

I miss him so fucking much.

But I'm not ready to face him or to stop screening his calls. As if on cue, my phone buzzes and I imagine it's him sending another message to add to all the others I haven't read.

I can't look at them yet, because if I do, I'll run right back to him, and I have to get on my feet first. I have to sort my career, work out how I'm going to salvage my reputation, or perhaps create a new identity. Change my name by deed poll. Get enough plastic surgery that I'm unrecognisable.

I can't hide out in Kate and Nico's apartment forever.

"Orange," Seb muses, a little furrow appearing between his brows. "Bold choice."

I make an effort to steady my breathing and pretend a wave of regret hasn't just assailed me. "I guess so." I refrain from explaining that I chose it to piss Jack off. To offend his sophisticated sensibilities. And he still bought the damn thing.

Seb continues examining the car, stroking the bodywork with a fingertip, as though he's checking it for dust. "Jack bought this car, right?"

A dark, tightly woven ball of fear plummets through me, as if any mention of Jack leads directly to the photo debacle, and suddenly Seb being a gentleman and not talking about them doesn't matter anymore, because I feel exposed anyway. *Totally fucking exposed.*

Am I going to feel like this forever now?

I have the sensation of zipping something up internally, hiding part of me away, just so I can turn to him and say, "Yes. Sort of... Anyway, it's new. I've barely driven it. Nico said it might be your thing. Or your thing for a while, anyway."

"Doesn't Jack want it?"

"Nope," I say with absolute certainty. Jack Lansen would not choose an orange car. "I want to get rid of it." Seb's brows rise, but he rolls his lips, and before any sound can come from his mouth, I let it all spill out. "I tried to buy it on his card, and it makes me feel guilty, knowing it's down here. It was a stupid thing to do. I want to sell it and pay Jack back."

Seb makes a dismissive noise that seems to come from right behind his teeth. "He won't care about the money." He assesses the car again, then his gaze snags on mine. "I'll help you out. I'll take it off your hands." He whistles. "This is one hell of a car."

I'm beset by the need to hug him. *Thank fuck.*

"Can you transfer the money to Jack? I don't want anything to do with it. I want to forget about the whole damn thing."

My chest aches. *Am I lying?* What if the only thing I ever have left to remember my entire relationship with Jack is this damn car?

This damn car, and a ruined reputation.

I become aware that Seb is staring at me, a contemplative look on his face. "You must be angry at Lydia, eh?"

Her name is so unexpected in this context, during this conversation, that I recoil. "Why?"

Seb looks uncomfortable, and I suspect he regrets raising this topic. "The photos. What she did was awful. God, I feel sorry for you."

My internal organs are imploding, shame crushing my insides. *I don't want to talk about the photos.* It's an effort to conceal the violence of my reaction, but I need to understand what the hell he's talking about. "What exactly did she do?"

Seb searches my gaze for some sign that I already know, but when he doesn't find it, his eyes widen. "Shit." He exhales a low sound. "Jack didn't speak to you?"

I shake my head, then remember the messages that came in from him last night and this morning. The flood of them, all unread, his calls all unanswered on my phone.

"Did he say something to you?" My voice sounds thready and my pulse is hammering. My legs feel like they're made of water.

"He came to see me in the office. He was worked up. Determined to try and work out how those photos were leaked. He had all sorts of questions about Lydia. Whether I'd been with her the night of the fundraiser." He tosses his head to make his hair fly off his forehead. It immediately falls right back where it was. "I was, but... not that way. She was only interested in Jack." *Of course she fucking was.* "Anyway, she had these photos she was looking at. She was totally distracted. I thought it was porn—" He breaks off, catching himself, cringing at what he's said. "Sorry."

His story has me hooked, and my shame has taken a backseat to the intrigue. I wave a hand to dismiss his concerns. "Go on."

"It was your photos. The ones Jack took of you. She'd stolen them from his phone at some point in the evening. As soon as he realised, he bolted out of my office like a prize-racehorse. Never seen him move so fast." Seb pauses. "He really didn't call you?"

"He did... but I didn't answer. He left a bunch of messages."

A beat of silence passes, during which I feel every ounce of Seb's judgment.

"Go listen to them." He rests a hand on his hip and exhales loudly. "This is none of my business, but I've never seen Lansen this cut up over someone. What went down with your photos was shit. Really fucking shit. But Jack's not entirely to blame, and you should listen to what he has to say." He turns back to the car, signalling that the conversation is over, even though for me it's just begun. I am buzzing with this knowledge. "I'll take the car," he adds, holding up a finger to indicate I wait, then pulls his phone from his pocket to make a call, I assume to clear the money with the bank or something, but my hand whips out and grips his wrist.

He stares in shock at where my fingers are clamped around his sleeve.

"Sorry. No. The car's not for sale." The words are tumbling out of me. "I made a mistake. I can't do it. I can't sell it. I'm going to keep it."

Seb tugs his arm from my grip and I let go. "Jesus, you and Lansen need to sort your shit out. The two of you are wasting my fucking time." He shakes his head, but I catch a hint of a smile and he winks as he adds, "Give him a kiss from me, won't you?"

Still shaking his head, he walks away, and when he's gone, I open my phone. My knees feel unstable, but I force myself to stay upright as

I scroll through the messages. A lot of them are just missed calls, but on a few of them he's left voice messages.

I listen to them one by one.

Fuck, El. I'm so sorry. This is all my fault. I should have deleted the photos when you asked. I should have got rid of them. I never, ever, imagined anything like this would happen.

What can I do, El? What can I do to make this up to you?

I need to talk to you.

El, please, call me back.

I don't recognise the sound of his voice. He sounds so serious, broken almost. *What have I done to him?*

Finally, I open the voice memo and listen to Jack's exchange with Lydia, and when I get to the end, I have only one thought.

That fucking bitch.

40
JACK

"You look fucking miserable," Matt Hawkston says. He's sitting at a table in a West End bar with me. We're supposed to be discussing the opening of a new hotel in Paris over drinks, but I can't concentrate. "You gonna talk to me, or stare at your phone all night?"

Guilt spikes. Matt's in the middle of a contentious divorce with his wife, Gemma, and I'm moping because Elly still won't talk to me, even after I sent her the voice memo of Lydia confessing she'd stolen my photos and shared them. I'd hoped everything might go back to normal once Elly had heard the evidence, but I was wrong.

I glance once more at my phone, reading over the only message she has sent me in the last few weeks.

Elly: *I listened to your messages, but I need time. I need to work out how I feel about all of this. Please.*

I've read it about a million times, but the words never change. It's been nearly a month since I last saw her. Weeks of begging Kate to let me up to see her and being rejected every fucking time. Weeks of my calls going unanswered. My messages being ignored. Sleeping in my fucking car outside Nico's building.

I'm absolutely broken over this. I destroyed the best thing I had going in my life, and even my attempt to fix it didn't work.

I give Matt the barest glance before I open Elly's social media. I keep compulsively checking it, even though seeing her face on the screen makes my heart ache. I'm reassured she hasn't taken her profile down, but at the same time she hasn't put up anything else since the party, and she must have told Derek not to either. But if she hasn't deleted everything, then there's a fragment of hope... maybe she hasn't given up entirely.

"Jack," Matt reprimands.

I put my phone down. "Sorry. You want to talk?"

Matt leans back in his chair and lifts his scotch to his lips. "Do I want to talk about Gemma?" He takes a sip of the drink. "Fuck, no. What's going on with you and Kate's friend?"

"Elly," I correct. "She's still living with Nico and Kate while she's searching for a new flat to rent." I blow out a sigh. "Things started happening for her, you know, with the music, and then the photos came out and all those videos... It's like a bomb went off and everything turned to shit. She packed all her stuff and left like it was all my fault."

"It was kind of your fault though, wasn't it?"

I clench my jaw. It hurts to know I'm the weak link that created this mess. I give the slightest of head movements to acknowledge that yes, I was culpable. "I'm doing everything I can to get those pictures taken down. You have to search pretty hard to find them now, but it's almost impossible to get every single one."

"You found out who did it?"

Rage roils in my stomach at the memory of Lydia's gloating face. "Yeah. A woman I dated." If I go into details, I'll lose my shit right here at the table.

Matt's eyes widen, and I swear he nearly laughs. "You dated someone who would do that? Didn't you notice that she was—"

I point at him, cutting him off. "Hey. None of that. You were married to Gemma for fifteen years. Clearly, we're both blind to the red flags."

Matt grimaces, but before he can say anything else, the door to the bar opens and Kate, Nico, and Seb walk in, heading straight for our table.

My heart clenches at seeing Nico and Kate together, hand in hand. Not only are they obviously in love, deliriously happy in one another's company, casting my misery into even harsher contrast, but they get to see Elly every morning. Every evening. At the weekend. She's walking barefoot around *their* flat now, and pain leeches through me at the thought that I don't get to witness those seemingly insignificant moments of Elly's life anymore. The way she flicks her hair over her face, or licks her bottom lip, or even the way she holds her tea with both hands like it's something to treasure. The light glinting on that damn nose piercing. They get to witness all of that, and it won't mean anything to them...

Kate kisses my cheek and sits next to me, and the others crowd around the table too.

I raise my hand in greeting, and Nico slams his into it, smirking as he says, "I know you love me, but please stop sending flowers. My place smells like a funeral home."

The others laugh, and I let out a groan. After the enormous floral delivery a few days after Nico's party, I reined it in, but I've been sending at least one bouquet to Nico's flat every day instead. *Pathetic*.

"At least he's not sleeping in his car outside the apartment anymore," Kate adds.

I cover my eyes with my hand. "Way to shame me," I say, indicating Matt and Seb, who are eyeing me with amusement. Seb snorts.

Kate ignores us both. "But, speaking of Elly," she continues, "I've had this idea. We were discussing it just now." She glances at Seb and Nico. "Elly's playing at the Marchmont tonight."

My heart goes into overdrive. "And?" I ask, steeling my expression so as not to reveal the overwhelming intrigue that's racing through me. *Am I going to get to see her?*

"And..." Kate pauses, her eyes flicking to Nico as though she wants to check he approves. He must give her some sign that he does because she says, "You should come. You never actually heard her play down there."

Adrenaline spikes in my system like I've downed a dozen espressos. I don't want to waste another second of my life without Elly, and if there's any chance I can see her in person, I'm going to jump on it.

I lean back in my chair, affecting casualness, although I have no doubt they can all see through me. "I don't want to... get in the way. Elly hasn't answered my calls."

Kate contemplates this as Nico signals to a waitress that he wants to order drinks. "I know," Kate says. "There was a lot for her to process, but I think she might be ready to see you."

"Think or know? I'm not coming if she doesn't want to see me."

"She wants to, she just hasn't said as much." *Jesus*. I roll my eyes, and Kate gives me a hard stare. "I've known Elly for half my life. I wouldn't suggest this if I didn't think it was a good idea." She sounds so sure of herself that I'm nearly convinced.

I glance at Nico, keen for his opinion. I can't outright ask him about the situation with Lydia and the photos, not with all these observers, but over the past few weeks, we've lined everything up so that she'll get what's coming to her. We must be close, now. And I'd feel a hell of a lot better about seeing Elly if I know that other matter is in hand. "What do you think?"

I know Nico understands what I'm really asking because he gives a short, sharp nod. "I think she's ready."

Kate, oblivious to our coded discussion, continues pleading. "Come to the Marchmont, please." She gestures around the table. "We'll all go."

I stare around at the Hawkston brothers. "You want to come to the Marchmont? It's not glamorous. Not like this place," I say, glancing around the luxury bar.

"I'd go anywhere to see her again," Seb says, smiling broadly.

Me too. Me fucking too.

"You're a deviant," Matt hisses at Seb. "This is Jack's Mrs we're talking about."

I pinch the bridge of my nose and close my eyes to the sound of Seb's raucous laughter, pretending I'm exasperated by him, when really I'm struggling to hide the stab of gut-wrenching pain that the term '*Jack's Mrs*' caused. Elly's not my Mrs. She's not my *anything*.

"Maybe all of us down there isn't a good idea," I mutter as I glance at Kate. "Does she know you're planning this?"

Kate looks contrite. "No. But if she wants to perform, she has to be able to do it regardless of who's watching, or what's going on in her life. Especially if she wants to get out of the Marchmont."

"Does she want that?"

"I think so, but she's scared. It's a huge deal to get out there and perform again after everything that happened. But she's been writing a ton of new songs. And Amy Moritz still wants to perform with her... she doesn't give a shit about the online chatter. Thinks there's no such thing as bad publicity. Thing is, if Elly doesn't want to miss her moment, she has to get over herself. Quickly."

I narrow my eyes. "Are you agreeing with me? Because Elly screamed me down for interfering with her music. For trying to change her and fix her and turn her into a product."

"Hmm. When we were younger she used to talk about it all the time. Being famous. Being a star. Getting her music out there. And then over the years of rejections she kind of... *shrank*. Some of them were so brutal that she gave up." Kate sighs. "I get that we shouldn't interfere, but when someone is so obviously holding themselves back... I don't see the harm in helping."

"Look at the two of you, trying to sort Elly's life out," Nico says, amused. "It's cute."

I scowl at him and drain the rest of my scotch. To be honest, all I care about is that Elly will give me another chance.

"I'll watch, but I'm not getting involved in her career ever again," I declare. "That's hers to manage however she wants."

41
ELLY

The Marchmont is busier than normal. Marcia's pissed because it means she has to work doubly hard, and we don't have the staff. All these people are here to see me. I never thought that putting my music out there... showing up on social media would make this kind of difference, and to see the impact trickling all the way down here, to the basement of the Marchmont, is mind-blowing.

Although, I guess they could all be here because they've seen me naked. The thought makes me want to vomit, but I can't hide forever.

I don't look into the crowd. I know it makes me look scared and amateur, but for now, it's the only way I can do it. Keeping my focus on the music and deliberately pretending there is no audience allows me to push through.

The crowd is appreciative tonight, but even so, my stomach is a tangle of nerves. On one of my songs, the crowd started singing the lyrics with me which has never, ever happened before. They already knew it. I almost stopped entirely and ran away at that point. But then a small voice pipes up that this is what I wanted.

All those years ago, when I first dared to dream of being a musician... I imagined it. Maybe not a little place like the Marchmont, but packed stadiums full of people singing my words back to me, waving their mobile phones like fireflies on a summer evening.

Could I have that? Is that even possible?

Maybe. Maybe not. But for now, I'm here, in the Marchmont, and for the first time, the crowd is here for me. Not for the cheap beer. Not for the shitty comedy act that was on stage before. But for me.

I'm slowly allowing the crowd's energy to feed me. Gaining in confidence. I'm *enjoying* this. And then I introduce my last song. The one I wrote after Nico's party.

"This one is called Playing Your Games, and I wrote it over the last few weeks. It's about someone…" A sudden knot of emotion forms at the base of my throat, but I swallow it down. I can't sing if I start to cry. I clear my throat and continue. "Someone I fell in love with, but it didn't work out."

I shift the microphone and begin strumming the opening chords in a combination that sends chills racing over my skin, and I can tell from the sudden hush in the room that I'm not the only one.

Playing your games will kill me,
You force me out and knock me down,
Hold me till I drown.
I'm afraid to play, afraid to lose
Every kiss is just another bruise.

The sound of your laugh will break me
Like the rush of a storm through broken seams,
But please, oh please, don't wake me,
From my twisted dreams.

As I continue, lost in the words, voice rising and falling through the melody, I realise when I'm a few verses in that the crowd are singing the chorus with me… and they've never heard it before. They've caught on so quickly. I've finally written something that resonates. And to think, it only took the worst heartbreak of my life to inspire it.

> *I can't be loved and I can't be saved.*
> *I can't leave and I can't go*
> *Because there's nothing else I'd rather do*
> *Than stay and play with you*
> *Even if it kills me.*

I move into the final verse, buoyed by the response, when I hear the shout. I can't make it out, but the sound jars me like a barrage of wrong notes, and I stop singing. I raise my head for the first time, staring out beyond the lights, making out the faces in the crowd.

Restlessness spreads like a disease and people shuffle in their seats, trying to see who shouted.

That's when I see the heckler. "You're no fucking good." He shouts again, clear enough that I can hear him. "If you're not getting naked, get off the stage."

Dread turns my insides to ice. For a few seconds, I do nothing. But I force myself to gather my wits. If I want to keep performing, I'm going to have to face people like this eventually.

I bring the microphone to my lips, affecting a smirk as I say, "Been there, done that. Sadly no t-shirt to show for it." I balance on one foot, kicking out the other to display my cowboy boot. "Still got these though."

Laughter, awkward and weak, trickles around the room. *Fuck, this is painful.* What was I hoping for? Raucous applause? I'm not a comedian.

A sleazy smile breaks over the heckler's face, and before I know it, he's barging towards me, dodging between tables at speed. He cups his hands about his mouth in a makeshift megaphone and yells, "Show us your tits! No one wants you with your clothes on."

Fear spreads like a web through my body, sticking me in place as the man lurches up to the stage, still rattling off insults I can no longer make out over the roaring of blood in my ears and the shocked murmurs of those in the audience.

A few tables away, someone stands up. "Stay the fuck away from her." The familiar voice makes my heart boom so hard I swear my ribcage rattles. *Jack*. He's here, rising from his seat to his full six-foot-four and marching towards the heckler, who is now only a few paces away.

Hope battles with the fear that's overtaken me, but the man is getting closer and Jack's still too far away. *Fuck*. The drunken heckler reaches out to grope me, and I let out a yelp, staggering back, using my guitar like a shield.

Just as his fingers are about to close over the neck of my guitar, Jack leaps to the stage in one massive step, grabbing the guy by the collar and hauling him backwards.

"Fuck off! Let go!" the man yells, appearing so small in Jack's grasp that he's like a puppet being dangled from its strings. Jack releases him, and he staggers a few steps backwards before righting himself.

People are shouting, squealing, and generally joining in on the chaos. Flashes explode as people take photographs on their phones.

"Apologise to her," Jack snarls. "Apologise, or your face and my fist are gonna get really fucking friendly."

Oh, God. "No—"

"Who the hell are you?" the man bites out, glaring at Jack and ignoring me. "I'll say whatever the fuck I want to her."

Jack's expression warps with a degree of wrath I've never seen on him. It looks like it takes every ounce of his self-control not to pummel the guy. But the man must be on a death mission because he barrels towards Jack head first, like he wants to use his skull as a battering ram.

At the last second, Jack pulls back his fist and strikes the man's jaw in a neat uppercut, sending his head whipping back. The man lets out a raw scream.

I squeal.

"Shit. Fuck!" someone shouts.

"Fight, fight," comes another voice, others quickly joining the chant.

"I fucking warned you," Jack grits out, pacing towards the man, whose face scrunches in terror as he stumbles to escape. His foot slips off the stage, and he loses balance, arms flailing. Almost in slow motion, he topples off the edge. His head cracks against a table, knocking pint glasses flying. A woman erupts from her seat, hands covering her mouth, as he collapses to the ground at her feet.

The event unleashes a torrent of latent chaos in the room, and everyone surges from their seats, yelling and bumping into one another. The heckler seemingly has friends, who forge through the crowd, surrounding him and hauling him up so his face is visible, revealing what looks like a broken nose, blood gushing down his chin.

Jack stalks towards the group of them, undeterred by the fact he's outnumbered. *Holy fuck, there's going to be a proper brawl in here.*

Fear seals my feet to the floor, my body seizing up and going numb with the shock of it. He can't possibly fight all those men. It would be violent and awful, but the thought unlocks something in my heart, unleashing a heat that scorches my lungs. *He wants to fight for me.*

"Stop," Kate screeches. I turn to see her pushing her way through the tables. Nico, Seb, and Matt jump from their seats too, heading towards Jack. Nico reaches him first, grabbing his arm and pulling him away, shouting something in his ear that I can't make out. Seb and

Matt hover nearby, no doubt ready to make sure Jack isn't charged with murder by the end of the night. Whatever they're saying to him, it must be registering, because he isn't making a move, despite the powerful, frustrated energy coming off him that tells me he'd rather be turning the man's brains to pulp.

The heckler's friends are lurching at Nico, Matt, Seb... anyone in the area. They look desperate to fight, but Seb looks more preoccupied with keeping his suit clean, stepping out of reach, whereas Matt and Nico are like bodyguards, rigidly sticking to Jack's side, preventing him from getting involved. Not that the men notice; they're so drunk that they start fighting with each other, throwing hapless punches and swerving into furniture. One of them knocks into another punter, who shouts back, and the brawl spreads through the bar like wildfire.

Marcia is suddenly beside me, grabbing my arm. "Quick. Out. Now."

But I resist, pulling back against her. "I'm not running this time."

Leaving my guitar on the stage, I hop down, scooping up a full beer from a table nearby, ignoring the shocked expression of the man whose drink I swiped.

When I reach the scuffle, the heckler is sitting on the floor, being propped up by a friend, and it's then, as I look closer, that I realise these are the same fucking men from the last time I was heckled in here. *Bastards*.

The man's bloodshot gaze shifts towards me. His face is a bloody mess, but I know he sees me, because he chokes out, "Go on. Take your clothes off."

I step right up to him, and in that moment he represents every single one of the people who's ever heckled me or abused me online.

I lift the pint of beer high over his head. "Fuck you." And then I pour the entire thing over his face, delighting in the way the bastard coughs and splutters, bringing up a mixture of blood and alcohol. *I hope that fucking stings.*

It's then that Marcia appears, yanking my arm and hissing in my ear, "Jesus, Elly. You'll scare all the punters away for good." Before I know it, security is ushering me out the back door.

It's only when I'm standing out on the street, the cold night air biting my cheeks, that I realise there's one person who really deserved a beer thrown in their face.

Lydia.

I can't do anything about that now. But there is one thing I can do that will show her I don't care about what she did. That I'm big enough to get through it. That I can really let all this shit slide off, just the way Jack urged me to. That she can't fucking touch me, no matter how low she's prepared to stoop.

I take out my phone, bring up Robert Lloyd's contact, and call. But when he doesn't answer, I send a text message.

Me: Hey Robert, it's Elly Carter. Sorry it's taken me so long to get in touch. If you still want to meet regarding representing me, you can get me on this number, but I understand if you don't. Please let me know, either way.

I wake to the sound of my phone ringing, the name Robert Lloyd flashing on the screen as I scrabble for the phone. "Hi, Robert." I sound stupidly breathy.

"Elly. Great to hear from you. I thought you were going to do a runner again..." He trails off, then collects himself. "In answer to your question. Yes, I still want to represent you."

My heart leaps, but I have to check he knows what he's saying. I need to know he has the full picture. "What about... the photos?"

He lets out a huff so loud and dismissive that I pull the phone from my ear for a second. "I don't care about the photos. They're gorgeous. You're gorgeous. It's all good. Most of all, your voice and your songs are absolute winners. Chart-toppers, Elly."

Did he just say what I think he did? Is this really going to be okay? Is it possible that my career didn't turn to a pile of steaming crap overnight?

I'm chewing hard on my lip to stop from smiling, just in case this is a dream. "Thank you."

A beat of silence has my pulse spiking. "I've been waiting for your call for weeks. What took so long?" he asks.

I blink back the tears that are rising. "It was all... it was too much. The photos, the stuff on the internet. It got me down."

"Ah." He pauses for so long I wonder if he has hung up, but then he says, "I get that. But in this business you need a thick skin. This may not be the worst that will hit you once we've got you properly positioned in the market. I need to know you can handle it, because if you can't, it'll break you. You have to be ready."

"I am."

"You're sure? Because I'm willing to bet on you. I've got your back, but I need to know you're gonna stay standing, no matter what comes your way."

"I will. I promise. I want this." This time, I really mean it.

"Okay. We'll get you signed on. Amy's keen to work with you. Does that sound good?"

My heart flutters, my palms grow sweaty. "Yes. Yes. More than good. I'd love that."

"Okay, then. I'll be in touch."

I hang up and lie back on my bed, revelling in the moment. *It's going to be okay. Everything is going to be fine.*

My heart sputters. How can anything be fine when I haven't sorted things out with Jack?

42
JACK

"This is a pretty mess, isn't it?" Mum says. She's sitting at my kitchen table, a selection of tabloid papers spread before her. She flicks to page six of one of them, where pictures of me yanking the bloke off the stage are spread, Elly in the background, clutching her guitar like her life depends on it.

Heir to Lansen Luxury Hotels leaps to defense of shamed viral sensation, Elly Carter.

Beneath it is a smaller image of Elly pouring a pint over his bloody face. *Good for you, El.*

"I told you you'd live to regret that girl," Mum adds. "The scandal. The shame. Good Lord. Look at all that blood." She jabs the image.

I clench my jaw, cursing the fact I let her into the house in the first place. I thought she was Kate, or I wouldn't have opened the door. She marched straight into the house like my poor behaviour was the perfect excuse to turn up and reprimand me, proving she's a 'good mother'. If she doesn't shut up, I'm going to kick her onto the street. "It's not a big deal. We've agreed to settle out of court. I'll pay him damages. Not that he fucking deserves them."

Mum pokes the paper. "It says he'll need reconstructive surgery to fix his face."

My phone buzzes, Nico's name flashing on the screen. I decline the call. I've been waiting to hear from him about news on Lydia, but I'm not talking about it when Mum's here. I glance back at her and shrug. "Again, not a big deal. They'll break his nose to re-align it. I've had it done twice."

Mum grimaces. She's probably remembering the time I broke my nose playing rugby. She always hated the sport; didn't want me ruining my 'gorgeous face'. "You're being very cavalier about all this. That young man could have pressed charges. Assault. Battery. They could have arrested you. Had you up in court." She rolls her eyes theatrically. "This could have been so much worse. I knew that girl would send you loopy."

"One more derogatory word about Elly, and I will force you out of this house and never allow you back in. There is nothing you can say or do to change my mind."

Mum's face sours like a pickle. "Darling. I wasn't saying anything bad about her. It's *you* that's gone loopy."

I rest my elbow on the table and point at her. "Cut the bullshit. I've had enough. I know what you meant, and *you* know what you meant. And I'm telling you right now, if you so much as hint at Elly being a bad influence or not good enough, or say anything disrespectful about her, I will quite happily live out the rest of my life as though both my parents are dead."

The colour drains from her face. "But you aren't even together anymore, are you?"

A wrenching sensation blasts through me at the reminder, but I don't let it show. I won't have the facts distorted by a display of emotion. "Irrelevant. I love her, and I'll love her for the rest of my life, even if she never forgives me. The memory of my relationship with Elly is more precious to me than actual time spent with anyone else, including you. I'd sacrifice the whole fucking world to have her back."

Mum draws up in her seat, and I brace for the theatrics. The tears. But they don't come. Instead, she says, "All right, darling. I hear you. You're in love."

Holy shit, she hears me? This has to be the first time she hasn't hit back with her version of reality, denying mine entirely. It's probably the best I can ever hope for from her.

An electric silence falls as Mum observes me. I pick up my phone from the kitchen counter, determined to ignore her as I search for Elly's latest song. The one she played last night. She released it yesterday.

She must have done it after the fight in the Marchmont. It's gone crazy on social media, especially after the news in the paper. The fight. The whole fucking showdown.

The song is going to be huge. And not because of all the scandal attached to it, but because it's damn good. You can feel the heartache and pain in it. And those lyrics...

"Have you heard from Lydia recently?" Mum's voice crashes into my head.

"No, and I don't want to. I'm not interested."

Mum leans back in her chair, crosses her arms over her chest, and tilts her head to one side. I know this look well. It's the *'I'm in the right, you're in the wrong, and I'm going to stare at you until you bow to my will'* expression.

But I'm not going to do that today. "You have crap taste in women, Mum. Lydia stole those photos of Elly from my phone. She spread them all over the internet. It was vicious and cruel, and the fact that you thought she was a good fucking match blows my mind. I'd rather cut my balls off and eat them than have anything to do with Lydia Archer again."

Mum's lips tighten further like she wants to suck them into her mouth. With a pop, she releases them and says, "You might be right."

I nearly choke on my next breath. I must have misinterpreted her earlier expression because that was not what I expected her to say. I'm immediately wary. "What do you mean?"

She pulls out her phone, scrolls a moment until she finds what she's looking for, and then turns the screen to me. It shows a glamorous headshot of Lydia, and when Mum scrolls down, there's a second image of her being ushered out of her house flanked by two police officers. "Breaking news. Lydia's been arrested."

It's happened, then. "Jesus. What for?" I ask, feigning surprise.

Mum's eyes narrow. "Sharing intimate photos. Your photos, I assume." She tuts and rolls her eyes. "Don't think I can't see you and Nico Hawkston all over this, darling." I hold my hands up in a *'this is nothing to do with me'* gesture, which Mum ignores. "You always have to fix everything for everyone, and if you love Eleanor as much as you say you do... Well. I dare say Lydia deserves it, but I find it all so hard to believe. She seemed so lovely. I'm quite shaken about it."

"I'm not. This is bloody wonderful news. She absolutely deserves it." I scroll through the article, then slide the phone back across the table to Mum. "Don't mention her to me again. Ever."

Mum's mouth flaps open and shut, audible puffs of air ejecting from it.

I want to laugh at how ridiculous she looks, but before the sound leaves my lips, a car horn honks aggressively outside, and we both pause to listen to it. Mum opens her mouth to speak again when the horn repeats.

With a scowl, she gets out of her chair and goes to the window, peering out. "There's an awful car out there. Dreadful orange thing."

Orange?

I'm out of my seat before I can process the fact my body has moved.

Mum's calling after me, but I'm skidding to the front door, the leather of my loafers sliding like ice skates. I haul open the door, and my heart stutters, missing a beat entirely when I see Elly getting out of that damn Lambo.

She's here. She's finally here.

When she reaches the top step, stopping so close I could touch her, we simply stare at one another. I notice all the golden threads in the blue of her eyes, the slope of her nose, the pale pink of her lips.

My Elly.

"That guy at the Marchmont lost his front teeth last night. Did you know that?" she asks.

"I did not know that," I confirm. *But I'm not fucking sorry.*

An awkward silence fills the space for a few beats.

"Can I come in?" I hesitate and Elly shrinks a fraction. "If you're busy—"

"No. It's not that," I blurt. "I'd love to invite you in, but Mum's here."

"Who is it?" Mum calls from the kitchen, and I see Elly stiffen just as Mum's heels clack out into the hall behind me. "Oh. Eleanor. You're back. What wonderful timing. Jack hasn't stopped talking about you." Mum paces until she's right beside me in the doorway, the two of us blocking Elly's entry. "I assume she's coming in?" Mum asks.

"She?" I say pointedly.

"Eleanor," Mum corrects.

I nod and shift aside. Elly's hesitant at first, but then she follows me in.

"Well," Mum announces as if this one word sums up a host of information. "I'll go then. Do try and behave yourself when I'm gone." She rolls her eyes to the ceiling. "Like an absolute animal last night.

Goodness." A shudder ripples through her before she turns to Elly, looking her up and down with a disdainful curl of the upper lip. "If you could try not to incite my son to violence, it would be much appreciated."

Elly shrugs. "Jack makes his own choices, Mrs Lansen. I think you know that."

Mum gives a disgruntled harrumph as she tucks the strap of her handbag tightly over her shoulder, tucking the body of it beneath her arm. She gives Elly another flick of a glance. "Your latest song. It's really... rather good." The admission sounds like it pains Mum to make it. "You've more talent than I gave you credit for. Well done."

Elly's jaw falls open, and I keep quiet, letting the compliment sink in. Mum's always responded to achievement. As a kid, I could always win her over by doing something good. Something exceptional. Winning some prize or game.

But it doesn't last, because Mum is nothing if not brutally honest. "You aren't who I would have chosen. I think we all know that. But I suppose we must try to get along, especially if you are set on Jack here." Mum glances at me. "He certainly seems set on you."

Before either of us can respond, Mum spreads her arms wide and wraps them around Elly in the most awkward hug I've ever seen. It's all pointed elbows and raised shoulders, as if Mum doesn't actually want any part of her body to come into contact with Elly's. It's so typically Mum that it makes me want to laugh, and the sight of Elly's alarmed eyes peering at me over Mum's shoulder only makes it worse.

Mum pulls back, nods at both of us as though this finalises the matter entirely, and lets herself out, closing the door behind her.

"That was... weird," Elly says under her breath.

I say nothing, not knowing whether Elly is referring to the compliment, the hug, or the fact that my mother's announcement that I'm 'certainly set' on Elly sounded almost like approval. I'm not sure how I feel about that last comment. I'd prefer to tell Elly myself how I feel, rather than have my mother out me. Not that Elly doesn't know, given I must have spent thousands of pounds on flowers over the past few weeks, and hours idling on the road outside Nico's apartment.

Elly twines a curl around her fingers, eyes landing on mine. "I noticed it's really hard to find my pictures online now." She keeps twisting that curl really tight. I want to reach out and loosen it, but I don't dare touch her. "Did you do that?"

My heart lurches like it wants to escape my body and spring right into Elly's. "I did whatever I could, yeah."

"Thank you." She tilts her head towards the kitchen where *Playing Your Games* is still streaming through the speakers. "Is that... my song?"

"Yeah." I shove my hands deep in my pockets. "It's really good. Is it...?" I can't bring myself to ask the question.

"About you? About us?"

"Yeah."

She sighs. "It was all.... very painful."

I nod, not wanting to agree and let her know how painful it was for me too. Not until I know what she's thinking, at least.

"I'm so, so sorry, El. I never meant for you to get hurt. I had no idea that anything would have gone down the way it did. I couldn't have predicted that Lydia—"

"Kate said you had Derek removing comments on my videos."

Guilt squeezes my gut. "Yeah. Sorry. I—"

"If I'd seen those, or you'd told me about them, maybe I could have predicted what Lydia was up to. Maybe not all of it... but some of it. I could have been prepared." She pauses, letting her shoulders drop. "I wish you'd mentioned it, rather than hiding it from me."

"I didn't want you to get upset." I let out a mirthless burst of laughter. "Turns out I can't control the world and all the people in it."

"But you can knock their teeth out and break their noses." I don't move. *Is that a compliment or a reprimand?*

"I'm sorry you had to see that."

"You looked like you wanted to do worse."

I tilt my chin in confirmation. *Fuck yes, I wanted to spread his guts out on the fucking floor.*

An awkward silence descends, and Elly fiddles with the sleeve of her sheepskin jacket. "I saw that Lydia was arrested. Did you do that too?"

I hesitate, unsure if she'll appreciate any more of my interference. But I won't lie to her, either. "With Nico's assistance, yes. I wasn't going to let her get away with it. She hurt you, and to me, that's unforgivable."

Her eyes soften and some of my tension fades away. "I always told you she was a red flag."

"You did."

Silence engulfs us, but it's not uncomfortable this time. "I spoke to Robert Lloyd this morning," Elly says finally.

"Oh, yeah?"

"Yeah. He still wants to meet. He's really enthusiastic. I think he believes in me."

"Of course he does. You're the whole package."

She blushes, her eyes dipping away from me for a second, and the air feels alive, as though all our unspoken feelings are quietly buzzing between us.

"About that song... the games." I huff a breath, not knowing exactly how to put this. "Was it really all so painful? Wasn't it worth it?"

She holds my gaze longer than is comfortable before she admits, "Yeah. It was worth it. You're worth every game."

A warming, fuzzy sensation expands beneath my sternum. "Does that mean you might want to... stay and play?" I ask, quoting her song. "Because I'd like that. I'd fucking love that, in fact. I'd love you to stay and play and never leave, actually."

So much for not telling her how I really feel.

"Even if it kills me?" she asks, half a smile on her mouth, but when I answer, I'm deadly serious.

"To be honest, if it kills you, then I'm dying too. I feel like I can't fucking breathe without you, and I've loathed every second of being separated from you. It's been agony. Not a day has gone by when I haven't thought of you. Wondering what you're doing, what you're wearing. If your feet are bare, or you're wearing those stupid pink slippers. I have ached with missing you. I don't want any more of those seemingly insignificant moments of your life to pass without me being there by your side, because, to me, nothing is insignificant. It's all precious. I want to be there when you wake up, and when you fall asleep, and every fucking second in between. So, yes. Please stay. I'm asking you... *begging* you, not to leave."

Her eyes are full of intense emotion when she says, "Yes, please."

I don't dare breathe in case I've misunderstood, and for a few seconds, I tune into the thump-thump of my heartbeat. "You want to stay?"

"Yes. I want to stay with you—*be with you*—and be happy and successful and let all the shit slide right off." A grin splits her pretty pink mouth. "I'm ready for that. I'm ready to let all the good stuff in. Really ready this time."

My heart explodes and before I can stop myself, I'm hauling her against me and kissing her, relishing her familiar taste and the feel of her tongue against mine as I wind my fingers into the curls I've missed so much.

"Fuck, I love you," I say, breaking my lips from hers. "Don't leave me again. No more messing around."

"No more games?" she breathes.

"Only if you want to."

She laughs, I laugh, we kiss, each swallowing the sound of the other. It's messy. It's perfect. I'm awash with gratitude that this wonderful woman is giving me a second chance.

"I want to. I always want to when it comes to you," she says. "But no more photos."

"Okay." I kiss her again, then whisper against her mouth. "There's something you should know though."

"What?"

"I burnt all my condoms."

She laughs. "I don't care." Our lips meet again, and the kiss is sensuous and frantic and calming all at once. "I love you," she says, when we break apart. "I never stopped loving you. Not for a single second. Even when I hated you, I still loved you."

I close my eyes and press my forehead to hers. Has anything ever felt as good as having Elly back in my arms? I don't feel worthy of it. Of her. She's far too good for me, but I'll take it because this woman is embedded deep in my soul, and without her, I'm broken.

"But you can't ever lie to me again," Elly adds.

"I won't. I promise. I love you. I've never loved anyone the way I love you, and I never will. You've changed my life, El. You've changed *me*. Being with you was the most wonderful experience I've ever had, and I swear I will never do anything to jeopardise that again. I'll devote myself to your happiness. Your wellbeing. Your safety. I'll—"

She presses a finger to my lips. "I get it, Lansen. You love me, and you're sorry." She kisses me hard on the mouth. "I forgive you, with my whole heart. Now... fuck me, before I change my mind."

What? I pull back to look at her, but she dissolves into a beautiful cascade of giggles.

"Don't tease me," I rasp, then shrug it off. None of it matters, as long as she's here. "Actually, do whatever you want with me. I'm yours, body and soul."

"Who said anything about teasing?" She grips my hand and pulls me towards the stairs. "I'm one hundred per cent serious. I love you, I've missed you, and I want to show you how much. I already showed up on your doorstep. What more do you want? I could go and sleep out there in the car for a week?" She points out the window, at where that stupid orange Lambo is parked.

Half a laugh sticks in my throat. "I definitely don't deserve you."

She grins. "Nope. But I'm feeling generous."

"Then I'm the luckiest man in the whole fucking world. I will worship you every day for the rest of my life. I love you, Elly Carter." *I'm never letting go again.*

She softens in my arms, and the look in her eyes is sincere when she replies, "I love you too, Jack Lansen. Always. Forever."

EPILOGUE

"Fuck me, that's an album cover," Seb says, staring at the proof picture in his hands.

"You're not holding back, that's for sure," Nico agrees, peering over Seb's shoulder.

We've all gathered in the Marchmont Arms this evening, on the ground floor where there's natural light. *No more basement for me.*

Under the table, Jack squeezes my hand. "I'm so proud of you," he whispers. I squeeze back and reach for the proof cover with my free hand. We've used one of the photos Jack took of me, lounging on the piano. The most tasteful one, and it has been edited, so it looks classy rather than porn-worthy. I run my finger over the album title, *Indecently Exposed*.

"Yeah. I'm done holding back," I say, a new sense of purpose swelling my chest. *I'm proud of me too.*

I'm releasing the new songs tomorrow, so we're celebrating. I signed up with Robert Lloyd and he got me a record deal almost instantly. Apparently, they were clamouring to sign me, because my scandal was a PR dream, rather than a nightmare. He kept saying that the photos were great, and we should use them for marketing purposes. It took me a while to get my head around it, but it turns out he was right.

I have over a million online followers now, and it's growing all the time, and most of that is on the back of what happened with those naked pictures. Singing with Amy Moritz at Nico's party helped, and I sang a number with her when she appeared at Wembley Stadium in the spring. It's been a crazy year, and my career has exploded. I could never have anticipated it.

"Fuck, not another one. This is a nightmare," Nico says, gesturing to a photographer who's lingering outside. He lifts a drinks menu and uses it to cover his face. "I'm going to have to stop hanging out with you if this keeps up."

Kate rolls her eyes. "Oh, rubbish, it's not like they don't follow you around sometimes."

Nico flinches. "Not like this, they don't."

Jack stands, and I grab his arm to stop him. "Where are you going?"

He jerks his head towards the window. "To get rid of him." I'm about to tell him not to bother when I change my mind.

"I'll come with you," I say, although really I'm saying, *'let's take a moment away from the others'*, and I can see the second Jack understands exactly what I mean because his eyes widen.

"Come on then," he says, tugging me out of my seat.

The others are so busy chatting that they don't notice as Jack and I disappear in the opposite direction from the photographer outside. I lead Jack out the back exit.

It's a warm summer evening. We've been together for six months, and I've never been so happy. I know, right down to my toes, that this is the man I'm spending the rest of my life with. Jack pulls me into him, here in the back alley, and kisses me with a ferocity that hasn't worn away even after all this time. We're still as eager for one another as we've ever been.

"You amaze me," he whispers as he pulls back from our kiss. "I can't believe all that you've achieved."

"You gonna take credit for it?" I reply, my tone teasing.

"Not even a little. This is all you."

I kiss him again. "I love you. I could never have done this without you."

"I love you too." He grins against my lips. "You know what else I love?"

"What?"

"These tiny signature skirts you wear." His hand slides up my inner thigh, and I feel every speck of want in my body dip to meet it. My skin blazes beneath his touch.

I let out a moan. "We're going to have to stop doing this if I get really famous. Can't be hooking up in public like this."

"This isn't public," Jack says, scanning the empty alleyway. "Not exactly salubrious though." He glances at the empty bottles around us and the industrial bins. "I think you deserve something better."

"Oh, yeah?"

He pushes away from me and pulls out a sheaf of papers from his jacket pocket, dangling it between his finger and thumb.

"What's that?"

"Your extended lease." He thrusts his other hand in his pocket and pulls out a lighter, clicking it to reveal the flame. "Move in with me. Officially."

I laugh. "I already live with you." When my lease ended, I stayed with Jack, but I demanded that he draw up a document and extend my lease, so I could keep paying rent. It was my way of instigating my independence, and I paid on time every month.

"I know. But there's always been the damn paperwork in the way, and I don't want that." He lets the flame approach the paper. "What do you say? Live with me. Stay with me. As my girlfriend, not my tenant. I'm deadly serious. I want you, forever."

I laugh and agree just before he lets the whole document burn, dropping the papers to the street when the flames get too close to his fingers.

"Ha!" Jack stamps on it. "You're mine now," he declares, yanking me into his embrace and kissing me so violently that my lips feel raw in seconds. "One day, I'm going to marry you."

Sparks explode beneath my skin. "Marry me?"

"Of course. You're the other half of my soul. As much as we laugh and mess around, and as fun as this is, I want you to know that I'm serious too. I'm in this for the long haul."

He kisses me softly, but passionately, his expression turning mischievous as he pulls back, still breathless from the kiss, and says, "Reckon we could fuck out here?"

Just then, a photographer appears with a huge long-lensed camera at the other end of the alleyway.

"Best not," I say, but I can't help smiling ear-to-ear as I grab Jack's hand and together we run down the back alley like a couple of kids, laughing and screaming.

"You..." Jack breathes, when we come to a stop a couple of streets away. "There is no one like you in the whole world. How did I get this lucky?"

I laugh. "It's your huge—"

He presses a finger to my lips to cut me off. "Nope. If you say this is just about my dick, I'll toss you over my shoulder and carry you home."

"—dick," I goad.

"That's it," he says, lunging for me. I twist out of reach, but he has a long stride and in two steps he has me in his arms, and he lifts me off the ground. I squeal and lock my legs around his hips, and my arms around his neck.

I'm not quite over his shoulder this way, but it's better because in this position I can see his handsome face when he growls, "You're in trouble now," making heat rage through me.

I press my lips to his, and the kiss is soft and tender this time, the passion behind it increasing with each passing second. I can feel his heart thumping through his shirt, beating right against my breasts. *He loves me.* I know it in every glance, every touch, every moment I spend with him.

I didn't know life could get this good.

I pull back, biting my bottom lip as I look up at him. "This is the best kind of trouble."

He flashes me a look of agreement. "Let's go home and play."

I answer without missing a beat. "Yes, please."

"All day?" he asks.

"All day," I confirm. "Every day. For the rest of my life. I love you, Jack Lansen."

"You do?"

"Yup. I'm sure. One hundred per cent," I reply, and I absolutely mean it.

THE END

Want more Jack and Elly?

Want to know what happens at Elly and Jack's first Christmas together?

You can find the bonus scene here:

https://dl.bookfunnel.com/k20an2r7km

Worth Every Risk

If you want more from the Hawkston Billionaires, you can order the ebook of Book 3, Worth Every Risk, using the QR code below. I love this story and can't wait for you to read it.

Afterword

Thank you so much for reading Worth Every Game. I truly appreciate the time you have taken to read my book and I hope you've enjoyed the experience. Putting creative work out into the world is always nerve-wracking, so I'm incredibly grateful for your support.

If you have a moment to leave a review, I'd really appreciate it. Or just shout about the book at the top of your lungs (preferably on social media, but to be honest I'm not fussy just so long as you are loud).

Joking aside, I always love to hear from readers so feel free to reach out to me at any of the places listed on the following page, or you can join my mailing list here:

KEEP IN TOUCH WITH RAE

Join my Facebook reader group, **Rae's Romantics**, where you can discuss my books, characters, and get information about upcoming releases.

You can also find me at my website
www.raeryder.com
And on Instagram & Tiktok
@raeryderauthor

Acknowledgements

I am going to keep it short and sharp this time. A rough draft never becomes a book without the help of a whole bunch of people. My book coach, Emily, my editor, Sarah, and Sido, (AKA SE Bouvier), who always reads the excerpts I send her and knocks them into shape at the last minute (usually when I've redrafted a section or changed something even after I've 'finished' editing). You've saved my bacon many times.

To my husband and my kids, who put up with me being constantly on my phone to market my books on social media. It's a bad habit (and painful necessity). I'm sorry that this whole writing endeavour takes my attention away from you more than I'd like. I love you all so much. One day, I'll outsource as much as I can so I can be more present when I'm with you.

And to all the beta readers and ARC readers who have helped me on this journey. Thank you so, so much for your time, your enthusiasm, your feedback and your thoughts. I appreciate you all.

Printed in Great Britain
by Amazon